All Planetary Shipping

P. Srigley

WigglesWorth Press & SrigleyArts.com

Also by Patricia Srigley

Universe Idol
Fire-scape
Scarecrow in the Graveyard

Unreal Estate Series, One Crooked House

Storyteller's Curse
Storyteller's Quest

The April-May June Series
1 – A World Apart
2 – Mad About Magic
3 – Message in a Bubble
4 – April Fooled

Deeply
Blue Wings

Moody Gasping Middle School Adventures
1 – Three Wishes Vending Machine
2 – Genie for Sale–Cheap

Library and Archives Canada Cataloguing in Publication:
Please contact the publisher for this information

ISBN 978-0-9810435-6-2

WigglesWorth Press & SrigleyArts.com
Montreal, Quebec, Canada

Contents

Part 1 – Megal

1. Gehenna

Skin. It hides everything. The new prisoner had a pretty pelt, nicely plump in a sea of skeletons. If I'd had the energy to lust after the girl, I would have edged closer, brushed against her softness, inhaled her fresh scent before it was gone.

I didn't try. I was one of the sea of skeletons, one of the wretched waiting to die.

Until I ended up on Gehenna Prison Planet, I had known only luxury and fawning from the time I cried my first tears, every wish filled as easily as a cup of milk, or as the years elapsed, a goblet of wine. In recall, such times had been lived by a man I was no more—a man who had not guarded his realm with the care it deserved. I paid the price now, for this man whose skin I wore, stretched taut over a pitiful collection of bones, decorated with sores and scars, my person as withered as the power I once assumed I had every right to abuse.

Skin hides everything. To this day, it hid the identity of my betrayer, but in my mind, I had narrowed it down to two—one I loved and one I hated. Or perhaps they had worked together to make me vanish from the Ice Planet, and awaken in hell, robbed of all things, even my illustrious name.

The plump girl moved closer, gracefully up the side of the mine pit, watched by hollow sunken eyes on all sides.

The third and hottest of the three afternoon suns edged overhead, searing down with stinging cruelty, sending inmates scuttling into the pockets of shallow caves where they would be trapped, until that mean sun slunk away, four long hours later.

I limped for the nearest shelter, dragging a twisted useless leg. One cave was as good as another. My only desire in a cave was its solitude. Too many new prisoners enjoyed inflicting pain on a ruined man, while they still had the energy to do so.

1

The girl followed.

Coincidence surely, but my heart beat faster—it didn't take much these days. And she drew closer still, purpose in her step. Perhaps not coincidence. An assassin? Unlikely. I was no threat to anyone now. My betrayer had hidden me here to suffer, rather than die. There is nothing like imposing a sentence of prolonged suffering to satisfy a vengeful heart.

I entered the cave and leaned against the rough stone, attending the entrance. She strode inside without hesitation. Her dark eyes examined every inch of my face. Those fierce eyes were not the eyes of a prisoner, even though she walked the same burning sand as me. Her skin was so plump and smooth, and her hair so glossy it gleamed. I longed to touch it, stroke it, smell it. She was the antithesis of all things Gehenna, and my mouth watered.

Skin. I was ashamed of mine. All of it: the gauntness, the stench, the unsightly scars, the man I was now. I lowered my eyes to stare at the ground.

"Megal? Is it you?" Even her musical voice caused pleasure, but that name! It was a name from another time and place.

I lifted my gaze and squinted in the dim light. If I knew this girl, I could not recall. "I was Megal once. Who asks for me by name?"

"I do, for another." She glanced warily over her shoulder, but none could enter the cave now. The suns would have cooked their skin. We would not be interrupted for hours.

"Who?" I rasped.

"Kyar."

That name caused more pain than being branded a prisoner, with a redhot iron—a scar that will never fade. The brand on her shoulder was still blistered and raw. "Kyar?" For the first time in years, I spoke the name of the brother who might have betrayed me, to claim my planets and stand in my stead. If his envy had driven him to such action, I missed him regardless. "Kyar, how is he?"

"Well enough. Megal, it is you?"

I nodded. She looked at me directly, then looked away. I couldn't blame her for avoiding the sight.

"Kyar has searched three years to find you. And you've been here, all along?"

Surely it was plain on my face. "Three years. It felt … longer."

"It must have seemed an eternity. Now that we have found you, we will free you from this place." She stepped closer. I could smell her now, still clean and healthy. I motioned her nearer still. I was surprised when she came close enough to touch, but perhaps she had a dagger hidden within the folds of her flesh. I didn't care.

She stroked my arm and the light brush of her fingers hurt. Everything hurt these days. And days were all I had left. I knew death shadowed me closely, creeping up to sweetly lick my skin at idle moments.

I laid my head on her shoulder and remembered Kyar. Three years. My little brother would be a man of twenty-one now. Her skin felt like a velvet pillow. I started to sob without shame. I had lost my pride so long ago, I couldn't remember having it.

She touched my patchy skull and murmured words I could barely take in, soothing me like a child. "It will not be long now. I have come to help you. Your home planet needs you, Megal. It has suffered these three years. Kyar has done what he can, but he has had to act in secret. Soon, you will be free, and together we can put things right."

Her words made no sense to me, yet all I asked was, "Who are you?"

"No-one of import."

I dried my eyes, pressing them against her rough tunic. While my mouth was so close, I kissed her neck with lips as cracked and rough as the stone that surrounded us. My tongue tasted the salty sweetness of her skin. She shuddered. Needless to say, it was not with pleasure, but revulsion. Following a hunch, I took her hand and turned the palm up. She bore a slave's tattoo. The mark was not one I recognized. My family did not own her.

"What shall I call you?" I asked.

"Whatever you wish."

I had not been a master for three years. I had been a slave to the prison. I saw now with a slave's eyes and felt with a slave's heart. "I would rather know your true name."

She gave me her beautiful name. "Sephine."

I should have asked about the plan to take me from this place. I was too distracted by the girl. My shaking hand stroked down her neck. Three fingers and a stump snuggled between her cleavage. I simply could not resist the temptation of such luxurious beauty. "Sephine," I whispered.

She stepped back, unable to hide her distaste.

"Please," I begged. In the past, it would have been an arrogant order, and she would have done exactly as I wished. I no longer believed I had

3

that right, nor did any man. She watched me impassively and held her ground. My lame leg had supported me for as long as it was able. I lowered, scraping against the rock wall.

The girl crouched too, close, but not too close. "Your brother sent me. I will see you off this planet."

"How?"

"It is better if you don't know. I am but a vessel to serve you, Nomad Megal." Her voice mocked a touch, which was no more than I deserved, crouched like a filthy animal in prisoner's waste.

The title caught me off-guard. Nomad—the ruler, and a ruler must always stand alone and apart. He does not belong amongst his people, but ahead of them, leading them. He shoulders the weighty responsibility of making the decisions that impact countless lives. And with his mantle of power comes isolation, and the inevitable loneliness that is just one more burden for him to bear. Yet men still crave the position of ruler, for all the power that it grants them.

The title was mine no longer. It belonged to whoever ruled my planets in my place. Yet from Sephine's words, that person was not my brother. I had thought him my betrayer, seduced by his jealousy, and benefiting the most from my disappearance, but if he was not ruling, and had sent Sephine to save me, I was wrong.

"Tell me, what has happened on the Ice Planet?" My neck gave out and my head lolled back, banging rock. Lacking the energy to raise it, I left it there.

Sephine didn't answer. She edged closer, opened her mouth wide, and exposed viper's fangs. Before I could move, she sank them deep into my neck. She was definitely not full-human, and she was an assassin after all. I finally had my answer. My brother must be laughing his head off right now, for what he had subjected me to—three years of unimaginable suffering on the hell planet, before he killed me off. And the woman … he had chosen well. Her skin was pure human. It hid the other completely.

But I was prepared. I had not survived Gehenna by chance. My hand slipped into my tunic and came out clutching a rare goran spine. What I had done to get that spike was so appalling, I never revisited the memory, except in the worst of nightmares. I deserved to be a prisoner after that deed.

The toxic tip penetrated her skin, before she knew I would fight back. Her fangs jerked out, ripping deep furrows through my skin. "No … Megal … you don't understand." The tragedy in her eyes faded to

4

blankness when she died. Her tears were still flowing as she released her last breath. It was quick for her. It wasn't for me.

The poison from her fangs burned like acid. I vomited what little was in my wasted stomach, before the paralysis crippled my body. Silent screams of agony tore through me when I could no longer breathe. The terrible pain was quickly followed by an icy death.

In spite of all that had come before, I did not welcome the end. Nor was death what I expected. My soul stayed trapped within my pathetic mortal remains, aware in the most distant way of what went on around me.

Sephine lay cooling and stiffening against my side, keeping me company. After the cave darkened, a siren split the air, signalling the time to line up and file inside the prison proper, for the hours of darkness.

After my extended stay, I knew the routine too well. Each inmate had a small bare cell, long enough to lie down with crooked knees, wide enough to cross in half a stride, but not high enough to stand upright. The cells were more coffin than room. There were waste holes in the floor. Rats crawled out of those holes in the dead of night, to nibble on extremities or open wounds.

Prisoners stood before their cells, until all were accounted for, then they stepped inside and the power grid activated. Any prisoner who tried to leave his cell before the grid was shut down again, died. Any prisoner who had a habit of sleepwalking, died. Any prisoner who ran screaming from a horde of rats, died. Each morning, there was a collection of the dead.

My mind drifted to my cell, where my jug of water and bowl of desert beetle larvae would be waiting—one serving a day, every day for three years. Not enough to keep a man alive, yet some men are too stubborn to die. Lately, the most stalwart of my clinging teeth, and my rotted bleeding gums, had made eating even that meager ration an ordeal.

The guards soon came to search the caves, seeking the missing prisoners. Sephine was hauled away first. I think the snickering guards had plans for her lifeless skin. I was kicked repeatedly. It was determined that I was dead. I wasn't quite sure myself, until the verdict was announced.

My body was dragged to my cell, tossed inside and left there.

All night long, hallucinations twisted my reality, until it was worse even than the one I knew. Over and over, I relived my time in the deepest desert tunnels, harvesting the explosive body fluid from the giant blast

5

beetle larvae that nested in the cool damp earth, so far below. The fluid was worth its weight in blackhole oil ten times over. A meager cupful could power a full-sized battleship for weeks.

Only the male inmates experienced the tunnels, rarely surviving more than a week. If an inmate lasted a month, he was sent back to the pits. I had survived the unstable fuel, the collapsing tunnels, and even the adult blast beetles, defending their nests with the explosive fluid that was their natural defense. But that night, I burned alive in the tunnels too many times to count.

The next morning, when the corpse collection passed by, I was robbed of my tunic and tossed into the cart, along with the other bodies. They smelled burnt, fried by the power grid. I lay amongst them, one of them. I screamed like the madman I was, yet I couldn't make a sound.

I should have been prepared for this moment. For three years I had known that only in death would I escape Gehenna's walls. The Nomad's vision that I hadn't understood, until I awoke as a prisoner on Gehenna, had shown me my awful fate when I was barely more than a lad.

No man ever left Gehenna alive. Every prisoner knew that truth. Only the females departed the planet, auctioned off for profit once a year, if they survived that long. It was the only day that the planet's security system shut down, allowing a parade of ships to dock on the planet. I had watched the ships come and go three times now. In my heart, I had sailed away with them, three times. There would be no fourth time.

The cart dumped the bodies in the desert, far outside the prison walls, and trundled away. Then it was just me and the other corpses. Perhaps we would become friends. I might have laughed hysterically, if I wasn't dead.

Daily, a gang of prisoners would collect the larvae that fed on the field of decaying flesh, gathering food for the inmates. It was a perfectly symbiotic relationship—we fed the larvae and the larvae fed us. Before my leg had been lamed, I had been part of that chain gang, and a more revolting task was impossible to imagine.

I ended up on the bottom of the day's dumping, protected from the searing heat of the suns. Night came coldly, yet the decomposing bodies wrapped me in a cocoon of warmth, almost pleasantly. I drifted away and knew nothing until a low light shone into my eye. A calloused thumb was holding up my left eyelid.

6

"This him?" The abrupt voice was deep and strong. It was tinged with an Alfreezian accent, identifying the man's birthplace as the northern glacier of my home planet.

A different hand checked my neck. It was bigger, softer, and gentler, as was the voice. "Hard to believe, but must be. Eyes are the Nomad's freaky colour. He's not crawling with worms, and he's been bitten— bitten bad. Sephine really went to town on his neck." That man's accent was a mixture of many.

"Sure he's not dead?" The Alfreezian sounded skeptical.

"Not positive, but Sephine's poison shouldn't have killed him, only make him appear dead. He's on the deathlist now, free to leave this hellhole." The words explained everything. I would disappear from Gehenna in death. Those who had stranded me here wouldn't know. Sephine had braved Gehenna to save me, and I had killed her. I wished I was dead then.

I was eased out of the tangled limbs with a great deal of cursing. And my handlers made a grisly discovery.

"Whitey, look there," the gentler voice moaned.

Whitey, the Alfreezian, said much worse. He had an impressive repertoire of curses. Sephine's corpse had been discovered. After he settled down, he said, "What killed her? No worms on her either. Check her body, Hanis." Whitey seemed a practical sort.

I was left lying naked and frozen on the exposed sand, while they investigated. They did not find the tiny hole left by the poisonous spine. Her death was deemed a mystery. The pair discussed bringing her along, but the idea was rejected.

"I can't carry two, not the distance we have to cover before the first sun rises," Hanis said.

"Probably better not to bring her anyway, since I'll not be the one to tell Kyar she's dead." The Alfreezian crunched closer to me again. "Matter of fact, neither of us is going to tell him." Whitey made it sound like an order. "He doesn't need to know. He'll assume she's still in the prison, and couldn't escape to meet us, despite her special talents. There was always that risk, so you won't say a word Hanis, not one."

Hanis didn't argue. He carefully rolled me in a blanket, tucked in the edges, and lifted me high over his enormous shoulder. "Are you sure this is all of him? He weighs no more than a sack of bones," he said.

"He is no more than a sack of bones," Whitey shot back.

I was bumped along on Hanis's solid shoulder for hours, fading in and out of reality.

After many miles, Whitey said, "The first sun is about to rise. We've reached the coordinates just in time."

The walking giant stopped and put me down. Almost immediately, there was a great swoosh of air overhead, followed by the sound of a whole lot of sand shifting and compacting. I knew it couldn't be a ship landing on the surface, not within the prison planet's impenetrable security lattice, yet that's exactly what it sounded like.

I was heaved onto Hanis's shoulder again, making my head spin sickly, as events unfolded in disjointed flashes of nonsense, amid constant noise and movement, and eventually voices and the familiar rumble of a ship's engine.

Had I truly left Gehenna Prison Planet? Alive? Or was this a flight of fancy, and I would awaken curled on the floor of my cell, sharing my flesh with rats? I couldn't decide what was real and what wasn't, before it all faded away.

After a long dark time, I did return to my senses and my body. I could move! And I didn't seem to be dead, unless I had ended up in Nirvana, but no—I had earned no place in that paradise.

I stretched out my limbs in a decadent bed of fur. The comforting hum of engines echoed from some distant place, like music.

"Megal?"

I turned my head and looked at my brother, after so long without him. I had hated him all that time, suspecting he had stolen me away and stranded me on Gehenna. And next I had thought him a murderer. Clearly, I had always lacked good judgment. It was plain on his face that he had suffered, too. Here he was sitting vigil by my bed. After nothing but inmates, Kyar's rather ordinary face was beautiful.

"Kyar. You're looking well—don't look a year older." I tried to smile with remembered charm. I no longer knew how.

He couldn't return the compliment and didn't try. "You're safely away from Gehenna. I'm so sorry it took so long to find you, Megal. You disappeared without a trace. Logic said you were dead, but I kept searching." He gently touched my shoulder, as if he thought I would break. His eyes were filled with regret, and worse—pity.

If I had had any pride left, I would not have allowed that emotion in any eyes that looked upon me. I shifted restlessly and discovered tubes in my arms.

8

"Stay still, Megal. You can't get up yet. The surgeon says you need food and rest. Lots of both, and more of the antidote for Sephine's venom." Kyar pulled his chair closer. He looked younger than twenty-one, with his freckled nose, plump cheeks and earnest blue eyes.

I was too drowsy to chat or confess my crime of murder. "Some plan you came up with." My voice was slurred.

"Liked it, did you?"

"It had its moments." My neck was heavily bandaged. I struggled to stay conscious. I couldn't. Kyar's voice faded away, asking about Sephine.

It took a week, a bucket of medicine, and several minor surgeries, before I was allowed out of bed. My leg no longer dragged, but still limped awkwardly. I showered for the first time in years and had a shock when I saw my reflection in a mirror. I smashed it off the wall and huddled in the corner, sobbing like the broken man I was. In my mind, I remembered a handsome golden-haired rogue, a beautiful flashy fellow. I didn't recognize the monster in the mirror. I didn't want to know him. I didn't want to be him!

Greely, the sallow-faced surgeon, and Kyar, were my only visitors in the weeks that I was quarantined in my sick room, occasionally coherent, more often not, wracked with fever chills and shedding the collection of parasites that were living within my skin. I vomited out more food than I could hold down, my malnourished stomach so unused to anything inside, it didn't know quite what to do with solid fare.

Kyar had again asked about Sephine. The only answer I could come up with was, "I was unconscious. I don't know what became of her." I had lost more than my pride on Gehenna, it seemed. I had also lost my courage. I was not nearly brave enough to tell my brother that I had killed her.

The doctor took my condition in stride, commending my progress as if I was a tot, and plying me with tonic like an oily space-travelling salesman. He seemed capable enough, in spite of his rough hands and casual bedside manner.

Kyar was more disturbed by what he saw, and tiptoed nervously around, never sure when he would be embarrassed to find me huddled and sobbing, or vomiting, sometimes both at the same time.

When Greely and Kyar arrived together one afternoon, I was finally alert enough to question my treatment. Without preamble, I said, "Did you not bring one of my clones along? I wish to shed this unsightly skin sooner rather than later."

Only the Nomad's line had spare suits of skin, bodies cloned without thinking brains. It was a tradition that dated back to a time when assassination was as commonplace as breakfast. And then there was the Nomad's Quest, which often resulted in the need for spare parts. Before a Nomad could hold absolute power, he had to make a gruelling journey across the ice, to a network of sacred caves and tunnels. The purpose of the Nomad's Quest was twofold. It reinforced the fact that as planetary ruler, the Nomad stood alone and must rely only on himself. If he survived the descent into the very deepest cave, a Nomad's vision was his reward.

The sacred cave was decorated with stalactites of glowing crimson, dripping ever so slowly, like blood. The Nomad would lie beneath and drink the drips, until he entered a world of visions. Like the hundreds of Nomads that came before, he would carve his vision into the wall of ice, and try to get home. If he survived the return trek, he often needed fingers and toes, sometimes whole hands and feet. The clones certainly came in handy then, giving up precious bits of themselves.

I had survived my quest intact, although I had not understood my dark vision, not until I awoke on Gehenna. Into the wall of ice, I had carved three suns and a skeleton, wearing my face.

My question about a clone was answered with an awkward pause. Kyar motioned Greely out, before he delivered the bad news. "All of your clones have been destroyed, Megal, by order of the Council of Icemen. They sanctioned the injection of vulture nanos. Your bodies were eaten alive."

What a gruesome sight that must have been.

The Council of Icemen was a planetary safeguard, in case a Nomad succumbed to madness, or died without leaving an heir. The council was the only thing that could overrule a Nomad, and the thirty men and women had to be in total agreement. Thirty against one Nomad.

When I was young, I used to visit the cold underground chamber where the clones were kept. I was morbidly fascinated by the dozen replicas of myself and Kyar, alive yet lifeless, lining one wall and nourished through tubes. Their muscles were stimulated by electronic impulses, making them jerk spasmodically and macabrely, almost like life-sized marionettes. Our clones—us, but not us. And now, all my clones had been destroyed. It seemed I would be keeping my ruined skin after all.

"Shame," I drawled, as if it was no matter. Kyar's revelation had raised more questions than it answered, namely, why my advising body of Icemen would want to destroy my clones.

Before I could ask, Kyar said, "One was stolen, a while ago."

"One clone? What became of it?"

His pregnant pause suggested that I was about to be told terrible news. Kyar did not disappoint. "It was ruling the Ice Planet for three years."

"What?"

"In your place, as you. Most believed it was you. I could tell it wasn't, but pretended I accepted him as you, since I couldn't prove otherwise, not while he held absolute power. I couldn't even have him killed off. He was never without his guards by his side. Never once."

My brother had seen the imposter within my skin. My legs failed me and I sank onto my bed. "Who violates my clone? Do you know?"

"Prin disappeared around that time."

Prin—Prin was a first cousin on my mother's side, and only a direct blood relative would be biologically compatible to wear my skin. The maternal line was never permitted power. Being born on the wrong side of the family had eaten at Prin, like a rotting sickness. He was the other I had suspected as my betrayer—but to be wearing my skin? How he must have hated that!

Prin had always loathed me, and truth be told, I had deserved his hatred. I had never been kind to my pinch-lipped, pious relative. I had gone out of my way to torment him, every chance I got. He was the worst type of fanatic, and now he was the ruling Nomad of Nine Worlds—my birthright. Or was he? Kyar had spoken in the past tense.

"Is he still holding power?" I asked.

Kyar gave his head a quick shake. "No, he left a few days before my own departure to find you."

"He left? Kyar, details!"

"He was deposed. You were deposed," he said, with a wince.

"Why? What had he done wearing my skin?" For a Nomad to be deposed, he had to commit the worst of acts. It had only happened twice before, in my planet's long history.

"He melted holes through glaciers, harvested ice caps, cracked the surface of the planet to reach what he believes lies below. He spent three years trying to prove that the Ice Planet is the original Green World."

"The first rock myth? Nothing but slush! Every damn planet thinks it's the first Green World," I decried. "And my people believe this was my doing?"

"Some of the Icemen don't, but enough do. Regardless, the vote was for your removal. Whether it was you or Prin, the Nomad had to be stopped, before he did irreparable damage to our world. They had the clones destroyed as tradition demands."

"What a bloody mess."

"Yes," Kyar agreed. And there was more to come. "Before they could contain Prin to face his crimes against the planet, he disappeared. Someone gave him the head's up and he fled, after he transferred all the soluble wealth he could access, into some off-planet account. He almost cleaned out the coffers, before he went on a bit of a rampage. He killed some Ice Guards and one of the Icemen."

I cursed soundly. Prin was free, wearing my skin, and filthy rich. And I would be blamed for his crimes. "And mother? She is aware of the imposter?" Why I thought of her then, I don't know. The shameful truth was in Kyar's eyes. "She thinks it is me? She does not see the difference?" I cried.

"You have to admit, you and Mother weren't exactly close in the years before you disappeared," Kyar said.

'Not close' was a most diplomatic description for the spectacular shouting matches that were the only conversation my mother and I had shared. She had disapproved of my lifestyle, cuttingly. I had defended my right to do exactly as I wished, rudely. She had wanted me to marry and produce little Nomads to secure the family line. I had almost laughed my head off over that. I believe it was the last conversation we had, before I was abducted from my Ice Palace, likely while I was in a drunken stupor and passed out on top of some girl whose name I wouldn't remember in the morning.

"Uh … you should know, Megal, you and mother have been the best of friends for three years," Kyar said, with an unexpected quirk of his lips.

"Heaven forbid."

Kyar didn't prepare me at all before he blurted out, "We aren't going home."

"We aren't?"

Kyar sank into the chair beside my bed. "We can't. There is a death warrant—an obscene bounty on your head, for your head."

My curiosity was piqued. "How much?"

"A thousand bizoux."

I hissed at the size of the reward. One bizoux was a windfall to the average man, most would sell their souls for ten. And I was worth a thousand!

Kyar pulled a folded page out of his pocket and handed it over. I took a peek and saw my face as it used to be. It was the face of a stranger. I had forgotten how beautiful I once was. And there, over my head, in big bold script, the promise of a thousand bizoux for my capture, dead or alive. Below was a list of my crimes. It was impressively long, with 'murder of a high official' heading the column.

I tucked the page in my belt and quipped, "Hell of a souvenir."

"Hell of a bounty. If I took you home, you would be iced, Megal. And even if you weren't, how would we prove your innocence? Prin could have been in a radiation explosion or something. He could look like you now. And you weren't on Gehenna under your own name, were you? You can't ask the prison to verify your stay, not after escaping. I can't take you home, Megal, not until this mess is straightened out. And I don't know how to do that, short of tracking down Prin and producing the both of you together."

"But …" I protested lamely. After years of merciless heat, I yearned to feel the bite of crisp air on my skin, and hear the crunch of ice underfoot. To swim in an ice crater, bubbling with steaming geyser water, would make me young again, if only for an imaginary moment. I hungered to see my family and friends, even as the wreck of a man I was now.

"There's more," Kyar continued.

"Of course," I said, weary and resigned.

When he chose to flash it, my brother had a saucy grin. Now did not seem the time, but there it was, spread across his face. "I had to break a few laws myself, to orchestrate your rescue. I'm not any more welcome on the planet than you, now."

"Kyar, what have you done?"

"What haven't I done? Stolen a ship, bribed officials, cleaned out a few private accounts (not mine), freed a few slaves (also not mine). Freed a couple of prisoners. Knocked a bunch of guards unconscious. Crossed restricted zones. Speeding. I can't remember everything." Kyar chuckled, enjoying himself.

I snorted. "So we are both outlaws."

13

"We are, for the time being, but you're the famous one."

"Infamous, I think. And the crew? How did you convince them to do this?" I had yet to lay eyes on the ship's crew, excepting Greely.

"It wasn't a matter of convincing. They are aboard this ship for a whole lot of different reasons. But you should meet them, Megal. They risked their lives to liberate you."

"When I am ready." I wasn't ready. I was drained by Kyar's news.

I had avoided mirrors for the last month. After Kyar departed, I gathered my resolve, such as it was, and faced my reflection. It was still a shock to see how Gehenna had remade me. I appeared more animate skull than flesh and blood man. My hair was almost nonexistent. I had more gaps than teeth. Scars and pox cut into skin, so deeply burned by three suns and blast beetles, it resembled melted wax. What was left of my nose was mashed and pointing to one side, framed by sunken, hollow cheeks. I looked like I had journeyed into true hell and decided to stay, cuddled much too close to the eternal flames.

The only part of myself that I recognized was the eyes. Their silver-blue colour was so light, they might have been made of ice. And that's exactly what they were called—ice eyes—rare on my planet, less rare in the ruling line, but still rare. I knew it was how Sephine had identified me.

I paged Greely. He came at once. I was his only patient on the ship. I said, "Fix the nose. Now. Replace the teeth. Might as well get it over with."

"If you insist, Nomad. My surgery is ready and waiting." Greely motioned for me to lead the way from my room. The good doctor had wanted to wait until I was stronger and healthier, but I was still the rightful Nomad Megal, so he did not argue.

The repairs were completed before two hours had passed. My appearance was improved, but not nearly as much as I had hoped. Vanity. I was surprised I still possessed even a ragged shred of that shallow emotion.

2. The FarGone 5

The next day, Kyar again suggested that I tour the ship and meet the crew, proving he judged me recovered enough.

I delayed. "Tomorrow."

Midday on the morrow, he turned up with a freshly pressed Nomad's tunic. It must have been mine once. After almost a month of recovery, it could still have wrapped me twice around. I donned it without a word and glanced in the mirror. I looked like a beggar, in spite of the richness of the embroidered cloth, trimmed with the pristine white fur that only the ruling line was permitted to wear. Leggings that should have clung tight, hung in loose folds on legs that were little more than twigs, and aspired to be sticks. The stubble of hair that had started to sprout on my head was as white and soft as the vermink pelt around my neck. I ran a hand over the unfamiliar softness on my head. It was lovely to have hair again, or the promise of hair.

"Stop preening. Come, the crew is assembled to meet you. I left them waiting in the galley with baited breath." Kyar was granting me no quarter this day.

Our roles had reversed, since my liberation from Gehenna. Now, he seemed the elder, and I the youngster who needed his guidance and protection. A broken man loves easily, if shown the smallest kindness, and I loved Kyar more than ever before, this brother who had resurrected me, and respected me, even when I cowered and sobbed. I had not earned his respect, yet he gave it. Others would not be so generous, or kind.

I preceded him down the snug corridor of the unfamiliar ship, and asked, "How many crew are aboard?" It was the first time I had been interested enough to ask questions.

"Twenty."

The number was surprisingly small. "And the ship?"

"Invisible. We are aboard a rusty shipper/transport, the FarGone 5, which appears to be delivering goods, although we don't have any, of course. The skin of this ship is misleading. Her hull keeps secrets." He smiled mysteriously.

I didn't know what to say about that except, "I see." Yet, I didn't. "Did this ship truly land on … Gehenna?" I could barely speak the name of the planet that had been my torturer.

"She did."

I glanced at Kyar. "But that is not possible. The security grid stops all mechanical and metallic objects from landing on the planet."

Kyar shrugged. "As I said, her hull keeps secrets, even from me."

Before I could question him about that statement, he added, "And no-one knows who is aboard her, except those already aboard. No-one knows the precious cargo I carry. I traded vessels, soon after we left the Ice Planet. I dumped the stolen ship and had this one waiting in low orbit over Coldstar, after I had raised it off the planet where it had been abandoned. The engineer, Venus, was still aboard, if you can believe that. She couldn't forsake her ship, she said. Anyway, I funded the parts and fuel she needed, and she had the ship flying in no time." Kyar was enjoying his subterfuge and I did not mind being called precious after years of torture.

Clearly, there were many more questions to be asked about the ship, but they would have to keep. We had almost reached the galley. I slowed my limping pace further and said, "And the twenty men? Do I know them?"

"You may know some. I handpicked this team. I trust each and every last one," Kyar stressed. "You should, too."

I only knew why he said that, after I met the motley crew waiting in the kitchen galley. The rusty shipper had no formal meeting room, as if I cared for such trappings now. The crew wore no uniform, another precaution in case we were boarded. Except for my own garment, clothes were casual and varied, even stained and wrinkled, as befitted the vessel.

Bodies snapped straight when Kyar slid the squeaky door aside. He waited for me to enter before him, as protocol demanded. The Nomad of Nine Worlds always leads the way, and walks alone.

I felt the imposter, pretending to be someone I wasn't—the arrogant man I used to be. I made an effort to walk without a crooked limp. I tripped. It hurt the bone that the surgeon had recently straightened as much as he could, given what he had left to work with. Kyar's hand shot under my elbow, to stop me from falling on my face.

Twenty pairs of eyes stared in dismay at the gruesome shell of the man who was being presented to them as their long lost monarch. Those eyes were quick to look anywhere but at me.

I laughed. It did not disperse the tension in the air, but made it crystallize. After three years on Gehenna, many would assume me mad. Perhaps I was.

Captain Glass was presented to me first. The name was familiar. Under my rule, she had been stripped of her captain's rank four years earlier, while in command of the grandest ship in my fleet—the flagship Glacius. I couldn't recall exactly why she had been ousted. Many of my lesser memories were elusive since my time on Gehenna, perhaps because of too many hard blows to the head.

The captain's long white-blonde hair was tightly braided to look too much like rope. I had spent days at a time, restrained by such bonds, and dragged around until my skin was sanded off. I backed away from the woman and moved quickly down the line of crew, mostly male and six female and Greely. Some darted glances at my face, most did not chance it.

The engineer, Venus, was a surprise. As hard as I tried to focus on her, I couldn't. I realized that she did not reside completely in my Universe. I suspected she had one foot in another dimension, although I had never heard of the existence of such beings. Her presence on the ship could explain the FarGone 5's impossible landing on Gehenna.

The one man I recognized easily was Oran'Jay, a cook who fulfilled a second darker duty. He had once ruled the kitchen in my Ice Palace, nestled snuggly in the Crystal Crater, on my home planet. He had never liked me. He did look into my face. It was clear he held the same opinion now. I nodded in appreciation. His emotion was a welcome relief, after all the embarrassed, evasive eyes.

Oran'Jay was not full human. His skin didn't try to be anything but green. Once upon a time, I had nicknamed him 'Frog', after a creature that inhabits most green worlds. The resemblance was undeniable, with his scrawny limbs, bulging eyes, big feet and mottled skin.

"Frog," I acknowledged.

"Corpse," he christened me. I suspected the name would stick.

I moved past him to a giant man with shoulders as wide as a captain's chair. "You took me off Gehenna?" I said.

"I did that." The mixed-up accent was familiar. The rough-hewn, shy face expressed surprise that I knew it was him. A prisoner's brand peeked out from beneath the edge of his short sleeve. One of the prisoner's Kyar had liberated, perhaps.

"I thank you for my life. What is your name?" I asked.

"Hanis Holly."

"Who was with you?'

He motioned to the small, sharp-featured fellow by his side. "Whitey."

"Mo White," the man introduced himself, standing stiffly. The Alfreezian. He was a twitchy fellow, with a narrow nose and narrower eyes. His demeanor was untrustworthy, yet I now knew better than to judge a man by his skin.

"My thanks as well. It couldn't have been a pleasant task, combing through rotting bodies, searching for my carcass." Why had I said that?

"I've done worse." Mo White's expression gave nothing away, yet I believed him.

I turned to address the crew at large, couldn't think of a single thing to say, and left rather abruptly. I hadn't collapsed into a crying heap, and congratulated myself that I was making progress.

It was another week before I ventured from my room again, and I only did so because the ship changed course so abruptly, I was flung off my bed.

I was not expected on the bridge. Everyone leapt to their feet, to stand rod-straight, when I limped across to Kyar and Captain Glass. Both were studying the viewing screen. Space almost always looked the same: black with pinpoints of light—stars.

"A change in course?" I inquired, propping myself against a thin yulithium pillar.

"Catching a comet. We'll ride the tail with the engines off, to make sure we aren't being tailed ourselves, even though it is unlikely." Kyar was certainly taking every precaution imaginable.

"That's wise," I agreed, and didn't know what else to say. Too many eyes were darting glances my way, and there was nothing for me to do on the bridge, except act as a distraction.

I fled back to my quarters and steam-showered for the first time in days—I was not yet in the habit of being clean. Wearing nothing but a tunic that was sticking to my still damp skin, I answered a timid knock on my door. Outside stood one of the shipkeeping staff. I remembered her name—Lillyth. She was sweetly appealing with delicate features, a petite build and large dark eyes. Her auburn hair was shorn short, as most women wore it on ships, due to the scarcity of water, yet hers still looked as soft as feathers. My tongue faltered, to be so unexpectedly confronted. I dare say, I gaped like a fish out of water.

Lillyth bowed with a jerk. She looked as skittish as a snow hare in a fox's den. "Do you desire company, Nomad?" she said, when my tongue remained mute.

"Company?"

"Companionship," she breathed so faintly, I could barely hear her. She toyed with the topmost tie of her tunic.

Then I understood. It had been a lifetime since I had any interest in, or energy for, a sensual act—except for the flash of hot desire I had felt for Sephine. But Sephine was dead, and the knowledge made my heart ache. I could do with some solace. And … pleasure. I wanted to know pleasure again, I couldn't remember what it felt like. For three years, the hands that touched me inflicted only terrible pain. I yearned to feel pleasure again.

"Companionship? I am honoured. Well, why not? Come in, Lillyth." I stepped aside and stumbled. An embarrassed blush heated my face. I tried to hide it by turning my back, to close the door. At the same time, I lowered the lights to a more romantic level. I settled awkwardly on the edge of the bed, as nervous as a virgin. In truth, I felt like one. I had never been with a woman as the man I was now.

I watched, enthralled, while she removed her tunic rather stiffly. There was nothing beneath it except her skin, which looked so soft, my hands twitched to stroke it. Her beauty was marred only by a rough scar at the base of her spine. She had once had a tail, before it was inexpertly removed. Lillyth was not completely human.

She stepped closer to the bedside and my breath caught in anticipation.

I kept my tunic on, not wishing to display my unsightly self. I reached out for her. Tentatively, I caressed her back, savouring the texture of her velvety skin. My hands came to rest on the graceful curve of her waist. My fingers explored the scar at the base of her spine. I turned her around and kissed it gently. "All better," I said, and guided her down to the bed.

I removed my tunic, before I settled beside her, craving to feel her skin against mine. She lay quietly, her eyes closed, while I pressed against her. I nuzzled her warm neck, tasting her with the tip of my tongue, smoothing a hand over her belly and gently undulating ribs. The sensations of Lillyth were so sweet, my hands started to tremble. They were shaking like an old man's when I cupped her small breasts. "You are so beautiful, so soft and sweet," I whispered and leaned over to kiss her nipple, drawing it into my mouth. She whimpered, but not in a good way.

I drew back and gazed at her still face. I waited until her eyes opened, before I asked, "What is it?"

She avoided meeting my gaze. "Could you turn the lights out?"

Too late, I realized she hadn't once reached out to touch my skin. I had been doing all the groping, and she had merely suffered my touch. My heart broke just a little bit more. Lillyth could not bear to look upon me, or touch my ruined skin, nor could I blame her. So why had she come to my room?

"Are you here by choice?" I asked.

"No-one is forcing me. It is my privilege to … to serve you, Nomad." Her tongue stumbled over the lie. I took her hand and checked the palm. She was or had been a slave. If Kyar had rescued her, she would do anything he asked, even cuddle with a monster. Maybe she already kept Kyar's bed warm at night. There were some things I would not share with my brother. And there was nothing in the world I would ask of a slave, after three years of being one.

My desire beaten down, I grabbed up my tunic, to cover the skin I had so foolishly forgotten to be ashamed of. I held the cloth before me, hiding as much as I could. "Go," I said, my voice coming out much too harshly. "Please," I added, ashamed when my voice broke on the word.

She was quick to toss on her tunic and run for the door. "I'm sorry, Nomad," she said over her shoulder, before she disappeared.

Furious with myself for being so blind to the truth, that no woman would ever willingly share a bed with me again, I needed to vent. I donned my clothes and went to confront the man I believed had sent Lillyth to me, placing the pair of us in an intolerable position.

I was right. It was my misguided brother, with memories of how shallow and self-serving I used to be. I was not that man anymore, and never would be again. I set Kyar straight on that point, and stormed away. For some reason, my brother was smiling when I left him.

I did not see Kyar again for two days. He couldn't leave the bridge, except to sleep briefly. Surfing on a comet's tail requires alert eyes, and many pairs of fast hands on the controls, to dodge the collection of churning debris. Regardless, the smaller particles that pelted the hull made it sound like we were flying through a hail storm.

No ships appeared on the sensors. We were safe for the time being.

As soon as we said farewell to the comet, Kyar called a meeting of the senior crew. Including Kyar and myself, eight sat around the worn dining table.

The ship's captain was beside me, her hair still unfortunately braided. The huge Hanis Holly and twitchy Mo White flanked Kyar. I was informed of their official roles on the ship. Hanis was the technical officer, and Mo was a cultural liaison, experienced in dealing with foreign planets and beings. He did not look the part.

Oran'Jay attended, but not as a cook. Greely was also present. Except for my regular skin regeneration treatments and tending the occasional minor complaint (usually mine), he didn't have anything else to do. The engineer, Venus, sat opposite me. It was hard to guess her age, perhaps because my eyes had so much trouble focusing on her physical body, even though she was sitting in plain sight. Trying to do so made my head ache, so I stopped trying.

"Well, we have some decisions to make," Kyar began, getting right to the point. "We have liberated the Nomad, and he is healthy enough, and of sound mind."

"Please, enough flattery," I drawled and stroked a hand over my softly stubbled crown. I loved touching the new growth.

Kyar continued, as if he had not been so childishly interrupted. "Since Nomad Megal is capable of ruling, it is time to track down Prin. We find Prin, we can all go home as heroes. Megal will reclaim his position as Nomad, richly reward us, and pardon all our crimes."

I snorted. "You paint a rosy picture, Kyar, so how do we find Prin? Many must be searching for him, since there is a fortune of a bounty on his head," I said, stating the obvious, then added, "my head." It was a bit confusing.

"True enough, but we have an advantage. I know the direction he took when he left the Ice Planet. Plus, I know Prin better than most. I spent three years cozying up to him, hoping he would let slip any clue as to what he had done with my true brother."

"And did he?"

Kyar pulled a face. "In a way. After he escaped, I searched his rooms and found the remnants of a burnt missive, scripted from a transmission from Gehenna. The scrap that was left made vague mention of a prisoner who walked with death. I deduced that it meant you. Prin must have had someone reporting to him, keeping him informed about your … circumstances."

Of course Prin would have been kept informed. Prin would have celebrated every minute detail of my misery. My chest tightened with rage, the strong emotion unfamiliar, after so many defeated years. "What direction did Prin take when he left the Ice Planet?" I demanded.

"I believe Prin was also going to Gehenna, to take you off the planet somehow, maybe through bureaucratic channels, or with a hefty bribe." Kyar shrugged.

I blinked in surprise. "To what end?"

"If your body was produced or identified as his, no-one would continue to hunt for Prin, you. That would be the end of the bounty warrant. Hell, Prin could even collect the bounty himself, through an agent acting on his behalf." Kyar's voice was laced with disgust. "So we had to beat him to Gehenna, hence the fastest ship I could lay my hands on. We got to you first, and I believe we got away without anyone being the wiser. That's why I have taken every precaution to be invisible. We can't have Prin killing you off and producing your skin, your DNA, to buy his freedom, and line his pockets with more of our planet's wealth."

"No, we can't. Find Prin. Deliver Prin to me." My voice was harsh with loathing when I spat my cousin's name. I hated the man, and I would see his brain removed from my clone's skull, as soon as it could be arranged. I would reclaim my birthright, and this time, I would not neglect my lands and people. I ached so deeply to see my home, it felt like a sickness.

Kyar nodded. "We'll find him, hopefully before he finds us. It might get a bit tricky, trying to avoid him and find him all at the same time— and if he suspects I have you, you can bet he'll be tracking us. It might give his location away."

It sounded complicated. I settled back and listened to the others discuss how to find and capture Prin. I offered no words, I was less informed than anyone.

Oran'Jay was as opinionated as always, his wide mouth shooting out words, as if an argument was in progress, not an agreeable discussion. His bulging eyes kept sliding me incredulous glances and I assumed the reason. In the past, I had been a man of too many words, my ears preferring to hear my voice over all others, even when I was spouting nonsense, which was most of the time. But Gehenna was guaranteed to change a man. I had changed so much, I barely recognized myself, inside and out. I preferred to listen now.

When my thoughts wandered and Sephine's dying face appeared out of nowhere, I shoved to my feet. My chair legs scraped the metal deck. It sounded like a harsh scream. I staggered out of the galley, seeking the refuge of my room.

Kyar came for me an hour later. I did not rise from my bed. "We will dine with the crew this evening," he said.

Even with my mouthful of new teeth, I was still in the habit of eating alone in my room. I shook my head and kept my eyes closed. I tried not to cry in front of him now.

"Megal." His voice was as stern as a father's. I hauled in a shuddering breath. He sighed softly and settled on the edge of the bed. "Megal, listen. I know that you don't like to talk about Gehenna, but anyone with eyes can see what horrors you have endured these three years." He took my hand and did not release it. "When you arrived on the ship, and I saw … you …" His fingers spasmed, squeezing mine too hard. "I thought I had found you, only to watch you draw your last breath. After three years of searching, I thought I was too late. Greely held the same opinion, but you fought death. You have survived the worst that a man can endure. I know it will take more time for you to adjust to a normal life, but the crew needs to see that you are capable of ruling again. They need to see even a shadow of the man you used to be. And when we find Prin, you must be strong. You must be the man you used to be."

"I will never be that man again, I do not want to be him. He was a fool."

"Be that as it may," he said with a quirk of his lips, "that man was strong-willed and decisive and confident. He may not have been prudent, he may have been brash and inexperienced and selfish, but those are traits of youth. If you had not been stolen away, you would have grown into a good ruler, maybe a great ruler. We'll never know, because you aren't that man anymore, but you are still the Nomad. You will rule the Nine Worlds again, as soon as we capture Prin. And I believe you will be a great leader this time around, but the others need to believe it. You need their support and their loyalty."

"When did you get so smart?" I choked out. It was a pathetic attempt at humour. "You should be the Nomad. You would have done a better job of it, then and now."

"I was born too late. And you're still alive, so you're stuck with the job," he said.

I sat up and made the effort to pull the shredded pieces of my soul back together.

"Go and preen. I'll wait for you," Kyar prompted.

I went and tidied up. Kyar had a gift waiting when I returned to him. Without a word, he handed me a carved staff. He must have stopped at a commercial planet, when I was too ill to notice. The fine wood and metal embossing showed rare craftsmanship. I was so overwhelmed by his thoughtful gesture, I couldn't speak to thank him. I hugged him instead. I didn't let him go until he clapped me on the shoulder and stepped back. I think he was a bit embarrassed. Before Gehenna, I had never hugged him and he had certainly never hugged me.

Walking more smoothly with the support, I accompanied my brother to the galley. We shared the end of the long table where we held our meetings. I made the effort to sit straight and converse intelligently. When Kyar was summoned to the bridge, I was left behind, awkward and alone.

Oran'Jay padded up before too many minutes had passed. I would have suspected him of compassion if he had been anyone else.

"Corpse," he greeted me and claimed Kyar's chair.

"Frog. Did you poison my food?" I hesitated to take another bite. Oran'Jay was a master at the art of poison. I had ordered him to such action in the past. Once, I had even had him tamper with the visiting Prin's lunch. My cousin had not left his room for two days after that meal. By then, the pretty girl he was wooing was sharing my bed. He had been in love with her, I think, and I couldn't even remember her name.

"Didn't poison your dinner. Might have spit in your soup, though." Oran'Jay winked a yellow-tinged eye.

I barked in laughter. It caught me off-guard. "After what I've lived on, Frog, I could stomach dining on shit."

"Not quite as fine as you used to be, are you?"

"Not even close." I found I was not minding his company.

"Ah, I only poison you in my dreams," Oran'Jay confided. Leaning closer, he turned serious. "And I don't want you dead. I need your Nomad's pardon to go home again."

"Why? You've been outlawed for your cooking?"

Oran'Jay ignored my smart mouth. "Before he disappeared, Prin had me kill off a few of his challengers. He laid the blame on me. He said I was acting alone, not on the Nomad's orders. I was about to join you on Gehenna, until your brother freed me, forcibly. I want to go home again.

Miss my wife and spawn." He revealed the personal emotion with obvious reluctance.

"You will have my pardon," I promised. "Did you know that an imposter wore my skin?"

"Of course I knew." Oran'Jay's rather pointy tongue darted out to lick his thin lips. "You never let me murder anyone, only make them sicken, or lose their memories." He sounded disgusted with me. "Now Prin, he liked killing. Always wanted the poison to work slow, and he liked to watch. Seemed to excite him in some perverted way."

"Who did he have killed?" I asked.

"I kept a list for three years. You can read it, if you can stomach it. Prin wanted Kyar poisoned next. It was the last assassination he ordered. As you can see, I didn't do it."

"Good thing," I said, my heart skipping several beats.

"Before he left, Prin blamed me for the last few murders, when I was only carrying out the Nomad's orders, as I am sworn to do. I would have poisoned him, if he hadn't taken off."

I lost my appetite and shoved my dinner away.

"Ah, come on. Eat up, Corpse. You're still skinnier than a skeleton," Oran'Jay chided, sliding my plate back in front of me.

"If the food had any flavour to speak of, perhaps I might manage it."

Barbed insults were still being exchanged, when Kyar appeared in the doorway. He motioned for me to accompany him. The meal was over for me anyway. We ended up in Kyar's room for a change. He poured out two measures of red brandy. I had not had a drink in over three years.

"Bad news?" I guessed.

He looked surprised. "No, a toast. To finding Prin." He clinked our goblets together.

"To finding Prim Prin," I said, recalling the name I used to call my cousin, when we were children. I drank deeply—such a toast required a drained cup, so I drained mine.

"Although he is not so prim anymore, what with all the murder and mayhem," Kyar said as he refilled my goblet.

"No, he certainly is not." I lounged back into the furred chair and sipped the second ration slowly. The first one had hit me with the force of a meteor.

The red tinge in the brandy came from a single precious drop of ice-blood per bottle. Ice-blood was incredibly rare, since it was found only on my home planet, and only in four locations. Three of those deep caves were stringently guarded commercial sites. Each and every drop of the potent red hallucinogenic liquid that trickled off frozen stalactites was collected—milked from my planet as if from her icy teats. The fourth cave, its secret location known only to the ruling line, was where every Nomad for thousands upon thousands of years had sought his vision. It was where I had envisioned what the future held for me.

If a person drank enough of the red brandy, they started having their own delirious fantasies. The drink was a much sought after export that made my planet a bloody fortune, almost literally.

Kyar finished his second drink and poured a third, as if he needed it. He held that cup up and toasted me. Kyar was growing maudlin from the fast consumption of the heady beverage. He never had been much of a drinker. We talked without consequence, and he poured himself a fourth. I nursed my second, refusing more. If I had known what he was about to say, I would have usurped the whole bloody bottle.

"And my Sephine, I still have to get her off Gehenna somehow. It shouldn't be hard, she can do a lot that pure humans can't. She'll be fine. You're sure you don't know why she wasn't at the rendezvous point?" Kyar asked, as he had so many times before.

"I don't know," I whispered, repeating the lie I had already told him, every time he asked. "You and Sephine were ... close?"

Kyar looked sheepish, and tipsy. "Didn't want to say anything, especially after what you've been through, but ... I'll tell you a secret. We got married as soon as we fled the Ice Planet. No-one knows, since she's a slave—was a slave. She wasn't even my slave, until I stole her away. Not a proper match for the Nomad's line, but love is love. Life was lonely with Prin as my brother."

It probably hadn't been much better for him when he'd lived with his true brother, but he didn't say that. I swallowed hard, trying to keep my meal down. I was truly sick with guilt. "You married Sephine? How long is the contract?"

"Until death. There's no-one else in the Universe for me. She's fantastic. Wait until you get to know her, I know you didn't have a chance on Gehenna. Once I determined that you were there, she insisted on going down to get you, since she has that special ability to make you look dead. And we had to get you off the planet fast, before Prin turned up. Did you have any chance to talk to her?"

26

"No." I shut my eyes when all I could see was her dying gaze. Kyar had loved her enough to sign a lifetime alliance. Such a marriage term was almost unheard of.

"Better tell you something else." Kyar looked as reluctant to speak as when he had told me that Prin was violating my clone. "You may have found yourself thinking about Sephine, uh, affectionately. Now that you know she's mine, I don't want you to feel bad about it. It's not your fault."

"Kyar, I have not been thinking of Sephine affectionately." I kept thinking of her dying. "What are you babbling about?"

"I'm talking about her bite. When she bites a man, a human man, there is a side-affect. Sort of an addiction to her poison—to her. It makes you want to be with her and close to her. So don't feel bad if you've been having desires for my wife. It's really not your fault, and you didn't know she was my wife, did you?"

"No, how could I? Has she ever bitten you?"

Kyar shook his head. "I fell in love with her without a bite. Anyway, I just wanted you to know that's why you might have been thinking about Sephine. She told me the addiction is supposed to fade within a month or two."

I nodded to acknowledge his words, giving nothing away, yet I wondered if I would stop seeing Sephine's ghost, when the feeling faded.

"Soon as we can, we'll take another trip to Gehenna. She knows to watch for me every half-moon, in the same spot we picked you up. She'll be waiting there."

She was already waiting there for Kyar, forever in the bone field. I should have told him about Sephine then, but I didn't. I couldn't bear to break his heart. And I seemed to have lost my courage on Gehenna, as well as my pride.

I poured Kyar another brandy and ran, but I did not seek my room. I toured the ship until I found Mo and Hanis. I ordered them to my quarters and shut us all in together. They looked anxious about being closeted with me.

"How can we serve you, Nomad?" Hanis asked, staying close to Mo.

"There is something we need to discuss. Have you told anyone of Sephine's death?" I asked pointblank.

"You know?" Mo gasped. "How did she die?"

I shook my head warningly. "Have you told anyone?"

"I haven't," Mo claimed, glancing at Hanis.

"Not me. I didn't want Kyar to hear by accident. The two seemed real chummy, if you know what I mean."

"I do. You will keep your mouths shut about this. It is one secret that must remain between the three of us, until I decide the time is right for Kyar to know the truth. Clear?"

"Yes, Nomad," they said in unison.

I dismissed them, but did not enjoy my solitude. I had killed my brother's wife. The knowledge festered inside me. Sephine's ghost drove me from my room. I paced corridors, unintentionally learning the layout of the ship.

The engine room was a surprise. The rusty FarGone 5 sported gleaming inner workings worthy of the sleekest jump-craft. This ship could probably create its own wormholes just by thinking about it. There were a number of curious upgrades that I didn't recognize. They looked alien and dangerous. I didn't touch anything.

After an hour of limping around the ship, rather like a ghost myself, I returned to my room exhausted, and found that I had company. It was almost like old times, finding a girl in my bed. Although this was no girl, but a mature woman at least twenty years my senior. And Captain Glass was technically on my bed, not in it, although it still seemed like an odd place to find her, especially out of uniform, which she was. She had donned a low-cut silky black tunic that clung to her breasts. They were larger than I had realized, and her legs were bare.

"Captain Glass?" I said, making a question of her name.

"At your service." She rose to approach me, her hips swaying. "I heard that Lillyth disappointed you the other night. Let me make it up to you," she drawled in a throaty voice that was nothing like the one she used on the bridge.

I was bewildered by her flirtatiousness, and her attire. Could she truly get past my repulsive appearance to screw my skin? And why would she want to? Aside from the fact that she was old enough to be my mother, I was hideous.

"No need to sacrifice yourself," I said, gripped by some swampy mixture of embarrassment and shame. I held my position by the door, simply mortified that sleeping with me had become a chore to be passed along, and gossiped about throughout the ship. "I am not yet in full health and still require much rest. My needs will keep."

She stepped so close, I could feel her warm breath on my cheek. We were nose-to-nose, and in her violet-blue eyes, I glimpsed some sort of dark perverted passion. "It is no sacrifice, Nomad. It would be a great pleasure." She leaned forward to kiss me. Her mouth was hot, hungry and almost painfully aggressive in its exploration of mine.

I certainly felt some stirrings, until her ropey braids swayed forward and lay over my arm. I expected them to take on a life of their own, to wrap themselves around me and tie me up, leaving me helpless, at the mercy of others. The touch of her braided hair made my skin crawl and I shuddered. One of her pointier teeth cut into my upper lip. I felt pain and tasted blood. The captain licked the blood and moaned.

I had known enough agony to last ten lifetimes, and rather frightened, I pulled back. "No, stop."

"Stop?" She didn't seem to understand my words, or perhaps believe them.

"Yes. Stop"

Her brow furrowed. "Why?"

"I think you should go." I jerked a hand at the door.

"You're telling *me* to go?" she asked incredulously.

"Am I not making my wishes clear?" I said, aiming to sound like the ruler I was, at least in name.

She laughed harshly. I had offended the ship's captain and her tongue got away from her. "You refuse me? You? If you held no great title, you could not pay women to lay under you. You would have to both blind and bind them to stomach your touch. Yet you refuse *me*?" she said, as if she truly couldn't believe it. "I brought you aboard this ship wrapped in death. You were as dead as a man can be, yet still live. You wore the scent of death, you were ... intimate with death." Her flash of anger transformed back into passion. She eyed me as hungrily as if I was a basket of fresh fruit, her breathing fast and shallow. The captain's moist red mouth looked about to eat me alive.

"Death excites you?" I guessed.

Her lips parted and she stepped close again. "Death satisfies me. And you're the closest thing to death on this ship."

In a flash, I recalled why she had been stripped of her high-level posting. She had been discovered to be keeping preserved corpses in her cabin on the Glacius—a collection of stiff, dead lovers. No-one had wanted to fly with her after that, in case they ended up in the same state.

Her passion was a lot too warped for my taste. If she loved death so, she might well murder me after the deed was done, to canoodle with my cooling, stiffening corpse.

"I have had more than my fill of death, Captain Glass, so I am going to refuse your very tempting offer," I said as diplomatically as I was able. I groped for the handle to open the door. "I think it is time for you to return to your own cabin. I find myself quite fatigued and in need of rest."

"Are you sure?" She took my hand and raised it to her mouth, to suckle hard on the ragged stump of what used to be my index finger.

"Uh, yes, positive," I declared, trying to ignore the sharp zaps of sexual desire shooting through my body, in spite of my distaste and fear. I reclaimed my finger and slid wide the door.

"Well, if you change your mind, you know where to find me." Captain Glass stepped out the door, her words left lingering in the air. Maybe I was a fool, but I did not call her back. I went to bed alone, haunted by Sephine's ghost. In my own way, I slept with death now.

Less than a week later, we passed over Coldstar, the ninth and smallest of my nine planets. The magnetic surface was a ship's graveyard for wrecked, contaminated and outdated vessels. They were simply released into the planet's atmosphere. They were drawn gently down to lie forever on the inhospitable rocky ground. The planet's gravity field was so weak that everything eventually settled to the surface perfectly intact. It was from Coldstar that Kyar had resurrected the FarGone 5, now the ship was back to visit its old stomping ground.

I stood on the bridge beside my brother. We watched the globe grow larger on the viewing screen. From space, it looked gray and drab, yet it was worth its own weight in the rare minerals that lay abundantly beneath the drab surface. A vast number of mining colonies thrived in the depths of the planet.

Kyar tapped my shoulder. "This is as close as I dare to go to the Ice Planet. I'm going to contact Jann and find out what's been happening at home. I'm hoping he's unearthed some news about Prin." Proximity to Coldstar ensured that we could not be traced by our transmission, even if someone managed to intercept and unravel the encoded communiqué.

I nodded my approval. We both trusted Jann with our lives. He was old, invisible and called no crater home. According to my brother, he was also one of the few Icemen who believed in my innocence—lucky for me. Jann had known my father, the former Nomad, and had tossed Kyar and me around in the air, when we were still small enough to believe we could fly.

Kyar sat down at the communications console and spoke his message. It would be scrambled beyond recognition, before it left the ship. The cypher-key to unscramble it was sent separately, to a different location.

I waited, limping impatiently around the bridge as though caged. Captain Glass ignored me. I didn't pace anywhere near her.

Jann took so long to respond, I returned to my quarters and had a nap. I slept until Kyar roused me gently. He knew I was inclined to awaken screaming about rats.

"Any news?" I yawned and rubbed my face awake. It was still a surprise to feel a proper jutting nose. Even though he was no cosmetic surgeon, Greely had done a decent job of restoring that small but vital feature. I could even breathe through it now, as long as I didn't have a cold.

"Not much. The planet's been quiet since Prin disappeared. Jann has heard a few rumours about our cousin's whereabouts, but nothing he can verify." Kyar sat down and kneaded his neck, revealing his tension.

"Are the Icemen ruling my planets, until this mess is straightened out?" I said, assuming the answer.

"Uh … no. There is something I haven't told you yet." It sounded like a confession.

I straightened on my bed. "Do tell."

"You're married."

"I am not married," I denied automatically. "Oh, you mean Prin."

"I mean the Nomad Megal."

"Ah, me." It hurt when I scowled. My skin was tight and tender after Greely's latest skin regeneration treatment. "Who is she? Have I ever met the mother of future Nomads?"

"You have."

My curiosity was piqued. "So, who is the lucky woman?"

"Daughter of an old family friend. Berle Frost's eldest. Do you remember Noel Frost?"

The name was familiar. The image of a tall, cross girl came to mind, sharing our dinner table whenever her father had visited mine. I remembered her voice best, cutting and colder than my planet. I used to call her Frosty Noel. I had not deemed her worthy of the attention of the man I used to be, when I was an arrogant ass.

"And how long has Prin been married?"

"Not long. The ceremony took place only a month or two before he escaped. It was arranged by her father. She barely saw Prin beforehand."

"And he did not take her with him?" I ran a hand over my head, trying to feel more growth.

"No, he did not. It was no love match, not like Sephine and I."

I cleared my throat, when it constricted as if squeezed by an unseen hand. "Well, she might be a match for Prin, but not for me. I didn't sign the contract and it will be terminated."

"It might not be that simple." Kyar studied his hands. "Berle Frost is now head of the mining conglomerate, for all nine worlds, and a Senior Iceman. There have been many changes while you've been gone. And if Noel is already pregnant with the next Nomad, it is your child that she carries."

I hadn't even thought of that. It was my genetic matter she had been exposed to, so any resulting offspring would be mine, even though I hadn't had the pleasure of being intimate with my wife, who believed she was allied to me, not Prin. Although the union might not last long, after I reclaimed my planets. Once she saw *me*, she might well terminate the contract herself. Or run screaming from not only the Ice Planet, but the entire galaxy.

"She is ruling the planets?" I guessed.

"Temporarily. It sounds like she is doing a fine job, too. She's smart and tough enough, that's for sure."

I hated her suddenly. "Wonderful," I ground out.

"So we are both mated. The half-moon on Gehenna is next week. We're going to swing by and pick up Sephine, then we will start tracking Prin in earnest." Kyar rose to leave.

I didn't want to go within a hundred galaxies of Gehenna ever again, and I could not avoid telling Kyar of Sephine's fate any longer. Plus, confession is supposed to be good for the soul. Maybe a confession would stop Sephine's ghost from tormenting me.

I motioned for him to stay. "Sit, Kyar."

Alerted by my grim tone, he did.

"About Sephine," I began, my heart aching for my brother. I just prayed he could forgive me for my actions.

"What about Sephine?"

"She will … not be meeting you, Kyar. She is dead," I blurted out.

Kyar's face crumpled until he looked like a lost little boy. "No!"

"Yes. She's gone. I'm so sorry, Kyar."

"But how? How?"

I could not meet his eyes. "She did not tell me of your plan, she just bit me." My fingers touched the scar on my neck. I gazed at the floor, anywhere but at Kyar's tragic face. "I defended myself, I had acquired a goran spine. I didn't know her intent and thought she was trying to kill me."

"You killed her?" Kyar backed away as if I was a monster.

"I didn't know, Kyar. I did not know. I'm so sorry." I reached a hand toward him, pleading for forgiveness and trying to offer comfort, all at the same time.

His eyes filled with tears. "Yet you did not tell me all these weeks!"

"It isn't the easiest thing to say. Please Kyar, forgive me. It was an accident. I am so sorry for what I did, but I did not know." I touched his arm.

He shoved me back and punched me in the nose, cracking the bone and knocking me to the ground. Before I could find my feet, he was gone.

Sick with grief, I blamed Prin for this, too. Not only had he ruined my life in every possible way, but because of him, I had lost my brother's love.

Anticipation to find Prin bit sharp and sweet in my soul. Revenge would be the greatest pleasure I had ever known.

It was time to hunt down Prin. It was time to wear the Nomad's cloak with authority. But first I paged Greely, to fix my nose, again.

3. The First Fare

After weeks of zigzagging across space like a lost snow goose, we had made no progress in learning Prin's whereabouts. Of course, the fact that we were trying to avoid him at the same time, made our task that much harder.

Kyar had not forgiven me, but now spoke to me on occasion, when it was unavoidable. While he grieved, I had stepped up and commanded the search. My determination overshadowed my good sense. I spent a fortune trying to track my evil cousin and we were soon running out of leads and funds. A ship needs fuel, the crew has to eat, most planets charge exorbitant docking fees, and bribes are dearer still. Jann regularly sent encoded missives, but forwarding us a financial transfer was traceable, and therefore too risky. Nor did he have access to the deep wells of wealth we needed. We were on our own.

Two months into our hunt, I called a meeting to announce that we were broke. I had already informed Kyar in a note. His written response had assured me that he already had a plan in place to solve our monetary problem.

When our ragtag group of eight was assembled around the table, Kyar rose to brief the crew, and I had a chance to study him. I was shocked by the change. A faded version of my brother stood before me, his skin lifeless, his eyes dulled.

Even his voice was lethargic when he outlined his strategy. "We are about to become a true shipper/transport. Our hull says that's what we are, so we might as well play the part. Transporting goods and passengers will pay our way. And we'll only go where we want to go, where our quest for Prin leads us. Those are the contracts we'll accept. The ship is already registered with A-1 All Planetary Shipping, as part of our cover, so now we will accept fares. I've already informed them that we're eager for some jobs."

"We are to become a common APS vessel?" Captain Glass made no effort to hide her scorn.

Kyar sank into his chair with a careless shrug. "For the time being—unless someone else has a better idea."

It was hard to tell if Mo White was serious when he said, "Piracy? Smuggling?"

"Not a chance. We don't want to attract any attention from the UGS, nor can we risk the Nomad." Kyar's scathing tone said what his words did not. The crew shared uncomfortable glances. No-one except Kyar and I knew why he now acted like he detested the very sight of me.

Regardless, I shoved to my feet to support my brother. "Becoming a shipper is ideal. We'll go where we want and get paid for it, completely incognito. Jann received a reliable report this very day. Apparently Prin conducted a traceable financial transaction in the Gashmore Galaxy, so that's where we'll travel first. Do you think you can arrange a fare to that sector?" I asked Kyar directly. Assigning him tasks was my way of attempting to keep him from drowning in his grief.

"Shouldn't be a problem." His tone was barely civil, and his jaw so tight, I half-expected the bone to break. "I'll check with the service. Parcels would be preferable to people, but if we have to take passengers, there are plenty of cabins available. No-one will recognize the Nomad for who he is. Just make sure everyone calls him 'Corpse'." The insult was poorly veiled by bitter humour.

I did not welcome the idea of strangers aboard what I had come to think of as my home. I had grown surprisingly comfortable with the crew. I played cards with Mo and Hanis, and some of the others. I had discussed the engines with the engineer, Venus, who refused to reveal her ship's secrets—even to me. Oran'Jay and I enjoyed exchanging snipes whenever we passed. Lillyth had spoken to me without blushing just the other day. The crew was beginning to feel rather like a big mismatched family, at least to me. I no longer felt the need to distance myself from other men, or put on airs, as I had in the past. I no longer believed that the Nomad Megal was better than his subjects—quite the opposite.

And soon there might be intruders aboard. I wasn't ready to be stared at like a freak, by those who were not used to my unsightly appearance. Greely still provided weekly skin regeneration treatments, but the deep healing was a slow process and would never undo all the damage to my scarred skin. Not even close.

"Try and book only packages," I said to Kyar.

"I might not have a choice. We'll have to take what we can get."

There was nothing else to discuss. Kyar went off to communicate with A-1. Later that night, he sent me a brief note, via Lillyth. It confirmed a shipping contract. He didn't state whether it was parcel or passenger. He didn't reveal a damn thing. I balled up the page and heaved it across the room. Except for the damage to my nose, Kyar was keeping all his anger inside, letting it fester and leak out in a steady flow of vitriolic actions. It wasn't doing him any good—or me.

Determined to clear the air, I strode off to his cabin. He wasn't there. I tried the bridge. He wasn't there either. "Where is Kyar?" I asked Captain Glass. Now that death and I were on cooler terms, she barely noticed me.

She pressed some buttons and checked her consol. "Cargo bay two, the largest one."

Off I went to the cargo bay. The door was closed. I wrestled the uncooperative heavy metal aside and limped inside. When something smashed into my chest with the force of a rocket, I was felled, unable to breathe at all. Was Kyar trying to kill me?

Apparently not. As I writhed on the ground, clawing at my chest, as if that would help the air find a way inside, Kyar appeared over me. His face was anxious, not gloating.

"Heavens, Megal! Couldn't you announce your presence?" He dropped to his knees and rolled me onto my side. "Breathe, damn it. Should I page Greely?"

I shook my head and dragged in a whisper of air. "I'll live," I rasped. "What hit me? A meteor?"

"Soar-board. I was riding around the empty space—racing," he amended. "I hit you pretty hard, I didn't see you until the last second."

To have my brother speaking to me civilly, and showing concern, was worth the small price I now paid. I spotted the abandoned board lying at my feet—longer than me and fiery red. The gravity-blocking engine mounted on the back was bigger than my fist. This board would have an impressive speed.

"No helmet, Kyar?" I wheezed.

His face closed up and he backed off.

I swore until I squandered my limited air, and collapsed briefly, before I managed more productive words. "You may not care if you die ... but I do. If you need a way to vent your anger, take it out on me—not yourself." I tried to stand and succeeded in sitting. Kyar did not offer assistance. "If I could give my life to bring Sephine back, don't you know

36

that I would?" I cried. "You act as if I meant to … do what I did. Nothing could be further from the truth. Nothing." I tried to stand again and managed to lurch unsteadily to my feet, swaying like a drunk. "Tell me how I might earn your forgiveness. I know I can't undo what I've done -
"

My brother lashed out, knocking me back to the metal planking. "No, you can't!" Kyar towered over me with clenched fists. "You can't bring Sephine back. You've taken her away, just like every girl I ever cared about. All you had to do was crook your finger, and off they would go, without a backwards glance. Why do you think I stopped bringing girls to meet you? It was like a game to you, wanting anything you couldn't have, only to toss it away once you had satisfied your own pleasure! And now you've taken Sephine—forever!" Kyar spun on his heel and marched for the door. At the threshold, he paused and said, "If I could have it to do over, if the choice was between Sephine and you …" His face twisted.

"It would be Sephine," I said. "Of course it would be. Your new bride or a brother you hadn't seen in three years, a brother who was never worth more than the title he was born to flaunt—there would be no choice. It should be Sephine with you now, not me."

"Not you. Anyone but her murderer!" Kyar slammed from the chamber, almost derailing the door. Maybe he never would forgive me. Until that moment, I hadn't realized the depth of his resentment over the past, and now I had killed his beloved. I hated the man that I used to be with a vengeance, but Sephine's death had been a tragic accident, not more than that.

I was trapped in the cargo bay, until I recouped the strength to open the unwieldy door. I refused to summon help—a sign that my pride was healing along with my skin. Or perhaps not pride, but self-satisfaction, since I would never be an arrogant, egotistical bastard again. Gehenna had seen to that.

It wasn't until the next day that I learned about our fare. Mo pulled me aside and reported that it was a retrieval from a restricted planet. He wasn't the type to worry, but the lines wrinkling his forehead proved he was worried now.

I couldn't allow Kyar's new recklessness to endanger the whole crew. I summoned him, and the senior staff, to our usual meeting place in the galley. I had no wish to further alienate my brother, and tried to be tactful when I said, "Um, Kyar. This restricted planet ... do you really think we should risk the UGS? Surely we can find another fare—a safer fare?"

"Safer fares won't pay a fraction of what we'll earn for this one little pickup and delivery," Kyar countered, unpleasantly smug. "And there is no real risk. It's a tiny planet in some foggy galaxy at the edge of the Universe. Even the Universal Guard Ships don't patrol that far out. The planet is stupid enough to have embraced a nuclear age, on their own planet! So they're not going to be around for long anyway." He laughed without amusement.

"But still ... did you not say that we should avoid drawing attention to ourselves?"

"Yes, I did, and who is going to notice what we do in the middle of nowhere, on a planet that is about to self-destruct? Not a bloody soul. This is the most profitable venture available at the moment, and I've already accepted the contract. It will take us less than a week to get there. We'll make the pickup and head directly to the Gashmore Galaxy for delivery," Kyar said, as if it had been decided, challenging my word as Nomad.

I was torn. I did not agree with his decision, yet I owed my brother more than I could ever repay. I nodded my consent, even though he hadn't asked for it.

At top speeds, and creating multiple ship-generated wormholes, which depleted our fuel supply quite alarmingly, it took six days to reach the restricted planet, sitting at the edge of the restricted galaxy. Not one planet in the whole expanse knew life thrived abundantly across most of the Universe, therefore ships were forbidden to even fly through the zone. Yet they often did, making unauthorized use of the galaxy's own wormhole, instead of squandering the fuel necessary to create a multiple wormhole detour.

We were doing a lot more than cutting across the galaxy. We were going to land on the tiny green and blue orb.

"Is the planet humanoid?" I asked Kyar, lounging around on the bridge to watch our descent. I had claimed the captain's chair and no-one had told me I couldn't sit there.

"Yes. This planet was seeded with our kind during the Spread, just like tens of thousands of other planets."

I yawned. "What are we picking up, anyway?"

"A girl," Kyar said, in the most matter-of-fact tone.

"What?" I stopped lounging and jerked upright out of the luxurious fur padding. Clearly, I should have asked my question sooner.

"Just one," Kyar said, as if I was overreacting.

"A girl? A living girl? Not cargo?" I had assumed we were retrieving cargo, given that it was a restricted planet. From the way the bridge crew was gawking at Kyar, I wasn't the only one in the dark about our mission. "You might have mentioned it sooner," I snapped, then asked a different question. "And why are we taking one girl off a restricted planet?"

He shrugged. "Long story I'm sure, but I only heard the short version. About twenty years ago, a spaceship crashed on the surface. The crew was stuck there until another ship could retrieve them. Anyway, one of the fellows did a little too much fraternizing with one of the planet's inhabitants."

"The pair wishes to reunite?" I guessed.

"Nope. The native female is long dead, but she did give birth."

"We are retrieving the child?"

"Yup, except she is no longer a child, since she was born about nineteen years ago. The father has been monitoring her progress from afar. It seems she has started to exhibit some disturbing, non-human traits."

This just kept getting worse. "The father is not humanoid?"

"Not pure human, half, I heard. Offspring looked fully human though, luckily. Given the circumstances, the father has decided it's high time to get the girl off the planet, for her own safety, and the planet's safety. Maybe the whole restricted galaxy's wellbeing."

I really didn't want to know how one girl could endanger a whole planet, let alone an entire galaxy, especially since that one girl would soon be sharing the same fragile hull that separated me from open space, but I had to ask. "Kyar, how is she dangerous? What is her father other than half-human?"

It was obvious that Kyar did not want to say. Instead he named the exact sum we were being paid for this pickup and delivery. The amount terrified me.

"What is her father, other than human?" I repeated.

"Catalystene."

With a curse, I shoved out of the captain's chair. "Are you insane?" I was too distraught to say it in a nicer way. "You want to bring a Catalyst aboard the ship? None of us will survive the journey, not as we are now."

"The girl's only a quarter Catalystene, if that, and untrained. We'll be fine."

I might have strangled my brother, if I was not so filled with remorse over killing Sephine, but I did put my Nomad's foot down. "I will not allow it. The risk is too great."

"When did you become such a swaddling infant?"

Kyar had crossed the line. I arched an eyebrow at the door, told Captain Glass to halt the ship, and hobbled off the bridge, leaning on my staff. Kyar followed with a belligerent scowl, looking more like the little brother from my past, than the one I had gotten to know, post-Gehenna.

In the privacy of my cabin, I said, "Kyar, what were you thinking?"

"I was thinking I want to find Prin. I thought you did, too." Kyar helped himself to my very finest red brandy, the darkest, most expensive variety. It had three drops of ice-blood in it. He drank far too much these days. "This payment will fund our search for a year. It will fund our search until we find our dear cousin."

I was tempted, but only briefly. "No."

"It's a bit late to refuse. The girl is already on her way to the rendezvous coordinates." Kyar swallowed the generous pour in one gulp, and served himself another. My level-headed brother was so changed by grief and heartbreak, a Catalyst might have already resided aboard the FarGone 5.

"She is meeting us of her own free will? To be taken from her home and planet?" I asked, incredulous.

"Well, no. Her father communicated discreetly with some of the inhabitants, the same ones he's been rewarding to watch and report on the girl. Of course, they don't know that their information leaves the planet, but that is no matter. He's bribed them to abduct her. They have no idea she'll be taken for a ride to the stars. The natives sound like a pretty clueless bunch." He smirked and emptied his glass.

"She is not coming with us of her own volition?" I sank onto the bed, feeling as queasy as if I was keeping company with a molting Decomp.

"Nope. She is already on the way to meet us, compliments of her abductors," Kyar said, acting foolishly triumphant.

Whenever I thought the situation could not get worse, it invariably did. And it seemed like we really didn't have a choice now. "For the sake of the planet's population, I suppose we do have to salvage this girl, since she has already been taken," I said. If she was enraged or upset, there might be catastrophic consequences.

I left Kyar drinking another glass of brandy, and returned to the bridge. "Resume course," I said, dropping into the captain's chair. We had almost reached the planet anyway.

The FarGone 5 landed smoothly in a clearing. There was no denying the captain's superb flying ability. I didn't even feel a thump when we settled into a field of greenery.

Mo scanned the immediate area and declared it safe and uninhabited by anything large or dangerous enough to be of concern. Kyar had planned to go with Mo and Hanis on this most important errand, but I doubted he was in any condition to do so now. Nor was I letting my drunken brother loose on a restricted planet—that scenario reeked of disaster. I opted to go instead. It had been too long since I had walked on anything except arid burning desert or hollow metallic floors. This planet wasn't ice and snow, but a green planet was the next best thing to home.

"Mo, you have the directions?" I verified, before we unsealed the hatch.

"Memorized." He tapped his temple.

We disembarked, wearing plain dark clothing and holding simple Scarnivian beamers. The handlights cast enough diffuse light for us to move through the darkness with ease. Mo had been monitoring something he called their television transmissions, and he promised we would fit right in. He had adjusted the universal translators accordingly. We each had one discreetly hidden inside our ears. And tucked in our belts, we had dartguns. They were loaded with a fast-acting sedative, just in case it all went wrong.

It was an extremely green planet. Abundant tangled vegetation hampered our progress. Hanis lifted a hand-laser off his belt and cleared a path wherever necessary, by slicing through branches. The breeze blew fresh and smelled fantastic, after stale recycled air.

The hum of engines was soon replaced by the buzz of insects and the rustle of leaves. The trees had a strong, sweet aroma. It was better than perfume. I did not mind any of it.

"Lovely!" Mo said, of the same opinion. He inhaled deeply, and we followed Hanis's forged trail.

We hiked for a good hour. We hadn't wanted to land too close to any of the planet's inhabitants. My awkward gait slowed us down, especially over the rough terrain, yet Hanis and Mo matched my pace as if it was their own. And Hanis did not offer to carry me. I appreciated his tact.

When we reached a sluggish river, Mo pointed to the right. "It's a couple of minutes that'a way."

We walked beside the water. I pulled out my Scarnivian scanner, aiming it straight ahead. It confirmed that some native humans were waiting inside a metal land vehicle. The scanner had trouble determining the number. It kept flickering between two and three. I smacked it against my palm and tried again. The number of life signs wavered between three and four. "Three beings, I think," I told Mo, choosing the common number.

We all but tiptoed forward. Never having met a Catalystene, and knowing the race only by reputation, I was filled with trepidation. I could only hope Kyar was right, about her influence being greatly weakened by her diluted parentage and lack of training.

A beige vehicle came into view, stopped beside a bridge. We flashed our lights, signalling our presence. A door opened outward and two shadowy figures hauled themselves from the small space. They were tall for a humanoid species, and unusually bulky. Hanis, who was huge to me, just matched their size.

I hung back, outside the circle of light. I didn't want to scare them with my face, and Mo was our cultural expert. He held his silence, waiting for the planet's inhabitants to speak first, so he could mirror their manner.

"You're here to pick something up?" A twangy voice asked vaguely.

"A girl. Liena." Mo matched the tone and abrupt speaking pattern.

"What are you going to do with her?"

"She won't be harmed, not that it is any of your business. You've already been paid for your trouble. The girl, now!" Mo ordered curtly. The less contact we had with the natives, the better.

When the pair opened a second door and hauled her out, the girl was so limp, I thought she was dead. Hanis took her and checked her over. "She's breathing. It's the right girl," he said and draped her carefully over his wide shoulder. That action struck a poignant chord inside me. Tears stung my eyes before I regained control.

The girl was significantly smaller than the two men. Maybe only the males grew so big on this green planet, or she was smaller because of her father's genes.

"Why do ya'll want her?" the twangy voice asked again, filled with curiosity.

"None of your business." Mo's hand rested on his weapon. He kept it there as we departed at the quickest pace I could manage, back the way we had come.

I kept a close eye on my scanner, to make sure we weren't followed. It didn't register anyone to the rear of us, so we were safe—unless the scanner was malfunctioning again. Scarnivian wares were the bane of the Universe, guaranteed to break down at the worst possible moment, but since the Scarnivians controlled a monopoly on most essential manufactured goods, and held patents on the bulk of the rest, a being really had no choice but to buy their substandard products and hope for the best. Repair shops thrived across all of space, thanks to the Scarnivians.

I plucked some sprigs of fragrant leaves off the trees we wove through, to make my room smell fresher. The tough lacey leaves came off the branches easily enough, and made my hands smell as tangy as the air. I picked a few extra, for the girl, so she would at least have the smell of home to console her.

"That went well," Mo declared when we reached the ship's hatch.

I didn't feel safe until we stepped aboard and sealed the door behind us. The ship smelled fresh, like the trees. Someone had been thoughtful enough to air it out, while they had the chance.

"At least the girl is asleep. If we can keep her sedated for the whole journey, we should be fine. Mo, tell Captain Glass it is time to depart. Hanis, bring our passenger to the brig."

He didn't move. "The brig?"

"I'm certainly not going to have her roaming the ship. The brig will be her quarters, until we get her the hell off the FarGone 5."

I escorted Hanis and his burden to the solitary brig. I pressed in the security code to release the door. I was one of the select few on the ship who knew it. The enclosed space was small and rudimentary, but compared to my cell on Gehenna, it was ten-star luxury.

When Hanis deposited the girl on the single bed, I had a proper look at her in the light. Her skin was nothing if not humanoid. She was rather slim and nondescript, with fine brown hair, clear skin, and a straight little nose. Thick dark lashes fanned against pale cheeks, making her appear all the more vulnerable—defenseless. I knew she was approximately nineteen, yet she looked younger. The only thing of note about her was a spattering of reddish-brown freckles across her nose and cheeks. I found those little spots of colour surprisingly appealing, in spite of the fact that they made her seem more child than young woman. It only increased the guilt that I was feeling over my unwilling actions.

A wave of sympathy washed over me. Liena would awaken in this cell on a foreign craft, far from her home, with no idea why. It reminded me too much of my own experience. I would never forget the terror of regaining consciousness on the hell planet, with no memory of how I had gotten there, and no hope of ever leaving.

"I'll have Greely examine her." I motioned Hanis out, laid a fragrant sprig on the bed beside the girl, and resealed the door. The less contact we had with her, the better, even if she was asleep.

I paged the doctor and sat outside the cell to wait for him, slumped against the wall. It was the middle of the ship's night, the walk had been long, and my leg was aching deep into the bone.

Greely was yawning and disheveled when he turned up, steering a small floating cart. The hum of the tiny gravity blocker was inaudible over the ambient noise of the engines.

I struggled to my feet. "You have another patient. Find out why she is unconscious, but do it quickly. She is part Catalyst," I emphasized, even though Greely already knew that.

"You can bet I'll make it quick. Could you open the door?" Greely didn't know the code.

I obliged and watched from outside. He donned gloves and performed a cursory examination, providing me with a running commentary. "Healthy specimen. Heart is strong, breathing is a bit slow and shallow." He threaded a fine wire into her vein, attached to a sensor. "Ah, there you go. She's unconscious because she is drugged. Nothing toxic, a little too much chemical sedative. She'll probably wake up in the morning with a hell of a headache, nausea, some lost hours, nothing more serious."

"Good enough. You can check her again when she wakes up. Once the drug clears her system, I would like you to prescribe her something that will keep her calm for the duration of the journey."

"As you say, Nomad Megal. I'm going to go back to bed then, catch some shuteye before our cargo wakes up." Greely departed at speed, eager to put some distance between himself and the girl.

After verifying the security measures, I shuffled for my cabin. It was already occupied—but not by a girl. I could not help but smile at the sight of Kyar, passed out on my bed. The space was plenty big enough for two, so I lay quietly beside him. I appreciated my brother's company, even though it was nothing more than his snoring body. I shifted until our shoulders touched. For the first time in years, I slept soundly and did not wake up screaming. It was Kyar's groans that roused me. He was clutching his head with both hands.

"Good morning." I made sure to sound overly chipper.

Kyar's groans segued into swearing when he sat up. "What the hell are you doing in my room?"

"I might ask you the same question."

His bloodshot eyes squinted around, trying to focus. "What am I doing in your room? What time is it? Did I miss the rendezvous?"

"You did, but our passenger is safely aboard. She probably feels as ill as you right now. Her abductors had her drugged. Do you want to meet her?"

"Not like this. Give me an hour." Kyar did look a wreck.

"I'll be in the galley when you're ready," I said.

He staggered out the door and I realized I needed a good cleansing myself. I had a lot of dirt and vegetation on me, after traipsing through the green woods for several hours. I also smelled of sweat. The fragrant sprigs I had scattered about the room made it smell lovely, but they didn't do a thing to mask my own odor. I headed into the steam shower stall.

When I was clean, I examined myself in the mirror. Greely's skin treatments had eased the worst of my burns and scars. I had gained a few more pounds. My hair was short and snow white, as if I was already old. It seemed appropriate. Even though I hadn't yet turned twenty-five, inside, I was ancient.

Slowly, I was starting to resemble myself, yet there was still a long way to go, before I could be called anything but repulsive. I hoped my appearance wouldn't terrify the girl.

I had time to eat and linger over a reviving hoarberry tea before Kyar turned up. I pushed the cup across to him. He looked like he needed some reviving rather badly. "Let's go," he growled and stalked out, still unwilling to sit with me, it seemed.

I would have lingered longer, to make a point, except I did not want Liena to wake up alone. I was on Kyar's heels when he turned toward the guest cabins.

"This way," I corrected him, heading for the brig.

"You've got her locked up?" Kyar cried. "After what her father is paying us?"

"For her safe arrival," I emphasized. "The brig is the safest way to get her across space. This is non-negotiable, Kyar. She is aboard the ship as you arranged, but she will stay in the brig. She will have no contact with the crew. Don't push it."

Kyar didn't. I think his head was too painful. When we reached the cell, the girl was sleeping exactly as I had left her. "Still not awake," I said, stating the obvious.

Kyar examined her with interest. "She's unremarkable to look at. You sure wouldn't notice her in a crowd, not even a crowd of one."

"Isn't that common for a Catalyst? To blend into the background, until they change and disrupt the normal pattern of the world around them. Like dropping a pebble in a pond, the ripples of change fade outward in all directions, going on and on and on," I murmured, inclined to worry, especially because the reaction was always strongest immediately around the Catalyst—the epicenter of the change.

"Uh, ya. Should we wake her?"

But Greely did that, strolling up with his tray and calling out a jovial greeting. The girl jerked upright and did an accurate impersonation of Kyar, that very morning, clutching her head and moaning, unaware she had an audience.

When she opened her eyes, she must have had a shock, but clearly, this girl was a master at hiding her emotions. She simply blinked once and rose carefully, her face an expressionless mask. She didn't say a word, and waited for us to speak.

"You are Liena," I said, giving nothing away.

"Who's asking?"

I could not speak my real name. "Believe it or not, I am called Corpse. It's a nickname."

"It suits you." Her tone was deadpan. And she had an attitude.

Kyar introduced himself by his second name. "Wisel." It was another precaution.

Greely got to be himself. "Greely, a surgeon. How are you feeling?" He motioned that I unlock the door. One girl should not be able to overpower three men, but since she was one-quarter Catalyst, I wasn't yet ready to risk it. I shook my head.

"I'm feeling like crap. Where am I? On a boat or something?" she said.

"A ship," I corrected.

"A cruise ship?"

"No, another kind of ship." I didn't want to startle her, and intended to ease into the truth, giving her time to adjust.

46

Her dark brown eyes narrowed. "A spaceship?" she guessed, much too quickly and accurately.

"Yes, the FarGone 5—an All Planetary Shipper, at least at the moment." I tried to smile and think I grimaced. After Gehenna, my face was sorely out of practice.

"Does this have something to do with my father?" she said, proving she knew a lot more than we realized.

"You are aware that your father is - "

"An alien," she cut in. "Yes, I am very aware. He left before I was born, like—left the planet. You can't get any more abandoned than that, can you? And my mother died giving birth. My fault, or so I've been told. My mother was from Earth, my planet. I've been locked up and studied for most of my life, until I escaped last year." What she said made no sense, but it did explain why her father wanted her off the planet now.

"Is this part of the short version of the tale, Kyar?" I inquired, overly polite.

He avoided my eyes. "Uh … no, I wasn't told about this."

I turned back to the girl for answers. "Why were you locked up and studied?"

"Because my father is an alien," she stressed with a heavy dose of sarcasm. She was talking to me as if I was a toddler, and not a very bright one at that.

"But how did the planetary inhabitants know he was not native to your planet?"

She sighed and wilted down onto her bed, rubbing her head. "I don't know, but they did. Where are you taking me?"

"To meet your father." I hoped she would accept this as good news.

"Oh. Maybe it's time." She began to look a little green around the edges and staggered up. "Bathroom?" she cried.

I pointed to the divided portion of her cell. There was no door, so Kyar, Greely, and I left, to grant her privacy. It gave us a chance to discuss what we had learned.

"But her home is a restricted planet," Kyar said. "They don't know about anything other than what is found on their own world, so how do they know about beings from other worlds?"

When neither of us had anything productive to say, we sought out Mo, our cultural liaison. He had an answer. "I saw it on one of their entertainment broadcasts. They believe in aliens, as they call anyone from another planet."

I nodded. It was the word the girl had used to describe her father.

Mo continued, "Although they've never actually seen them. Or maybe they have. Even though it's forbidden, I suspect quite a few spacecraft pass by here. Some of them must land, like we did, or crash, like Liena's father's ship."

It made sense. "And somehow the natives learned that Liena's father was an alien," I surmised, "so they locked her up and studied her. Even her name is a jest, isn't it? What a life." I felt a surge of anger against the unknown Earthlings.

"And now you've got her locked up again," Kyar said.

I ignored his barb. We headed back to the brig. Liena was stretched out on the bed, as pale as snow, looking smaller than before. I felt like a brute for abducting and caging the girl. I unlocked the door, allowing Greely entrance. He donned his gloves to give her another cursory examination.

She sat up on the bed and allowed it, her face stoic, as if she was used to being poked and prodded. I suppose she was. After he declared her healthy, I sent the doctor away.

Kyar and I entered her cell, wanting answers. We sat together on the bench that was affixed to the wall. The girl perched on the edge of the bed. She studied us, as much as we studied her.

"What happened to you?" she asked me. "Were you burned by acid, or in a chemical fire or something?"

"Or something. How did the beings on your planet know that your father was an alien?" I asked again, using the proper terminology from her world.

"Honestly, I'm not sure. I grew up in a secure, artificial environment, always watched and studied and ... and always alone. But I never exposed my differences." She smiled with satisfaction and looked rather wicked, adding, "Well, a few people did find out, but they didn't live long enough to tell anyone what I could do."

Kyar glanced at me in alarm.

"Did you kill them?" I asked.

"Not on purpose. It just kind of happened because of what I can do."

She was not supposed to know such things. "What can you do?" I moved my hand closer to my dartgun.

"Want me to show you?" Her eyes narrowed on my hand.

"No. No, just tell us."

"I can change. But don't you know that? Aren't you like me?"

48

I shook my head. "My brother and I are humanoid. Your father was part Catalystene. That's why you can create change."

"Oh. I thought you were like me. I thought someone was finally like me."

She looked so sad, I said, "Your father and his people will be like you. Soon you will meet him."

"Where is he?" the girl asked.

"We're delivering you to the Gashmore Galaxy. He's waiting there to meet you. It's a couple of weeks away at speeds faster than you can conceive of."

She wrinkled her brow. "If you say so. But how can you be human, if you're not from Earth?"

It was time for a brief history lesson. "You'll find humanoid species throughout the entire Universe. Ages ago, many green planets were seeded with humans. The first humans originated on an unknown green world, and thought enough of themselves to spread, like a rash, or a plague. This universal seeding is referred to as 'The Spread'."

"You're kidding, right?" Liena said skeptically.

"No. And finding the original Green World has become an overblown universal quest. Some even believe my world was the original home of the very first humans, although it's an ice planet now. Anyway, these original humans travelled the length and breadth of space, even travelling multidimensionally, planting their kind everywhere. Humans survived all over the Universe, and they thrived, multiplied on a grand scale. Of course, each planet's environment affected how the race developed, from that point on. Many humanoids will look different from what you're used to, especially those that ended up mating with other species, creating whole new races."

"That's really incredible. And my planet doesn't know any of this, although lots of people on Earth do believe in aliens."

I resumed my barebones history lesson. "And now humans have a tendency to consider themselves superior to all other races, and they enslave other beings, when they can get away with it." I didn't reveal the shameful fact that my illustrious family had owned slaves, and probably still did. Once I ruled again, that would change, and not just for my family, but on a grand planetary scale. I could see quashing a number of rebellions in my future.

"No kidding?" Liena said.

The universal translator wasn't sure if that was a question. I said, "It is the truth. Your world simply isn't aware of any of this yet, and won't be for some time, if it survives." I had my doubts about that, given the little I had learned about the planet. While we were on the surface, Captain Glass had ordered their air, soil and water analyzed. It was all toxically polluted. Mo also reported that their television transmissions showed a population entertained by violence and prone to war, with a history of enslaving the members of their own race, or massacring them. If they did survive to explore space, they would fit right in with the rest of us.

"Ya, I know my planet is in big trouble. Most people do know it, they just don't do anything about it." Liena seemed to deflate, looking fragile and sad. I was barely aware of reaching out to grasp her hand, because she seemed so forlorn.

When we touched, it felt like I was being sucked into a black hole. Her dark eyes bore into mine as if she had swallowed my soul. Even her face wavered, growing rough and scarred and dark, her eyes lightened, her hair shortened and whitened. The ship lurched violently and seemed to spin in circles, until Kyar yanked me back.

I didn't know what had just happened.

The girl did. Her face smoothed out and looked like her own again, rather than mine. "I'm sorry," she cried. "I wasn't prepared for you to touch me. You can't touch me, skin-to-skin, unless I know you're going to, so I can block the reaction. Oh Megal, I'm so, so sorry about Gehenna," she whispered.

She hadn't merely looked like me, she had *been* me. She had changed into me. Liena started to sob as if her heart was broken. Arms wrapped protectively tight around her body, she rocked on the bed. If she had lived my three years of hell in brief seconds, who could blame her.

Kyar steered me out the door, skirting wide around the girl. He made sure to lock the brig securely. I wouldn't have made it out of the cell, if not for my brother. What had transpired between Liena and I had left me so disoriented, I barely knew where I was.

As soon as we were in the corridor, Kyar asked, "What did that feel like? She changed into you right in front of my eyes. I've heard about it, but I've never seen a Catalyst do that. It was so fast, and she knew your memories! Guess I was wrong about the strength of her abilities. I wonder what changed outside of herself." He was babbling. "Something had to change, to balance the change to her. I know that much about Catalysts." He seemed awfully distraught over nothing.

I merely felt sleepy and yawned, craving my bed.

"And why did the ship shake? Right. The ship did shake." Kyar didn't take me to my cabin. He hauled me along with him, to the bridge.

Captain Glass was leaning over the sensors, as intense as I had ever seen her.

"What made the ship shake?" Kyar demanded, stepping up to her side and studying the data.

"No idea. Nothing. I can't figure it out. There are no other ships in the area, nobody fired on us. No spatial phenomena. Nothing." She pressed more buttons, her braid swinging wildly.

"Then it must have been the Catalyst," Kyar stated.

I settled into the captain's chair, humming a cheerful melody I recalled from happy childhood days. Kyar was more useful, he reported what had happened, so the rest of the crew would know to never touch the girl.

"And we're stuck with her for two weeks?" Mo sounded scandalized.

So drained I could barely keep my eyes opened, I left Kyar in charge. I stumbled back to my cabin and fell onto my bed. I was asleep before I could even toe off my boots.

4. UGS

slept around the clock. I would have slept longer, except Kyar banged on my door and walked in. He no longer woke me gently, but went out of his way to startle me with loud noises.

"Good morning." I yawned.

"So far it is not a bad morning," he said, without confidence. "I want to talk to the girl again. Come with me."

I wanted to see Liena, too. "Sure." I rose and sauntered for the door.

"Uh, Megal ... perhaps you should dress first." My brother was studying me with disbelief. I was wearing nothing but an impressive collection of scars. I laughed heartily and tugged on a tunic and leggings. Kyar's gaze changed to one of bewilderment. I laughed harder and hugged him. He backed away as if he was frightened.

"Are you okay?" he asked. "Or does the doctor have a secret stash of Seventh Heavens or Cloud Nines?"

"No happy pills for me," I declared, twirling my staff as I limped into the corridor. "Let's go see Liena."

Kyar followed more slowly. "Sure about the pills, Megal?"

"Positive, I am quite happy enough."

"Ya, I can see that." He didn't seem to believe me, about the pills. Highly addictive and banned across the Universe, I doubted we even had any aboard.

Humans that took such artificial enhancers were never again satisfied with real life, and became highly prone to suicide. On Gehenna, vials of the pills were occasionally smuggled in, hidden somewhere on, or in, a prisoner's person. Men would, and did, kill for just one pill on the prison planet. I had never succeeded in getting my hands on one, and now that I had my life back, I knew enough to avoid them.

"Check with the good doctor," I said breezily.

"Did you drink your breakfast?" he asked next.

In answer, I tossed my arm around his neck and breathed in his face.

52

He shoved me away, his face wrinkled with disgust. "Heavens, Megal, could you not brush that new set of teeth the doctor gave you? Your breath smells like a Decomp."

"Surely it can't be that bad." I grinned, showing off my teeth. We were almost at the brig anyway. Too late to do anything about my breath.

Liena was still locked up. I couldn't remember why I had put her in the brig. She was sitting on her bed, staring wanly at nothing. At our appearance, she smiled. She had a kind heart, I did know it. I unlocked the door and entered. Kyar hung back.

"Is it morning, Megal?" she asked.

"Morning on this ship. Have you been fed? Do you have all you need?"

She nodded without conviction. She looked like she needed a warm hug. "I'm going to touch you. Be prepared," I said. She just watched me quizzically.

"Close your eyes and picture me in better days, when I was pretty," I advised. Since she knew my memories, she could.

"Oh Megal, I don't need to do that," she said. "I know how you look inside, and that is what matters."

It was such a nice think for her to say. "Ready?" I smiled into her eyes.

She offered a tentative and very sweet smile in return. "Okay, ready."

I wrapped my arms around her and hugged her small frame tight. She hugged me in return, and stroked my back as if to soothe the many whip scars. She had shared my ravaged soul, and we rocked together, both trying to offer solace.

"What the hell is going on?" Kyar demanded.

We drew apart. Liena said, "There is nothing to worry about, Kyar. Will you stay and talk, Megal? There is so much more I want to know." There was no trace of her former attitude. She just looked at me with such pity in her eyes, it would have upset me, if I hadn't been so happy.

"How would you like to dine with me in the galley?" I asked. Keeping her in the brig was simply ridiculous.

"Oh, yes, I would love to see the rest of the ship with my own eyes, rather than through your thoughts and memories. Another person's memories aren't at all the same as seeing something with my own eyes. And I've never been on a spaceship. Of course you know that."

"I do." I held wide the door and she walked out. Kyar protested. I ignored his objection. He came along, staying close.

In the galley, we claimed the end of the long table. Liena studied everything. She seemed especially delighted to meet Oran'Jay, when he carried over our lunch himself. He didn't usually wait on me, or anyone, so maybe he wanted to meet the girl.

"I call him 'Frog'," I confided, as soon as Oran'Jay left.

"He does look rather like a giant frog," she said. I assumed her comment was because she knew all my thoughts, until she said, "We have frogs on my planet. But they aren't very big. You can hold them in your hand. Some are even poisonous if you lick them."

I laughed with abandon, trying to imagine why any being would want to lick a frog.

The crew stared at me and the girl as if they had never seen an odder sight, but everyone was perfectly polite. Kyar sat beside me. He was tense and kept scowling down at the meal he didn't even taste.

After lunch, I took Liena on a tour. Kyar followed, with Mo and Hanis in tow now. Once she had seen all there was to see, on the admittedly small, shoddy craft, I tried to relocate her to a more comfortable cabin. Kyar was having none of it. Mo and Hanis backed him up, and wouldn't follow the orders I tried to impose. Liena intervened at that point. She said the brig was just fine, so I didn't come to blows with anyone. Not that I felt like fighting. I was too happy inside for anger and punching my friends.

I walked her back to the brig, where we talked for the longest time. I learned quite a lot about her ability to change. If she was asleep or unconscious, and someone touched her, skin-to-skin, there was no reaction. Yet, if she was awake and unprepared to be touched, the change happened instantaneously, like a knee-jerk reaction. She could block the reaction, consciously, as long as she was anticipating the contact. It was how she had been able to hide her ability from her jailers on Earth. That and they mostly touched her with gloves on, because they were scared of catching alien bugs.

I was interested to learn that she could change into animals, not just people. She claimed she could change into any living thing, as long as their mass was comparable to her own, within about thirty-five pounds. The greater the size discrepancy, the harder it was for her to hold the form, so she couldn't do it as long. If there was minimal size discrepancy, she could hold another's form almost indefinitely.

We shared dinner in the galley, and she returned to the brig to sleep. When I retired to my cabin for the night, I dreamed blissful visions all night long and awoke rejuvenated. As soon as I showed my face the next day, Kyar insisted that Greely check me over. The doctor declared me as healthy as I could be, after three years on Gehenna. He confirmed that I was substance free.

For a week, I knew nothing but such warm, fuzzy days, as content as I had ever been. If my head had been clearer, I would have known such euphoria was not natural and could not last. But even if my head had been clearer, the last thing I would have been worried about was UGS.

Seven days after we brought Liena aboard, the UGS waylaid us. An exuberantly armed Universal Guard Ship closed in on us in the middle of a particularly barren patch of space. There was nowhere to hide.

The crew was summoned to the bridge in a panic. I was lounging with Liena in the brig, and almost didn't bother to go, in spite of the urgency in Captain Glass's voice. I only went because Liena said I should.

I meandered down the corridor, trying to remember if I had locked the brig door, since Hanis and Mo had already gone ahead. Kyar was most insistent about the brig door being kept locked, which was just silly. I forgot all about it, when I stepped onto the bridge and saw the sinister Universal Guard Ship looming large on the viewing screen.

"We have company," I observed.

"Really?" Kyar said, with exaggerated sarcasm. "I hadn't noticed."

"But the UGS don't normally patrol this zone of space," I said, ignoring his tone.

"No. Maybe they *changed* their routes recently," he insinuated.

I felt the need to defend our guest. "Nothing to do with Liena, I'm sure."

"Regardless, they want to board the ship for a routine inspection. I'm not sure if I believe them. Maybe they know something."

Captain Glass eyed me, then turned to Kyar. "Well, what do you want to do? Outrun them? Allow them aboard? Bribe them to leave us alone?"

"The last would be my choice." Kyar rubbed the back of his neck. "But we don't yet have the funds for that." He glanced in Venus's direction. "You can outrun them?"

"In my sleep." It was the first time I had seen the engineer animated. Her eyes appeared lit up from inside. Briefly, she flashed a more solid form, then slipped out of focus again.

Being the Nomad, I asked, "Does anyone want to know what I think?"

"No!" every last person said with gusto.

"Megal, your brains are mush," Kyar said, adding, "I am hoping it is a temporary change, but until Liena is off the ship, I am in charge. Go sit down over there." He pointed toward the corner.

Mildly offended, I claimed the captain's chair instead.

"Okay, maybe it is a routine inspection." Kyar paced restlessly. "We'll allow them aboard. We aren't carrying restricted goods, and we can't be accused of smuggling. They won't know where Liena originates from, not by looking at her." He stopped abruptly. "Yes, best to face them now, get it over with. I don't want to be chased across the next ten galaxies."

"So we let them board?" Captain Glass said.

"Yes," Kyar said decisively. "But get Liena out of the brig first. They will ask awkward questions about that." He pointed a finger at Mo. "Mo, stash her in your cabin, say she is your companion. And stay with her, but don't touch her. Hanis, go meet the Universal Guards, bring them to the bridge first."

Mo and Hanis departed to carry out his instructions.

Captain Glass communicated with the UGS, verifying that they could board. Everyone awaited their arrival with bated breath, except me. I hummed a happy tune, the one that had been stuck in my head for days. Their shuttle docked against our magnetic starboard hatch, rocking the ship gently. When Mo dashed onto the bridge, flushed and wild-eyed, even I knew something was wrong.

"Liena is gone!" he gasped.

Kyar turned to me with an accusing eye. "Did you not lock the brig?"

"Um …" I tried to remember, my thoughts twirling and foggy and still happy.

Kyar shook his head with weary resignation. "I think I have the answer."

"Universal Guards are already aboard," Captain Glass said. It was too late to delay them.

Universal Guards are a stern, bossy type of humanoid. It's their mission to enforce common law across the vast expanse of space. Most of them take that duty pretty seriously. They have been known to slip a little profit in their pocket, to look the other way on minor infractions, but never on anything truly significant.

Three such beings tromped onto the bridge with Hanis, their boots polished and their buttons shiny. The trio of females was looking awfully dapper for the nether reaches of space.

Everyone stood at attention, while I continued to loaf in the captain's chair, amused by the big fuss over nothing. The guard chief's rank was recognizable, because she carried the longest dartgun and sported the most metal rings around her wrist cuffs.

Captain Glass stepped forward to address her; the captain is always the one responsible for the vessel. "Captain Glass of the FarGone 5, a shipper/transport under contract with A-1 All Planetary Shipping."

"Universal Guard Chief Zandee." The big-jawed woman surveyed the bridge. Her gaze stopped on me and I saluted with a grin. She frowned and turned her attention back to Captain Glass. "What is your destination? Your cargo?"

There was a prearranged cover story in place. Captain Glass spouted the false information and produced the phony paperwork for a mundane pickup and delivery of Scarnivian robotic composting units. The documents were examined and returned.

"Scarnivian units," Zandee said in a belittling tone. "Cheap crap. Unreliable. So your cargo bays should be empty, if you haven't picked up your goods yet."

"The bays are empty," Captain Glass verified.

"Then you won't mind if we have a look-see, before we go on our way." Zandee was not asking. "And we'll check the rest of the ship, since we're here."

She began with the bridge, touring the perimeter silently. She wasn't one for small talk. Zandee stopped before my chair and stared down, frowning again. "Your name?"

Kyar had created a false identity for me, if I could only remember what it was. I couldn't. "You can call me Corpse," I said with a wink.

She frowned. "That is your name?"

"That's what they call me."

When Kyar signaled frantically to the captain, behind the guards' backs, Captain Glass intervened. "This is one of my engineers. He was a little too close to the ship's worm-hole vent when it misfired a few months ago. There was a minor explosion and he still hasn't fully recovered." She shared a significant glance with Zandee. Was I being assigned brain damage now?

"He looks familiar." Zandee's eyes narrowed.

"Perhaps I remind you of someone else who blew up." I thought I was funny and chuckled.

Zandee had no sense of humour, or I wasn't as funny as I thought. "No, that's not it. We'll tour the rest of the ship now." Brow furrowed, she moved along, flanked by her lieutenants.

"Stay put," Kyar growled at me in passing. He and Captain Glass accompanied the visitors. I didn't feel like staying put, I wanted to see Liena.

As soon as they were out of sight, I left the bridge, trying to guess where I might find her. I played a game of hide-and-seek, avoiding the Universal Guards, while I searched the cargo bays, the galley, and then the engine room. I had a surprise there. The gleaming technology was blackened and rusty, much of it draped with oily cloths. Venus was as soiled as her engines, making her look far more tangible than she usually did.

"Love what you've done with the place," I quipped.

She smiled. "Camouflage."

"Well done. Have you seen Liena?"

"No, she isn't here and I've been into every nook and cranny."

"UGS should be here soon," I warned and continued on my way. It was getting tricky to avoid the guards, so I opted to hole up in my cabin. I reclined on my bed, daydreaming about sledding on my home ice. I must have drifted into a nap. I was deep in euphoric dreams when my cabin was invaded.

Kyar hurtled into the room, waking me abruptly. "We have a problem," he gasped out.

"Liena still missing?"

"Yes, but it's worse than that. The chief guard, Zandee, she kept saying you looked familiar, then she got a funny look on her face and clammed up about it. I think she might have recognized you. The UGS would have been informed to watch for you, well—for Prin. And you do look more like yourself than when we brought you aboard."

"You're imagining things." I didn't bother to rise.

Kyar stepped close and yanked me up. "Look, since Liena touched you, you don't seem to give a damn about anything. Nothing concerns you, but this should. If Zandee has guessed who you are, she will take you back to the Ice Planet to claim the bounty. Do not doubt that you will be iced there."

"That should please you. Sephine's death will be avenged. You can claim the title of Nomad. Why don't you turn me in to Zandee?" I suggested.

Kyar did not find me amusing. He looked hurt. "I don't wish you dead, Megal. What are we going to do?"

"No idea."

Kyar raised his eyes to gaze at the ceiling, as if the answers might be engraved on the metal struts overhead. "Why am I asking you? Don't leave this room. I'll be back."

I lay down to resume my nap. Before I could fall asleep, I had another visitor. "Liena!" I smiled and patted my bed for her to join me. She didn't.

"Megal, those uniformed women—I overheard them talking. One of them knows who you are, she was talking about your eyes. She plans to turn you in for the reward." Liena's face was the picture of distress.

"Kyar figured as much. I guess I'll be going home sooner than I expected," I said, accepting of my fate. At least I would walk on the ice, one last time—one very long and naked walk to my death. Even the Nomad's line can't survive prolonged exposure, when their skin is all they wear. I had seen others iced. It was a slow and torturous journey to depart the world of the living.

"But there must be something we can do." Liena bit her lip and scanned my room. She was thinking hard. "We're not that far from Earth really, are we?"

"Not at top speeds. But why Earth?"

She shot me a panicky glance when tromping boots sounded from down the corridor. She moved to lock the door. "It's my home planet!"

"So?" I wasn't following her train of thought at all.

"How far from Earth? Tell me," she pressed urgently.

"At top speeds, we're under a week away, although I don't think we have the fuel to do it," I mused.

"But the Universal Guard Ship will?"

"Of course. They never lack for fuel."

"A week, that should be manageable, the size discrepancy is minimal," she murmured to herself. A heavy fist hammered on my door and Liena jumped.

"Hello?" I sang out.

"Zandee here. I want a word." Her voice was deceptively mild. It was too late to make a run for it.

The last thing I expected was for Liena to step close. We tended to keep a safe distance from each other, as a precaution. "I'm going to touch you with my defenses down. I am not going to block the reaction. I will become you, Megal," she said.

I blinked in confusion. "Why?"

"Because it will be me that goes with the UGS. Not you. Once I'm aboard their ship, I'll change into Zandee. I'll just have to hide her, tie her up or something. As commander, I'll be in charge. I'm going to order the guard ship to fly to Earth." She was talking fast and I had a hard time keeping up.

"You're going back to your home?"

"Yes. I didn't want to leave it. Now that I have the opportunity to go back, I'm going. The planet needs me, I don't have time to explain why. You have to promise you won't come after me. I'll save your life and you'll let me go. Deal?" She stared into my eyes. I saw how desperately she wanted to go home. It was a feeling I knew too well.

Although I couldn't fathom why she felt that way. "Why do you want to go back to a planet, where the inhabitants kept you locked up?"

"I'm not locked up anymore, Megal. And I have made dear friends that I care about. I miss them, and they need my help."

"Then we have a deal." I smiled. "I will miss you, Liena."

"Me too, Megal."

The banging on the door repeated, more urgently.

"I'll be right out," I called.

Liena didn't just touch me, she leaned close and kissed my cheek. I grinned and replaced my cheek with my lips. For a brief moment, I was kissing her, and then I was kissing myself. My lips were softer than I would have expected, and timidly gentle, but that would be Liena in my form.

The ship shook violently, almost knocking us off our feet, and we parted. I faced my twin. It was disconcerting. I really was as ugly as sin in three-dimension. I certainly wouldn't have kissed me.

"Clothes," Liena gasped and opened my closet. She shed her own garments, stepped into leggings and yanked on a Nomad's robe. My scarred skin and wasted body was not a pretty sight. I was glad she covered it up so quickly.

"Now hide!" Liena ordered in my voice, already moving for the door.

I scooped up her clothes. "Liena?"

"Yes?"

"Safe home. And please keep my skin covered, until you turn into Zandee." I arched an eyebrow and she managed a smile.

I hid in the closet while she went out to meet the guards.

The close contact with Liena had drained me. I must have fallen asleep in an uncomfortable crouch. When something disturbed my slumber, I had no idea how much time had passed.

It was a battle to raise my eyelids. I tried to figure out where the hell I was, and why my knees were throbbing. When a dangling edge of vermink fur tickled my face, it all came rushing back.

My head was clearer than it had been in a week—because Liena was off the ship? A faint noise confirmed that someone was in my room, outside the closet. Surely not the UGS? I eased the door opened, just a crack.

Kyar was seated on my bed, head in his hands. The only other time I remembered seeing my brother cry, as a grown man, was when I told him about Sephine. But he was sobbing now, soundlessly. I couldn't bear the sight.

"Kyar!" I tripped out of the closet. I fell down beside him and wrapped both arms around his shuddering frame. "Stop. Stop this." I rocked with him, holding my brother with all the strength in my thin arms.

"Megal?" he choked. "I've gone mad."

"What? No. Of course you haven't." I held him even tighter, my own eyes filling with tears when I shared his distress.

"I saw the UGS haul you away with my own eyes. Yet here you are. Madness is the only rational explanation," he rasped. "I've lost Sephine and now I have lost you, too. And I've lost my mind." He pressed his head against my shoulder. I felt like his older brother, for the first time in many long years.

"Kyar, it was Liena that left with the UGS. She changed to take my form," I explained, as briefly as I could. "She is going to transform into Zandee next, and order the Universal Guard Ship to take her home. She wants to go home. I've promised we will not pursue her. I have lost us a fortune, Kyar. Will you forgive me?"

His body relaxed limply against me. I stroked his hair until he stopped shuddering. He said, "Megal, you are really here?"

"I am, but I've cost us a great fare."

"Worth it, I suppose." Kyar sat up and dried his eyes, pulling himself together admirably. He did not say that he had forgiven me for Sephine, and I did not ask, but I knew there was peace between us. "The crew is going to be in for a bit of a shock," he added, his voice not as steady as his demeanor.

I grinned. "Don't tell Oran-Jay. I'll give him a fright."

"Only if I can watch."

"Deal." It was the second deal I made that day, and both worked out rather well.

5. The Walking Dead

The next day, Kyar contacted A-1, in regards to another shipping contract. He wasn't sure if they would grant us one, after losing Liena. Luckily for us, they did. The ship was running on blast beetle fumes and worm-hole oil residue at that point, and we were quite desperate to get as far from the Universal Guard Ships as we could. If Liena's plan didn't work, they would be coming after us, all lasers firing.

Kyar called a meeting of the staff. He announced that he had both good news and bad news, and that we would soon be picking up some passengers. They were willing to pay up front, and were traveling in the direction of the Gashmore Galaxy. That was the good news.

"And the bad news?" I asked, when he hesitated to say more.

"Uh, ya, about that ... look, you know I really didn't have a choice here -"

"Surely it can't be that bad. We've survived a Catalyst, after all," I remarked. "What could be worse?"

"A Decomp," Kyar said lightly. Everyone around the table laughed. "I'm not joking. And it's three Decomps, not one."

Everyone stopped laughing and began to look rather nauseous. I jumped in. "As long as they're not molting, we'll manage."

Kyar grimaced. "Uh ... it is their molting season. Their own ship broke down and they are quite desperate to get home."

I didn't care how desperate they were, or how desperate we were. Even I couldn't support Kyar now.

Captain Glass surged to her feet. "No, no, no! You never get the smell of a molting Decomp out of a ship. I won't allow it. Not for one day, not for one hour. Not for one minute!"

Kyar tried to make the bad news sound like good news, when he said, "It will only be for about nine days. They aren't going quite as far as the Gashmore Galaxy. They'll pay ten times the regular fare, since most ships won't transport them."

"No ships will, including mine!" Captain Glass bit out.

Given that she enjoyed cuddling with corpses, her attitude confirmed exactly how disgusting Decomps could be during molting season. A half-humanoid species, often called the 'walking dead' or the 'living dead', their spongy outer layer of skin rotted off once a year, while they still wore it. It sloughed off all over the place, leaving a rancid trail. Their body odor was as foul as one might expect, and their food of choice was more repulsive than their pelt. They also had a gaseous problem that was legendary.

"Nine days in a confined space with three molting Decomps. And I thought Gehenna was bad," I said. It was the first jest I had made about that place.

"We don't have a choice," Kyar repeated, and leaned back in his chair, arms crossed. "I know it's going to be rough, but we'll survive. We're rendezvousing with them tomorrow. I'll distribute nose plugs."

The gathering dispersed with an enthusiastic amount of griping. I accompanied Kyar back to his cabin, pleased that he let me. It was lovely to have his companionship again. We had a lot to talk about, including Liena and the Decomps.

"Nice to have you clear-headed," Kyar remarked, settling on his bed.

I claimed the chair. "Was I that bad?" The memory of my time with Liena was so clouded, it felt like a dream.

He snorted. "Worse. But you were happy, quite a change."

"Yes." It had been a lovely change.

"We owe Liena a great debt. She saved our ship from being impounded, and she saved your life. I hope she makes it home."

"She should. Once she turns into Zandee, she'll know how to act and how to run the ship. Liena is resourceful." I frowned, trying to remember more of what she had told me. "She said her planet needs her, but didn't have time to explain why. At least she is aware of what she can do, and does know how to control it."

"It would appear so."

"And tomorrow we welcome Decomps aboard." I shuddered. "The crew will not love you for this."

"I should have said it was your idea."

"You should have," I agreed.

We talked until dinner and ate together, aware it was the last meal we would enjoy for some time. Once the Decomps came aboard, the crew would probably give up food.

Kyar was the only one who welcomed our three passengers onto the FarGone 5, but the whole crew knew when they arrived. Within minutes, the reek had permeated every inch of the ship. Nose plugs didn't work miracles. The odor was so pungent, it could be tasted. It made eyes water and noses run, plugs or not.

As soon as the funds were in hand, Kyar had the stocks replenished and the ship refueled. Fully provisioned, we left the rendezvous planet behind. The depressing gray surface of that tiny globe had not inspired any urge to stretch our legs on land.

Venus promised she would cut two or three days off the journey, and the FarGone 5 managed the creation of extra wormholes without distress. Between wormholes, the ship flew with deviant speed that made no sense to me. Unless it was somehow multidimensional, although I didn't see how that was possible.

I stayed mainly in my cabin that week, to avoid the Decomps. When restless, Kyar and I snuck into the largest empty cargo bay. We enjoyed wild soar-board races around a makeshift obstacle course. Kyar had produced a second battered board from some storage locker on the ship. I got that one. He kept the shiny red racer and won all our contests.

The soar-board allowed me to move with ease, since I only had to stand on the thing. There was no awkward limping when I raced Kyar. I felt like a whole man, until I dismounted.

We played as if we were lads again. It had been so long since I truly had fun, that I never wanted the stolen moments to end. A touch of the happiness that Liena's change had generated, lingered on inside me. It helped to balance the misery of Gehenna.

The reckless distraction of the soar-board races seemed to take Kyar's mind off Sephine. The Decomps also helped there. Kyar was the liaison between the gross beings and the rest of the ship, and if anything can distract a man from his problems, it's hanging around with molting Decomps.

Although I saw much repulsive physical evidence of the beings, I only came face-to-sloughing-face with one of them, when Oran'Jay lost his temper and threw a fit over the food he was required to prepare for the paying guests. I happened to be in the galley, picking at a piece of bread that tasted more like the fouled air than bread, when Oran'Jay surged out of the kitchen, eyes bulging more than usual, his face and chest covered in a splash of gore.

I tossed my bread in the recycle unit and prepared to run. I wasn't quick enough.

"Do you know what they eat? Have you any idea?" the cook sputtered.

I really didn't want to know more than I already did. "If it's what you are wearing, I think I do." I backed for the door. I should have attended my rear. I actually bumped into the Decomp, and that squishy warm contact made me cringe. Too much of the being's skin stuck to my clothes. I might have shrieked before I gathered myself.

"Sorry, so sorry. Didn't see you there," I stammered.

"No, I don't imagine you did." The voice was dry, unlike the oozing flesh.

My eyes found his face, and I swallowed a whimper. It was leaking various fluids, and looked to be shredded. Some flesh was dangling right off, ready to abandon that body. Who could blame it? But the eyes were intelligent and amused—bright green in the field of bloody red.

I tried to be polite. "Are you enjoying the trip?"

"It has been fine. Fast, but that is not a complaint. I look forward to arriving home. As a species, we only travel when absolutely necessary. We do not enjoy the experience, especially at this time in our cycle."

"No, I don't imagine you do," I said agreeably, willing my stomach to hang on a little longer.

"It was sheer bad luck that our ship broke down. Granted, it is a Scarnivian vessel and doesn't have a reputation for reliability, yet we keep it perfectly maintained. It should not have failed us." The Decomp was getting downright chatty.

And I was losing the battle with my innards. "Well, you'll be home tomorrow."

"Yes. I have come to check on our dinner. It is delayed, and I couldn't find Kyar to pass the message."

I swung around. Oran'Jay was standing dumbly, wide mouth slack. "Oran'Jay, dinner almost ready?" I prompted.

"Uh, ya." Meeting the Decomp had taken the wind out of the cook's sails. "It will be brought to your cabin directly."

The Decomp nodded. "Lovely. We are quite famished and what you are preparing looks delicious." He motioned at what decorated Oran'Jay. The man's hand was a nightmare of dangling lines of dripping skin.

"Uh … ya." The cook scuttled away. I would have laughed if I hadn't been about to lose my meager ration of bread.

"Nice to have met you." The Decomp didn't hang around. He was wise enough to know better, you could see it in his eyes. He moved gracefully away, leaving several bits of himself behind. I no longer judged a man by his skin, but what lay on the floor was enough to have me limping fast for the privacy of my cabin, and a very long steam-shower.

I didn't try eating again until the passengers disembarked and the ship had been aired out, thrice. Captain Glass was right, the stench didn't depart with the Decomps.

There was a spontaneous celebration that night. Everyone emerged from their cabins as though coming out of hibernation. Oran'Jay refused to cook a scrap and got utterly drunk. No-one blamed him, and many joined in.

Lillyth had been the one to clean up after the Decomps, all week long. She had spent the day de-goring their cabins and looked like a pale shadow of her former self. Even though it was completely unheard of, and something I would never have done before Gehenna, I poured Lillyth a generous measure of my precious red brandy, and served her myself, playing the part of waiter.

We had almost reached the Gashmore Galaxy, and now had sufficient funds to keep our ship running for several months—longer if we were frugal. The situation looked promising. A wiser man might have realized that meant we were destined for trouble. It arrived without warning, as trouble loves to do. It began with Kyar's casual mention that A-1 had offered us another shipping contract, and then it snowballed into an avalanche.

6. Coffin-shaped Crates

"No Decomps!" The cries rang out on the bridge when Kyar mentioned A-1's offer of another job.

"Only parcels," I warned my brother, the Nomad again now that my brain was functioning.

Kyar flashed his boyish grin for the first time in ages. "As a matter of fact, we are talking about parcels."

"Good enough," I said. I couldn't have been more wrong.

The cargo was loaded onto the FarGone 5 as soon as we docked over a gelatinous purple planet. The surface of that orb wobbled and rippled alarmingly, as if the planet's orbit was unbalanced. The massive shifting was visible even from our docking deck, high above.

I remained in my cabin, after a small nondescript ship docked against our side. Zandee had recognized me. There was the risk that others might as well, although it was slight. No-one but UGS would have been staring at my wanted poster day-in and day-out.

As soon as the ship was moving again, I set out to find Kyar. He was in cargo bay two, backed by four rectangular metal boxes, each one the same as the other. They were longer than a man, and wider. In fact, I could have comfortably napped in one, except for the chilled temperature of the hold.

"What's inside?" I inquired.

Kyar eyed the nearest container, as if trying to see through it. "I don't know."

I frowned. "What do you mean you don't know?"

"I don't know," he repeated. "A-1 guaranteed the safety and legality of the contents. They said we had to keep the boxes at just above freezing at all times. We don't have to know what's inside."

"I disagree. A-1 has already saddled us with a Catalyst and a trio of molting Decomps. I can't say I trust their prudence." I joined Kyar in eyeing the cargo, waiting for him to say it. I didn't have to wait very long.

He shoved one of the boxes and it didn't move. "Damned heavy. I suppose we could take a peek."

"I suppose we could," I agreed.

"Although …"

"What?" I asked.

"They did say not to open them," Kyar admitted.

Nothing is guaranteed to grow curiosity more than such a constraint. "It is our ship, Kyar. We have every right to know what we're transporting, for our own safety and wellbeing," I stressed.

He tapped his chin. "True."

Neither of us sounded like the voice of wisdom. Again, I waited for Kyar to make the first move. He was responsible for the metallic coffin-shaped crates lying in front of us. No longer a cautious fellow, he began prying at the lid of the nearest one. I helped—I went and fetched several tools from Venus.

It took a great deal of effort (on Kyar's part) and one broken pry bar, before we gained access to the interior of one of the crates. At first glance, the contents were disappointing.

"Blankets?" Kyar tilted his head, his hands holding the hinged lid angled open. "Why would anyone bother to put blankets in heavy metal boxes? Or transport them across space? It makes no sense."

I poked at the fuzzy purple cloth. It was kind of prickly. "I don't think they are blankets, Kyar, unless they are intended for very tough-skinned beings."

"Take some of them out. Maybe there's something underneath." He propped his shoulder under the lid and stuck one hand into the box to help.

"Ouch!" he exclaimed. "The cloth really is picky. What the hell is it?"

We stopped tugging on the material. I scratched my arm absently. Kyar scratched his stomach, then his hand. We eyed the purple cloth with all the suspicion it deserved. I began to feel itchy all over. Kyar rubbed his neck and dropped the lid back in place. He resealed the crate in-between frantic scratching.

"You're getting a rash," I pointed out helpfully, motioning at his face.

He scowled at me. "I'm not the only one."

We ran for our rooms to shower. Before we even arrived at the nearest door (mine), Kyar was erupting in purple boils—big ones, everywhere. I was in the same sorry state.

"I don't think those purple things were blankets," Kyar said, his lumpy face miserable.

"No." I fought to open my door, with rapidly swelling purple fingers. It was a nearly impossible feat. As soon as we stumbled inside, I paged Greely, barely able to manage the buttons on the wall panel beside my door. Kyar settled carefully into a chair, with much wailing about boils in unseen places.

While we waited for the doctor, I cast Kyar dark glances, as if this was his fault more than mine. We held our silence, no doubt both feeling the fool.

Greely bustled in, took one look at the pair of us, and backed out of the room. He opted to shout through the closed door. "What have you lads been into?"

"The new containers in the cargo hold," Kyar admitted.

There was a pregnant silence.

"Do you know what's wrong with us?" I asked.

Greely didn't reveal much when he said, "I do."

"Is it fatal?" Kyar sounded merely mildly curious. Without Sephine, he did not value his life overly much.

"Unlikely, or you would already be dead. Don't leave the room, I'll be back."

When Greely returned, he was sealed from head to toe in a silver isolation suit, and breathing through a biofilter mask. "It may be too late for precautions, but one can hope. At least I didn't touch you. At least you're only starting the second stage," he said, his voice muffled by the suit.

"Second stage of what?" I demanded.

"Spox."

"Spox?" both Kyar and I said, clueless.

All we could see of Greely were his accusing eyes. "Spox is a biological security agent to stop smugglers—or snoopers, from prying where they shouldn't." He poked one of my lumps with his gloved finger and it hurt like hell. "Pretty rare, since it takes careful handling. It's too easy for the wrong beings to get infected. But I've treated it a few times, enough to recognize it. You must have touched something in the boxes that penetrated your skin."

"Yes," I said, shame-faced. "The top layer of the crates, the picky purple blankets. Is there a cure?"

"Nope. It has to run its course, not a slide on the ice either. If it's the most common strain, you won't enjoy stage five." If Greely was smirking, we couldn't see it, but I suspected he was. He truly did lack the compassion you would normally find in a healer.

I muttered, "I'm not enjoying stage two." I could feel a boil erupting in the worst possible place.

"There must be something you can do," Kyar appealed.

"Not much. Once the stuff gets into your system, you simply have to see it through. I can give you something for the pain."

"Now would be good," I said. "And how long does this last?"

"A week or two. It depends on the strain, and everyone reacts a little differently. Kyar, you'll have to stay quarantined here for now. We don't want to further risk spreading this around the ship."

Greely went off to get us some medicine for the pain. He came back steering a floating cot. Kyar and I would be roommates. I suspected this was going to get very ugly.

Greely's potion knocked us out for the night. When it wore off, I awoke screaming from a nightmare about a horde of rats gnawing on my skin. It wasn't rats. It was the burning boils. No inch of my body had been spared. Kyar was already in the bathroom, and from the agonized screaming, even the simple act of urinating must be akin to torture. Ignoring my bladder, I decided that I felt no urgency to experience the same for myself.

When Kyar staggered into sight, he was a monster. The ripe purple boils were as large as penguin's eggs. He was walking on tiptoe with his legs splayed. Lying back on his cot brought tears to his eyes. "Get Greely in here!" he sobbed.

My fingers were too swollen to press the buttons on the wall panel. Neither of us moved, while we waited for our tardy physician. He didn't arrive until well after breakfast, and then he did not show the appropriate sympathy for our condition.

"More painkillers, lots of painkillers," Kyar gasped.

I had a better suggestion. "A sedative. Make sure it lasts a week. I want to be unconscious for a week."

He shook his head. "Stop being such a baby. You're only in stage two. I can't sedate you, you need to drink a lot to wash the toxins out of your body. No, not red brandy—water! I'll give you some more painkillers, and lots of water."

He did just that, providing two jugs and some orange pills.

I downed the pills and asked, "What's stage three?"

He avoided my gaze. "Ah, you don't need to know that yet. Drink more water."

"Stage four?" I tried.

"You'll find out soon enough. I'll sedate you for stage four, no problem then." The bridge of his nose wrinkled. Greely was cringing behind his mask.

"Stage five?"

"No way am I going to tell you about that. Better if you don't know."

I threatened him with the brig. He threatened me with jettisoning every last orange pill out through the waste hatch, and into open space. Greely won. The only good news the doctor delivered, was that stage five was the final stage.

Kyar and I didn't enter stage three until the end of that week, when the boils started erupting like miniature volcanoes. I dragged myself to the bathroom, renamed the torture chamber, and my face in the mirror would have made a Decomp sick. The worst of stage three was the vomiting, which wouldn't have been nearly so bad if I wasn't sharing my small cabin with another who had the same affliction.

The erupting boils and the uncontrollable vomiting convinced Greely that we no longer needed his personal attention. He simply shoved our supplies through the door—jugs of water and orange pills we could no longer hold down. Stage three was, without question, far worse than stage two.

There was a short period of respite between stages three and four. We were no longer considered contagious, and we stopped vomiting. Lillyth came to clean my cabin, took one look, and said we could clean it ourselves. She didn't stay to visit. Not one member of the crew stopped by to wish us well or cheer us up.

Greely decided we could benefit from some medical attention again and deigned to drop by. He slapped some foul smelling ointment onto our healing boils, and wrapped us in bandages from head to toe, so the medicine would stay on. He left only the most necessary parts uncovered. I could see little of Kyar, except his eyes, so like mine, but a darker silver-blue.

It was the very worst time to have visitors aboard the FarGone 5, especially visitors who wanted to take over the ship, so of course they chose that time to come calling.

Kyar and I were the last to know about the untimely company. We were in the middle of a heated argument over who should scrub the bathroom, when someone marched in without knocking. The woman was not a member of the crew. She was tall and vaguely familiar.

"It smells even worse in here than the rest of the ship," she said by way of a greeting.

Kyar identified her for me. "Noel? Good heavens, what are you doing here?"

I didn't know how to address my wife, so I sat down on the bed and held my tongue, covered in bandages, and deeply embarrassed about my condition, the state of the room, and the stench.

She ignored me anyway. "Kyar? It is you?" He nodded. "Then you know exactly why I am here."

"Do I?"

She crossed her arms tightly, protectively. "I knew you were helping your criminal brother to escape. I knew if I found you, I would find him. And I really, really wanted to find him. And now I have." She smiled so coldly, I felt like I had fallen through thin ice into a frigid lake. Noel's strong, noble features were drawn, emphasized by tightly-tied dark hair.

Kyar tried to explain. "No, Noel. You've got it wrong. I've found Megal, but the real Megal, not the imposter you married. There are two Megals—remember the clone that went missing?"

Noel wasn't in the mood to listen. She shook her head and looked down her straight nose at Kyar, planting her hands on her hips. "And now you've become smugglers. Smugglers!" She sounded quite shrewish.

"Certainly not," I said, too sick and exhausted to display any proper outrage.

Noel shot me a glance sharp enough to cut a man in half. At least the loathing was directed at Prin, not me, except she didn't know that.

She didn't waste words on me, but focussed her attention again on Kyar. "That so-called doctor of yours tells me you have a case of smuggler's spox, so of course you are smugglers. And don't feed me that slush about Megal not being Megal. I'm not stupid. I've tracked you down and taken over your ship, and I will see Megal returned to the Ice Planet to stand trial for his crimes."

"Taken over the ship? What do you mean you've taken over the ship?" I demanded

"Noel, listen!" Kyar cut in desperately. "Prin was the imposter inside the clone. He had Megal stashed on Gehenna, for three years. I only just found him, barely alive. Take his bandages off and you'll see that this Megal is not the one you called husband."

Noel didn't spare me another glance. "That's nothing but slush, Kyar. Now, get up and trot along to the brig. You will both share that space, until we reach the Ice Planet."

Neither of us was inclined to move, not until she invited in a hairy stranger, with bulging muscles and a sinister dartgun.

"What's in the darts?" I asked. If it was merely a sleeping draught, I was going to beg the fellow to shoot me. I was going to snore through the next stage of spox.

"Fuzion nanos," Noel said, with nasty satisfaction. Being shot with fuzion nanos was almost as bad as being shot with vulture nanos—the microscopic critters that ate you up inside, while you still lived. Fuzion nanos targeted the cartilage and joints, hardening and fusing every last one, until a person couldn't move an inch, ever again.

It seemed Noel really had taken over the ship.

I followed Kyar's lead and hauled myself painfully up. We didn't trot to the brig. Kyar moved like an arthritic old man. I hobbled worse than usual, because the big hairy fellow had relieved me of my staff. We didn't see one member of our crew along the way. Noel marched behind. I could feel her eyes impaling my back, still trying to kill me.

At least the brig was clean. I chipperly pointed that out to Kyar, and claimed the narrow single bed. "One cot please, with a side order of soup," I ordered from my prone position. My humour earned me a frown, otherwise I was ignored. The door was locked tight, and we were left alone for hours.

When night arrived, we were still in the brig, without an extra cot, and certainly no soup or food of any kind. By such time, I had claimed the floor and Kyar was napping, more or less comfortably, on the bed. That's when the symptoms of stage four struck me. Kyar did his best to tend me, until the middle of the night, when he succumbed as well.

Stage four was particularly horrible, since Greely wasn't handy to sedate us or put us out of our misery, and we only had one bed. It wasn't as messy as stage three, but it was much more disturbing. Greely later described it as a flash fever. It felt more like my body was on fire, and the inside of my head was smoldering slowly away, until nothing was left except glowing coals and smoky ash. I honestly couldn't say how long stage four lasted. I was delirious with pain for most of that time, convinced I was back on Gehenna, being branded by hundreds of red-hot brands, all at once, over and over again.

When I finally regained my sanity, I was on the bed. Kyar had already recovered from the fever. And Greely was there. I smiled at him, as happy to see his face as if he was an angel.

"Your fever has finally broken. Back with us?" he asked.

"I think I am."

He sat me up and handed over a jug of water. I drank it all. As soon as I could speak, I asked, "Have you taken back the ship?"

He shook his head and glanced over his shoulder. I spotted Noel and her furry-faced companion lurking outside, still clutching weapons.

I saluted them, before Greely lowered me back down. I spotted my brother hovering and said, "Kyar, you've recovered?"

"Faster than you." He had to rub it in.

"I don't suppose that was stage four and five combined?"

It wasn't. And Greely was right, stage five was the worst. Kyar and I succumbed about the same time, and it was downright gruesome. Even though Noel allowed the doctor to attend us, there was little he could do to help, other than nearly overdose us on the orange pills.

It turned out that there were two reasons the doctor had kept our healing boils covered. The first was that he didn't want us to see what was developing inside our skin. The second was that the foul smelling ointment instantly killed what burrowed its way out of our flesh. The spox was less a virus and more a species of parasitic, egg-laying worm. Each of the boils had nourished an egg, the heat of the fever hatched those eggs, and now the worms were boring their way out. Greely didn't mention the worms, not until it felt like we were being stabbed by an armoury's worth of pointy daggers, and something started squirming about inside the bandages.

I screamed in terror and writhed as if I was on fire. Kyar couldn't control himself either, and the hard floor made it that much worse for him. I cursed and staggered up. "Take the bed, Kyar. Greely, get him up."

The doctor maneuvered Kyar onto the softer surface, then started unwrapping our bandages, revealing the tiny green-spiked fiends that had bored their way out of our skin, only to become coated in the ointment that was lethal to them. They were so small to look at, yet felt as big as snakes when they pierced my tender flesh.

Greely collected the dying worms and dropped them in a beaker of acid, just to be safe. Soon, both Kyar and I were coated in blood and mucus, and the worms were still coming, cutting us up in their bid for freedom.

About halfway through the exodus, Noel clapped a hand over her mouth and ran. I was surprised that she had lasted as long as she did, then again, my suffering was probably sheer entertainment to my wife.

By morning, Kyar and I were finally out of worms. A cot had appeared at some point. We both collapsed and slept like the dead.

When I awoke, I was alone in the brig. I sensed that I had been asleep for a very long time. I was staring at the ceiling, in a stupor, when Noel turned up with the same hairy dartgun-wielding fellow. I had decided that he was her personal bodyguard, or maybe her lover. Prin had abandoned her, after all. She could have sought sexual satisfaction elsewhere.

"What have you done with Kyar?" My voice sounded like a rusty hinge.

"Your brother is fine. He is cleaning up in his cabin. You need to do the same. You're repulsive. Get up." She lacked even a trace of sympathy.

I didn't move. I wasn't sure I could. "The crew is unharmed?"

"Yes. Locked together in the largest cargo bay."

"I do hope you have been feeding and watering them, and seeing to their needs." I was surprised there was a thread of steel in my voice, given that I felt as weak as a hatchling.

"Of course we've been feeding them," she snapped impatiently. "I have no wish to harm anyone but you. Now get up, or I'll have Carn drag you to your quarters."

So the hairy fellow had a name.

Being dragged was the last thing I wanted, in my present condition. I managed the great feat of sitting up, then standing. I set my jaw and limped all the way to my cabin, even though it felt like a ten mile hike across broken glass—the boils had not spared the soles of my feet.

Once there, Noel posted Carn outside the door. She followed me in. "Alone at last." I winked. "Have you missed me, my love?"

She looked me over from head-to-toe. "Go and clean up. I've honestly never seen a more sickening sight."

The mirror in my bathroom confirmed it. At least that room had been scrubbed until it sparkled. Poor Lillyth. Now it was my turn. I downed a couple of orange pills, so I could endure showering off a thick layer of dried blood, greasy ointment, and who knew what else—probably worm poop. I followed it with a steam cleansing.

When I stepped out of the stall, there were no towels. I certainly wasn't about to don my disgusting tunic, and the remnants of bloody bandages that lay heaped on the floor, like a collection of poorly skinned pelts. Assuming my chamber was empty, I limped out of the bathroom to find something to dry myself. Too late, I noticed I still had company.

Noel was standing stiffly by the door, eyes already on me. I started to retreat, then changed my mind. Noel had already seen my exposed skin, now and when Prin had no doubt strutted about in it, sharing what was not his to share with her.

"Don't mind me, no towels," I muttered and limped to the cupboard.

She blushed and averted her eyes, then she looked again. I tried not to feel ashamed of my skin. Yet shame was all I could feel, and embarrassment. Even the spox marks couldn't hide all the damage Gehenna had done to my mortal coil. I was a pathetic wreck of a man, and I knew it.

"What happened to you?" she said. It sounded like an accusation.

"Not as pretty as you remember me?" I quickly tucked a towel around my waist, even though, to my raw, sore skin, the cloth felt like it was fashioned from pins.

"Not as I remember you." Noel left it at that.

I couldn't read her tone, and tried honesty. "Three years on Gehenna happened to me. Not what anyone would call a picnic. Rather like three years of having spox." There was too much truth in that statement, and I attended to drying my chest as gently as possible. She watched, without taking her eyes off me. It was unnerving. I yanked the nearest tunic on over my still damp body, before I patted moisture off my legs.

"How long before we reach the Ice Planet? Should I don my Nomad's robe, one last time?" I asked, and even managed a light tone.

"Not yet. We are still some days away."

I slid one raw leg gingerly into a pair of soft worn leggings, and said, "How did you get aboard?"

She shrugged with false modesty. "I politely asked permission, said I had news. Captain Glass did not see me as a threat—an advantage of being a woman. And I am your mate. Once aboard, the dartguns inspired everyone to cooperate."

"I see." I finished dressing and settled on the edge of my bed, needing a moment to recover from dressing.

"Get up." Noel motioned at the door.

"Can't I just stay here? I promise not to run away." I smiled with self-deprecation. We both knew I couldn't run to save my life.

"Get up, Megal, unless you want to get dragged."

I stood up. "Not when I've finally gotten clean. So, back to the brig for me?"

"It's where you belong."

I approached the door, and Noel. She stood defiantly in place. I stopped in front of her. We were the same height, and I looked deep into her eyes. They were as dark and impenetrable as black ice, and yet, they had a wounded air about them. "Prin hurt you, didn't he?"

"Stop laying the blame for your crimes at your cousin's door."

"What did he do to you?"

She just shook her head and told me to shut up. That was not going to happen. I had one more pressing question that I had to ask, while we were alone, to satisfy my curiosity. "You do not carry our child?" I said, watching her face carefully.

Her breath caught and her brow furrowed, as if my question had confused her. She didn't answer.

"Do you?" I prompted.

She whispered, "No, of course not. You know that."

My stolen skin had already kissed her so many times, but I had never felt her lips with mine. It wasn't fair. My recent life had been anything but fair.

Driven by the need to erase Prin's vile trespass, I leaned across the small distance that separated our lips. She watched me clinically, but with a puzzled tilt to her head. My lips brushed hers as lightly as a snowflake. She didn't stab me to death, so I deepened the kiss.

For a hard woman, she had soft lips—the softest lips I had ever touched as the man I was now. I reached up to cup her face and she flinched ever so slightly, then relaxed when I stroked her cheek. I moaned softly into her mouth and parted her lips so my tongue could touch hers. I couldn't resist her sweetness.

My hands smoothed down her back, tracing her spine to the seductive curve of her waist, gently massaging too-tense muscles. I found the hem of her top and shifted the cloth aside. I was rewarded with skin that was smooth and velvety and warm. It was as tantalizing as her lips. I breathed in her scent and pressed closer, overwhelmed by too many enticing sensations. When she reached for me and wrapped her arms around my waist, I felt such pleasure and longing, I never wanted it to end. Perhaps

I had been too long without a woman's tenderness, to feel such intense yearning in my soul over a kiss shared with one who hated me, but I began to tremble with need. "Noel," I whispered against her lips, and even my voice shook.

She must have remembered that she hated me then, or else she took a peek at my face, because she shoved me away—hard. I didn't want to let her go, yet respected her wishes. I stepped back, although letting her go caused as much pain as having a limb ripped off. She stared at me with an expression in her dark eyes that I couldn't read at all. Was it some sort of shocked dismay? Was she disgusted that she had kissed and touched a man who was as hideous as a monster?

I did not want her to see how profoundly our physical contact had affected me and smirked as I would have, before Gehenna. I arched an eyebrow at my bed. "Technically, we have an alliance, so if you want to -"

"What are you playing at, Megal?" she demanded.

"That was not playing. That was anything but playing," I said in earnest.

"You're always playing. Have another look in the mirror, husband. Alliance or not, I will never sleep with you. No-one will." She flung opened the door and stomped out.

Her words hurt, even though she was merely stating a fact I already knew. "Ah well, it was fun while it lasted," I called glibly, trying to hide my hurt. I limped out of my cabin, probably for the last time, and said, "Perhaps you can let Kyar roam free. He is not the criminal."

"Perhaps I will. Rumour has it that you killed his wife."

Those words cut through me like a dagger. I faltered and banged into the wall. "I don't want to talk about it."

Noel turned to look at me. "You really did kill her?"

"Yes." I shoved away from the wall and picked up the pace. I couldn't wait to reach my cell. We shared no more conversation.

Someone had cleaned up the brig in my absence, probably poor Lillyth. The blood soaked sheets were gone, as was the cot. Worn out by the time on my feet, I took more orange pills and slept until a tray of food arrived. It was carried by a different stern-faced fellow, one I had not yet seen.

"Not poisoned?" I asked.

"Try it and see." He slid the tray into my cell and left.

I dug in, too hungry to resist. And if it had been poisoned, he probably would have said it wasn't. The mammoth stew was delicious. I knew it wasn't Oran'Jay's cooking, so he was probably still locked up.

No-one came to visit me for two days, except for the food-carrying fellow. He resisted all my efforts to engage him in conversation. I had nothing to do but sleep and recuperate. My worm-hole wounds were healing nicely. I wondered if Kyar's were doing the same. I missed my brother, and given that I might not have many days left, I wished to spend them with him. I wanted to apologize for Sephine, and for the past, again and again, while I still could.

In the middle of my third day of solitary confinement, Noel herself brought my tray. She came inside and sat down as if planning to share the meal. Before I could produce any smart remarks, she said, "I've been thinking."

"Really?" I helped myself to a vegetable root. "What about?"

"The crew has been pleading your case. They are very convincing, and loyal. Kyar, as well, supports you. I don't understand his devotion, especially after what you did to Sephine."

I lost my appetite and tossed the food back on the platter. "It was an accident, a tragic accident that I can't undo, no matter how much I wish I could. And I don't want to discuss it."

She nibbled on a root and studied my face as if it was a riddle. I was being examined, like evidence. Her free hand reached up and felt my hair, tugging hard at a bit of it. It was just long enough to tug now.

"Ouch! It is real," I assured her.

"Yes. And white, snow white. It used to be golden." Her fingers felt the ragged edge of an ear lobe that had been bitten off—by another prisoner, not rats. My cheek was next, the deepest scars explored. Then my hand with the missing finger. "How did you lose that?"

"Blast beetle blew off some, rats took the rest."

She examined the stump closely. "It looks like an old injury."

"Almost three years." It had been one of the first things I had sacrificed to Gehenna.

"And your back?"

I attempted a dismissive shrug. It felt more like a nervous twitch.

"I saw it the other day." She bit her lip, drawing my eyes to the rosy pinkness. "Under the spox marks, there are so many scars. They look like cuts from a whip." She nibbled her root, waiting for me to explain.

"On Gehenna, the guards consider a whipping to be a bloody good show," I said, emotions tightly under control.

"The brand ... certainly looked real."

"Because it is."

She rose. "Show me."

I stood and lowered the tunic to my waist, stopping there. She didn't need to see more, even though she already had. She turned me into the light and leaned close to my shoulder, tracing the brand of a prisoner—a circle of chain, filled in with bars. No hope, no escape. Noel's gentle touch was not what I expected. It had me closing my eyes in painful longing. My skin drank in her tenderness.

"It looks old, too." She turned me around to study my back, running a hand over the rough ridges, some old, some not so old. She hissed as if in pain and I faced her again.

"And the leg?" She wanted all the answers.

My crooked lower limb was visible through the leggings. "Happened on Gehenna," I said shortly. The details were irrelevant. "Does my body support Kyar's account of things?"

She nodded. "It does. But other ... things have made me question who I allied with. You are Megal?"

It could have been a stupid question, but it wasn't. "I am."

"You did not ally with me?"

"No. I was vacationing on Gehenna around that time." The truth came out flippantly.

"So I did unite with Prin?"

"Yes, Prin, wearing my stolen skin, violating my clone." My voice shook with rage. "And it would have been Prin that you shared a bed with. Did you not see the imposter?"

She shook her head, eyes shadowed. "I didn't know you well, at all. You never had time for me, when my father brought me to visit. I was not as pretty as the other girls who were always hanging around you."

"I was a foolish man, a complete ass. I like to think I am not that man any longer," I said. "No-one leaves Gehenna unchanged. Well, most don't leave Gehenna at all, ever. Only some of the women leave alive, if they survive their sentence. They're sold into slavery at an annual auction. I've heard that that fate can be worse than the prison planet." I found that hard to believe myself.

Noel motioned for me to redress. She sat down primly. "You're so thin. Eat something, Megal."

I had a question of my own first. "You said other things are not consistent with the man you allied with. What are they?"

"Your concern for your brother and the crew. The other Megal thought only of himself."

That sounded too much like me, before Gehenna.

"Their loyalty to you is freely given, and ..." Noel trialed off, blushing. If I hadn't seen the crimson wash of colour with my own eyes, I wouldn't have believed it.

"And?" I prompted, tying my tunic in place.

Noel dropped her gaze, her long, dark lashes fanning her cheek. "And Prin lacks your ... touch."

"Ah, I see." I was certainly pleased to hear that. I cocked an eyebrow at the cot. "Does that mean you want to -"

"Heavens no, Megal! Settle down and eat your dinner."

I ate and she nibbled. We finished the meal together in surprisingly peaceful silence. I simply enjoyed the company and the food, and daydreamed about replacing Oran'Jay with whoever was cooking my meals now.

After I had eaten, exhaustion claimed me hard. Healing requires a lot of energy, and I still had much healing to do. I sagged back on the bed, and was surprised when Noel covered me with a blanket.

"Sleep, Megal." She picked up the tray and left.

I slept, too tired not to. Plus, there was nothing else to do in the cell. When I awoke, the brig door was ajar. My staff was leaning against the wall. Noel had made her decision. I was free. I picked up my staff, going so far as to embrace it in a hug, and smiled to have my life back—once again.

I immediately sought out Kyar. I found him on the bridge, with the proper crew back in place. When I was spotted, I was cheered as a hero and a friend. My heart swelled and threatened to choke me. I tossed an arm around Kyar's shoulder and said, "Are we still heading for the Ice Planet? To finish me off?"

"We are not. Noel gifted us with a solid lead for the other Megal, a lead that she did not explore, because she came chasing after the FarGone 5. She and her crew have returned to their own ship and sailed off. Noel said to tell you that she will take good care of your planets, until you can reclaim your title of Nomad."

"I bet she will." My disappointment that she had left, without so much as a fare-thee-well, caught me off-guard. "So, where does this lead take us? Where has Prin been lurking?"

"You won't believe me," Kyar said. The crew bobbed their heads in agreement.

"Of course I will. Where is our dear cousin now? Gashmore Galaxy?"

"Not even close. We've been heading in entirely the wrong direction. Prin is on Earth," Kyar declared.

He was right, I didn't believe it. "Earth? Liena's home? That's wrong. We were there, it must be me that was sighted, not him. Maybe the UGS started the rumour. They did take me into custody after we stopped on Earth." My explanation made more sense than Prin skulking around on the restricted planet.

"That's what I thought until Noel provided details. Unless you were on Earth for weeks before we landed there -"

I cut in. "You know I wasn't."

"Exactly. So it was Prin. Noel believes he is still holed up there."

"Liena did say her world needs her. I wonder if that has to do with Prin." It all seemed too much of a coincidence. We would probably need to find Prin to get answers. And at the moment, I was more interested in reuniting with my brother.

I enticed Kyar off the bridge and we shared dinner in the galley. Together, we looked like a pair of spotted humans. His worm-holes were nicely closed up and healing faster than mine. He said that Greely would start my skin regeneration treatments the very next day.

"Those spox were really something, weren't they?" I said, trying not to remember the worst of the affliction. "How did Greely recognize the condition so quickly, if it is as rare as he claims?"

We were alone in the room, so Kyar shared a secret. "Greely used to heal pirates, smugglers and their ilk. He rode a pirate ship, and made a profit from treating them, instead of turning them in. He got caught and is no longer licensed to practice anywhere in the Universe. He was happy to have a position on this ship. He will earn a Nomad's pardon?"

"He certainly will. More than that if he wants it. If not for him … well, I don't even want to think about what would have happened if those demonic little worms had infested the whole ship. Speaking of which, what became of our cargo?"

Kyar swallowed a bite of stew. "It's still aboard. It never got delivered."

That was not good news. "But hasn't A-1 asked about their containers?"

"A few messages came in, while Noel had charge of the ship. The last one said that the cargo has been rerouted to a new destination, still to be announced. I sent A-1 a return communiqué this morning, explaining that we had other business to take care of, before we could deliver the cartons. I said we would deliver the shipment when we could." Kyar scratched at a red spot beside his ear. "Frankly, they were kind of upset. They said we had to get the cargo delivered on schedule. Anyway, it's their tough luck. They can't do anything from halfway across the Universe, now can they? Forget about the containers, it's time to focus on Prin."

I nodded in agreement and Kyar proceeded to fill me in on all that I had missed. He reported that we were already headed for Earth, and should arrive in less than a fortnight, if all went well.

I figured we were due for some good fortune, proving I still wasn't a wise man.

7. Pirates

Two days later, I was roused from a deep sleep when the ship bucked wildly. I had endured a particularly gruelling skin regeneration session with Greely and really didn't want to be disturbed. All my spots were gone, but my skin was too tender to touch. I had taken three orange pills to fall asleep. I no longer thought of the doctor as an angel, quite the opposite.

Any notion of returning to the sanctuary of slumber was thwarted by Captain Glass. She broadcast to the ship at large that we had company. Nor did she sound at all pleased about this unexpected development. I donned my softest tunic and went to investigate.

Everyone was already on the bridge. Even the hostile ship hadn't waited for me. It was looming large on the viewing screen, and it wasn't a Universal Guard Ship. There were no markings on the hull. This vessel was shiny black, sleek and sexy, and powerful—all the things that the poor FarGone 5 wasn't. At least the ship wasn't really big. It matched us for size.

I moved to stand by Kyar. "Have they said hello yet?"

"No," he growled.

I frowned. "What are they waiting for?"

"An engraved invitation? I don't know. How would I know?" Kyar was grumpy. His spots were gone too, so he must have been feeling every bit as tender as me.

I claimed my favourite chair and waited, like everyone else.

It wasn't long before a rough voice communicated exactly what the black vessel wanted. "FarGone 5, A-1 All Planetary Shipping has sent us to retrieve the cargo you have aboard your ship. The client has an urgent need for the contents. They cannot await your delayed delivery. I have the tracking number to verify the transfer of the cargo to my ship. I am sending that information over now."

85

I shared a puzzled glance with Kyar and he muttered, "Guess they did hunt us down."

In less than a minute, the information appeared on the main consol. "It looks legitimate," Captain Glass murmured, verifying their invoice number against our own.

"Why do you think they need the cargo with such urgency? What is in those containers? Maybe we should borrow a couple of silver suits and have a quick look-see," Kyar proposed. He was getting curious again.

I prodded him with the end of my staff. "I don't care what is inside those cursed boxes. Let's get them off the ship, while we have the chance." I stood up. "Captain Glass, tell them to dock against the cargo hatch. We'll even help them cart the blighted things onto their ship."

Captain Glass forwarded the spirit of the message, not my words. Kyar and I went off to his cabin to find a few more orange pills. We barely had time to sit down, before we felt the nudge of the other ship magnetically linking with ours. Their captain had managed the maneuver nicely. Kyar was asking me what I thought of Noel, when there was a much bigger bang. It vibrated the deck beneath our feet.

"I wonder what that was," Kyar murmured, not overly concerned.

Seconds later, something whizzed by our door. It sounded like the discharge of a very serious weapon, one that lacked finesse. I leapt for the wall panel to communicate with the bridge. Kyar scrambled under his bed, but not to hide. He came out clutching a dangerous looking long-gun. I had never seen him hold anything like it before.

Captain Glass had time to gasp, "Pirates! We've been tricked," then the ship-wide broadcast cut off abruptly.

"Kyar, do you have another one of those?" I cried, all too aware that we were in serious trouble. Pirates left no survivors to bear witness to their crimes.

"No, just the one." He moved for the door, eager anticipation stamped on his face. "You stay here. You're not up to a firefight." Multiple blasts were now echoing from all over the FarGone 5.

"I can help defend the ship."

"Megal, you can't run, you're not … strong. Stay here. It's better for everyone if you just hide." He slipped out the door.

Words hold such power. I don't think Kyar meant to wound me, yet he did, with his words. I was not a useless invalid. I was a man who had defended his life so many times, I couldn't recall them all. My body might not be as able as another man's, but it took more than physical strength and speed to survive.

Anger grew inside me, replacing the hurt. I listened to the silence outside the door, and rashly slid it open. The corridor was empty. The blasts were sporadic now. It was hard to pinpoint their source.

Carrying my staff under my arm, so as not to make a sound, I shuffled cautiously toward my quarters, then I bypassed them. The stillness from the cargo area drew me to investigate. The hatch that connected the FarGone 5 and the pirate vessel was wide open. The four rectangular metal boxes were lined up, still on our side, but ready to be confiscated, as was Kyar's shiny red soar-board. We carried little of value, and the pirates must be sorely disappointed. At least A-1's crates were still sealed—a blessing to be sure. And for the moment, the area was deserted.

Looking at the boxes, I had an idea, but it wasn't one that I wanted to attempt, not unless the ship was in dire straits.

I believed it was and acted accordingly. Greely's medical room was my first stop. It too was empty. I helped myself to a scalpel and a silver isolation suit from his closet. Carrying both, I headed for the engine room. Tromping boots had me ducking quickly inside, where there were lots of handy nooks and crannies, as Venus called them.

I stayed hidden while two small humans, dressed in scruffy layers, gave the engine room a cursory sweep. They went on their way, believing it empty. The fragment of conversation I overheard was neither encouraging nor unexpected. The pair spoke callous words about leaving no witnesses, and casually mentioned blowing something up. The only thing in range was the FarGone 5.

It was confirmed—the pirates had won the short skirmish and intended to kill everyone. Strongly motivated to put my nebulous plan into action, I donned the overlarge isolation suit and borrowed a pry bar. Carting the tool, I snuck back to the cargo hold.

Two of the containers had been moved. Two had not.

Desperation granted me strength. I was able to force open the weakened lid of the container that had already been breached, by Kyar. I stood the pry bar between the lid and the bottom, propping it open. Covered from head to toe, I spliced off a square of picky purple blanket with the scalpel. I couldn't resist looking below the remaining purple layers, and what I saw, sealed beneath a thin layer of frosty glass, staggered me. Surely I was hallucinating. I looked again. No, my eyes were working.

Clomping steps approached from the other side of the hatch, from the invading ship. I carefully positioned a corner of purple cloth, sticking out and brushing the handgrip on the side of the container, then yanked free the pry bar to close the lid. Whoever picked up the container would become infected.

The footsteps were getting too close. I dodged through the nearest doorway, out of sight. I pressed against the wall of the empty cargo bay and held my breath, listening to the thumping that was so close to where I hid. When the noises faded away, I peeked out. One more of the containers had been carried off, but not the one I had tampered with. That would be next.

I smiled with satisfaction, feeling anything but weak and useless. Yet there was still much more to do. The riskiest part of my ruse still had to be put into action.

I snuck back to my cabin and very carefully attached the swatch of spox infested cloth around the floor-end of my staff. Only then did I remove the isolation suit and don my finest Nomad's robe. As an afterthought, I tucked the bounty missive discreetly under my belt. It might be useful as a distraction, depending on how events unfolded.

Quite terrified of what I carried on the end of my staff, I limped through the corridors. I stepped brazenly onto the bridge, and barked, "What the bloody hell is going on?"

My eyes darted everywhere, relieved to see no prone bodies, especially Kyar's. He was sitting strapped to a chair, as was Captain Glass, and the rest of the bridge crew. Venus was there, too, all tied up. She was the only one who appeared to be injured. There was blood dripping down from her head and her eyes were closed. She was also as solid as I had ever seen her—as solid as anyone else on the bridge.

I just hoped the missing members of the crew were merely locked up elsewhere, and not slaughtered.

The FarGone 5 was being held hostage by half a dozen humanoids, waving around brutal blasters with careless disregard. None looked pure human. One man was acting as if he was the new captain. His appearance made me shiver. His breed of human had clearly developed on a planet with too much gravity. His body was thick and squat, and his head had been pulled partially into his body, eliminating his neck entirely, and flattening his skull, making him a good head shorter than me. His squashed face turned toward me, and he laughed. "What have we here? Where have you been hiding, old man?"

I leaned weakly against the nearest console, emphasizing my frailty, while toying with my staff. "I was napping in my quarters. No-one thought to wake me. You've taken my ship, then?" I waved a hand around the bridge. "Are you shopping for anything in particular?"

"Merely looking. We hoped to find a lot more than we did, based on the urgent transmissions we intercepted, but your cargo holds are sadly bare, a waste of our time. Not to mention the odor we've had to endure. Your ship reeks! What are you dressed up for?" He stepped close and flicked the fur at my neck. I had to look down into the deeply recessed eyes.

"Your esteemed visit, of course," I quipped, with a bob of my head. "Take whatever you want, little that it is, and leave us in peace. That is all I ask."

"Ask all you want. Beg. It won't do any good, but it will entertain me." The villain gave me a hard poke in the chest, knocking me back a step.

I tried to stand straight. "And you are?"

"The man who is going to blow you up. Call me Jancko. And you?" He poked again. It was going to leave bruises.

"Corpse."

"Suits you. It will suit you much more in a few minutes." He flashed his blue-tinged teeth at his men and they shared a snide guffaw. "Well, Corpse, we have wasted enough of our time on your ship. We will be taking a few of your crew along, since you lack anything else of value." He pointed to Captain Glass. "Her, and the other women. They're the lucky ones. The rest of you will soon be bloody space pulp."

A weapon was raised in my direction. It was time for more drastic action. "There is more on this ship than you realize," I mentioned, coolly casual.

Jancko's eyes narrowed. "Tell me."

"There is something very valuable on board, and I will tell you exactly where it is, but only if you leave the crew healthy and the ship intact. One thousand bizoux will be your reward for that good deed."

Over the pirate's shoulder, Kyar met my eyes. He shook his head ever so slightly.

"You are in no position to bargain." Jancko stepped closer and grabbed the neck of my robe in one hand. With his superior strength, he only needed one arm to lift me off the ground and shake me. His men were highly entertained. After Gehenna, this belittling treatment was nothing new, yet I did not appreciate my crew, and especially my little brother, seeing me thus.

As soon as my feet were back on the deck, I corrected him. "Actually, I am in a position to bargain. You've already revealed your intent to destroy the ship and you will never find this treasure unless I tell you where it is." I might have gloated. I shouldn't have.

Fast as a rocket, his fist flew. I went down easily. Someone cried out, I didn't think it was me. My ears ringing and my nose spurting blood, I bellowed, "I just got that nose fixed. Twice."

Jancko didn't care. He loomed over me. "Where is this fortune?"

I held out a hand for assistance to stand. None was forthcoming. I struggled to my feet and faced the bully. "Beating me will not inspire me to talk. Nothing you can do is worse than what has already been done to me. A fortune for the ship's freedom—that is the bargain. You can take it or you can kill me." I leaned back against a yulithium pillar, truly needing the support now.

He reassessed me. My words had been truth, and I think he knew it. But he was not ready to give in. We knew his face and ship. We could identify him to the UGS.

"Perhaps you would care more if I killed someone else," Jancko mused.

"Unlikely." I kept my eyes fixed on his face and tried to look like an uncaring bastard. I did not glance in Kyar's direction.

He scanned his prisoners: Captain Glass, Kyar, Hanis, Mo White, Greely, Venus and a few of the bridge crew. Everyone sat stoic.

One of his men said helpfully, "That one didn't like you hitting him." Kyar was poked with the end of a blaster.

Jancko shifted his weapon, aiming it at Kyar. Kyar didn't blink.

"Ready to talk?" Jancko asked me.

"As a matter of fact, I am." My plan was not playing out quite as I had envisioned, yet the situation might still be salvageable.

"Now is the time." Jancko's voice was liberally laced with threat.

In answer, I slipped the page from my belt and handed it to him. "That's me," I said, in case he couldn't tell. "In better days, check the eyes."

He looked between me and my image several times. "*You* are worth a thousand bizoux? You are the treasure?" He roared with laughter, before he passed the page around to his men, so they could have a good laugh, too. "Well, I guess you will be taking a ride with us. You'll have a fantastic view when we disintegrate your ship, but first, a little business to take care of." I had no idea what he meant, not until he raised his weapon, pointed it at Kyar, and blasted a gaping hole in my brother's chest.

"No!" I screamed too late. The deed was done. "No! Kyar." I lunged toward him to stem the flow of blood. My brother's eyes were wide and staring at nothing. "No," I sobbed, drowning in grief.

"Was he a friend of yours?" Jancko inquired, motioning for his men to bring me along.

I fell against Greely, trying to think through my shock. What I had seen in the coffin-shaped crate flashed before my eyes. I murmured desperately in Greely's ear, before I was dragged away. The rest of the crew was left tied to their chairs, to die with the ship.

Surrounded, I was escorted through the corridor. Overcome with grief, I was barely able to stay on my feet. It was reason enough to be clumsy with my staff. I jabbed everyone in the leg, especially the flat-headed captain. Him, I targeted twice, before he wrenched my staff away and tossed it aside.

At the hatchway leading onto their ship, the last coffin-shaped crate was no longer there. My heart sank, for now I needed it to be safely aboard the FarGone 5.

By the time we stepped onto their ship and edged around the rectangular containers stolen from the FarGone 5, my captors were scratching as if they had a bad case of fleas. The first boils were starting to bloom. The pirates began to cry out in fear and pain. With a bellow of rage, Jancko lunged at me, assuming my guilt. I ducked behind one of his men, who was distracted by his burgeoning boils.

"What is this? What have you done?" Jancko roared.

I answered him with a lie. "My whole ship is treated with a biological protective agent, a strain of spox—that's what you smelled. We are immunized against it, you are not. It is fatal, but only after a prolonged and very painful incubation period."

Jancko reached for his weapon. Already, his fingers couldn't hold it. His men were in the same condition, but they could still run—sort of. They could keep up with me, at least. I needed another delay.

"There is an antidote," I declared.

They stopped coming after me. I reached into my pocket and produced a vial of the orange pills that I kept handy these days. I held it up and rattled the three pills. "Looks like enough to save three of you," I bluffed.

91

"Let me board my ship and depart in peace, and the pills are yours." I didn't expect them to agree, my words simply made the bluff seem more believable.

"Give me the pills!" Jancko tried to shove past his men.

"Certainly. Enjoy!" I heaved the vial over their heads, as far down the corridor as I could. It landed and kept rolling. They all went for it, rather than me, clumsily wrestling each other now.

As fast as I could move, I limped back toward my ship. When I passed the stolen cartons, I checked the one nearest the hatch. It was the crate I had tampered with. I tried to shove it, staying far away from the purple edge of cloth. I lacked the strength.

Cursing, I scanned the corridor and spied the soar-board propped against the wall. Perfect. I shoved the red tip under the heavy container and at the same time, activated the gravity-blocker at the other end of the board.

I could hear the pirates getting closer again. The soar-board lifted the end of the container and I shoved. It inched under, raising it higher. I shoved again and it slid fully underneath, floating the crate off the ground.

The pirates were almost upon me.

Leaning on my prize, I guided the floating container through the hatch, banging walls on both sides. With not a second's grace, I slammed the hatch on Jancko's lumpy red face. His wild eyes told me that, in spite of being the captain, he had not been one of the men to get an orange pill.

I forced the locking bar into position, released the magnetic seal and reversed the current, separating the intimate union of the two vessels. Now, if only I had been quick enough. I left the coffin floating where it was and hobbled for the bridge, wishing I could run.

The crew was still restrained, fighting their bonds. Venus was conscious and no longer a solid form. I avoided the sight of Kyar's limp, mutilated body. I yanked a knife out of my boot, to cut Greely's bonds, freeing him. I gasped, "It's in the container, just inside the cargo hatch. Wear gloves when you move it!"

He nodded and shook off his bonds, while I continued freeing everyone.

Captain Glass was already back at the controls when Greely ordered Mo to move the container to his treatment room. Fighting tears, I cut Kyar's body free. Greely assessed his condition.

"Died instantly," he said, shaking his head. "He might have been dead too long to save."

"No, he'll be fine," I cried, trying to lift my brother.

Hanis touched my shoulder, as gentle as he always was. "I'll bring him, Megal."

I stepped aside. Hanis scooped Kyar up and carried him away, trailing a thick line of dark blood. Greely went with them. I intended to go along, except my legs gave out. I fell into the nearest chair.

Captain Glass had the pirate ship on the viewing screen. The shiny black hull was floundering in space, trying to gain control. I could imagine the scene on their bridge, with every crew member covered in big purple boils, their fingers unmanageable, perhaps tearing opened each other's gullets to get at undigested orange pills.

"Why aren't they attacking?" Glass asked, baffled.

I had forgotten to tell the crew what I had done. As briefly as possible, I explained about the spox.

"Clever idea. Do you want me to blast them?" The captain asked, her eyes gleaming.

There are times for mercy, but this didn't feel like one of them. Jancko had murdered my brother and his men had laughed. They would have slaughtered my entire crew without a second thought. After this incident, they would hunt us to the end of the Universe in a quest for revenge.

"Blast them," I ordered, and felt no remorse.

They fired on us first and missed by a thousand miles. Our captain returned the favour. She did not miss. After three direct hits, their hull exploded, the fragments shooting out in all directions. The valiant FarGone 5 hurtled out of there, barely ahead of the cresting wave of projectiles.

As soon as we were clear, I told Captain Glass to resume course for Earth. I made my way to Greely's treatment room, terrified to arrive. Until I knew otherwise, I could still hope for my brother's survival.

Hanis and Whitey were seated on the floor outside, blocking the narrow corridor with their legs, and Lillyth was there. "Has the rest of the crew been released?" I asked.

She nodded. "We were locked in the smallest cargo bay. Two were injured, but they will recover."

I sank to the ground with them. Waiting.

"How did you know about Kyar's clone?" Mo asked.

"I saw it when I was removing a scrap of spox-cloth, to infect the pirates. I couldn't believe my eyes at first."

"Do you think it's a coincidence? That Kyar's clone or clones were on this ship?" Lillyth asked.

I had had some time to draw my own conclusions. "No. I think we were carrying Kyar's clones aboard our ship, because Prin arranged it. I think Prin knows exactly where I am. And I think he planned to kill both me and Kyar, as soon as we delivered the clones to him. He was probably planning to become Kyar next, to rule the planets once he eliminated me." I was pretty sure I had it all figured out.

"Smart plan. Sounds like Prin," Mo agreed.

Hanis simply nodded and leaned back against the wall, his hands still red with my brother's blood.

We discussed the situation from all angles, the conversation taking our minds off Kyar's battle against death. It was an hour before Greely made an appearance, his weary face giving nothing away.

I lurched to my feet. "What news?"

"I have transplanted Kyar's brain into his clone. The clone is healthy." Greely sucked in his cheeks and sighed. "Look, I won't know more until Kyar wakes up, if he wakes up. He was dead longer than he should have been, before I made the transfer. There wasn't time to properly warm the clone ... I won't know his condition until he awakens, or doesn't."

"When do you expect him to wake up?"

He shrugged. "I'll call you if there is any change, one way or the other."

"Please do." I limped away, feeling the need for privacy. I had almost reached my quarters when Oran'Jay approached from the other direction. He must have been locked up in the small cargo bay, since I hadn't seen him on the bridge. He was kindly returning something that belonged to me.

Before I could scream 'no', he tossed me my staff. I felt the graze of rough picks dig into my leg, as if it was happening to someone else. It wasn't, it was happening to me. I decided then and there that I must be cursed.

I chased Oran'Jay with my staff, until the burgeoning boils made it impossible. I never caught him.

There are many things a man should never have to endure once in a lifetime. Twice is simply cruel jest. Spox is one of those things.

Kyar was on his feet and in good health, before I reached stage five.

8. Restricted Planet

With Kyar and I indisposed, Captain Glass set a slow and meandering course for Earth, where we all believed Prin was hiding. A-1 tried to contact us repeatedly. Captain Glass did not respond. She didn't trust them, given that Prin had gotten the clones aboard our ship. He had to be in contact with someone in that organization, but it was impossible to know if A-1 was unwittingly involved, or as thick as thieves with my conniving cousin.

The first day I was back on my feet, the crew held a celebration. Both Kyar and I were alive and well, and the ship was closing in on Prin. It was reason enough to make merry, and I enjoyed being toasted for my quick thinking. I didn't mind everyone, especially Kyar, knowing that I hadn't been useless against the pirates after all. Maybe next time, he would have some faith in his older brother, if he could overlook the fact that I had also gotten him killed.

After two recurrent doses of spox, after watching Kyar die, I simply reclined in my chair and sipped red brandy, perfectly content to be exactly where I was—with the crew that I now thought of as dear friends.

Such moments are rare in life, and must be savoured fully. As Nomad, when I'd had everything I wanted at my fingertips, and a beautiful skin to strut about in, I had never felt as at peace with myself as I did now. Seated by my side, Kyar looked younger and happier in his new body. The heartbreak that had plagued him, appeared to have disappeared. And tomorrow would be soon enough to figure out what Prin was plotting.

Tomorrow came too quickly.

With morning's clear resolve, I contacted A-1, then summoned the crew to the galley. Before I shared my big news, I repeated my belief that Prin had plotted to become Kyar and rule my planets again, as my brother, after murdering every last one of us when we delivered the clones. If we had not been boarded by chance by pirates, if I had not peeked in the container, we would have walked right into his trap, completely unprepared and defenseless.

Everyone agreed that my reasoning was sound. Prin always had been a schemer, thinking many moves ahead, as if life was a strategic game with people as the expendable pawns. Now we would be one step ahead of Prin. I had already formulated a plan, gift-wrapped with a pretty bow on it, and I couldn't wait to share it.

I cleared my throat loudly, before my triumphant reveal. All eyes focused on me. Trying not to smile, I said, "I spoke to A-1, and I've obtained the new delivery co-ordinates for the crates. I have assured them we'll make the delivery without delay."

Kyar was the one to put the rather obvious pieces of the puzzle together. "The new delivery coordinates are on Earth?" he guessed.

"They are."

"The delivery coordinates will lead us straight to Prin," he added.

"They will. And I've confirmed delivery. A-1 has even offered us a bonus to convey the packages to the restricted planet, with the stipulation that *we* accept the risk. I agreed to their terms."

"Walk right into Prin's trap? I don't think so," Kyar said, proving himself a cautious fellow again.

"Prepared," I stressed. "Walking into a trap when you know it is there, is a very different thing from doing so blindly."

"But still, we don't know what Prin will have in store for us. We don't know what we need to be prepared for, so how can we be ready? With Prin, it could be anything."

"I think we can be prepared, Kyar. He can't know that pirates boarded us, that we saw what was inside the crates. He won't have a clue that we are aware of his trap. That gives us the advantage."

"I still don't like it." Kyar leaned back in his chair, his jaw set at a stubborn angle.

"Swaddling infant." I tossed his own words back at him, with a smirk.

Mo was the first one to support me. "It's our best chance to catch the bugger. We all need Prin to prove Megal's innocence, so's he can rule again. We all need a Nomad's pardon, for one reason or another. If A-1 is sending us to Earth, it confirms Prin's location, doesn't it? We have to make the delivery, hang the risk."

Enough heads nodded. Oran'Jay, Captain Glass, Hanis, Greely, Mo, myself. Kyar surveyed us with resignation. "I guess that's it then. We will step into Prin's trap."

"No, Prin walks into our trap," I corrected him.

He refused to show any enthusiasm, yet accepted the decision with good grace. We remained around the table and chatted for a bit, trying to guess what mad scheme Prin might have dreamed up. The possibilities were endless, and deeply disturbing.

We stopped meandering and flew with purpose toward Earth, generating one wormhole after another, like a chain. It was lucky we were fully stocked up on fuel.

Only when we orbited high above the surface of the planet did Mo made an unsettling discovery. He was mapping the delivery co-ordinates when he slammed a hand down on the console with such force, I expected it to buckle.

"Problem?" I inquired.

"When we find Prin, I'm going to pound his face into bloody slush," Mo ground out, then glanced at me. "Unless you want to reclaim your undamaged clone, Megal, then I won't."

The words were startling. Evict Prin's brain and reclaim my last clone? To look beautiful again? To walk with ease? To run? It was so tempting, yet, to even think of intimately inhabiting the same body that Prin had abused, made my own skin crawl. Still, wasn't that a small price to pay for the strength and good health I would regain?

"I'll have to think about that," I murmured. "So, what is the problem?"

He gestured at the consol. "The co-ordinates on Earth."

"Yes?" I prompted.

"It's the exact same spot where we picked Liena up. Same river, same damn bridge. A-1 has made a notation that this is for our convenience, since we're already familiar with the location, but I'm not so sure. If you ask me, this stinks of Prin."

The significance of his revelation was not lost on anyone on the bridge. It gave us all pause.

"Prin is taunting us. How long has he been playing us like a puppet?" Kyar burst out.

Mo growled, "In cahoots with A-1. Bet he found out that a Catalystene needed transport to the Gashmore Galaxy. Once he knew that, he probably started the rumour himself, about Megal being sighted in that quadrant, to keep us distracted and off his tail."

"Speaking of a foul stench, do you think he was responsible for the Decomps?" I asked Kyar, who had been the one to book that shipping contract with A-1.

"Could have been, I suppose, if he arranged for their ship to be sabotaged, so they couldn't make it home. A-1 did seem awfully eager to give us the fare, even though we lost Liena," he said, and cursed. A man never welcomes being played for a fool, and the fact that Prin was behind the manipulation made it that much worse.

I had never credited my cousin with having a sense of humour, but perhaps I was wrong. Saddling us with molting Decomps was diabolically funny, unless you happened to be sharing the ship with them.

A related thought had me sinking into the captain's chair. "Do you think he sent the pirates? To obtain the clones and murder us all?" That would have served my cousin's purpose.

"No." Kyar sounded certain. "No. Prin hates you, Megal. You can bet he's spent three years drooling over the reports of your suffering. He will settle for no less than killing you himself, now that you've escaped Gehenna."

Oran'Jay held the same opinion. "He'd plan a torturous end for you, and he'd watch. Mark my words."

Knowing Prin, I tended to agree with them. I mulled over this latest development. It didn't really change our plans. Prin would still set his trap, intending to murder us and claim the clones, unaware that we knew exactly what he was up to. And we would defeat him at his own game.

"Hold this orbit," I told Captain Glass. "Let's examine the meeting site and determine how best to defend ourselves. How much time before the exchange?"

"About six hours," Mo answered. He returned to studying the console instead of abusing it. "As I see it, the main problem is that we only have one container to deliver, and it's empty. We won't fool Prin for long."

"Luckily, Prin only needs one clone, and the coffin holds a surprise." I said. Greely and I had already prepared for this.

"The coffin isn't empty," the doctor said. "It holds Kyar's original body, looking like a clone. Chest is all covered up, empty head is fused together. Whole thing is encased under ice-glass. Prin won't be able to tell that it isn't a perfectly healthy clone, not until it's too late."

Mo nodded in appreciation. "Nice touch."

I thought so. "And we explain the missing cargo with the truth. Pirates boarded us and managed to steal most of our shipment, before we fought them off."

"If we get as far as conversation," Kyar said.

It was very possible that we wouldn't. Prin might blast first and ask questions after, if anyone was still alive to speak. Then again, he was more likely to blast my feet off, so he could torture me rather than kill me, after he had eliminated everyone else.

So we planned our safeguards as best we could, with no idea what we were about to face. We dared not scout the area or lie in wait. Prin was sure to have scanners trained on the location, watching for any suspicious activity. Of course, we did the same. Our scanners showed no unnatural movement in the vicinity.

As the exchange time edged closer, we all grew tense and silent. I was almost shaking with anticipation to capture Prin. I had decided that I would reclaim my skin, as soon as it had proven my innocence. I would be strong and healthy again, and Prin would die, since he no longer had a body to call his own. Sadly, he wouldn't experience Gehenna for himself, but he would pay for his crimes. Not normally a sadistic man, I hoped the removal of his brain from my skin would be performed without anesthesia. I could arrange that.

Kyar betrayed his nerves by repeating what had already been discussed, over and over. We would walk into the trap, and do nothing until Prin showed his hand. Six of our number would go, no more. More would have aroused suspicion. The six included myself and Kyar (neither of us trusted the capture of Prin to others), Hanis Holly and Mo White, Borelle, a strong strapping young man who was an expert in weaponry. And Greely, of course, in case of medical emergencies. If anyone was forced to assault Prin, I needed my clone kept alive.

My brother did not once suggest I stay behind, and I appreciated his unspoken faith in me.

All of us were armed with blasters in plain sight. It would be expected on an unknown planet. And discreetly, we carried small dartguns. Those weapons were loaded with neither vulture nanos nor fuzion nanos, since Prin could not be damaged. They held a powerful sedative instead, one that would drop him in his tracks.

Beneath our shirts, we wore impenetrable shielding. More protection would have been nice. We didn't know how much support Prin had with him on the planet, but we couldn't risk alerting him to the fact that we were onto him.

The exchange location was the bridge over the small river where I had first laid eyes on Liena. The scheduled time was the earliest morning, when the sun was starting to rise over the eastern edge of the planet. Then and there we would face Prin, and I would have my justice and my revenge.

Captain Glass brought the ship down in full darkness, much closer to the site than when we had last visited Earth. I wanted the FarGone 5 nearby, in case we needed support. Tensely, we assembled by the cargo hatch, surrounding our crucial cargo—Kyar's lifeless skin. Everyone double-checked their weapons and scanners.

"I can't believe we are within a mile of Prin," Kyar murmured.

"So close." My heart was pounding too hard inside my thin chest. I hated the waiting, but we had all agreed that we should let Prin arrive first, to see how many men we were up against.

Captain Glass soon communicated that information to us. "One being is on the bridge." Her strangely hushed voice came strongly out of the console beside my ear, as if she was speaking right into it. "A second is at the far end of the bridge, on the opposite side of the river, standing out of sight. There is no-one else in the area."

"Only two. You're sure?" Kyar asked.

"Positive."

"Well, I guess this is it." He cocked an eyebrow at the hatch. "Ready, Megal?"

"Do you have to ask?"

We turned on our Scarnivian scanners. They doubled as communicators, one of their latest products. I hoped that they were more reliable than their regular scanners, since our lives might depend on the small devices. "Captain Glass, inform us if there is any change, any at all," I said, testing the thing. We would be keeping the channel open at all times.

"I will. And be careful." Her voice came out of my hand now. It sounded like she cared.

It was time. I led the way with Greely, me watching my scanner and Greely clearing vegetation where necessary, with a handheld laser. We were followed by the four coffin-carriers, struggling through tangled branches and crowded tree trunks. The plant life was as thick as the last time we walked the planet. The dark sky lightened almost imperceptibly as we hiked, until it was glowing orange. Earth really was a paradise planet. It was just too bad the inhabitants were determined to spoil it.

When we emerged from the green wall, the dark shape of the bridge faced us, arcing picturesquely over the glinting water. The gracefully curved wooden surface was no more than fifty paces across.

100

And on the apex of the bridge, one figure stood alone. It could have been anyone, unmoving in the near dark, wearing a capped hat and silhouetted against the brilliance of the rising sun. But it wasn't anyone—it was Prin masquerading as me. I could tell.

"It's him," I breathed to Kyar.

"Ya, I see him."

We kept moving.

"Stop," the figure on the bridge ordered. We all did. "You have something for me?"

Mo put down his corner of the coffin and pulled out some documents, acting as if this was any regular A-1 delivery, not a clandestine transaction on a restricted planet. "We have some bad news," he called. "Only one of your packages has survived the journey. We were boarded by pirates. They managed to make off with three of your crates, before we destroyed their ship. But we saved this one. Do you want to accept it without the rest of the consignment?"

There was a long pause. The shadow on the bridge stood indecisive, then said, "Yes. The two biggest fellows can bring it to me for inspection."

Hanis and Borelle were obviously the largest, even in the dim light. They each took a side and hauled the carton up the gentle rise of the bridge. Their boots sounded hollow on the wooden surface, thudding much slower than my heart.

Before they got too close, Prin pulled a head-covering down from his hat and donned long gloves. He was prepared for the spox cloth, and the mask hid his identity at the same time. Tricky.

Prin had the key. He unlatched the crate and moved the cloth aside. He nodded his approval and relocked the crate. The gloves came off, but the disguise stayed in place. He spoke quietly to Hanis and Borelle. They carried the crate the rest of the way across the bridge to the other side.

Only then did I notice the boat. Hanis and Borelle struggled down to the far shore, waded into the water, and loaded the crate onto the small craft. Was Prin ensuring the safety of his clone, before trying to blast us? I felt over-exposed and kept my eyes on him. Still, he didn't move. I might have shot him with the sedative then, if not for his hidden partner on the same side of the bridge as Hanis and Borelle.

Biding my time, I waited until both men crossed the bridge safely and were back on our side. Prin motioned to Kyar and I. "Bring the

101

documents, I'll sign receipt of one crate," he said, his voice muffled. Mo handed me the papers.

Covered as he was, we could walk right up to Prin, without recognizing his face. "I guess this is where he kills us," Kyar joked badly. He stepped forward.

I followed, with no intention of dying, and every intention of seizing Prin undamaged. We walked toward him as if we were naïve fools. The nape of my neck began to tingle. Something wasn't right. I couldn't put my finger on what it was, but I knew.

I slipped my hand in my pocket and palmed my small dartgun. I stayed behind Kyar, so Prin couldn't see what I was up to. When I was close enough not to miss, I stepped out from behind Kyar and took a clear shot. My dart hit Prin in the chest. He crumpled slowly down, hitting the wooden bridge with a hollow thump.

"That was too easy," Kyar said, as if he was reading my mind.

"It really was," I murmured.

We hurried up to the unmoving figure. I wrenched off the head covering and saw my face as it used to be, unmarred and smooth. Too perfectly beautiful. Prin wasn't completely senseless yet and tried to speak. I didn't give him the chance. I wouldn't normally strike a man when he was down, but this was Prin, so I made an exception. I punched him as hard as I could in the face and his nose broke with a loud snap. It did feel odd, like I was breaking my own nose, which had already been broken far too many times. He sagged onto the bridge, his nose bleeding profusely. Kyar aimed his blaster at Prin's head, as if Prin might spring to his feet at any moment.

I winced. "Not the blaster, Kyar. Not the face."

He raised one eyebrow at me. "Look who's talking."

"I know, I know. I couldn't help myself."

We both gazed down on our hostage and Kyar said, "Uh, Megal … what's happening?"

Prin didn't look as much like me as he had before I punched him. He was beginning to look more like a girl with brown hair and nondescript features. The wind picked up around us and it began to rain, even though there were no clouds in the sky. And then Prin looked exactly like a girl we knew very well. We were both gaping at Liena, when the boat's engine fired to life below. Things started to make sense, in an awful way.

"Megal, look," Kyar gasped.

I followed his glance. A familiar blonde head was shining in the new daylight, driving away in the boat with the coffin.

"Prin." I glanced at Kyar, stunned. He raised his blaster and aimed at the boat, saying, "Sorry about your skin, Megal."

"Oh, just do it."

But he had no chance to blast the fleeing Prin. The boat was attached to something well-hidden, and so basic, I felt like a bloody stupid fool when a microfiber rope tightened around my ankles and pulled them out from under me. Kyar came along for the ride. Both of us were yanked painfully over the bridge railings. At least our vests absorbed the worst of that impact.

I grabbed my brother when we flew through the air. I was still holding him when we landed on water that felt as hard as a metallic deck. The boat had a powerful engine. We were dragged along, half in and half out of the water, and the waves felt like hammer blows on my skin. I was breathing as much water as air, making my thoughts fuzzy. How did Prin dream up this stuff? I had no doubt that he would drag us behind the boat until we died. So Prin had won. No doubt he was laughing his head off, or my head off, on his speeding boat.

A powerful blast almost blew my feet off. I thought that Prin was trying to blast us, as well as drown us, until we stopped speeding through the water. We began sinking instead. Kyar's blaster fired in the boat's direction and I realized the truth of the matter. Kyar had kept his wits about him. He had freed us from the rope with his blaster.

I had no strength to kick to the surface for air. I floundered, until Kyar locked strong arms around me and brought me up. We both choked and gasped, desperately hauling in air. My brother didn't let me recover. He pulled me toward shore, where the vegetation grew thickly, even under water.

The boat fishtailed and came speeding back, nose pointing straight at us. We would never make the shore in time. "Release me," I shouted to Kyar.

He did and we sank under the surface. I hauled out my blaster. Even though the last thing I wanted to do was ruin my beautiful skin, I fired straight up when the boat passed overhead. My blast hit the boat's back end, but it didn't slow down. It turned again and raced back toward us. I was long out of air and fought to aim my weapon. I lost track of Kyar in the churned up water and hesitated to fire, not wanting to hit him instead. The boat passed overhead and kept going.

103

Half-drowned, I kicked to the surface and aimed my weapon at Prin's back. He swerved as I fired. I missed him by several yards. Before I could try again, the boat reached a curve in the river and was gone. My ears full of water, I strained to hear if the vessel was coming back. I couldn't hear a thing. Nor could I spot Kyar. I kicked in a circle and located my brother, floating face down.

"Kyar! Kyar!" I released my blaster to the depths and stroked toward him. Fear must have granted me strength. I succeeded in flipping him over. His eyes were closed and he had a terrific lump sprouting on his forehead, but he coughed and started breathing. I got a hand under his neck and struggled to tow him toward the shore. I cursed my weak body when I floundered and started to go under. Neither of us would have made it, if Hanis hadn't surged into the water like a walrus. He dragged Kyar onto the land. Borelle helped me ashore.

"Where's Greely?" I cried.

"Right here." Greely bent over Kyar and said, "Relax, Megal. He's all right. Big bang on the head when the boat hit him. Guess you didn't see that?"

"No."

"We'll carry him back to the ship, where I can examine him more thoroughly. Let's get moving." Greely motioned for Hanis to lift Kyar.

We struggled downriver toward the bridge, surrounding Kyar. The wind and rain had died as quickly as it had appeared, and I attributed it to Liena's changing. She was still unconscious, looking completely like herself again, except for her swollen nose. I felt like the worst sort of brute for knocking her out with a dart, and punching her in the face.

Mo was guarding her, weapon in hand.

"Wake her," I said to Greely.

He opened his medical kit, pulled out a dart, and stuck her with it. In less than a minute, her eyelids fluttered opened.

"Liena, what the hell is going on?" I demanded.

She gazed at me blankly, blood all over her face. I removed a cloth from Greely's kit and mopped up the worst of the blood. "I'm so sorry I hit you, I thought you were Prin," I said.

She nodded and winced. "I know, Megal. We have to talk. Prin forced me to help him. I have to tell you …" She faltered and worried her lip. I could only assume her news was bad, since she was not eager to share it.

"I'm going to help you up, if you think you can stand," I said, so she would know to put her defenses up.

"I think I can."

I assisted her to her feet. She leaned against the bridge railing for a moment, steadying herself.

"We can talk on the way to the ship, when you're able to walk. Greely can fix you up there," I said and turned to Greely. "Get Kyar back to the FarGone 5 for treatment. We'll catch up."

Everyone went with them except Mo. He trailed after Liena and me, granting us enough space to converse privately, yet keeping a close eye on her, as if he didn't trust her fully.

"Liena, how did you end up changing into Prin, as me?" I prompted, in no mood to wait patiently for answers.

"He knew who I was, Megal, and where I lived. He turned up at my door, blaster in hand," Liena began.

I heaved a sigh of frustration. "It makes sense. He is somehow involved with A-1 All Planetary Shipping, the company that has been assigning us our shipping contracts."

"Including the contract to ship me," she confirmed. She would know everything Prin knew, since she had shared his vile thoughts.

"Yes." My steps dragged worse than usual. I felt so disappointed that we did not have Prin in captivity.

Liena linked her arm through mine as we walked. She went on to describe how she had been forced to participate in Prin's evil plot. Before Prin presented himself to her, he had planted a destructive biological agent on the restricted planet. "He was going to release it and destroy my whole town, every living thing, if I didn't help him. I really had no choice but to co-operate, Megal."

"Did he speak the truth?"

"He did. I knew when he touched me, so I could transform into him. He didn't realize that I would know his thoughts as well as his body." She swallowed hard and her grip on my arm tightened. "He really is a dreadfully wicked man. Anyway, I know where he has hidden the weapon, and it's the only one he has, so I'll retrieve it. I'm sure he won't hang around on Earth, not now that you know he's here."

"Oh, I have every intention of tracking him down, before he can flee," I said. Prin could not fly a ship off the planet without us being able to track it. We had him as thoroughly trapped as a fish in a flooded crater. It would simply take a little bit longer to corral him, I reassured myself. Captain Glass would be following his trail down the river even now, with the ship's sensors. We would catch Prin, it was simply a matter of time.

It was a relief to reach the ship. "Come in and Greely can fix your nose. And if you would like to come with us -"

She shook her head and darted a glance inside the hatch. "My nose will be fine, I can change it, make it straight. But there's more, Megal."

"More?"

Her face kind of crumpled. "I learned *all* of Prin's thoughts. There is something you need to know. I didn't want to say it in front of anyone else." She ended up whispering and glanced significantly at Mo. He was standing a few paces away, waiting for us to enter before him.

"Go ahead in," I told him.

He didn't move.

"That was an order."

He cocked an eyebrow at me, amused that I would assume the mantle of Nomad that I had shed, in favour of friendship and camaraderie. I smiled. "Liena is no threat to me. I will be in directly."

"You have five minutes," he said, as if he was the one in charge. He ducked into the ship.

"Tell me," I said, since I only had five minutes.

She bit her lip and her eyes dampened. "It's about Sephine."

I still couldn't hear that name without my heart feeling stabbed. "What about her?"

"Megal, Sephine is alive."

My head spun. "No. I saw her die. You must be wrong. Why would you even think it?"

"I don't think it. I know Prin's thoughts," she stressed. "He pieced most of it together—your escape from Gehenna. He is aware that Sephine aided you. She is alive and on Gehenna. That spine didn't kill her. She is far more resilient to toxins than pure humans. She only appeared dead, as you did. She revived, and the guards found her and brought her back into the prison. Prin has been receiving reports on her, from the same guard that kept him informed about you, Megal."

It was fantastic news. Sephine was alive, and we would save her from Gehenna. I hadn't killed her! "But this is wonderful news! Thank-you for telling me."

"There's more." Her expression proved it was bad.

"Ah, of course. Go on."

"Sephine is going to be auctioned off of Gehenna in six days. You have to get to Gehenna in time for the auction, or she may truly be lost to Kyar, forever." Liena knew as much about Gehenna as I did, after

106

sharing my thoughts. That place did not keep records. They got their money and cared not where the prisoners went. The ones who weren't purchased, provided a dramatic finale to the auction, by being executed and dying en masse.

"Next week? We can't make it there in time." Gehenna was simply too distant from Earth.

"The FarGone 5 can," Liena said. "I learned a lot about your ship when I was your guest. The ship is … alive in a way that I could sense, since I was touching her when I was inside her hull."

"Venus seems linked to the ship," I said, not quite sure where I was going with that thought.

"More than linked," Liena said cryptically. "And you haven't seen her true speed. You can make it if you leave now."

That was a problem. "Prin?"

"You can't do both Megal. You can save Sephine, or you can track and capture Prin on this planet, but you can't do both. There is not enough time," she stressed, squeezing my arm.

To let Prin go? When we had him? It broke my heart. Yet to imagine Kyar's happiness to find Sephine alive. There really was no choice to make. "Sephine it is," I said. "Liena, are you sure Prin won't harm your world?"

"He can't. He only had the one nano weapon. He won't have that for much longer. I expect he will be gone from this planet as soon as the coast is clear, as soon as you've flown off. But what about Kyar's clone?"

I shook my head. "There is no clone. Kyar's dead body is in the coffin. Kyar already made use of the clone, and his old body will never breathe again. It was too badly damaged by the pirates that boarded us."

"Pirates? It sounds like quite a story. I wish you had time to tell me more."

"Likewise." We smiled at each other. "Uh, Liena, when you turned into Prin, what change did that create?"

"I don't know. The change is not always obvious to me." She grimaced. "Sometimes I have no idea what it is. Now, you better go. Venus will get you there in time. You will save Sephine."

If only I could capture Prin, too.

Liena hugged me goodbye, holding on tight, as though loath to let me go. "Be careful, Megal. After sharing his mind, I fear for anyone who tries to stop Prin."

"Oh, I will stop him. It will just take longer than I had hoped."

Before I stepped through the hatch, she told me her Earth address, so I could let her know how it all turned out, if I was ever back this way. I promised I would, if I could. I stepped into the ship and sealed the door, wondering if I would ever see Liena again. I had certainly never expected to see her a second time.

Prepared to make myself extremely unpopular, I limped for the bridge. As soon as I stepped into view, Captain Glass motioned me over. She did have Prin on the sensors, tracking his movements. She pointed to a bright red blip. "Prin has just reached a small settlement. I can't pinpoint him amid all the other life signs, but I know he is there. If we send out a search party, they'll be able to track him down."

It almost killed me to say, "Let him go. Set a course for Gehenna. We must reach it in six days."

The entire bridge crew stopped what they were doing and gaped at me. "Did you take a hard blow to the head, like your brother?" Captain Glass said.

"No. We have a more pressing mission than capturing Prin. Set course for Gehenna, now."

She didn't move. "I will do no such thing. Explain yourself."

They did need to be told. They had a right to be told. "Get the ship moving, and I'll explain."

The ship rose off the planet with what felt like great reluctance. As we hurtled into the blackness of space, I said, "Kyar and Sephine are married. When she came to Gehenna to rescue me, I thought she was trying to kill me. I killed her with a goran spine. That is the reason Kyar was so upset with me, not so long ago." No-one had been able to figure that out. "To make a long story short, Sephine is not dead after all. She is on Gehenna, about to be auctioned off with all the other females. If no-one buys her, she will be executed. If she is bought, we'll probably never find her again. We must reach Gehenna before the auction, or I doubt Kyar and Sephine will ever be reunited."

I had been too brief. I had to answer a whole lot of questions, about how I knew Sephine was alive, and about Liena and Prin. When the questions finally trailed off, I said, "I know I am asking too much of you, to let Prin disappear, but I promise you, we will find him again. The clone is useless to him, so he will still be coming after me. As soon as we have reunited Kyar with his wife, we will track Prin."

Everyone did not agree with my choice, but the crew didn't mutiny. Captain Glass kept the ship on course for Gehenna. Before I left the bridge to check on my brother's condition, the ship was spinning into its first of a chain of generated wormholes.

I found Kyar lying on his bed, as pale and still as his dead body had been in the crate. Greely was sitting in the bedside chair. He had helped himself to a glass of red brandy. It had been a harrowing morning, and I did not fault him for drinking on the job.

"How is he?" I brushed Kyar's hair aside, to see the lump on his forehead.

"Ah, he'll be fine in a day or two. Took quite a whack, but no permanent damage. Minimal bleeding in his brain." Greely stood up and stretched. "Are you going to watch him?"

"I am going to watch over him." There was nothing I would rather do than sit vigil by Kyar's bed. "The crew will update you on our destination," I said, since I didn't want to talk about or even think about Gehenna. I settled in the still warm chair and followed Greely's example, helping myself to Kyar's store of brandy. I felt the need, after all that had happened on the planet called Earth. Kyar and I had almost died, and Prin had gotten away, taking my beautiful skin with him.

And I was headed for Gehenna, again.

I refilled my glass, telling myself that I wasn't drinking alone. Kyar was keeping me company in his own way. I toasted my brother's slack face, imagining his reunion with Sephine, and his true forgiveness, since I hadn't killed her. But perhaps I wouldn't tell him that she was alive, not until I had seen her with my own eyes.

Prisoners died in droves on Gehenna, or were maimed so badly, death was the better alternative. Since Prin last received a communication, something could have happened to her. I dared not raise my brother's hopes, only to dash them again. The more I sat and thought about it, the more convinced I became that he should only be told about Sephine when she had been safely liberated. Unfortunately, that would mean my feet would be walking upon Gehenna's burning sands once more.

Kyar lay unconscious for another day and a half. In that time, I informed the entire ship that Kyar was to be kept in the dark about our mission to rescue Sephine. Until we had proof that she was alive, he was to know nothing.

When Kyar finally opened his eyes, the first thing he said was, "Did we get Prin?"

"Not quite yet," I said. "We are following our cousin's craft at a distance, waiting for the opportune moment to board his ship and take him by force."

Kyar tried to sit up. I laid a hand on his shoulder, holding him down. "You took quite a blow to the head, Kyar, when Prin's boat hit you. Greely doesn't want you on your feet yet. He has prescribed another day or two of bed rest. And he wants to keep you sedated." It was a lie. I wanted Kyar kept sedated, until I could present him with his beloved.

"I feel like I could use a bit more time in bed," Kyar agreed. "Wake me when we're going to board Prin's ship."

"I will, don't worry. Now go back to sleep."

Kyar was still dazed enough, or sedated enough, to accept my words without question. He went back to sleep.

I managed to keep him abed for another two days, with Greely's help. By then we were less than two days from Gehenna. Even with its exceptional wormhole capability, the FarGone 5 was travelling at a speed I didn't understand. I had never seen a ship match it. I was becoming convinced it was truly multidimensional travel, which was supposed to be a universal myth.

When I visited the engine room and pressed Venus about it, too curious not to, she was as tight-lipped as every other time I broached the subject. She was also looking exhausted, and even less tangible than usual, vibrating extra fast, as were the engines. Trying to focus on anything in the engine room hurt my eyes. I was glad to go on my way, even without answers.

I spotted Kyar heading for the bridge and intercepted him. "What are you doing up and about?"

"Stretching my legs," he said.

"But isn't it time for your sedative?" I asked.

"I refused the last one. I'm feeling fine."

"Then come and eat lunch with me." I linked our arms as if it had been decided, trying to take Kyar with me.

"I already ate lunch." He reclaimed his arm and kept going, the wrong way, toward the bridge.

"But I haven't. You can keep me company. We have much to discuss." I tried to catch up and stumbled into the wall.

He turned around and steadied me, saying, "We do have much to discuss, Megal. You are awfully patient about capturing Prin. It seems a bit strange. No, it seems a lot strange. I'm going to see how far ahead of us he is. Our ship is traveling so fast, I don't see how he could be staying ahead of us." Clearly, Kyar had figured out that something was fishy.

I trailed him to the bridge, tempted to tackle him to the ground. I wasn't strong enough. Captain Glass wasn't there. She had to sleep sometime. Mo was sitting in for her, enjoying her chair. At Kyar's appearance, he quickly turned off his console, hiding our course and proximity to Gehenna. Kyar could not help but be alerted by that action.

"Okay, what's going on?" he demanded, surveying the mute crew.

All eyes turned to me. I was the one to lie or reveal the truth. I opted for lying. "We're chasing Prin. Dr. Greely said you had to rest your brain for a good week, so we have not kept you informed. You should return to your cabin and have a nap. Or we could have lunch."

No-one stopped him when he approached the console and reactivated it. He studied our course and checked the sensors. "No ships ahead, none behind," he said. "Megal, what the hell is going on? Of all the bloody places in the Universe, why are we closing in on Gehenna?"

"Kyar, let's talk in your cabin. Come with me, please." It was a word I had never used before Gehenna.

Kyar narrowed his eyes. "And if we talk in my cabin, will it be truth that I hear?"

"If I can't avoid telling you the truth, then I suppose it will be." It seemed I had no choice except to tell him about Sephine, but it wouldn't be in front of so many eyes.

I limped for the door, Kyar on my heels. In his quarters, I settled him with a brandy before I said, "I have news that will be of great interest to you." I poured one for myself, feeling the need.

"Oh, just spit it out, Megal."

"I would prefer to wait until it has been confirmed, before I tell you, in case the information is wrong. Will you give me two more days?"

"No. By then we'll have reached Gehenna. Tell me this news now."

I sat down across from him. "Kyar, I've received a very reliable report that Sephine is alive on Gehenna."

"Sephine is alive?" His expression was one of bewilderment, not joy.

"She lives, Kyar, as a prisoner."

He set his glass down. "But how could you possibly know that?"

"Liena told me." I drank deeply.

"Liena?" He raised his hands, palms up, questioningly.

"When she transformed into Prin, she knew all his thoughts." I went on to explain everything, as succinctly as possible. Kyar sat as still as an ice statue the whole time. I concluded by telling him about the auction and our deadline, and poured myself another brandy. My hand shook, remembering Gehenna.

"You let Prin escape?" he deduced at once. "So that Sephine could be saved?"

"Of course. I will see you reunited with your wife, Kyar, if it's the last thing I do," I vowed.

"She's alive," he murmured, more to himself than me. He picked up his glass again and downed the contents.

I couldn't read his face, it was closed to me. "You will see her soon, less than two days." I smiled.

Kyar did not. "And Prin?"

"We'll pick up Prin's trail, as soon as we have Sephine back. We will find him again." I was promising a lot on nothing but hope.

Kyar walked to the door and opened it. "I want to be alone." He made a shooing motion, as if I was a pet.

I stayed put. "Are you sure you don't want to talk about it, Kyar?"

"Yes, Megal. I'm sure. Get out."

"Well then, I will leave you alone." Rather offended, I stepped out into the corridor. Kyar shut the door, closing me out.

I stood in the corridor, trying to make sense of Kyar's reaction to my joyous news. I had expected celebration, elation, some display of happiness. I had seen none of that. Perhaps he didn't believe that Sephine lived. Maybe he had to see her with his own eyes, before he could celebrate. It was understandable. Hope can be a deeply painful emotion, especially when it is dashed.

I returned to the bridge. I sat quietly, filled with dread as Gehenna drew closer and closer. I wanted nothing more than to turn the ship around, and travel even faster in the opposite direction. When I thought I might vomit, I returned to my quarters. I made it just in time. I was so physically sick, it felt like I was losing my guts along with my last meal.

Two days later, we landed on Gehenna with no time to spare. The auction was starting. I verified how many bizoux we had in the safe-hold. Eighty-five. It was more than enough to buy double or triple that number of prisoners. And we only intended to buy one.

Gehenna's security lattice was turned off. Hundreds of motley craft were parked beside the prison compound, on the barren surface of the dirty planet. It looked like we were the last to arrive.

I was standing by the hatch, waiting to open it, when Kyar appeared at my side. I had barely glimpsed his shadow these last two days, and respecting his desire for solitude, I hadn't pestered him. But I appreciated his presence now.

Seven days ago, I would have bet my very life that I would never willingly step onto Gehenna's sand again, and here I was doing just that. The awful memories of the place had not yet had time to fade. Perhaps they never would.

Kyar opened the hatch when I couldn't move. He stepped out first. I couldn't let him face this ordeal alone, and convinced by feet to move. I followed him outside. The sounds and smells slammed into me with the force of a sledgehammer. I wanted to scream like a madman, or cower beneath my bed like a small child who believed in monsters. Hell, I was a man who believed in monsters, and I had met all kinds of them on Gehenna.

I controlled myself for Kyar, who had to be feeling more disturbed than me, imagining his wife suffering this place for so long. I touched his hand, mine as cold as ice and shaking like an old man's. "Soon, you will see her soon," I murmured, praying she hadn't been mutilated beyond all recognition, praying she looked a whole lot better than I did, when I left Gehenna.

He nodded. "You stay here, Megal. We'll get her."

"No. Sephine saved my life. She is here because of me. I know how this place works, I'm going." And I would not let my brother endure this ordeal without me by his side.

Clutching my staff, I led the way. The pouch of bizoux clinked on my belt. Hanis, Mo, Borelle, Greely, and even Oran'Jay, came along. I hadn't anticipated such an escort, but welcomed it. I felt safe, surrounded by so many loyal men—loyal friends.

We wore casual clothes to blend in, and wide-brimmed hats to protect against the sun. Only one hung overhead now, still hot enough to burn skin. The auction would be over, before the second sun made an appearance.

Two guards with gigantic blasters flanked the stone archway. They allowed us entrance into the prison courtyard, where the auction was held. I did not recognize either guard. I ducked my head regardless, glad of the camouflage of my hat.

Kyar accepted an auction list. Mo helped himself to a second copy.

We settled together on metal benches, beneath an awning that sheltered us from the worst of the heat, as the sale got underway. It was scorching enough to fry a penguin egg, even under the sunshade, yet I was shivering.

The crowd of men was thick and smelly, and as boisterous as if they were attending a fight to the death. Many of the women would be bought as companions for whole ships. Some ships bought dozens of women, for the purpose of reselling them at a profit. Older, damaged women could be purchased cheaply, then worked to death. And the ones who were not purchased, would die on that same auction stage in a few short hours. The more callous spectators would stay for that show.

On display before us, with no protection from the sun, were the ranks of female prisoners. They were lined up three deep, pressed against the curving stone wall, on both sides of the platform. Too many to count, each had a number scrawled across her forehead.

I scanned for Sephine and didn't spot her. I didn't know if I would even recognize her now. Kyar was doing the same, squinting against the bright light. I borrowed his list. Almost nine hundred prisoners were to be auctioned off. Some were listed by name, more were not, merely by the number that corresponded to their forehead. Beside each recorded number was the female's species. Most were listed as part-human.

Sephine's name was not listed. We would have to wait for her to be brought before us.

The auction moved along at a fast pace. Most prisoners were purchased for less than a quarter of a bizoux. The youngest, prettiest and healthiest earned the prison as much as one bizoux, never more. The ones that no-one bid on were shoved to one side, wailing or stoic with despair.

When more than eight hundred had been presented, I was growing frantic. I still could not spot Sephine in the remaining number. Nor could Kyar. Several times he had shaken his head, as if he believed me wrong.

Number eight hundred and forty-five stepped up on the platform from behind. We both gasped. Sephine had been out of sight the whole time. I rose to my feet. Mo pulled me down.

Sephine was not plump, as I had last seen her, but she was still shapely. For a Gehenna prisoner, she looked fantastic. Her hair was luxurious, flowing down past her waist. Her skin was bronzed, not burned. I had to control myself when I wanted to bound right up onto the platform and scoop her into my arms. What was this madness? According to Kyar, the addiction to her poison should have worn off long ago, yet from my irrational response, it had done no such thing. I wasn't cold any longer, but overly hot. Sweat trickled down between my shoulder blades.

I shook my head to clear it and looked at Kyar, grinning with elation. "Told you she was alive."

"Seems you are right," he said, rather flatly.

I motioned for Mo to do the bidding.

He started with a flourish, "One bizoux." We all expected it to end there. It didn't.

"Two bizoux," one of the prison guards said.

"Three," another guard countered.

"Five bizoux," called a voice from somewhere in the crowd behind us, so not a guard. An excited murmur echoed through the assembled bidders.

The voices reduced to a stunned silence when Mo said, "Six bizoux."

"Seven," countered the same voice from the rear.

I turned around to discover who was bidding against us, suspecting there was more to this than a random desire for a pretty prisoner.

Mo said, "Eight."

Our competitor said, "Nine."

I spotted the fellow when he spoke. He was an average-sized, nondescript humanoid, with a long thin face and thick purple-black veins that coated his head like hair.

"Ten." Mo sounded pissed.

"Eleven." The fellow saluted me. I scowled back.

I spoke in Mo's ear. He said, "Fourteen."

"Fifteen," our opponent said with a flourish.

I elbowed Mo. "Twenty," he barked.

"Twenty-five."

Everyone in the compound was enthralled by the bidding war, including the guards. And Sephine— her eyes were on our group. I smiled to let her know everything would be fine, then sent Hanis over to find out who the rich fellow was.

Mo said, "Thirty."

Our competition said, "Thirty-five."

"Forty."

No-one could believe it when the fellow said, "Fifty."

"Slow the bidding down," I advised Mo, deeply worried now.

He said, "Fifty-one."

The other fellow didn't co-operate. "Fifty-five."

"Fifty-six."

"Sixty."

"Sixty-one."

"Seventy."

"Seventy-one."

"Eighty."

Hanis was back, with dreadful news. "That fellow sends you his regards, Megal. He says that your cousin said to say hello."

"Prin," I growled. So he was behind this, but why did he want Sephine? What was his game now?

Mo glanced at me questioningly. Everyone was waiting. I nodded and Mo said, "Eighty-one."

And Prin's cohort said, "Ninety."

We had run out of bizoux, and the prison did not honour credit. Prisoners were paid for in hard coin or they did not leave. Everyone was straining their necks to watch Mo. It was his turn to bid. Even the auctioneer motioned for Mo to continue, as if he didn't want the excitement to end.

And Sephine was watching, desperate yearning in her eyes. She had saved my life, she was my brother's wife, she was his life and happiness.

Like a laser cutting through me, I suddenly knew what I had to do. I could save Sephine and give my brother back all that he had lost, if I was strong enough. No man was that strong. I looked at Kyar. My little brother. I owed him more than I could ever repay. For him, I could do this.

I rose on legs that shook. I had never needed my staff more than when I walked forward. Kyar hissed for me to come back. I continued slowly up to the platform. I stopped before the auctioneer. Very clearly, I said, "One thousand bizoux."

There was a strangled cry from Kyar.

I turned to see if Prin's partner could beat that. He looked apoplectic, proving he couldn't. Sweat poured off me, wetting my clothes so thoroughly, I might have been standing in the rain, except it never rained on Gehenna. The air shimmered in the heat. The crowd wavered as if it was an illusion. Maybe I was merely having a terrible nightmare. My eyes found Kyar, head in his hands. No, this was real, yet it was still a nightmare.

Everything happened very quickly after that. We were escorted to stand under the awning, where payment was made. Sephine fell into

Kyar's arms. He embraced her, but his eyes were on me. I untied the sack of bizoux and pressed them into Mo's hands, knowing the ship would need them.

I dredged up a smile from somewhere, for Kyar's joy. "I give you back your wife, little brother. You are the Nomad now. You can pardon the crew," I said softly, before I turned to pay for Sephine with my life. "I am Nomad Megal, Nomad of Nine Worlds. There is a one thousand bizoux bounty on my head, dead or alive. I am your payment for this prisoner." I removed my hat.

They knew my name, and my bounty. I was famous, I was worth a fortune. They approved the payment.

I was barely allowed to say farewell to anyone. Kyar gripped me hard, his face tormented. Even Oran'Jay cared. He slipped a small metal capsule into my hand, whispering, "Tuck it in your gum, Corpse. If you ever need a painless end, bite down hard, and you'll have it."

I nodded. The pill might come in handy. I slipped it into my mouth and said, "Thanks, Frog."

Before my crew had moved out of sight, I was relieved of my tunic, kicked to the ground and brutally beaten with my own staff. An infamous Nomad was fair game, and highly entertaining to abuse.

Since I was as valuable to them dead as alive, the guards were not very careful. They gave the crowd of bidders a great bloody show.

I merely wished that they had waited, until those who cared about me were further away. Kyar tried to stop it. Mo and Hanis were smart enough to restrain him. I saw their tussle through a wash of red, numb at that point.

One of the interesting things about being beaten to a pulp, is that you really don't feel very much pain, not after the first dozen blows. Following that, it's as if the violence is happening to some other poor soul.

When I lay like a true corpse, it wasn't fun to hit me anymore. I was dragged into the high-walled prison, and I knew I would never leave Gehenna again.

Gehenna was another thing that no man should have to endure even once. I was probably the only cursed soul who would sample all Gehenna had to offer for a second time. I took great comfort in the hard lump hidden high in my cheek. If I ever saw Oran'Jay again, I was going to kiss his green face.

PART 2 – Kyar

9. Kyar's Quest

"Kyar, there's nothing you can do. Come with us, don't look," Mo ordered sharply, keeping a firm grip on Kyar's arm. Stronger and bigger, Hanis forced Kyar away. Sephine stayed close by his side. He had his bride back, but he had lost Megal. He realized he was crying then, helpless to stop the vicious violence being done to one he loved.

Everyone kept him moving toward the ship.

Oran'Jay sidled up. "I slipped him a poison pill. He can die painlessly, anytime he wants."

Kyar knew the words were meant to be comforting, yet they were anything but. He was steered aboard the FarGone 5. He was left in Hanis's charge, while Oran'Jay and Mo disappeared together without explanation, back toward the prison with the pouch of bizoux. The ship took off as soon as the pair returned.

In minutes, the dusty brown planet was nothing but an ugly speck in space. Captain Glass automatically set a course for the Ice Planet. Kyar supposed he was the Nomad now that Megal had officially given himself up. It would be a mere formality to claim the title.

"Come with me, Kyar." Sephine wrapped an arm around his waist and led him off the bridge. Everyone had been speaking in hushed voices, and he had been staring at the viewing screen, yet seeing nothing. She took him to his cabin, kissed him sweetly on the lips, and put a brandy in his hand. Kyar tried to pull himself together. Sephine was the one who should be attended to after months on Gehenna, not him.

"Sit, Sephine." He handed her his drink and poured himself another.

She looked fragile, her cheekbones prominent, her eyes shadowed. There were no scars on her skin, except for the prisoner's brand. She had survived Gehenna relatively unscathed, at least at first glance. "How are you?" he stroked her cheek, puzzled that the obsessive love he had felt for her was not clawing at his innards like a caged snowcat.

"I survived. That is all one does on Gehenna. And I did what I had to do—to survive. It's good to be off that planet." Her mild words left too much unsaid. "And you, Kyar? You seem ... different." She brushed a fingertip over his eyebrow, which in his original skin had been divided in two by a childhood scar. No longer.

He hadn't yet had a chance to tell her about switching skins. "I am different. Pirates boarded us. I was blasted and died instantly. Luckily, we had one of my clones aboard—long story. I'll tell you it sometime. Anyway, Greely transferred my brain into the new clone, so here I am."

She nodded as if that explained things, as if there were things to explain.

Kyar studied her closely, welcoming anything that took his mind off the sights and sounds of the vicious beating that kept playing over and over in his head. "Is that why ..." He wasn't quite sure how to ask about why his feelings for her had calmed.

"You are no longer addicted to me, now that you have changed bodies," she said frankly.

"But ... did you bite me?"

"Once, by accident, when we were loving each other. Just a little bite. It does happen, especially when I've had too much to drink," she confessed, kissing his cheek.

"But ... the feeling never faded, not until I switched bodies. You said the addiction was temporary."

"It is, or it should be. I suppose everyone can react a little differently."

Her vague nonchalance didn't quite ring true. Kyar wasn't sure he believed her words. He looked her directly in the eye. "Was I only in love with you because you bit me?" His whole world seemed to be spinning out of control.

"I hope not, Kyar."

"Is that why the prison guards were bidding on you? Because you bit some of them?" he guessed. That had seemed peculiar.

"Yes, I bit a few guards, so they would give me things, proper food, clean water, a larger cell, protect me from the other prisoners, excuse me from the dangerous jobs, things like that." Her eyes stared defiantly into his.

"You had to do more than bite them, didn't you?" he alluded, but gently.

She held his gaze. "I did what I had to do, to survive."

"I'm glad you survived."

119

"I always survive," she declared.

When she stepped into his arms, he accepted her comfort. He held her against his chest and said, "Your life should have been easier after marrying me. Not harder. I shouldn't have let you set foot on Gehenna. I should have found another way to rescue Megal." He sighed from the deepest, saddest part of his soul. He stroked Sephine's back, fighting to keep his grief in a box, so it wouldn't overwhelm him.

"Did you ever love me?" he asked, surprised by his own words.

"I did love you." She kissed his neck lingeringly. "And I always will. You're very lovable, Kyar."

Kyar detached himself and poured a fresh drink. He knew he would be finishing the bottle—anything to stop the vivid memory of Megal's torture.

"Love makes no guarantee, bites do. I can bite you again." Sephine leaned against his shoulder.

"No." He stepped back. "Megal must still be in love with you since you bit him, if the craving—the addiction—never faded for him," he mused. "Is that why he saved you?"

"Saving me did not allow him to be with me, so no, I think he did that for you. He loves you as much as I do. That's why he wants you to be Nomad now." Sephine kissed him again, muddling his thoughts, when he was trying hard to figure out what it all meant. If he did manage to get Megal off Gehenna alive, for a second time, it would be damned awkward if his brother was still in love with his wife, given that the craving lasted much longer than she had claimed. Maybe it was even an everlasting addiction.

Kyar stilled when the significance of that thought was simply too shocking to ignore. If Sephine hadn't been stabbed by the goran spine, and had returned to the FarGone 5 with the Nomad Megal, he would have been addicted to her—in love with her. And Sephine had known exactly that.

Kyar tossed back another drink. If he'd had any emotional energy left to spare, he might have been furious with Sephine for manipulating him. He might have suspected that she had volunteered to save Megal, only to end up as the Nomad's allied wife—a much more powerful position than merely the Nomad's brother's wife. As it was, his heart had taken enough of a beating, without venturing down that dark path. Kyar simply felt empty and defeated, and Sephine had been through her own hell.

"I'm going to get Megal off Gehenna, if he's still alive after … after what they did to him," he said, the alcohol making his thoughts slow and lumbering. "If I find Prin, Megal can … will be proven innocent, then he will be released. Even Gehenna can't keep an innocent man, especially a powerful Nomad." His words sounded logical and positive. Kyar took comfort in them. "We do know Prin was still on Earth just days ago. And he communicated with a representative to buy you from the prison, probably to hold you hostage and use against us." Prin was the slimy type to indulge in blackmail. Kyar put down the bottle with a bang. Drinking himself into a stupor wouldn't help Megal. "If Prin has left the planet Earth, he couldn't travel half as fast as this ship. If we revisit Earth, we can find out what ship he is using, possibly track it," he mused.

"Megal said you were to be Nomad now." Sephine kissed him, confusing him again.

He eased her away. "No. No, not like this." Usurping his brother's position felt so very wrong.

"Go then, tell your captain to change course for Earth." She moved him toward the door. "I am going to enjoy a very long, steamy shower. If you want to join me after you've delivered your message, please do so. I've missed you, Kyar." She kissed him lingeringly.

Kyar wasn't sure how he felt about getting naked with her. He wasn't sure how he felt about her in his heart, given that she had likely planned to trade up from him to Megal. And just how many prison guards had she been sleeping with? Such thoughts were more than enough to dampen his burgeoning passion.

He stepped back from her and opened the door. "Enjoy your shower, Sephine. I will be on the bridge." Filled with resolve to capture Prin, Kyar hurried there. As soon as he reached the bridge, he said, "Change course for Earth. We are going to track Prin."

Captain Glass nodded at him. "About time, Kyar." She altered course so abruptly, anyone unlucky enough to be standing up, fell down.

Oran'Jay and Mo took Kyar aside. Mo said, "I hope you don't mind, but I used a handful of bizoux to bribe some of the guards to look out for Megal, to keep him alive—if he is still alive, and to slip him extra food and water. One guard will be sending regular transmissions, to let us know how he's doing."

"Thank you. I'm glad you thought of it. I … I wasn't thinking at all."

Mo patted him on the shoulder. "I knew you'd want me to do it."

Kyar nodded and sat down in the nearest chair. He was not ready to return to his quarters and Sephine. He was nervous to be around her. Frankly, she scared him now that he could see her with clear eyes, without the addiction to her that her bite had caused. Her venom was more potent and long-lasting than he had ever guessed, and it would allow her to manipulate anyone she bit. It was a scary power she possessed, and a sneaky one.

The trip back to Earth was almost as quick as the one to Gehenna, yet it felt like it lasted a month.

Before they even reached Earth, a brief transmission arrived. It simply said, "Nomad Megal lives." Kyar had hoped for more. Alive could mean many different things, and from what he had witnessed, death might be preferable to Megal's alive.

Kyar had moved into his brother's quarters, not ready to be intimate with the wife who had used him, and plotted to betray him to become the Nomad's wife. And yet, she would be the Nomad's wife, if Kyar stepped into his brother's boots.

The rudimentary space that had been Megal's home seemed to echo with emptiness. On the small ledge beside Megal's bed, he discovered Liena's home information. It was written in an almost indecipherable scrawl. No doubt, it was hard to write with only the three lesser fingers. Megal's childish script tugged at Kyar's heart.

It was a lucky find, because Liena would be a big help. She might even know if and when Prin had left the planet. She would definitely know what ship he had at his disposal, since she had shared his thoughts

When the FarGone 5 reached Earth, it orbited until darkness fell. It landed for a third time on the restricted planet. Kyar, Mo and Hanis walked the streets of the town, nearest the bridge they knew too well. They asked an Earth human for directions, and had no trouble finding Liena's dwelling. Her small square home was on the edge of the town, surrounded by a wall of vegetation. It ensured privacy, and was not unexpected. She was hiding from those on the planet who knew she was only half-Earthling.

Kyar rapped on the door. He was so relieved when Liena answered, he almost hugged her, before he remembered she had to be prepared to be touched. To say she was shocked to see him was an understatement.

Liena gaped at him, as if he was an apparition, not solid flesh and bone. "Kyar? Come in. What … what are you doing here? Mo, Hanis, come in, sit. What has happened?"

"It's Megal," Kyar blurted out. "He's back on Gehenna."

"Oh no. No. How did that happen?"

Kyar did enter and sit then, feeling the need. "It was the only way to free Sephine. He traded himself for her freedom."

Hanis and Mo settled on comfy chairs, in a room so sparsely decorated, it could have been on a spaceship. Liena sat opposite him. Kyar went on to explain about Prin's representative bidding against them, and the awful choice Megal had made. He did not describe the terrible beating. It was not something he could put into words, nor was it something Liena needed to know. As it was, what he told her left her visibly shaken. She had lived Gehenna through Megal's memories. She knew firsthand, what it would be like for him to be back there.

"So, we need to find Prin," Kyar concluded. "You know his thoughts, do you know what he planned to do next? Where he intended to go? And we need to know what type of ship he is piloting."

"Of course," Liena said. "The ship is a Scarnivian Disc, a single family craft."

"It is a common enough ship," Kyar said. Regardless, the information was very helpful, as long as Prin did not switch ships. "He is travelling alone?"

"Yes."

"And do you know where he planned to go from here?" He leaned forward, elbows on his knees.

"He wasn't sure himself, but even if he had been, that will have changed. His circumstances have changed. He didn't get a useable clone, or kill you, or kill Megal." Liena worried her lip. After a reflective minute, she added, "I think Prin will return to the Ice Planet."

Kyar did not agree. "He wouldn't dare."

"If you had ever shared your cousin's sick, twisted mind, you'd know that Prin would dare anything," Liena countered. "I've shared a lot of minds, both animal and human, but I've never experienced anything like Prin. He's so manipulative, without conscience, and sadistic. What repulses other men, attracts Prin. He is nothing like Megal. Beneath it all,

Megal is … rather sweet and honourable, and vulnerable. I know he wasn't that way before, but Gehenna didn't just damage him, it remade him, or maybe he was always that man inside." She shrugged. "It's hard to believe that Prin is related to you and Megal."

"You can't pick your family," Kyar said.

"True enough."

And if Liena had been able to choose, she probably wouldn't have opted for her mixed parentage.

"But the Ice Planet? Why would he go back there?" Mo asked with skepticism.

"It's his home," Liena said. "He still imagines himself as the Nomad. He intended to rule as you, Kyar, this time around. And he wants to rule again, so he can prove the Ice Planet is the original Green World. He is completely obsessed about that. What if … what if when he gets home and finds out Megal is on Gehenna … what if he tries to prove that he is the real Megal, the innocent one? That's the type of twisted plotting he loves."

Kyar shook his head. "He couldn't get away with it. Too many know the truth now. A few simple tests would unmask him as the imposter. He would have to prove who he is, before he can rule. He won't be able to do that."

"That's good, but maybe he's desperate enough to try. Everything has fallen apart for him. Prin thrives on being in control and it's slipping away from him. I really think he will go back to the Ice Planet. He's been researching a type of bio-weapon that will destroy or melt ice, but he hasn't got it to work properly yet," Liena said.

"Thank heavens for that," Kyar said, heartfelt.

"He's still working on it, Kyar," Liena warned.

"Perhaps we should head back to the Ice Planet, then." Kyar was missing his home. If he returned and temporarily claimed the title of Nomad, it would allow him unlimited resources to track down Prin. And he could pardon all the crew who had helped him. They deserved that. He stood up. "Is there anything else we should know about Prin, before we try and catch him?"

Liena clenched her jaw, eyes haunted. "Never trust him, not an inch. He's not really sane. The world he inhabits is the one in his head, his own warped reality. Nothing else matters to him." Her eyes darkened further. "I wish I could do more to help. Poor Megal."

"We'll get him off Gehenna, don't you worry," Hanis said gruffly.

"Please let me know how it all turns out, if you can. And if there's anything I can ever do, you know where to find me," she said.

"Thank you, Liena. I will try and let you know." Kyar took a few steps toward the door. "Unless you want to come along for the ride. It will be quite an adventure."

"Tempting." Liena smiled sadly. "But I can't, I am needed here. Maybe another time." She walked them to the door, where she opened a little closet. She motioned to a gallon-sized green and black vat, sitting on the floor under some hanging coats. "I did retrieve Prin's bio-weapon, if you would like to take that away with you please. I'm not too comfortable having it in my house, let alone on my planet."

"We'll be happy to dispose of it. It's the least we can do," Kyar said.

Hanis stepped forward and hoisted the vat into his arms. They hurried back to the ship with Prin's evil weapon, and took off immediately, rising silently into the sky.

At a quick clip, they arrowed toward the Ice Planet, scanning for Scarnivian Discs all the way. They didn't find the one Prin was piloting. Kyar contacted Jann, to announce that he was coming home to claim the Nomad's title.

Eleven days later, they reached the translucent blue orb that was the most beautiful planet in the Universe. Every last crew member squeezed onto the bridge to watch home grow bigger and bigger, until it filled the viewing screen completely. Kyar's heart filled with emotion, most of it regret, that Megal was not standing by his side to share the moment. Sephine was. She stepped under his arm and held him close. He did not push her away.

Captain Glass landed the ship on the edge of the Crystal Crater, home of the Nomad's Ice Palace. The FarGone 5 was small and light enough to perch on the thick perma-ice, without leaving a crack.

They were expected. A tremendous fanfare met Kyar when he stepped out into the invigorating wind, howling across the bare surface of the planet. Kyar filled his lungs with the frigid pure air and looked around in a daze. He had stepped into some sort of planned ceremony. A row of Icemen bowed before him. A white Nomad's robe was laid over his shoulders, while chimes and horns filled the air with music. Handfuls of snow were tossed into the wind to swirl around him. He was being welcomed as the Nomad. It was a bittersweet homecoming.

Feeling as much an imposter as Prin, Kyar went along with it all. He walked beside the ceremonial line of thirty Icemen, nodding to each one.

Jann was the last. His wintery blue eyes, thick beard and barrel chest were unchanged, as always. Jann had a timeless quality, like the ice he called home.

Kyar's mother stood beside Jann, regal and composed, not a white hair out of place. Her long blue gown was so slick, the snowflakes skated right off, not daring to settle. "Kyar, welcome home." She pecked each of his cheeks briefly with cold lips.

"Mother." Kyar acknowledged and moved on to Noel Frost. "Noel, you've … heard?"

She nodded, and gripped his hand. "I'm so sorry, Kyar." Her eyes dampened, gazing into his. There was no doubt that her sympathy was heartfelt.

"We'll talk later," he murmured.

"Or sooner, Kyar." She bowed and he moved along, greeting other family members and officials, until he reached a drop-off and could go no further. There, spread out below him, was the Nomad's Crystal Crater.

At about five miles across, it was small for an inhabited crater, yet it held the most influential population on the Ice Planet. The centrally located bowl was reserved for the ruling line, their extended family, highly-placed officials, the Icemen and their families—and added to that, an army of servants and menials.

In the center of the crater, the Ice Palace jutted high over everything. It had always been Kyar's home, yet he had lived in it as the Nomad's brother—Megal's unnoticed shadow. Now he was the Nomad. Everything as far as the eye could see belonged to him, at least for a time.

The outer ice walls of the palace glistened under the brilliant sun, the thick layer of soft drippy shapes flowing down from the tallest towers. The palace had an ever-changing façade, as ice melted and reformed at the mercy of the weather. Cold outside, the interior of the building would be toasty and warm, naturally heated by underground hot springs that also provided a flow of steamy water, to fill the vast bathing pools on the ground floor, and meet all the castle's needs.

Inside the castle, a permanent yulithium framework supported insulated walls and screens of woven metal microfiber, and sheets of glass, which allowed diffuse light to softly illuminate the interior, at least during the daytime. Floors were lined with more of the same, and carpeted to be soft and warm underfoot. Tapestries and fur, and sheets of embossed metal decorated the walls. In the most opulent tower—the Nomad's— rare wood lined the inner walls and floors, imported or

126

harvested from the few green craters that dotted the southern tip of the southern-most glacier.

Kyar stood on the lip of ice, staring down at his home. His home. It was his now. All of it! A hungry longing tugged at his soul, catching him by surprise. With Prin out of the picture, this could all be his, forever— if Megal did not survive Gehenna.

Deeply disturbed that he had even had that thought, Kyar turned toward the vehicle that would carry him down to the bottom of the Crystal Crater. Along with the ragtag crew of the FarGone 5, he boarded the plush trolley reserved for the Nomad and his guests. As soon as they were settled on fur-padded seats, the vehicle spiraled smoothly down and around the curved side of the crater, on slick tracks that led directly into the base of the Ice Palace. Ten floors and a collection of turreted towers loomed overhead.

"Quite a to-do for a bunch of criminals," Mo growled, bringing Kyar back to reality.

As soon as he stepped out of the trolley into the humidity of the palace, he was welcomed by more family and friends. There were simply too many bodies to greet individually, so Kyar waved in all directions. Sephine stayed pressed against his side, as he wormed his way through the crowd. They eventually reached the elevator that would carry him up to his wing, on the second highest level of the Palace. He did not merit a tower. Only the greenhouse level was higher than Kyar's quarters, but it had to be. The food plants that grew there required a lot more light than he did.

Overwhelmed by the emotional homecoming, Kyar craved some solitude. He didn't get it. His mother, Noel and Jann arrived on his heels. And servants were waiting to attend him, now that he would be Nomad. Kyar had never had servants in plural before. He had made do with one, and that had been more than enough. Now, he felt surrounded.

"Oh, Kyar." His mother embraced him with rare affection. Kyar wasn't quite sure how to respond. He didn't have a chance to say a word, before she burst out, "Jann has told us everything. Prin was masquerading as Megal for three years?"

"Yes, Mother."

"And you found your brother?"

"For all the good it did. He's back on Gehenna now, to pay for Prin's crimes, and Megal is still the rightful Nomad. I'm simply borrowing his title so I can get him out of there, so I can get him home," Kyar said firmly. He also needed to remind himself.

Noel was the one that asked, "How is Megal?"

"Alive, last we heard." Kyar did not distress her with the rest.

Jann clapped a wrinkled hand on Kyar's shoulder. "We'll get your brother home, one way or another. You can summon the Icemen and work out a plan, as soon as you get back from your quest."

"My quest?"

"You can't be Nomad unless you walk the quest. You know that."

Kyar did know that, he had simply forgotten. There were too many pressing matters filling his head. "But I don't have time to walk a Nomad's quest. It takes more than a month. Megal has to be freed from Gehenna as soon as possible. He's ... not in good shape. And Prin may turn up to cause even more damage. There must be some way to postpone the quest."

"There isn't," Jann said implacably. "Wish there was, but there isn't. Without the quest, your authority will not be recognized."

"Tradition is everything," Kyar muttered. He had lived on the Ice Planet all his life. He knew that inconvenient truth as well as he knew his own name.

"Sit down, Jann, Kyar, everyone. Let us discuss this more comfortably." His mother was always aware of the niceties. She turned to Sephine. "Ice wine for everyone," she ordered. Kyar had forgotten to tell his mother about his marriage.

"Um ... Mother. This is Sephine. She isn't a slave, she is my wife." He put an arm around Sephine, who was looking rather anxious. His mother had that effect on people. "Sephine, this is my mother, Pin Aurora."

"Your wife?" his mother said blankly, her nostrils and lips pinching. The expression reminded him of Prin. "But ... she is a slave."

"Not anymore. Sephine is my wife. We have a lifetime contract," Kyar said, rather defiantly. He motioned to the trio of hovering servants to fetch the ice wine. All three left the room. He hoped they would bring some food back with the wine, because he was starved. He should have mentioned it. He still could.

Kyar strode off to do just that, leaving Sephine to handle his mother. He rather hoped she would bite the woman and ensure her loyal devotion. There was no denying that his mother could be difficult, but unlike

128

Megal, Kyar had always managed to keep peace with her, until now anyway.

After he made his wishes about food known, their small group sipped wine together. They enjoyed mountain goat cheese and crisp walrus rinds, while they discussed the topics of the most urgency in regards to the planet. Kyar postponed making any decisions about his own course of action, until he had time to think, settle in, and figure out what to do with Sephine.

That night, Kyar curled up in his own warm bed. He was home again, yet felt quite untethered. When Sephine joined him without an invitation, he did not have the strength to send her away, especially when she let her robe fall to the floor. She was a vision of beauty, and he was feeling quite ravaged by loneliness. Cocooned together in vermink fur, she kissed him and stroked his skin. They had not shared a bed since she had been liberated from Gehenna. The more she kissed him, the hungrier he grew for her. Her skin was so velvety and smelled uniquely of her.

Kyar had been struggling to figure out how he felt about his bride, without the addiction to her, and with the knowledge that she had used him and likely intended to end up with Megal. Yet her hands and her mouth and tongue birthed a desire in him that he could not deny, or control.

Kyar kissed her shoulder. Knowing that he might soon be away for more than a month, his lips continued on, finding a more interesting place to nibble. "It's been so long," Kyar whispered, his tongue tasting her skin. She was as sweet and earthy as imported honey

"Yes, far too long." Her mouth welcomed his, hot and wet and voracious.

"Don't bite me," Kyar groaned.

She didn't, she did something much more pleasurable than that. They got little rest before the sun rose, then they slept past noon. No-one dared to disturb them, what with Kyar being the future Nomad and all.

The Council of Icemen and Noel Frost summoned him to an assembly the next afternoon. They wanted to officially verify his intent to be Nomad. The last thing Kyar wanted to do was spend a month freezing his ass off, when he could be cuddling with Sephine, but he didn't really have a choice. If he was going to save Megal, he had to be the Nomad. And if he was unable to save Megal, by walking the quest, Kyar would be the true Nomad. He agreed to walk the Nomad's quest.

The very next day, after a night with little sleep and a great deal of lovemaking with his wife, Kyar set out alone across the glacier. He yearned to return to Sephine, yet he kept walking, wrapped in fur and pulling a light sleigh loaded with a supply of basic essentials. He was barely out of sight of the Crystal Crater when a wolf sled raced up to him.

"Hop on," Jann called.

Kyar did. "Isn't this cheating?" he asked with a grin.

"Are you going to be the Nomad?" Jann shot back.

"Not for long." At least that was the plan.

"There you have it. And you haven't got any clones left, not since Prin destroyed those he didn't steal, so we wouldn't realize he had acquired them. We can't have you freezing your parts off, now can we." Jann flashed teeth as white as the snow.

"True," Kyar agreed. He had learned the fate of his clones during his first assembly with the Icemen. It proved that Prin had had significant inside help. A-1 had probably picked up Kyar's clones for Prin. The traitor who had arranged to have them shipped had already been identified and jailed, so at least he was no longer a threat. Hopefully there were no more traitors in the Ice Palace.

Jann slowed the sled to a crawl. "Take the dogs, head due north. Someone else will meet you further along," he said and stepped off. The white wolves raced Kyar out of sight. They cut days off his journey, and the larger sled was loaded with an insulated tent, blankets and more food. There was even a heat-rock to keep his tent warm. Jann had thought of everything.

Halfway to the caves, Kyar reached the shore of a massive flooded crater. Due to the hot springs that fed it from below, it never froze. It was so vast, he could barely see the other side, although that probably had more to do with the mist that rose off the water than the distance itself.

Kyar had just turned left to make the long detour around it, when a gigantic leathery pterodactyl soared over him and landed. A flock of the flying reptiles had been imported to the Ice Planet from a distant galaxy eons ago. They had been bred as carriers, and manageable numbers of them had flown over the Ice Planet ever since. With a wingspan of up to twenty-five feet, the beasts made ideal ships to move people from one crater to another, with no harmful impact on the planet's fragile environment. Pterodactyls were cold-blooded creatures that could not generate their own warmth, so they spent their non-flying time penned in small covered craters that were warmed by cracks in the ice, that released hot vapours. And when in flight, the beasts did generate enough of their own warmth through exertion.

Kyar waved to the fellow who was piloting the pterodactyl and hurried over. One of the youngest Icemen, Uris Monk, offered Kyar a lift. Kyar was happy to accept. The dogs were released to find their own way home and Kyar had an aerial ride the rest of the way to the caves. Their location was marked only by a common enough tower of stones. Such structures could be found all over the planet to help travellers find their way, when there were no other landmarks at all, only flat ice as far as the eye could see.

Upon landing, Uris said, "I'll wait for you." There was a small heated crater beside the caves, so Uris and his pterodactyl would be comfortable enough.

"Much appreciated," Kyar said, eyeing the small mouth of the caves with trepidation. If a person didn't know better, they would assume it was a very minor crater, no more than a pock mark really. But that little black hole in the ice looked hungry to Kyar, like it wanted to swallow him up, and never spit him back out.

Uris clapped him on the shoulder. "Let's get your gear sorted, and make sure you have enough rations and water."

"Yes. I've heard it's a gruelling trek to reach the deepest cavern," Kyar said.

Megal had told him all about the caverns, when he had arrived home from his quest. His brother had been far too thin, frostbitten, and badly bruised from tumbling down an ice shaft, one that he had been lucky to scale out of. His face had looked quite gruesome, too, stained as it was by the red drips that had rained down on him, when he drank the sacred blood of his planet to gain his vision. It was undeniable proof that he had succeeded at his quest.

The bloody colour took weeks to fade away entirely. No amount of scrubbing could remove it. Despite all the hardship he had endured, or perhaps because of it, Megal had been triumphant and exhilarated. Kyar stopped thinking about his brother in cheerier times, when his heart cramped.

Kyar and Uris shared a hearty mutton stew, before Kyar laced on spiked boots and shouldered his pack of essentials. "I'll be as quick as I can," he said, ready to depart.

"Don't be so quick you slide down an ice shaft," Uris warned. "I'll wait as long as it takes, just be careful down there."

"Oh, I will." Kyar activated his Scarnivian beamer, banged it a couple of times to get the light to stop flickering, and descended into the eerie black mouth. It led into a virtual maze of ice tunnels and caves. At least he had a hand-drawn map, compliments of Jann—a map that was not supposed to exist.

The trip down was a combination of climbing, falling and sliding, even with the boots. As bad as it was, Kyar knew the return trip was going to be many times worse.

He descended deep into the perma-ice, until he lost track of time. Thanks to the precious map, he found the sacred cave, only getting lost once.

The cavern was a fluorescent glowing red, and downright spooky. Even though it wasn't particularly large for an underground cave, at about fifteen yards across and maybe five yards high, it was a truly awesome sight because of the ceiling of brilliant diamond stalactites that dripped dark red fluid. The colour appeared almost magically from the clear crystalline points. Kyar would have enjoyed exploring the mystic space, if he'd had the energy to spare.

He lay beneath one of the lowest stalactites and drank the bitter red drops that looked too much like blood. Many landed on his cheeks and ran down the sides of his face, in the same pattern that he had seen on his brother, all those years ago. Drops landed in Kyar's eyes and stung like vinegar. He lost his grip on reality, when a world of imploding stars filled his brain.

A flood of visions clouded his mind, but only one recurred over and over. It was his true vision. It stayed sharply with him when he floated slowly back to the real world. Unsettled, he didn't understand any small part of what he had seen.

When Kyar could stand again, he stumbled toward the wall of pictures and carved his image with his knife—three figures laid out in a ritual funeral. And there was a fourth figure, with a knife jutting from their back. He knew the knife was symbolic of betrayal.

He was backing away from his disturbing vision of death when he spotted Megal's carved vision. Even though his brother had never revealed what he had seen, Kyar recognized the three suns arced over a skeleton. It wore his brother's face. The suns were red in the wall of white ice. Thick, clotted blood decorated them. Megal's blood, frozen forever in time.

Kyar traced the carved skeleton. So Megal had known he would face death on Gehenna. Or did this image mean he would truly die on the hell planet, this time around, his bones lying there forever? Maybe Kyar's mission to save his brother was destined to fail, and Megal was fated to die on Gehenna.

Kyar shoved the knife into his boot and started climbing back to the surface, tormented by the possibility that he had wasted three years of his life, only to prolong Megal's suffering.

His churning thoughts wouldn't stop, and the red drops had left him dizzy and confused. Climbing out of the caves was an ordeal that almost finished Kyar. It was days before he finally saw blue sky at the end of the steeply angled tunnel. He was crawling on all fours at that point, quite unable to stand.

Monk was waiting, a cozy camp set up. He assisted Kyar into the tent. Kyar collapsed on rough fur, never intending to move again. Monk let him sleep until the next day, fed him hot stew, and flew him halfway back to the Ice Palace. Kyar stumbled along for almost a week before Jann turned up on his dogsled. He gave Kyar a lift the rest of the way, ensuring they had the chance to talk privately.

"Won't people wonder how I did this journey so quickly?" Kyar asked. It had been less than three weeks.

"You are the Nomad now. They will accept your word. Just say the wild beasties helped you or something," Jann said.

"Did you do this for Megal?" Kyar could not resist asking.

Jann looked highly insulted under his ice-coated beard. "Not a chance. He was little more than a lad when your father died, but Megal completed the quest without help. It took him more than two months, but he didn't freeze anything off. He was always tougher than anyone thought. Well, he's proved that on Gehenna, hasn't he?"

"Yes. What's been happening while I've been out of touch?"

Jann clicked his teeth to keep the wolves moving. "The FarGone 5 received another transmission last week. Your brother is still alive on Gehenna, and I pray those guards you bribed are looking out for him. Other than that, little of note."

"Any news of Prin?" Kyar asked.

"No sign of the slimy bugger. I never did like him, you know, even though I tried to, since he was your kin." Jann shook his head.

"I don't think any of us liked him," Kyar said. Prin had not been likeable. Even as a child he had been preachy, sneaky, and inclined to tattle and whine.

Kyar was allowed one day to thaw out, before the Icemen summoned him again. At that assembly, he was officially named Nomad Kyar. His first act was to order all the planet's ships to hunt down Prin in his Scarnivian Disc. His second act was to officially pardon the crew of the FarGone 5, and assign them to the Ice Planet's flagship, the Glacius. Lastly, he declared Megal's innocence and wrongful confinement on Gehenna. It was a most productive assembly.

Sephine's first act as the Nomad's wife, was to move them into Megal's tower. Kyar felt like a trespasser in his brother's home, but he had missed Sephine dreadfully. He didn't want to risk making her unhappy, so he made no protest.

To celebrate the new Nomad, a great feast was held two nights later. Everyone in the palace joined hundreds of invited guests, to revel in the grand hall. With Sephine by his side, Kyar ate and drank too much. Everyone sang his praises and honoured him. After years of suffering under Prin's misrule, and then having no Nomad at all, the planet was ready to embrace Kyar with opened arms.

Entertainers had been flown in from as far as the north and south icecaps, to perform before him. Daring stunts had the crowd gasping. Kyar's favourite display was by a skilled team of icicle archers. They launched dagger-sharp bolts of ice at a pair of their own, whose only defense was handheld fire-lasers, and the beautiful couples' acrobatic dance moves. If they had missed vaporizing even one of the projectiles, they would have been killed. But they didn't, they evaded the deadly barrage and turned it into nothing but hot spray, and they did it with showy flare.

Kyar didn't see his bed until halfway to dawn, and it was through bleary, tipsy eyes. Even then, he didn't sleep. He lost himself in loving Sephine. He experienced enough pleasure to leave him weak and trembling and aching for more. He believed he was falling in love with her, naturally.

The next day, neither moved from a tangle of naked limbs, not until his mother invaded the tower. She declared that she wanted to get to know Kyar's chosen mate. Her servants followed, carrying a feast. They served it up, course after course. Kyar's new servants didn't look happy about that, not until he told them all to take the afternoon off. Late afternoon, Noel visited, to privately discuss issues that she had been struggling with as acting Nomad.

Kyar didn't leave to track down Prin that day, or the next, or even the next week, but he did post rich rewards for any information about Prin's whereabouts. And he waited for news.

No news came in, but invitations did, from surrounding craters. Kyar and Sephine were entertained lavishly, each and every night without fail. After a lifetime of being second to a charming, flashy, rogue of a brother, Kyar was now the one who held power and respect. A stronger man might have resisted the seductive pull of the Nomad's title, and all the perks that came with it, but Kyar could not. His brother's carved vision had shown that there might be no hope for Megal, so Kyar decided to enjoy his own life as the Nomad of Nine Worlds, if that was his destiny. He wished his own Nomad's vision had been clearer about the future, yet it was a riddle. Was he the betrayer, or the betrayed? Surely he was not the betrayer, although he did feel twinges of guilt that he was not doing more to help Megal.

Kyar had discussed Megal's carved vision with Sephine, with no mention of his own. She had concluded that it was Megal's fate to die on Gehenna. Then she had pulled Kyar into bed to comfort him. The more Kyar was with her, the hungrier he grew for her skin. No matter how tired he was at night, he could not sleep until he had loved her. And he could not start the day until he had loved her again.

After a life of hardship, Sephine was thriving. She had made peace with his mother somehow. Kyar did not question the details, but enjoyed the results. And Sephine adored dressing up for their endless soirees, donning richly embroidered and fur-trimmed robes that matched his own. Servants were always arranging her hair in complicated braids and curls, or massaging her with creams, or painting her skin with decorative dyes.

Kyar would reluctantly leave her to her ministrations, while he attended daily meetings with the Icemen. At the assemblies, Kyar had only to state his wishes, and they were carried out. It was exhilarating to hold such power in his grasp. The planets were running smoothly under his rule.

When a report came in that a minor southern glacier had developed a small crack, he dismissed the Icemen's concerns as overblown. He was in a hurry to get back to Sephine, before she had her hair done for that evening's banquet. There was something he wanted to do with her in his private hot pool, something that required both of them to be underwater.

Hungry for his wife, Kyar ended the assembly early and hurried back to Sephine. He found her in the sitting room with Oran'Jay. The green fellow was stomping around clutching a missive. Sephine didn't look at all pleased, in fact, she looked viperously pissed.

Kyar eyed the paper. "What is it?"

"Message from Gehenna, if you're not too busy to read it," Oran'Jay snapped.

Sephine grabbed the note with a quick hand. "Nothing you have to worry about, Kyar. Lunch is ready. The cook has prepared marinated reindeer, as you requested. Oran'Jay, you will excuse us."

Kyar didn't move. "Is Megal … dead?"

"Read the note," Oran'Jay bit out.

"Sephine?" He held out his hand.

She smiled and stepped close, kissing him deeply. "Megal is alive. You can read it after lunch, so the meal will not be spoiled by the delay."

The reindeer did smell delicious. And Kyar had a second appetite to appease. Sephine had not yet had her hair styled. "I'll read it right after lunch. Thanks for bringing it by, Oran'Jay."

With a curse, the cook slammed from the room, eyes bulging in their sockets. Kyar didn't worry about it. He stuffed himself, then enticed Sephine into the hot pool. She must have misplaced the note. Kyar never got it. Nor did he ask for it.

The next day, Kyar was waylaid on his way to meet with the Icemen. Oran'Jay, Mo and Hanis were waiting for him by the elevator.

After he greeted them, he asked, "How is life on the Glacius?"

"We declined the post, stayed on the FarGone 5," Oran'Jay said and shoved him into the elevator. He pressed the button for the ground floor.

"I'm going to the fifth level." Kyar reached for the panel.

Oran'Jay moved to block it. "Not today, you're not."

"Kyar, we have to talk privately. You need to come with us," Mo stated, less aggressively.

Kyar trusted them and said, "Sure. Why didn't you just say so?"

"Not sure how you'd react." Oran'Jay stayed planted in front of the panel, like a sentry.

Outside the elevator, Kyar's escort loaded him into a trolley. It was hauled straight up the side of the crater on its pulley. He was leaving the Crystal Crater, it seemed. It was a great distance to travel to simply talk privately. He began to feel anxious when he was ushered into a small shuttle craft, perched on the edge of the crater.

"Are we taking a trip? I have to be back by dinner," he mentioned.

"Don't worry about it." Mo prodded him inside and sealed the door. The ship took off, but it didn't fly far. It landed beside the FarGone 5, barely out of sight of the Crystal Crater. Noel was the last person he expected to see motioning to him from the hatch of the rusty little shipper, but there she was.

Her voice carried across to him on the wind. "We'll talk in here, Kyar."

Kyar followed her onto the ship. In the galley, Kyar was startled to find the entire crew seated around the long table. Had they all declined the post on the Glacius? "What is this about?" he asked no-one in particular, staying on his feet.

Noel appeared to be in charge. She was the only other person standing. "Did you not read the note from Gehenna that Oran'Jay delivered yesterday?" she asked.

Kyar flushed with shame and mumbled, "Uh … not yet. No."

"Told you so," Oran'Jay informed the assembled group, rather smugly.

"It seems you are right, Oran'Jay." Noel sat down and tapped her fingers nervously. The rest of the crew waited for her to speak. "We proceed according to plan," she finally said.

"Plan? What plan? And right about what?" Kyar asked.

Captain Glass and Venus rose. They left the room without a word. Kyar was advised to sit. He did, and waited for someone to tell him what was going on.

The engines began to hum and the ship shook. He didn't need a viewing screen to know that the FarGone 5 had just taken off. The Nomad had been abducted. Kyar felt a surge of panic at leaving Sephine behind. He leapt to his feet and shouted, "Turn the ship around right now, or you will all be jailed!"

Noel shook her head. "Not yet. We will turn the ship around, Kyar, after you listen to what we have to say, not before. I would advise you to sit down and shut up." Clearly, it was an ultimatum.

Kyar sat down with a scowl. No-one spoke to the Nomad in such a manner. "Tell me why I am here, but you damn well better stay in orbit over the planet."

Noel glanced at Oran'Jay, who began to spout lies. "I've been doing some research on your wife's origins, on her non-human side. Turns out that she's at least half Parasquit. Not a lot is known about the race, but

I've found out she doesn't have to bite you for you to be addicted to her. She can affect you more subtly, with a lot of physical contact like sharing her saliva and sweat and … other bodily fluids. The addiction develops more gradually, without you being aware of it, but it's just as potent. She's been clouding your mind, Kyar, and she knows exactly what she is doing."

"You're full of slush. Turn the ship around," Kyar ground out.

Noel leaned forward. "Kyar, we've all noticed that you haven't been yourself. The man we know wouldn't leave Megal stranded on Gehenna."

"I haven't left him on Gehenna!" Kyar smacked the table hard for emphasis. "I have ships searching for Prin, and rewards for information posted. I'm doing what I can, but Prin has disappeared without a trace. What the hell do you want me to do? Give up my own life to find Prin? I've already wasted more than three years trying to save Megal, and look how that turned out!" Kyar realized he was shouting in a rather high pitch.

Noel didn't shout back. She slid a paper across the table. "This is the latest message from Gehenna. The transmission arrived yesterday. Read it."

Kyar didn't want to, yet felt he didn't really have a choice. He was being watched. He picked up the short missive. It stated that Megal was alive, but he'd had his tongue cleaved off in an altercation with some other prisoners. Knowing Megal, he had probably been shooting off his mouth with smart remarks. And still, he was alive.

Kyar left the dining room and sought out his old quarters. He reached the bathroom before he threw up. After he recovered his poise, he returned to the dining room. "Take me back to the Ice Planet," he repeated, "or you will all be iced." Kyar needed to see Sephine. He needed her comfort.

Hanis and Mo shared a resigned glance, and moved to flank him. "Come on, Kyar," Mo said.

"Where?"

"To the brig," Mo said.

"You wouldn't dare."

Apparently, they would. The pair took him to the brig and locked him up.

10. Asylum

Kyar was trapped in the brig for four days, before he began to suspect there might be some truth to Oran'Jay's words. After four days without Sephine, and three days of Greely's so-called antidote, he felt different—more like himself.

Greely had taken a blood sample on the first day. He concocted what he claimed was a counter-agent, for what Kyar had been absorbing from Sephine. Greely had been injecting him with four darts a day since. If Kyar refused them, Hanis and Mo simply held him down, while the doctor stabbed him.

When he awoke on the fifth day, Kyar knew that he was clear-headed in a way that he hadn't been for months. He faced his shadowy reflection in the metal wall and didn't like what he saw.

After being wined and dined and stuffed like a Solarus goose, his cheeks were as plump as the belly that hung over his belt, And Megal? Megal was reliving hell, because he had loved his brother enough to sacrifice himself to restore Kyar's happiness. And how had Kyar repaid him? He closed his eyes in shame. Months had passed in a whirlwind of heady pleasure for Kyar, while Megal suffered on the hell planet. Kyar touched his reflection in the metal. Was he the betrayer from his carved vision? No—Sephine was the betrayer. Kyar was the betrayed.

It was time for him to act, to search for Prin himself, since no-one else could find a trace of the rat. Liena had believed that Prin would find his way back to the Ice Planet, yet there was still no sign of him, so Liena must have been wrong.

Kyar hollered for Noel until she came.

"Is this another threat to have me iced?" she asked tersely.

"Uh ... no. Sorry about that. Look, maybe Oran'Jay was on to something."

She crossed her arms, arched one graceful eyebrow, and waited.

"I do feel more like myself now, and I haven't in months. I guess Sephine was using me." He dropped down on the narrow bed and kept spilling his guts. "I think the only reason she went to Gehenna to save Megal, was so that she could bite him and come back as the Nomad's mate." He shook his head in disgust. "Sephine was just one more girl using me to get to Megal. And now that I've ended up as Nomad, Sephine's scheme has changed. She wants me to retain the title. She wants Megal to die on Gehenna. Any way I look at it, she's been using me, manipulating me—betraying me."

"You're finally catching on." Noel did not uncross her arms. She was not going to make this easy on him.

"Yes. Can I come out now?"

"Only if you are willing to help Megal."

Kyar nodded. "More than willing. You must know …"

She unlocked the cell and escorted him to the dining room. The crew was waiting around the table, as if they had never left it. Kyar apologized for his threats. Everyone forgave him. They apologized for kidnapping him and locking him in the brig. He forgave them. Once they were all friends again, they got down to business.

Noel had spent the last five days productively. She had accessed all the reports from ships out searching for Megal. She had also gotten her hands on the files of information bought with reward bizoux. For the rest of the day, they reviewed every scrap of data, no matter how trivial it seemed.

They were still at it when Captain Glass contacted them from the bridge. "Kyar, half the Nomad's fleet has just surrounded us. If they don't hear your voice in the next two minutes, they're going to blast the FarGone 5 into the next galaxy—their words. Could you come and tell them that you are alive and well, and here of your own volition?"

"My pleasure. Time to stretch my legs anyway." Kyar strode off to the bridge and said hello to his fleet. Once he had assured them of his good health, they insisted on sending over an armed party, to verify that he didn't have a blaster pointed at his head.

One ship docked against the main hatch and the FarGone 5 had visitors. Several Icemen and a couple of Ice Guards were accompanied by Sephine. She was the last person he expected, or wanted to see, but there she was reaching out to embrace him.

He stepped back quickly. "Hello, Sephine. Keep your distance please," he managed civilly enough, even though he wanted to throttle her.

"But Kyar, what has happened? You disappeared and we all feared for your life. May I not kiss you? I have missed you so. Haven't you missed me?" She reached out again.

He wasn't foolish enough to close the distance. "I missed you too much, if you know what I mean. Our alliance will be formally ended. The FarGone 5 is taking a trip to find Prin, and I'm going along."

"I'll come too. I can help find Prin, and I can help get Megal off Gehenna," Sephine said with a touch of desperation. She knew he was on to her.

"No, Sephine. You've already done enough to help Megal." A being would have to be earless to miss Kyar's sarcasm. "You will return to the other ship now."

"But Kyar, I must speak with you privately. There is something you don't know."

"I think there's a whole lot that I don't know, but I'm figuring it out. Goodbye Sephine," he said with unmistakable finality, signalling the Ice Guards to take her away.

"Kyar, I'm pregnant with the next Nomad," Sephine cried, a hand on her stomach. "I'm your wife, the Nomad's wife. You can't discard me when I'm pregnant with your heir."

Kyar swore viciously. "I don't have time for this. I'm going to find Prin, so I can get Megal off Gehenna. He's the rightful Nomad, not me. His children will be the next to rule, not ours. Stay in the Ice Palace until I return, then we'll settle this."

She shook her head wildly. "Kyar, you're the Nomad now. Why would you want to give that up? We have such a wonderful life, and our children will rule next, don't you want that? Megal won't be able to rule, even if you do get him off Gehenna alive. He won't be able to speak a word, useless, an invalid. He was barely sane the last time he escaped Gehenna. He must be quite mad by now."

Kyar didn't want to hear another awful word. He motioned more emphatically to the Ice Guards. "Get her out of here. Return her to the planet, but don't let her get close enough to bite you or even lick you," he ground out.

Sephine was escorted away and she made no further protest. Kyar didn't watch her leave. Real or not, he had been happy with Sephine. He would miss that happiness. He just hoped she was lying about being pregnant, like she had lied about everything else.

The two ships separated, and the FarGone 5 was alone in space.

"Let's get back to work." Noel put a sympathetic arm around his waist and urged him toward the galley.

"Back to work," Kyar murmured. It would take his mind off his battered heart.

After many more hours spent reading reports, Noel suggested they zip on over to the Bane Star Cluster, a truly decadent little corner of the Universe, where information could be bought as easily as a pair of socks or a towel. Seventh Heavens and Cloud Nines were plentiful, coveted by men and women who had lost all hope. The most recent Prin sightings originated in that quadrant, and everyone agreed it was the best place to start searching.

Captain Glass set a direct course, and a fast one. The ship arrived in the middle of the Bane Star Cluster in under a week. It docked over Asylum, a planet with only three hours of daylight per cycle. The remaining twenty-seven hours of darkness were devoted to sheer decadence on a scale most beings couldn't handle, at least not for more than a couple of days. Kyar had never visited the world, but he knew Megal used to vacation on Asylum regularly. Kyar had never accompanied his brother. Megal wouldn't allow it. He claimed that Asylum was something you experienced alone.

From space, the ocean was swirling with currents of purple and green and turquoise. There were no large land masses. Instead, a prolific collection of small islands decorated the surface, making the planet appear as if it had a bad case of spox.

Before they descended, Mo reluctantly revealed that he, too, had spent some time on Asylum. "Too much time, long ago. Another lifetime." His closed face was warning enough to ask no questions. "I worked for the woman who owns one of the most exclusive pleasure islands on the planet, and she owes me a favour. I'll start with her, see what she can tell me. Hanis, Oran'Jay, you'll come with me."

"I'm going too." Kyar was curious to see the legendary world.

Mo vetoed the idea. "Kyar, you're the Nomad now. You can't go risking your skin, and that's exactly what you'd be doing if you came with us. The air down there makes beings crazy, they lose their inhibitions. I don't want to have to watch your back as well as my own. Wait on the ship, we won't linger down there, believe me. We'll find out what we can about Prin, and be back before you can miss us."

Kyar was not inclined to cool his heels on the ship. He was restless after being used by Sephine, and in the mood for a little craziness. And

Megal had come here often enough. He had always returned to the Ice Planet in one piece, more or less. Sometimes he had looked a shadow of himself when he got home, but he had always recovered.

Kyar said, "There are three of you going. You can watch my back if you feel it is necessary."

Mo scratched his chin. "Borelle better come too." That made four babysitters.

Noel surprised them all when she said, "I'm not going to be left behind. I've never visited the planet. I want to see what all the fuss is about." No-one could persuade her otherwise, and Mo certainly tried.

The ship landed on the thumb of a mitten-shaped island, in the middle of the three hours of daylight. Mo said the island was called Asylum, like the planet, then he muttered something under his breath about 'insane asylum'.

After instructing Captain Glass to keep the ship on recirculated air, and all the hatches sealed tight, Mo allowed them to disembark. In hindsight, Kyar wished Mo had locked him in the brig again, instead of letting him experience Asylum. Four babysitters were not enough after all.

***

A pillow being lifted off Kyar's face woke him up. Greely tossed it aside. "You've been abed for two days, Kyar. Time to get up. You're needed on the bridge, but Mo wants to see you in the galley first."

Kyar struggled into a sitting position and groaned with gusto.

"Need any medical treatments?" Greely inquired, a distinct gleam in his eyes.

"Not sure. I'll let you know. Get out." Kyar managed to stand, shower and dress, feeling a thousand years old. The red suction marks that had covered his body, everywhere, had started to fade away. He walked to the bridge at the pace of someone as old as the glaciers. He dropped onto the nearest chair as soon as he reached it, then remembered he was supposed to go to the galley first.

Captain Glass and most of the bridge crew were at their stations, hard at work. Too hard at work. Were they trying not to laugh? It did seem so. Without a word, Kyar rose and limped off the bridge. Muffled laughter followed him. He hadn't even asked where the ship was going, and he had no idea, but Mo would tell him.

Kyar made it to the galley without falling down. Mo and Hanis were waiting, with Noel. Oran'Jay sauntered up with a carafe of cocoa and

143

joined them, grinning from one tiny green ear to the other. There was no doubt, Kyar was going to be on the receiving end of a whole lot of ridicule in the days to come, for his adventures on Asylum, and the embarrassing condition he had been found in.

"What is the ship's destination?" he asked, all business.

Mo looked awfully pleased with himself when he said, "The Ice Planet."

"But ... why are we going home? Did you discover nothing about Prin's location?" Kyar helped himself to a cup of cocoa, wondering why Mo looked so smug about the disappointing news.

"I discovered a whole lot. More than I ever expected to."

Kyar perked up. "Tell me."

"Sheer luck that I ran into some staff that knew Megal from the old days, when he used to be a regular on the island."

"And?" Kyar prompted.

"He was spotted last month. He spent some time on an adjacent island. He stopped by Asylum Island, before he departed the planet." Mo gloated, as he had every right to do.

"Prin," Kyar breathed.

"Definitely Prin. The island he visited, the Isle of Mar, is a refuge for undesirables, citizens who aren't welcome on most other worlds. Some really dark stuff goes on there, all of it against universal law, I'm sure. Prin must have felt right at home."

"Uh ... shouldn't we visit that island? Get more information about why Prin was there?" Kyar said.

"We've already been to Mar. You slept through it. You were lucky to miss it." Mo was as tough as mammoth toenails and even he looked momentarily shaken.

"What did you learn?" Kyar felt a bit like he was pulling teeth, and he lacked the energy to do anything so strenuous.

"I managed to acquire a list of who's been squatting on Mar lately." Mo tapped the pages in front of him. "We ran the names through our data stream. One of them stood out for Noel."

"Who?" he asked her.

"A bio-engineer, who was discovered to be creating hybrid nano weapons, illegally of course. He's universally banned from working with nanos ever again."

"I'm sure he's respecting that ban," Kyar said with appropriate sarcasm. "And Prin met with him?"

144

Mo nodded. "He spent at least a week with him. Before Prin left the planet, he was overheard by one of the staff, saying that he was going home."

"Home?" Kyar gasped.

"Home to the Ice Planet," Mo confirmed.

"So Liena was right." Kyar should have had more faith in her.

Oran'Jay hissed through his row of sharp, crowded teeth. "Bet he's already burrowed into the Ice Planet. I just wish we knew where, and what exactly he's up to."

They all nodded.

"So we are going home to find Prin," Kyar said, stating the obvious. The Icemen would be happy to see him back, after his abrupt and unplanned departure. They had been sending urgent messages, saying he was needed on the planet.

"Home to capture Prin." Mo raised his cup and everyone drank to the sentiment. Even though the crew had been pardoned for their crimes, it was clear that they remained loyal to Megal, and wished to bring him home.

The week that it took to reach the Ice Planet passed quickly. Kyar slept through much of it, still recovering. The Icemen sent several more communiqués, and were relieved to hear that Kyar was almost back. Clearly, there was something urgent they wanted to discuss with him, but they were waiting to do it in person.

The day before they arrived home, Kyar and Noel found themselves in the galley alone. He still tended to be more embarrassed around her than the others, given how he had been found on Asylum, probably because she was a girl. He had been avoiding her whenever possible.

"Let's talk, Kyar," she said.

Kyar swallowed hard and cleared his tight throat. "Sure, what about?"

"Oh, stop being so embarrassed. What happens on Asylum stays on Asylum," Noel declared. "We need to concentrate on finding Prin. We have to get Megal off Gehenna. He won't last long in his present condition."

"I know." Kyar couldn't even imagine what hell Megal was enduring, if he was even still breathing. "You're still Megal's legal bride. If we get him off Gehenna, you'll hold that position, if you want it," he reminded Noel.

She shook her head. "It was Prin I allied with, not Megal."

"Did you realize he wasn't Megal when you married him?" Kyar asked. They had never discussed this.

"No. How could I? I didn't know a clone had been taken." She paused and worried her lip. "I did know something was wrong. Megal had no trouble attracting girlfriends, but the first night I was with Prin, as Megal, he was very cruel. He enjoyed being cruel. Inflicting pain … excited him." There was a haunted look in her eyes. Prin had hurt her.

"He will pay for all his crimes," Kyar said, with emphasis.

Noel nodded. "Anyway, I had never seen Megal act that way, cruelly, so it did seem out of character. I thought maybe he had been forced into a union with me and wanted to punish me." Noel shuddered, adding, "I'd always had something of a … an affection for Megal. He never lacked charisma, did he? Or wit or beauty. Maybe it's true that women are drawn to bad boys that are unattainable." She gave a self-deprecating little smile. "I was disappointed that he was so horrible, anyway, it wasn't him—it was Prin."

"I knew you fancied Megal. Most girls did." Facts were facts. "I assumed that's why you agreed to the union. If we can't capture Megal's clone in one piece, he will need your support when we get him home. No more girls will be lining up," Kyar said.

"I know." Noel gave a tight little smile. She rose and left, rather abruptly. Kyar had the distinct impression that he had said something wrong, but he didn't know what it was.

The next day, they landed beside the Crystal Crater. There was no grand ceremony this time. The ice had a deserted air. Kyar and Noel were escorted directly to an assembly. All thirty Icemen were in attendance, their faces as grim as gravestones.

As soon as Kyar sat down, Jann rose to his feet and said, "Welcome back, Kyar. As you have probably surmised, we have a problem. That small crack in the southern glacier isn't so small anymore. And there are two new splits in the ice surface, in the same area." Jann showed no alarm. Regardless, Kyar's heart felt like it rose up to block his throat.

"The ice … our planet is cracking apart?" he gasped.

Jann nodded and another Iceman rose. He read the highlights of an official report. The ice experts did not believe the cracks were occurring naturally. The report made dire predictions about the catastrophic consequences of what was happening.

From all accounts, the Ice Planet was in the first stage of an environmental disaster, a meltdown, and they had always taken such care with their fragile ice. Already, two inhabited craters had been destroyed. People had died in those craters, unable to escape the collapsing ice.

"Can anything be done to stop it?" Kyar asked, shocked to the core.

Jann sighed. "The icers don't have any recommendations yet, other than evacuating the craters that seem to be at the most risk. They're still investigating. A team of scientists have descended into the first crack, trying to find out what's causing the problem. There is no sign of melting or anything impacting with the ice. There haven't been any icequakes. Nothing! They haven't found a single clue to explain why the ice is cracking apart. Everything seems normal, except for the fact that our ice is being destroyed."

Historically, the ice had never done that before. The Icemen fell silent, waiting for Kyar to decide what should be done.

Of course, Kyar strongly suspected Prin. How could he not? His cousin was back on the planet and according to Liena, Prin had been working on a nano that could destroy ice. If he had perfected the weapon on the Isle of Mar, this was probably the result.

Kyar laid a hand on the thick report in front of him, to steady himself. "We'll wait to hear what the icers discover down in the fissure. I'll fly over the site tomorrow. Tonight, I'll have a look at the reports. But first, I will update you on Prin's latest activities, which I have no doubt are directly responsible for what is happening to our ice."

"Prin?" more than one Iceman gasped.

"Yes, Prin." Kyar went on to explain what Prin had been up to. Noel contributed, in-between skimming through the icers' reports.

Kyar was asked a lot of questions that he couldn't answer. Afterward, several long-winded Icemen had to have their long-winded say, and an involved discussion broke out. By the time the assembly was concluded, the dinner hour had come and gone.

Kyar ended the assembly and left the room quickly, before he could be corralled. Jann and Noel followed on his heels. Jann said, "Kyar, Noel, we'll eat together. Give us a chance to talk."

Kyar wasn't sure where to take them for dinner. He didn't know what had become of Sephine. "Where should we eat?" he asked wearily. The day had been long, the assembly even longer, and now he might have to face Sephine.

"Let's eat in your rooms," Jann said. "If you're trying to avoid Sephine, she's still squatting in the Nomad's tower."

Kyar swore.

"No-one could tell her not to, could they? She is still the Nomad's wife. You haven't decreed otherwise," Jann said, as blunt as he always was. And he was right.

"No, I haven't. I'll take care of that problem tomorrow," Kyar said. It seemed he had a lot of problems to address, without delay, not the least of which was that his world was cracking apart. And then there was Megal.

"Any news from Gehenna?" he asked.

"Only silence," Jann said with regret.

11. Green World

K yar was glad to be back in his own rooms, rather than Megal's opulent tower. It felt like coming home. His cook had been informed of his return and there was a meal waiting. Kyar settled at the end of the modest table. Jann and Noel took the nearest chairs, facing each other. Silently, they ate the delicious salad of vegetables, grown overhead, and a generous portion of steamed fish.

Over cocoa, Noel highlighted what she felt were the important points from the icers' reports. "The first crack started near a green crater and tracked northward. It's abnormally straight for a crack, and straightest where it began to form." She slid a page in front of Kyar. It was a scanned map of the first fissure's path. The beginning of the split was almost ruler straight. The icers had circled the abnormality with a red marker.

"And the second fissure?" Kyar asked.

"It exhibits the same bizarre characteristic. Start's straight, just like the first one. The third split is the same. All three have continued to widen exponentially," Noel said. "All the cracks start near green craters." She made that bit of information sound significant.

"I don't think there is any doubt that this is Prin's handiwork," Kyar said.

"I agree. I don't think anyone believes otherwise, not after what we told them today. Slush." Noel leaned back with slumped shoulders, looking as burdened as Kyar felt.

They started when the outer door sprang opened. Sephine strode in, as if she had every right to do so.

"Welcome home, husband. You should have informed me that dinner was served. And we should be eating in the Nomad's dining room." Sephine looked magnificent in a fur-trimmed silver gown, and presented herself with an annoying amount of self-assurance, given how they had parted.

"You weren't invited, Sephine," Kyar said coldly. "I will discuss our situation with you tomorrow, in private. Go back to the Nomad's tower. It will be the last night you spend in that luxury." Simply looking at her filled him with disgust and self-loathing. He had been too easy to fool and manipulate, not once but twice. There would be no third time.

Sephine didn't leave. She settled gracefully at the other end of the table, as if presiding over them.

"You are not welcome here, Sephine. Leave, or I'll have the guards escort you out. As a matter of fact, that's not a bad idea," Kyar said.

"Wrong! That is a terrible idea. I carry the next Nomad, your heir. I wasn't lying about that, Kyar. We were intimate enough times, weren't we? If you don't believe me, the palace surgeon will confirm it," Sephine said, ignoring the reluctant witnesses to their confrontation. "Your mother is thrilled that the family line will continue to rule the planets. You always were her favourite."

Kyar glared across the table. "The planet surface is cracking apart. There won't be much left to rule, if we don't figure out how to stop the disaster. Our personal situation comes second to the planet, so go back to Megal's tower and stay out of my sight, or I might just have you removed from the entire crater, heir or no heir, mother or no mother." He meant every word of the ultimatum.

"Still a bad idea, Kyar." Sephine didn't budge.

Jann shoved to his feet. "I'll summon the Ice Guards on my way out. I'm not leaving you alone with *her*!"

Sephine simply said, "Another crack in the ice will form tomorrow. If I had a vested interest in what happens to this world, I might be motivated to stop the destruction of the southern glacier, and what will come after."

Kyar could not credit her words. They were simply too shocking! "You're full of slush, get out!" he shouted, fully prepared to toss her out himself.

There was no need. Sephine rose with aplomb. "We'll talk tomorrow, I'm sure. Goodnight, Kyar." She sauntered out, as cool as an icicle.

Kyar moved to the wall panel and summoned a couple of Ice Guards, to make sure Sephine reached the Nomad's tower and stayed there. She had just proven herself too dangerous to roam freely about the palace. All she had to do was bite someone—anyone, to ensure they did her bidding.

Noel had three goblets waiting when Kyar dropped back into his chair. "Sephine is lying," he said. He downed the brandy in one gulp.

"If she isn't, we'll sure as hell know by tomorrow. And if she is speaking the truth, she'll have the answers we need." Jann tossed his drink back, too, and thrust to his feet. "I'll keep you informed, Kyar."

"Please do." Kyar didn't show Jann the courtesy of escorting him to the door. He was simply too drained to make the effort.

Noel sipped her brandy while Kyar sank deeper into despair. Like a pool of quick-slush, it sucked him down. He was soon wallowing in self-pity. "I've been Nomad for less than half a year and my wife is destroying the planet. Megal did a better job without even trying," he muttered. "Do you think Sephine truly knows something about the ice splitting apart? Or is she hoping to manipulate us?"

"I don't know, Kyar. Sephine will do anything to hold onto the power that she has with you. She clawed her way up from slavery to Nomad's wife, didn't she? And she does have the ability to inspire men to spill their secrets and do her bidding." Noel moved to the glass window to watch the show of coloured lights dancing in the northern sky. It was not as spectacularly flamboyant as the sky over Asylum, but in Kyar's mind, it was more beautiful, because it was his home sky.

Noel touched the glass. "She could know something, I suppose. She has been on the planet, while we've been away."

"True enough. Sit, Noel. Talk to me." He motioned at the chair.

She shook her head. "Tomorrow will be a busy day. I'm going to accompany you to survey the cracks."

"Good idea. We'll plan to leave mid-morning, barring any disasters. Maybe we'll even get lucky and find some sign of Prin."

"Unlikely, but one can hope. Goodnight, Kyar." Noel saw herself out. Kyar was quick to lock and bar the door after her. He didn't want to wake up, bitten by his wife. Now that he wasn't under her spell, she terrified him.

His rooms felt too quiet after weeks of hearing the ship's engines. He avoided the bed he had once shared with Sephine and fell asleep under a blanket on the couch. Urgent banging on the door roused him. The tinge of diffuse light coming in, proved it was morning, but barely.

Jann barged in as soon as Kyar unlocked the door. "The icers have sent a message. A fourth crack is already forming. Let's go have a word with your … with Sephine."

Another confrontation with his wife was not how Kyar wanted to begin his day. "Give me a minute," he said and went to freshen up. When he returned, Jann was pacing. Everyone was doing a lot of that these days.

"Come on, come on!" The old fellow rushed them all the way to Megal's tower. Two guards were standing vigilantly outside the door at the base of the tower. They bowed before Kyar and stepped hastily aside. He still wasn't comfortable with the subservient gesture. It always made him feel like an imposter. At least nobody bowed to him on the FarGone 5, nor did he expect it.

They climbed the spiral stairs and entered the luxurious Nomad's suite. As always, walking into Megal's rooms caused Kyar a sharp pang of loss. Two servants were already preparing Sephine's breakfast, yet she was nowhere in sight.

"Wake the lady up, now," Kyar said.

The nearest woman bobbed her head and disappeared down the hall to the Nomad's bedroom. Sephine took her time turning up, with her hair arranged perfectly and a silky white gown covering her down to her fur-tipped toes.

Playing the part of a gracious hostess, Sephine invited them to sit and poured them steaming cocoa. Kyar ignored his, as did Jann, perhaps fearing poison. "What do you know about the southern glacier?" he demanded, his hands itching to wring the truth from her.

"It is not what I know. It is what I will reveal," she stressed. "And at what price."

Jann put a restraining hand on Kyar's arm, when he would have lunged at her. "What is the price?" Jann asked.

"I will hold the position as the Nomad's wife, and our child will rule after Kyar." Sephine smiled like a viper. "I'm not asking for much and what I know will save not only the southern glacier, but the rest of the planet. What's happening in the south will spread, without end."

"What exactly is happening?" Kyar demanded.

Sephine gave a little shrug, not inclined to say a thing.

"Are you responsible?"

She shook her head. "It is not my doing."

"Who is responsible?"

Sephine blew on her cocoa, before she said, "You already know."

"Prin—using specially created nanos to destroy the ice," Kyar stated, watching her reaction.

Sephine sipped calmly, giving nothing away.

Jann growled, "Can what's happening be stopped?" She nodded. "And you know how to stop it?" She nodded again.

Kyar and Jann shared a speaking glance. No discussion was necessary between them. Kyar shoved to his feet. "Well, I think we'll fly on down there and figure out how to stop the cracks for ourselves."

"If you don't act quickly, it will be too late," she warned. "And I promise that you won't be able to stop the destruction, not without me."

Kyar gazed down at her and sighed. "Look, Sephine, what you are asking, it's not something I can agree to. Megal will be Nomad soon, and I won't be. So you can't hold the position of Nomad's wife, unless you want to ally with Megal, and I can't speak for my brother."

"You will have to speak for him, since he will never speak for himself again," she shot back. "And he is in love with me since I bit him, so he will agree to the union. He will welcome it, if he doesn't die in the meantime."

Kyar had experienced an addiction to her venom firsthand, and knew that Megal probably would want nothing more than to be with Sephine. "And is a union with my brother agreeable to you? You've seen Megal, and he will not be in better shape now," Kyar said frankly, yet feeling the traitor.

She shrugged. "I'm a survivor, Kyar. I've shared your bed. I dare say I can share your brother's. I'll just make sure to drink heavily and douse all the lights."

Kyar's jaw dropped in astonishment. "Was my touch so displeasing to you?" She had never shown a trace of anything but enthusiasm, delight and satisfaction, when they had lain together.

"You're very needy, Kyar, with all your cuddling. And since you've gotten fat, you're quite sweaty," she said spitefully.

Clearly, he had been both a blind and a stupid man as far as his relationship with his wife was concerned. It was almost funny how clueless he had been. "Regardless, Megal is already allied with Noel, so he can't marry anyone else," he pointed out, getting back on topic.

Sephine dismissed his concerns. "That relationship can be annulled. She carries no Nomad's child."

"You don't know that for sure. She was on the FarGone 5 with Megal," Kyar said.

Sephine laughed. It was not a nice sound. "Noel's father is wealthy and high-ranking. She has no need to touch that ruined skin. She will end the alliance."

"Perhaps she sees beneath his skin."

Sephine waved a hand dismissively. "I doubt that. But we can cross that bridge when we come to it. At the moment, you have a choice. You can save your planet or let it crack apart, killing everyone who can't get off the surface in time, and that will be the majority of the population."

"And you would let that happen for your own gain," Kyar said.

"In a nano second." She smiled again, so coldly that Kyar had to suppress a shiver.

Jann spoke up before Kyar could. "We'll go have a look for ourselves."

"You will be powerless to stop the damage being done to your world."

"Then tell us how to stop it," Kyar cried.

Sephine actually yawned. "You know the terms for that. You are speaking in circles, Kyar, and I grow weary of it."

Then and there, he made an impulsive decision. "We're leaving for the southern glacier immediately, and you're coming with us." He grabbed her arm and hauled her to the door. She made no protest, verbal or otherwise. Kyar ordered the Ice Guards to come along. Jann went to fetch Noel, and notify the crew of the FarGone 5 to prepare for departure. The ship was larger than they needed to skim to another part of the planet, but Kyar preferred it over any other vessel.

Within the hour, they were airborne. It took less than half an hour to reach the site of the damaged ice. The entire crew assembled before the viewing screen, looking down at the first and largest crack. It was bigger than Kyar had expected, wider than the widest river, and so long it disappeared from sight over the horizon.

Oran'Jay hissed at the sight, while most of them were speechless with horror.

A small cluster of vessels glinted from one section of the fissure. Captain Glass banked the ship and coasted in circles while Jann made contact, hoping for some good news. There was no news at all. The scientists were still trying to reach the bottom of the chasm. As yet, they had not discovered the source of the problem, even though the ice was cracking apart before their eyes.

"We'll land," Kyar decided. "Assess the situation down there."

"Don't take too long assessing," Sephine drawled near his ear.

Kyar jerked away from the feel of her warm breath, in case it contaminated him. "Lock her in the brig," he told the two guards posted on the bridge. He took great pleasure in watching her be led away.

He left the FarGone 5 to meet with all the planetary experts—scientists, environmentalists and icers. Almost the whole crew came along. Everyone wanted to help.

They had an informal meeting on the edge of the fissure. The wind was calm and the sun was behind a haze of cloud. It was a beautiful day, except for the fissure and the fatal sound of sharply crackling ice coming from deep below. Kyar wondered how long it would be safe to stand on, and more importantly, park their ships on.

The icer in charge was someone he had already met. Klaus Undar knew more about ice than anyone on the planet, and he was mystified by what was happening. "I've taken samples from the top, the middle, and the lowest part of the crack. The ice is normal. Not a thing wrong with it, except that it's crawling apart, as if it's shrinking, for no bloody reason!" His long grey beard flapped up and down, keeping pace with his mouth. "There is no run-off, so it's not melting. Well, you can see that for yourselves." He motioned at the offensive chasm with a huge mitten.

And they could. The ice was as dry as it should be. Klaus pointed out marks that they had carved inside the crack. After two days, the marks were still there, proving it was not the surface of the ice that was disappearing.

"We've analyzed the air, the sky, and the surrounding outer space. Nothing is beaming at the crack from a ship. Whatever is causing this, we can't find it," Klaus said.

Noel stepped forward. "But you haven't reached the bottom of the crack?"

"We're trying. Getting down there is a lot harder than you'd think. The ice—the crack, it doesn't open up straight down to the bedrock. Near the bottom, everything narrows. It's like trying to find your way through a maze of honeycomb passages. The team will follow one tunnel, only to find it blocked, then they have to climb up and out, and start all over in another passage. They're having a really tough time."

"I'm sure they are," Noel murmured.

"What about blasting straight down?" Kyar asked. "Opening up a passage for ourselves."

Klaus looked scandalized. "The ice is too unstable. It might collapse like a table whose legs have been broken. That's the last thing we should do." He didn't say 'leave this to the experts', but it was implied.

Kyar led his party back to the FarGone 5. As soon as they were aboard, he visited the brig. Sephine was reclining on the bed. Kyar spoke to her from outside the cell. "The icers haven't discovered how Prin is using the nanos, or how the nanos destroy the ice," he said, watching her face closely.

"And they won't. Prin is too clever." The name was mentioned a little too familiarly.

"Do you know him?"

"We met recently." She wasn't giving much away.

"Where?"

"It doesn't matter where. It won't change anything."

That was probably true. "So you're not willing to tell me what Prin has done to cause this?" Kyar asked again.

"I will tell you, if you give me your word that I will remain the Nomad's wife and mother of the next generation of rulers. I'm getting tired of saying it, Kyar, and you are squandering time you don't have to squander."

Discouraged, he rejoined his crew on the bridge. Everyone was looking morose. Kyar sighed and said, "I think I must agree to Sephine's ultimatum. Her terms, what she gains, it is a small price to pay to save our world."

"Oh, Kyar," Noel said, with sympathy, but she did not try to talk him out of his decision. No-one did. Every last one of them would have made the same sacrifice, yet it did look like they felt bad for him.

With a heavy heart, Kyar returned to the brig and unlocked the door. He motioned Sephine out.

"Does this mean you agree to my terms, Kyar?"

"I do, as long as what you tell me stops this disaster." He didn't try to hide his resentment.

"Excellent choice, Kyar. We will both benefit greatly from our bargain." She smiled with self-satisfaction. He kept a safe distance, even though two guards stood nearby.

They all relocated to the galley, where the crew was assembled, waiting to learn how to save the planet.

Sephine took her place almost demurely, eyes downcast. She tucked her skirts around her, before she said, "Prin has recently developed a nano that will destroy ice on a grand scale, as you have already figured out. The nanos are tailored to eat ice—that's the simplest way to explain it. The ice is their food and they reproduce at an exponential rate, until they run out of ice. As soon as they run out of ice, they dissolve, causing no further destruction."

"And he has released them in four different locations," Kyar assumed.

"He has, so far." The threat was strongly implied.

Noel asked, "How do we stop the nanos?"

Sephine indulged herself with a dramatic pause, before she said, "There exists a second and more aggressive type of nano. It moves faster than the first, and reproduces faster. And it feeds on the ice-eating nanos. It will stop the spread of the first. It won't repair the ice, but it will stop the destruction."

"Why would Prin create something to stop his own little monsters?" Jann demanded.

"Prin likes to be prepared. Once he finds what he is looking for, he can hold the whole planet for ransom."

"Proof that the Ice Planet is the original Green World," Kyar muttered in disgust.

Sephine nodded. "His quest, his reason for being."

"Where can we find this second nano? If it exists."

Sephine tucked a curl behind her ear. "Oh, it exists, and it is closer than you think"

Kyar heaved a sigh of frustration. "Stop playing games, Sephine. I've agreed to your terms. Where are the nanos that will save the Ice Planet?"

"You didn't used to be so impatient, Kyar," she drawled and plucked an ornate comb out of her elaborate hairstyle. "The nanos are right here."

On closer inspection, the four shimmering jewels on the comb had liquid centers.

"But … surely we will need more than that," Noel said.

"No, it's enough." Sephine said. "One for each crack. The nanos do reproduce exponentially faster than the other. Do the math. You can stop all four cracks."

"How did you convince Prin to trust you enough to hold onto the nanos that will stop his destruction?" Kyar asked, not yet sure that he believed her.

"I had a little nibble of your cousin. I don't think he truly understood my nature."

"He didn't realize how addicted he would become to you," Kyar stated.

"If you must speak plainly, then yes, he didn't realize how much influence I can have over a human man. Even though he wears Megal's skin, he didn't taste nearly so sweet. And now he trusts me completely, so he entrusted me with half his precious nanos. He believes I am helping him in his quest. Ridiculous notion. There is nothing to gain by proving that this is the first Green World—no wealth, no power, nothing worth anything." Sephine snorted in disgust, making her opinion of Prin quite clear.

It was hard to know which of the pair was the more dangerous. It was lucky they were not united in Prin's cause, or they might well have been unstoppable.

"Where do we need to deposit the nanos?" Noel asked.

"Just break the glass jewel and release the nanos below the ice in each of the cracks, where Prin released his. That's where they will work the most effectively," Sephine said, adding, "the sooner the better."

"But the icers haven't been able to reach the bottom of the cracks," Kyar said.

"The green craters," Noel said at the same time, a few leaps ahead of him.

"Yes. Prin released the nanos at the base of the ice, so no-one could find them, not that they could have stopped them," she said with a careless shrug. "They devour the ice from the bottom up, and it pulls apart, hence the cracks."

Kyar leaned forward. "Do you know exactly where Prin released his nanos?"

"Yes. Check the four green craters, where the ice and land touch. Point the compass due north, then move five degrees east. That's where you'll find the mouth of Prin's tunnels."

"The craters have already been checked. No tunnels were found," Mo said.

"Prin resealed the ends of the tunnels with ice. The plugs are only a couple of inches thick. Break through them and you'll have access to the tunnels. They burrow through the ground under the ice, then angle back up into the ice. Prin brought along a Scarnivian moler to do the digging, then he simply released the nanos at the end of his tunnels."

"How long are these tunnels?" Noel asked.

Sephine thought about that for a moment. "A mile, perhaps two."

"And Prin is acting alone? Except for you?"

"He is a loner, and that is one of the nicer things I can say about your cousin," Sephine drawled.

Kyar picked up the precious comb. "Where is Prin now?"

"Somewhere on the planet. He is likely in or near one of the four craters, gloating over his success." She smirked.

That sounded right to Kyar. Prin was too egotistical to miss witnessing his destructive show.

Everyone moved very quickly after that. Sephine was put back in the brig until her information was proved true. Kyar summoned Klaus Undar and explained the situation. The four faux jewels were removed from the comb, and four teams were organized, one for each of the four craters.

Noel, Kyar, and their party were assigned the crater near the newest fissure. With still six hours of daylight left to them, they might be lucky enough to find Prin, as well as deposit the nanos. Mo, Hanis, and Klaus Undar made up the rest of their team. Klaus carried their ration of the precious nanos, sealed inside a vial to keep it safe.

A shuttle deposited the party of five in the bottom of the crater. The small crater had a diameter of about ten miles. The green space was dotted with evergreen trees that would be called dwarf on any true green planet. The ground was rocky and uneven, not nearly as inviting underfoot as smooth ice.

With dartguns tucked handily in their belts, they surveyed the surrounding forest silently. Kyar would have felt safer with a blaster in hand, but he wouldn't risk damaging Megal's stolen clone. Megal needed it now more than ever, if he was to live a normal life.

A short hike north brought them to the seam where ice met land, at the coordinates Sephine had provided. Hanis hammered mightily at the ice with a pickaxe, until the plug fractured inward. The entrance to the tunnel had been completely invisible. They wouldn't have found it without Sephine's information.

Mo bent down to peer inside the dark entrance. "The passage angles down into the earth under the ice, as Sephine said. So, a mile or two trek to reach the location where Prin released his nanos, if she's not lying," he said.

"Then let's go." Kyar took a step toward the entrance.

Mo blocked it. "The tunnel might be unstable, Kyar, it might even be booby-trapped. Klaus and I will take the nanos in, while you three wait here. Hanis will guard you." Mo had gotten protective of Kyar, now that he was the Nomad.

Kyar was about to argue when Noel said, "It's a wise idea. We'll wait here."

"Good. We'll be as quick as we can. Hanis, keep a sharp eye out." Mo clicked on a Scarnivian beamer. It flared and went out. He banged it and it came back on. Klaus pulled a second light from his pack. The two men ducked into the tunnel, and disappeared.

"Be safe," Noel called. No answer echoed back. They were already gone.

"We might as well get comfy. It will probably be a long wait," Kyar said.

They collected deadwood and branches, and started a crackling campfire burning. Noel, Hanis and Kyar sat close, enjoying the rare treat of burning wood on a planet that had hardly any trees at all.

Night fell around them. Kyar contacted the ship to say that they would hold their position until Mo and Klaus reappeared. Captain Glass updated them on the other groups. The rest of the tunnels had been located, and three other teams were presently in the process of transporting their nanos into those passages.

Kyar was still talking to the FarGone 5 when something rumbled in the distance. The ground trembled. "What was that?" Kyar asked Captain Glass, surging to his feet.

"I'm not sure, but we felt it up here, too."

Then it happened again, but stronger.

"The ground is shaking down here," Kyar cried. "Do you know what's causing it?" And then it trembled for a third time, violently enough to knock them to their knees. It was followed by profound stillness.

Kyar staggered to his feet. "FarGone 5, are you there?"

"Still here, but barely. Our sensors are showing that two of the cracks have collapsed in on themselves. Hell of a mess on the surface, but your fissure is still intact." Captain Glass reported.

"And the teams trying to deliver the vials? Did they make it? Did they survive?" Kyar asked.

"I don't know. The cave-in appears very widespread. I don't see how anyone could have survived, I really don't. Can you get your team out? In case this happens again?"

"I'll try. Keep me informed." Kyar signed off. He immediately attempted to reach Mo on his communicator. "Nothing but dead air," he said. "I don't know if they're too deep in the rock or if something has happened, from all the shaking. Slush." He thrust the communicator in his pocket, unsure what to do next.

Noel's head jerked up in alarm. "What's that?"

Kyar expected more shaking. Instead, his ears picked up the sound of howling, getting louder by the second. A pack of wild wolves raced down the side of the crater, chunks of ice sliding with them. Had the animals picked up their scent? Or were they upset by the environmental catastrophe? Kyar wasn't about to wait around and find out.

"Head for the tunnel!" He thrust Noel forward. Hanis grabbed their packs. They were close to the entrance and tumbled inside the tunnel, before the dogs reached the crater floor.

12. Tunnel Vision

"I don't think the beasts will chase us in here, but let's go a bit deeper, just in case. Wish I had a blaster," Hanis said, pulling out his dartgun.

"That might bring down the walls," Noel gasped.

Kyar led the way with his light. They jogged along, straining their ears for any sound from ahead or behind.

The passage was undamaged and mainly clear of debris. The Scarnivian moler had done a good job, creating a smooth, circular passage through the rock and frozen ground.

When no wolves could be heard howling at their rear, Hanis called a halt. "We don't want to go too deep in case the ice shakes again." He was barely out of breath. Kyar, on the other hand, was panting like an old man. The excess weight he carried on his frame, tended to rob him of breath and tax his muscles.

"It doesn't sound like the wolves are following," Noel said, her eyes too wide. "They probably don't like confined spaces any more than I do."

They listened again. Noel must have had the keenest ears, because she tensed and pointed ahead. "Did you hear that?"

Both men said, "No."

"Listen." Noel edged forward. They followed closely. After a dozen or so paces, Kyar heard an echo of indistinct sound, little more than a vibration. He skirted around Noel until Hanis caught his arm and yanked him back.

"I'll go first," he said. He took the light out of Kyar's hand, and the lead. For a big fellow, Hanis could move fast, and as silent as a shadow.

They hadn't travelled far when they came to a fork. The two branches of the tunnel angled away from each other, in a 'V' shape.

"Slush, Sephine didn't mention this," Kyar said.

They strained their ears again, trying to pinpoint the elusive sound. Kyar noticed something on the wall of the left passage. "I think we have our direction." He pointed to a scratched arrow.

Hanis grinned. "Bet Mo thought of that. I'll go check it out." He started moving again.

Kyar glanced at Noel and said, "I think we should stick together."

"Yes. Probably best, since we're already down here."

They followed Hanis. The passage leveled off. The noises ahead grew more distinct, until the knocking sounded like rocks banging together. The narrow tunnel began to widen out, as if the Scarnivian moler had made multiple passes, not just one. It seemed peculiar, if all Prin had wanted was a passage to deposit his nasty nanos.

The banging grew louder. "Almost there," Hanis whispered, gripping his dartgun firmly. Kyar tried to keep up. His lungs and heart were telling him there wasn't enough air in the tunnel, even though his brain was quite certain there was plenty.

Their light was all that lit the profound darkness. Hanis must not have wanted to make them a target, if they were walking into danger. He adjusted the beam to its lowest setting

Noel gasped and grabbed his arm. "More light, Hanis," she hissed.

"Are you afraid of the darkness?"

"No, look at the wall! Look!" She shook his arm.

Hanis adjusted the beamer to a brighter setting. Kyar almost shrieked. "What the hell?" he gasped.

Embedded in the tunnel wall were countless human skulls and assorted bones. Blank eye sockets peered out at them in a most accusing manner. For trespassing in their final resting place, perhaps?

The skulls were piled haphazardly, one atop the other, buried in layers in the ancient clay earth. Kyar crouched and touched the fine white powder and larger fragments that coated the ground. It wasn't rock or ice, but bone.

"What is this place?" Hanis handed the light to Kyar and stuck his fingers into the eye sockets of a nearby skull, protruding out of the wall. With little effort, he pried it free. Dirt and clay fell out through the hanging jaw. He brushed clay off the skull. "It's really old. The back of it has been smashed in."

They all jumped when the banging ahead sounded louder than ever. "We better check that out first," Kyar said. "The banging is from something alive, while these bones had been dead and buried for ages. They aren't going anywhere."

He adjusted the beamer to its lowest setting, and they hurried through the wider passage, able to walk side-by-side, glared at by skulls on both sides. There seemed to be no end to the grisly remains.

The light was so low, they almost stepped off solid ground into open space. The noise was coming from what appeared to be some sort of pit. Kyar increased the light again and aimed it downward.

"Mo!" Noel cried.

Their friend was about twelve feet below, sprawled on a mound of earth and bones. He was the source of the noise. He dropped the two skulls he was banging together. "About time," he groaned, his sweaty face twisted in pain.

"Oh, Mo. How badly are you hurt?" Noel called down.

"One leg is broken." He motioned to his right limb. It was bent in a way no human leg should bend, right in the middle of his thigh.

"Where's Klaus?" Kyar asked.

"Gone ahead with the nanos. Ground … collapsed beneath us when the earth shook. Klaus fared better than me. He was pretty banged up, but he should … should make it." Mo moaned and shifted restlessly. "Hanis, do you have the med-kit? My leg is bloody killing me."

Hanis scrambled over the edge and down the steep slope, in a tumble of loose debris. Kyar and Noel climbed down more slowly. The incline was also packed with skulls and bones. Every last one looked human.

"Glad you found me," Mo said through clenched teeth, when they reached him. "I thought this might be my final resting place, with all these other bones."

Noel crouched beside Mo and gripped his hand. "Your poor leg. Are you hurt anywhere else?"

"Just the leg." He must have squeezed her hand too hard. She winced.

Hanis dug out the medical supplies and handed Mo a dose of orange pills. He swallowed them like a starving man. At least they worked fast. The tension went out of him and his eyelids drooped.

"What now?" Hanis said.

"Can you carry Mo up that slope?" Kyar asked.

Hanis squinted at it. "Ya, I can get him out of this pit."

"My light is over there." Mo pointed. Hanis retrieved it and turned it on. It still worked.

Kyar glanced at Noel. "As much as I want to get the heck out of here, I think we need to make sure that Klaus released the nanos."

Noel nodded. "Our planet is more important than our lives. I'll go with you."

"No, you go with Hanis. I'll be right behind you, with Klaus."

"You're not going alone, Kyar." Noel stood up as if the matter was settled, which in her mind, it was. "Hanis, be careful. We'll see you topside."

Hanis said, "Don't dally."

"We won't." Noel patted him on the back and set off. Kyar hurried to catch up. Together, they climbed out of the pit on the far side. Bones packed that area as well. They were traversing one massive gravesite. Tens of thousands of skeletons would be a conservative estimate.

Noel managed the steep slope with the agility of a mountain goat. Kyar was more like a lumbering old bear, but he made it. And then they ran. Or she ran and he lumbered. The passage narrowed until it was a tunnel again. The walls were blessedly bone-free.

About a half mile farther along, they found Klaus. He was flat on his back, eyes wide and staring at nothing. Kyar flashed the light in his eyes and Noel shook him. There was no reaction, or pulse. He had died trying to deliver the nanos. The little gem was clutched tight in his fist, over his heart.

"Oh, poor Klaus." Tears overflowed from Noel's eyes as she crouched beside his body. She gently shut his eyelids, before she worked the stone free from his fist. She stowed it carefully in her pocket.

"What killed him?" Kyar asked.

Noel performed a cursory examination, pushing Klaus's bulky pack aside. Under the thick fur coat, the man's chest was purple. It looked like a couple of his ribs were broken. Perhaps one had punctured a lung or a vital artery. He had not fared better than Mo after all.

"Internal injuries, at a guess." Noel closed his coat, as if his body might still feel the cold. She rose and dashed tears from her eyes.

"There's nothing we can do for him, Noel. Let's get the vial to the end of the tunnel. I don't want to be down here any longer than necessary," Kyar said.

"I know. I don't either." Noel took a deep, shuddering breath.

They started moving again. The tunnel began to angle upward. Kyar judged it to be a good sign—up was toward the ice. The ice was where the nanos had to go. They trudged on, until they reached the ice layer of the planet.

What used to be solid ice was eaten away and half gone, leaving behind a honeycomb of ragged caverns that wouldn't last long. Kyar was surprised that this ice shelf hadn't collapsed already. The surrounding ice was filled with low-level noise—a barely audible, high-pitched crackling symphony.

Noel immediately removed the precious stone from her pocket. She stepped toward the nearest solid ice. On close inspection, it was strangely porous.

She banged the gemstone on the ice. The gem cracked and broke, releasing a gelatinous glob of light pink gel. The reaction was instantaneous. The gel liquefied to run thinner and thinner. It expanded outward, at an ever increasing rate.

"It looks like it's working," Kyar said, although he couldn't be sure. He didn't know what was supposed to happen.

"It moves amazingly fast, doesn't it?" Noel leaned closer to watch.

"Yes, but this is not a show we should stick around for." Kyar gripped her hand and they ran, back the way they had come, down the sloping tunnel through the earth, and past poor Klaus. He looked so abandoned, sprawled on the earth in the dark, frigid tunnel. If they could have taken his body along, they would have. Alas, he was a big man and the tunnel was long. Add to that, it might collapse on them at any second.

When they neared the pit, Kyar could hear voices. It seemed odd. Hanis and Mo should be long gone. Maybe Hanis had waited for them after all, or needed their help to move Mo.

Kyar reached the edge of the collapsed pit. He stopped dead when he saw who waited below. He turned off his light, but it was already too late. He had been spotted, and heard. The loose debris his foot had dislodged went rattling down the slope.

Noel was slightly behind him. She stepped backwards into the darkness, without making a sound. Kyar didn't think she had been seen.

"Join us, cousin," Prin ordered, from his seat beside Mo. Hanis was leaning against the rock on Mo's other side, held at bay by the dartgun Prin had balanced on his knee. Kyar would have bet his life the weapon held something far more lethal than sleep-darts.

"You're okay, Hanis?" Kyar asked.

"Ya, but Prin knew you were here." There was a slight emphasis on the 'you'. Kyar hoped Prin did not know about Noel. She might be their only hope now.

Kyar stood exactly where he was. "I've been looking for you, Prin."

"And I've led you a merry chase. At least you can call me by my real name now, not the name of your poor brother. I hear he's back on

Gehenna." Prin laughed in a sniveling tone that could never be mistaken for Megal's good humour. "Now get down here."

Kyar didn't move. Prin picked up a skull and brought it down viciously on Mo's leg, the broken one. Mo fainted and Hanis surged to his feet, to lunge at Prin, in flagrant disregard for the dartgun.

"Hanis, don't!" Kyar cried and slid down the slope, desperately trying to formulate a plan. At least Noel was hidden. She was smart and resourceful. She would come up with a way to stop Prin.

Kyar approached his cousin. When he was about ten feet away, Prin said, "Stop right there." He aimed the dartgun at Kyar, who froze in his tracks. "Drop your weapons, all of them, and empty your pockets."

Kyar did, not wanting Mo to get pummeled again, or worse.

"Where is Klaus?" Prin asked. He was awfully well informed.

"Dead, about a mile down the tunnel. He died of his injuries, from the fall into this pit, I would guess, unless you killed him."

"If I had killed him, I wouldn't be asking about him, now would I." Prin narrowed his eyes until they were slits. Even though he wore Megal's beautiful skin, he did not look nearly as attractive. It had to do with the pinched expression around the mouth, and Prin was looking even more peevish than usual.

"What do you want from us?" Kyar demanded. "I've already delivered the nanos to the end of this tunnel—the nanos that will stop the ice from disappearing." He wasn't sure if it was a mistake to reveal the information, yet talking might grant Noel more time to come up with a way to stop Prin.

Prin's lips pulled down in petulant displeasure. "It is no matter now. I've found what I was searching for, but it is not what I expected to find." Prin picked up a femur, the longest leg bone found in a human. He ran his thumb over the length, shaking his head in regret.

"What are all these bones?" Kyar asked, "Do you know?"

"I do, and I'm going to bury this whole graveyard, as soon as your mate repairs my Scarnivian moler." He shifted his dartgun to point at Hanis. "Blasted machine broke down, just when I was starting to plug the tunnel to this bone pile." With no forewarning, Prin tossed the femur to Kyar. "Have a look."

Kyar caught the bone and ran his light over it, examining it. Lightly etched lines marked the surface, running the length of the bone—straight and true lines. The bone had not been gnawed on by a hungry predator with fangs.

He ran his thumb over the etched lines, as Prin had done. They looked to have been made by a very sharp blade. He dropped the bone and picked up a smaller rib that was lying by his boot. He held it close to his light. It had been cut cleanly through and had the same linear marks as the femur. He approached the sloping wall of the pit and pried out a skull, seeming absorbed, while edging a little closer to Prin. The skull was bashed in like the other one they had seen. He held the skull in his hand and turned to Prin. "Did all these humans die unnaturally?"

"Every last one." In a fit of temper, Prin picked up another bone and heaved it at Kyar, who ducked.

"But there are thousands upon thousands of skeletons."

"And you can read the marks as well as I can, cousin. You know exactly what happened to these humans." Prin's lips pinched so tight, his mouth was ringed with white.

Kyar nodded. He had hunted all his life, he had carved meat off enough bones to recognize the marks left behind. "So the humans on our planet were hunted in the past. Why does that evidence need to be hidden?" he asked, to keep Prin talking. And he was curious.

"They weren't hunted!" Prin screeched. "Look at the marks again!"

Kyar did. The pattern of lines was very organized. He lined up three femurs. The marks were more or less the same on each bone—repetitive. "Not hunted, butchered," he said.

"I'll let you in on a little secret, cousin. But first - " Prin stood up and motioned for Hanis to start walking up the steep slope. "Out of the pit, both of you." He helped himself to Kyar's light.

Kyar followed Hanis up the slope. Mo wasn't going anywhere, he was still blessedly unconscious. Prin climbed up behind Kyar, keeping a safe distance between them, so Kyar couldn't knock him out with a dislodged skull or something equally hard.

When they all stood together in the tunnel above, Kyar chanced a peek over his shoulder. He couldn't spot Noel in the darkness, on the opposite side of the pit.

"Move. Faster," Prin snapped.

They walked until they reached the split in the tunnel. "That way." Prin indicated the right branch, the one they had not explored. They turned down it. About a dozen steps later, they found the Scarnivian moler. It was almost plugging the tunnel.

"Fix it," Prin ordered Hanis.

"If I can." Hanis looked doubtful.

"Let's hope you can, because if you can't -" He aimed his weapon at Hanis's chest and made a clicking noise with his tongue. Maybe he thought he was being witty. "It comes with its own toolkit, in the rear compartment." Prin stepped aside. "Fetch it," he said to Kyar.

It was a tight fit, but Kyar managed to worm his way between the rock wall and the blade. His clothing saved his skin from being scraped off. He found the small toolkit and tossed it over the blade, to Hanis.

"Try and start the machine since you're there," Prin said.

Kyar climbed into the tiny cab and closed the hatch, sealing himself into the clear bubble. The control board lit up, proving the machine still had power. Kyar pressed the button labeled with the universal symbol for 'start'. The moler blade turned once, weakly. The cutting lasers flickered and blinked off.

Hanis raised a hand signaling 'stop'. Kyar pushed the door open and waited, holding his position while Hanis dumped out the toolkit. He scowled at the meager contents. Through the bubble, Kyar could see small pliers, an adjustable wrench, a skinny screwdriver, and what must have been the tiniest laser in the Universe.

"Not much here, but I'll do my best," Hanis said.

Kyar didn't care if Hanis ever got the machine working. He hoped the added delay might let Noel stop Prin, somehow.

"Repair the moler or I'll shoot you full of fuzion nanos," Prin said matter-of-factly. "And that is a fate worse than death," he added, as if they didn't already know.

Hanis said, "Try the engine again."

Kyar pressed the button. The round blade rotated about a foot and ground to a halt. The lasers flared once and went out.

"Well?" Prin demanded petulantly.

"It looks like the blade has come unseated. It's no longer balanced. I need access to the whole machine to repair it," Hanis stated. "It's too boxed in here to work on it, isn't it?"

"Tow the machine, then," Prin snapped. "The tunnel is wider at the fork. It's not far. Kyar, you push."

Kyar moved to the rear and shoved on the back of the bubble. Hanis donned his leather mittens, gripped an edge of the blade, and pulled. Prin helped by spouting more threats and waving his dartgun carelessly around. The machine inched forward, slowly.

By the time the moler sat in the wider fork in the path, both men were drenched in sweat, despite the dank chill in the air. Hanis moved around the blade and Kyar whispered, "Take your time. If you can stop Prin without destroying Megal's clone, do it." Hanis winked his agreement.

"Sit there," Prin barked at Kyar, pointing across the tunnel.

Kyar lowered himself to the ground and rested his back against the rock, about eight feet from Prin's false face. "You were going to tell me a secret," he reminded his cousin, hoping to distract Prin from watching Hanis.

"Ah yes. About the original Green World, and about the Spread. Quite a story, but no-one will ever know it, except us." Prin sighed and stared pensively off into the distance. For just a moment, he looked exactly like Megal. Kyar closed his eyes in pain, wishing that it was his brother with him, unravaged by all the harm done to him.

"The Ice Planet is the original Green World," Prin said baldly, yet without the elation Kyar would have expected.

Kyar's eyes widened. "You've found proof?"

"You've seen the proof."

So far, Prin wasn't telling much of a story.

"The bones," Kyar stated. It was the only thing of note in Prin's excavated tunnel.

"Yes. The Spread had a very different purpose from what humans have always believed. Very different." Prin sat down and laid his weapon across his lap.

Since Prin had mentioned the Spread in the same breath as the bones, Kyar made a not so wild guess. "Humans were deposited around the Universe for a different reason?"

"As food. We were nothing but meat!" Prin ground out. "And this original Green World was home to those who fed on us. It was their home as well as ours. This planet is nothing but a wasteland of death, where we were conquered and butchered for meat!"

"You couldn't have figured all of that out from the bones, so how do you know?" Kyar truly was interested in hearing Prin's answer.

"I've been trying to prove that the Ice Planet is the original Green World for years. I've gathered historical data from so many planets and species that I've lost count. I've found clues, bits and pieces—things that made no sense, until I discovered this bone-yard on my way out of the tunnel, after I'd deposited my nanos. I was curious enough to do some additional excavating, examined the bones, dated the strata layers … and now I know." Prin was paying no attention to Hanis.

"What species butchered us as food? What species called the Ice Planet home when it really was a green world? Did you find out?"

"Of course I found out. I know exactly which species devoured us by the millions and planted us across the Universe, so they wouldn't have to cart their food around when they became a race of space travelers, after their sun cooled and their world froze.

"Are you going to keep me in suspense?" Kyar demanded.

"You have one of their descendants riding aboard your ship," Prin hissed.

"Who?"

"The green fellow—Oran'Jay. The poisoner," Prin spat out with a spray of spittle.

Kyar frowned. "Oran'Jay is half-human."

"But the rest of him is Amphaxion. In its pure form, the race was a lot bigger and stronger. They diluted their bloodline, travelling and breeding indiscriminately with any species whose women would open their legs to them. In latter times, they even began to breed with their meat source." Prin curled his lip like a rabid wolf. "Worthless beings. As if they could ever be better than humans. As if any race could ever be better than us. We've survived and thrived, we've populated the Universe, we've proven our superiority. No-one needs to know our shameful beginnings, that we were livestock once. Meat! No-one will ever know our planet was once a blood-red slaughtering ground."

"So you're going to bury the evidence. Wise move." Kyar nodded his approval. "You're right, no-one does need to know this humiliating ancient history."

Prin slumped back into the wall, strangling his dartgun. "Hanis, how are the repairs coming?" he bellowed.

"Too soon to tell," Hanis called back.

Prin needed more distracting. "It's ironic that you're the one who unearthed the proof that our race began as nothing but conveniently placed meat. And now you'll have to hide the evidence that this is the original Green World." Kyar chuckled. Prin raised the gun and pointed it at his head.

Before Prin could shoot, the Scarnivian moler blade spun once, then twice. It picked up momentum until it was an invisible whirl. The collection of lasers flashed and flickered through the spinning blade, ready to vaporize tracks of solid earth, leaving the rest to be displaced by the yulithium blade.

If they didn't need Megal's clone, Hanis could have simply chased Prin down the tunnel and chopped him into tiny little bits. Alas, that was not an option.

Hanis turned off the moler and stepped around the blade. "It's working for now, but I can't say how much longer it will hold up. The whole machine is shoddily put together. The parts are cheap, and you've made miles of tunnels already—I'm surprised it's lasted this long. Anyway, I might need to repair it again, just warning you," Hanis said, holding up his hands as if in surrender. "So don't get mad at me if it breaks down again. I can fix it again."

Prin snorted. "You had better hope so. Walk ahead of the moler, back to your pal Mo."

Kyar had a very bad feeling about walking in front of the destructive vehicle, especially when the driver was someone he wouldn't trust to hand him a soup spoon.

As soon as Prin stepped into the cab, Kyar grabbed his light and shouted, "Run!" Hanis was already moving. Together they pelted back toward Mo. The moler immediately gave chase. It moved faster than Kyar would have expected. He had to run hard, belly bouncing like jelly.

Hanis gasped out, "I repaired the moler, but I made a little change to the cabin."

"What?" Kyar panted.

"Prin won't be able to get out. Door won't open from the inside, and the bubble is shatter-proof." Hanis grinned like a rogue. Kyar would have hugged him, if they hadn't been running for their lives.

"You guessed he would bury us with the bones?" Kyar said.

"It was as obvious as the nose on my face. That's why I told him he might need me to repair his moler again. Didn't want him to kill me back there." Hanis stopped talking to run harder. The moler was gaining. The brilliant laser beams flashed too close to their heels, spraying up chunks of earth. The whole tunnel was filled with blinding, flickering flashes of light.

"Almost at the pit." Kyar skidded to a stop when he nearly ran right over the edge. And Mo was gone!

"Climb down." Hanis shoved Kyar when the moler seemed about to run them right off the ragged edge of land. Kyar scrambled down the slope with Hanis, barely ahead of the jutting, spinning blade that would have made mincemeat of them. The moler skidded to a halt, the blade jutting dangerously out over the pit. The blade turned off, and the silence was a relief. The machine made one heck of a racquet. Its running lights stayed on, lighting up the whole scene as if it was daytime.

Prin was struggling to get out of the cab. When he couldn't, he began hammering his fists against the clear bubble, as if he was having a child's tantrum. When that did no good, Prin lifted his dartgun. He pointed it at them. It was no blaster, and even a blaster wouldn't have penetrated the shatter-proof cab. Hanis saluted, a huge grin on his sweaty face.

Prin reacted. With a snarl, he tossed his gun down and hit switches. There was a loud click below the track. The blade roared back to life, spinning in reverse. Prin drove the vehicle against the tunnel wall. Debris began to spray into the pit, pelting Kyar and Hanis. It felt like they were standing in a bruising hailstorm. They retreated out of range.

"What's he doing?" Kyar asked Hanis.

"Plugging the tunnel. Given enough time, he'll seal the passage with rock and earth."

"And trap us on the wrong side, with no way out," Kyar cried. But it would take a while. "You fixed that moler a little too well, I'm thinking. Or did you make any other adjustments?"

"I didn't have time."

When someone tapped Kyar on the shoulder, he jumped a foot.

Noel was standing right behind him. He hadn't heard her at all. Given the noise the moler was making, he wouldn't have heard an army thundering up behind him.

"Where's Mo?" he asked.

"A little further into the tunnel back there. It almost killed us both to get him up the slope, but I'm glad we did." The place where Mo had lain was rapidly being buried in rubble.

"I'll go check on him," Hanis said. He climbed the slope and disappeared into the darkness.

"What now?" Noel asked.

"What now," Kyar repeated, wishing he knew. "Well, Prin is trapped inside the cab of the moler, but it can still move. He's sealing the tunnel, trapping us down here."

Noel studied the machine in action and rubbed a hand across her eyes, leaving a streak of dirt. "How is Prin trapped in the cab?" she asked.

"Hanis disabled the handle on the inside, simple but effective."

"So he really can't get out at all," she said, as if it was important.

"Nope. What are you plotting?" Kyar nudged her with an elbow. In answer, she reached over her shoulder and produced a blaster. "Where did that come from?" he asked.

"Klaus had it stashed in his pack. I searched it, looking for something to help us, while you were keeping Prin company. I found a spare light, and this. Could we blast the moler?"

Kyar shook his head. "The bubble is shatter-proof, and even if it wasn't, I won't risk killing Megal's clone." That was not an option.

They watched the moler until Hanis slid back down the slope to join them. "How's Mo?" Kyar asked.

"As comfortable as he can be. He's passed out -"

Noel cut him off. "Hanis, we need to stop that machine. What's the best way to shut it down? From outside the cab?"

"I don't know if there is a way." Hanis scratched his chin and watched the Scarnivian moler move to the opposite side of the tunnel and dig in.

"If we blasted the blade, would Prin be safe in the cab?" Noel was back to that.

"Probably. Or you could blast the ground under the moler. It's close to the edge of the pit. The moler might fall right in. The clone should be secure enough inside the cab."

Noel glanced at Kyar, a deep frown-line between her eyebrows. "I think we have to risk it. We can't let Prin seal us in the tunnel. He'll escape and that won't help Megal, will it. And it certainly won't help us."

Kyar thought about it until the earth shook hard. A cascade of rock came down around them. They huddled together, their backs pressed against the far side of the slope. The shaking strengthened, followed by a terrifying rumble that sounded like it was all around them. The ice above must be collapsing in on itself. But was the tunnel deep enough in the earth to be unaffected?

The shaking tapered off. The ground stilled and the rumbling echoed to silence. The tunnel had held. Kyar released a breath he hadn't been aware of holding. "I think it's over. Everyone okay?"

"Yes, and I think the ice gods have intervened at the opportune moment." Noel was smiling. Kyar followed her gaze and gasped. The Scarnivian moler was teetering on an edge of cracked ground. Noel aimed the nose of the blaster at the rock beneath the moler tracks and fired. That was all it took to bring the machine crashing into the bottom of the pit.

A triumphant whoop split the air, from Hanis, almost loud enough to bring down more rock. Kyar didn't cheer, he was too afraid that the clone had been damaged beyond repair.

They scrambled over loosely piled earth to reach the moler. It was lying on its side. The cab had survived the fall—and so had Prin. He was groggy and moving restlessly.

"Let's restrain him while we can," Kyar said.

Hanis yanked open the door and hauled Prin out by the scruff of the neck. He strapped Prin's hands ruthlessly behind his back, with the fellow's own belt. Kyar retrieved the dartgun from the moler. He tucked it safely away in his pack. He almost couldn't believe they had finally captured Prin, and mainly unharmed.

"Tie his ankles, too," Kyar said. He wasn't taking any chances.

Hanis yanked a loose wire from the moler's undercarriage and lashed Prin's ankles together. Prin's slitted eyes fell closed. He seemed to pass out completely.

Hanis tossed Prin over his shoulder and said, "I can't carry Mo, too, and we need to get out of this tunnel before it collapses."

"I know. We'll manage Mo. You just worry about getting Prin out," Kyar said.

Hanis started struggling up the slope. Kyar and Noel went to get Mo. As gently as they could manage, they maneuvered him between them, down into the pit and up again. At least he'd had a double dose of orange pills. He was barely conscious, and it was for the best.

The slow, limping group struggled through the tunnel that was now littered with crushed piles of rock and bone. They were able to move a little faster when they got past the debris. Halfway to the surface, they met up with a search party. Some of the crew from the FarGone 5 had come to find them, proving the tunnel to the outside world was still open.

"Borelle, Oran'Jay! Wonderful to see you," Kyar cried.

"Likewise. And look who you've captured!" Oran'Jay cackled and poked at Prin.

Borelle was quick to scoop up the groggy Mo, relieving them of their burden.

"Thanks. How much further?" Kyar gasped, struggling for breath.

"Not too far." Oran'Jay yanked Prin's head up and smacked him across the face until he woke up.

"Don't hurt the clone," Kyar said.

"I can hurt him a bit." Oran'Jay grinned and punched Prin in the face. He released the hair and Prin's head flopped against Hanis's back, lolling loosely. "Now, let's bring that worthless brother of yours a present."

Kyar couldn't wait to do just that.

Part 3 - Megal

13. Twice Cursed

had no intention of living the hell of Gehenna twice. I planned to die quickly, and get it over with. Yet each day led into the next, and as much as Oran'Jay's little pill called to me so seductively, I resisted the temptation. But oh, I loved that little pill. I cherished it and kept it tucked in my cheek. One hard bite and my suffering would be over. The pill was my salvation, especially when I was sent to the tunnels to harvest the fuel from the blast beetle larvae. I tried to explain to the guards that I had already done my time in those tunnels. They didn't care, nor did they believe me, even though I now sported two prisoner's brands, proving this wasn't my first stint on Gehenna.

At that point, I led a gang of prisoners in an escape attempt, trying to tunnel around the blast beetles and under the thick stone walls—as if there was anywhere to go after that. It was doomed to fail. The guards caught us and we were strung up and whipped, and assigned another month in the tunnels. I was held responsible. My fellow prisoners took their own revenge. It was far worse than anything the guards had done.

After I could no longer speak, the pill began to whisper to me, a sweet sweet voice in my head. I gave it a name—Sugar. By that time, I was talking to it inside my head. I knew I was losing my mind, as so many did on the hell planet, yet I couldn't stop my sanity from slipping away. Sugar's voice soothed me when I needed it most, and that voice was soon a part of me. I lost track of time.

And one day, a grand ship appeared overhead. It was circled by smaller vessels and they were coming down to land. Had I been on Gehenna for one year? Surely not. For some reason, it struck me as hilarious that I had been on Gehenna for a year and still lived. I laughed until tears ran down my face. I was losing precious moisture, yet I couldn't stop laughing.

Sugar told me to hush. She didn't like it when I made a spectacle of myself. I tried to stop laughing and started sobbing instead, a wreck of a man bawling in the dirt. One year. Was that not long enough? 'Sugar? Can I go now? Will you take me away?' *No, not yet. Hush Baby.* 'Please Sugar?' *No Baby, you can hang on a little longer. Get up. Go in a cave if you're going to cry.*

The conversation in my head was interrupted by several guards. "Nomad Megal?" One bowed before he kicked me. Everyone knew who I was—the object of ridicule.

The other yanked me to my feet.

They took me into a section of the prison that was normally off-limits to the inmates. It was cooler within the thick stone walls. I was shoved into a large underground room, sparsely furnished and filled with elegant bodies—the minister of the prison, countless official types, and Kyar. Kyar was there, or I was imagining him.

They stopped their intense conversation when I limped in. Kyar approached and touched me gently on the shoulder. He was wearing a Nomad's robe. He was a lot chubbier than I remembered, and his eyes were so sad. 'Kyar, it's so good to see you.' *He can't hear you, Baby.* 'He can't?' *No, now shush. Listen to what they're saying.*

My ears still worked, yet I had trouble following the train of the conversation. Kyar was doing most of the talking, presenting documents to the officials. Someone else was escorted in. It was me, as beautiful as an angel. 'Look, Sugar. I can go now. I'm an angel.' *That's not you, Baby. That's Prin.*

I started shivering hard, because the room was so cold, or maybe because Prin's malevolent gaze felt like a frozen blade scraping across my skin. I edged closer to Kyar and tried to say my brother's name. All I could do was grunt.

Kyar heard me and put a big warm arm around my shaking skin. His jaw clenched and he released me, but only to remove his Nomad's robe. He draped it over my shoulders. It swamped me, but it was so warm and smelled like my brother. I pulled it tight around me, like a security blanket, and rubbed my face on the so-soft fur.

Kyar shared a few clipped words with the prison officials, before he guided me out the door. He moved half a pace behind, following protocol, leaving me to lead the way. I wasn't capable of walking alone and turned to my brother, waiting for him to guide me.

He swallowed hard and stepped close again. "We'll walk together," he said, and linked arms with me. He started moving at my limping pace.

'Where is he taking me, Sugar?' *Home Baby, I think he's taking you home.* 'I want to go home.' *I know, I know you do. You'll be home soon.*

I walked with Kyar, out of the prison. Behind us, Ice Guards flanked Prin on both sides, all the way to a spacecraft. It was not the FarGone 5. It was much bigger and as lavish as a ship can get—the flagship Glacius. I yearned for the shelter of the FarGone 5.

Inside the hatch, lining the extravagantly wide corridor, the crew stood at attention—Hanis, Mo, Borelle, Oran'Jay, Greely, and many I didn't recognize. Even Noel was there, with tears in her eyes. I had missed Noel, and thought about her a lot on Gehenna.

'What are they all doing here, Sugar?' *I think they're escorting the Nomad home.* 'Me?' *Yes, Baby.*

Silently, Kyar moved me through the bodies, who greeted me with affection and emotion. And so much damn pity in their eyes. I just kept walking with Kyar and Sugar, ending up in an elaborate medical chamber. Prin came in there, too, with his escort. The Ice Guards chained his wrists and ankles to a surgical table, before they departed.

Sugar wanted me to look my cousin in the eyes, so I limped closer. My own face sneered back, triumphant despite the prone position, and the chains. Some superficial scrapes and bruises marred the beautiful skin, but nothing that wouldn't be healed in a week.

"Look at you, Megal," Prin drawled. "I don't think I've ever seen a more pitiful sight. You have no idea how pleased I am that you haven't died yet." He did look pleased.

Kyar moved to my side. "Are those really the last words you want to speak, Prin? No request for forgiveness? No apology?"

"Never." Prin studied me for a long moment. "Your brother is quite mad, you know. I can see it in his eyes. You're a fool to place him back in charge of the planets."

"The planets were ruled by a mad fool for three long years. Now they will finally be ruled by the only one who should be Nomad," Kyar declared loyally.

If I could have spoken the words, I would have told Kyar that I was mad, and undeserving. Sugar wanted me to touch Prin, make sure he was real.

I reached out and felt Prin's smooth cheek with my palm. My grotesquely broken and bent fingers had been chewed by rats. Rot had

179

set in. They smelled foul and looked horrific against his smooth pale skin—my smooth pale skin. My other hand was in even worse condition. I had been robbed of several more fingers by the prisoners who had taken my tongue. And what they had done to me with those severed fingers …

Don't think about that, Baby. Never ever. Sugar's soft whisper soothed me.

Prin jerked back as far as his restraints would allow. "Keep your monster of a brother away from me, Kyar!"

"I would beat you to death if you weren't wearing Megal's skin. But I've come up with a better idea. Greely suggested it, actually, and it's brilliant." Kyar put an arm around my shoulders as if to prepare me.

"A fate worse than death, I'm sure," Prin said.

"You call Megal a monster. Well, you will be that monster soon. Once your brain is removed from the clone, we're going to put it right here." He touched the top of my bald, scabbed head.

Prin refused the offer with a curled lip. "No thanks. That would be a fate worse than death."

"Do you really think this is a choice you get to make, Prin? It has already been arranged. Greely is preparing to perform the operation as we speak." Kyar looked at me. "Is that okay with you Megal, if we put Prin in your … ruined body? We need him alive a little longer, there is a problem on the Ice Planet, and he is the only one who has the information that will help us," Kyar said vaguely. "He hasn't been willing to share his secret, and we haven't wanted to torture it out of him, not while he is wearing your skin. Once he is out of your clone, we will make him reveal the truth. So, is it okay?"

'Is it okay, Sugar?' *Sure, it's okay.* I nodded my head.

"After he has told us where we can find what we need, you can have him sent to Gehenna, or iced, or jettisoned into open space. It will be your choice, Megal." Kyar kept a steady arm around me.

I nodded again because Sugar told me to.

"Greely is going to perform the surgery, to switch your brains right now. Your body is in pretty bad shape. I'm sure you can't wait to be healthy and whole again. Are you ready?"

'Am I ready, Sugar?' *Yes, Baby.* I nodded, wishing I had a tongue to tell my brother that I loved him. I rested my head on his shoulder.

"Megal, I'm sorry it took so long to get you off Gehenna—again. It shouldn't have taken this long." His eyes were so much older than the last time I had seen them.

180

'It's okay, Kyar,' I wanted to say. All I could do was grunt.

His face tightened and he kissed my cheek. "We'll talk soon. You'll have to tell me how you lost your tongue."

I shook my head. Never would I tell him that morbid story.

Greely bustled in, as rough and casual as ever, yet avoiding my eyes most determinedly. He told me to lie on the second palette. Once I was prone and feeling helpless, he ushered my brother away. I tried to say, 'Don't leave me, Kyar.' He didn't hear my pathetic whimper. I missed him as soon as he was gone.

Greely seemed hurried. "Relax, Megal," he advised me. The ice bed was freezing, which made it hard to do so. His hands were shaking when he injected me with a sedative. I didn't think that boded well for the coming brain surgery.

"I am sorry, Megal, if it means anything," he said, as I sank into a cold dark lake in my mind. 'Can I go now, Sugar?' *Yes, Baby.* I kept sinking, all the way to the deep, black frozen bottom of nowhere. Prin laughed all the while. Perhaps he was as mad as I was. It took days to float back to the world of noise and light.

I awoke disoriented. The world came back to me in fragments. Making sense of it was like trying to fit the pieces of a puzzle together, while seriously drunk. 'Where am I?' Sugar was still tucked high between my gum and cheek, but she didn't answer me. 'Where am I?' I fought to open my eyes. Everything was blurry and slow to come into focus.

Voices were talking around me, talking about me. Kyar and Greely were doing the talking. Noel was the first to notice that my eyes were opened. She said, "Prin is awake."

Kyar stepped fully into view. "Finally." There was no affection on his face, quite the opposite. And why was I being misnamed Prin? I tried to ask, and grunted. Wasn't I supposed to have a whole tongue by now? I gazed at Kyar helplessly.

Someone appeared behind his shoulder—me. No Prin. He was still in my clone, and I remained in my ruined skin. And Prin was walking around freely. 'Sugar, what's happening?' Suddenly, she was there again. *I don't know, Baby, but I don't think it's good.*

"How is he?" Kyar asked Greely.

The surgeon stepped closer and checked me over, still avoiding my eyes. "The patient seems fine. He's recovered from the transfer." The doctor disappeared from my limited field of vision.

"Lovely. Then it is time to lock Prin in the brig," Prin said, as if he had every right to do so. Two guards lifted me off the table and dragged me away. I would have kicked and screamed, except I was still too drugged. Had Greely made a mistake? Mixed-up the brains? It didn't seem possible, or likely. No, Prin must have gotten to the doctor, paid him off somehow, or kidnapped his family. Blackmailed him. Something. It was the only logical explanation. Trust Prin to cook up such a madcap scheme.

The brig on the FarGone 5 was much larger and airier than the space where I ended up. My new cell had black walls and could be crossed in three paces. There were no bars, only a thick solid door without even a window. It had a small slot with a sliding panel. It opened and closed from the outside. The toilet sat in the corner, fully exposed. A narrow bed was the only other thing in the room. It was clean and there was a blanket. The space was more box than cell, yet it was still an infinite improvement over Gehenna. It was all relative, I suppose.

I was shoved inside. The solid door to the isolation chamber was slammed shut. I crawled onto the cot and passed out. Over the next day or two, I did little more than sleep and eat the meager rations that appeared through the slot.

All the injuries I had accumulated on Gehenna, had been tended and bandaged while I was sedated, probably so they wouldn't fester to the point where they killed me. Kyar had said they needed Prin alive, so I was being kept alive, but little more than that.

While unawares, I had also been washed and redressed in soft clean clothes. I'm sure it wasn't for my own comfort, but so that those who had to interact with me, wouldn't have to endure the stench and filth of Gehenna that I had brought aboard on my skin.

Even with the medical attention, my hands were ruined. I had to eat like an animal, slurping directly from my bowl with my mouth. With half my tongue gone, I was also inclined to choke.

I knew my meals were drugged, because every time I ate, I fell asleep for hours. I ate the food anyway. After Gehenna, my body was starved and wasted. Nor was sleep such a bad place to be, especially since my cell was completely rat-free.

When I could stay awake, I talked to Sugar, but even she seemed to be fading from my mind.

I think it was three days before I had a visitor. I was surprised it had taken Prin so long to turn up and gloat. He slid the door closed behind him and leaned against it, gazing down at me with such flagrant delight, he was almost glowing. I sat up on the bed, heart pounding too hard. I had to wait for him to speak, since I couldn't.

"I'm so glad you're still alive," he said significantly, as he had before the surgery. And now I truly understood what he meant. "And I still need you or you would be dead," he hissed.

I didn't doubt it.

"Nothing to say?" He chuckled at what he thought was a witty comment.

I rolled my eyes.

"You will be questioned later today. You will provide the answers that I am about to give you, and as a reward, I will allow you to continue living."

How could anyone believe that continuing to live my life was a reward? I began to laugh like a madman. I laughed hysterically until tears ran down my cheeks, and still I couldn't stop. Prin lost patience and slammed me against the wall, his arm pressed into my throat, stopping my breath. "How's this? As a reward, I won't kill you slowly and painfully. I'll kill you quickly and mercifully."

I didn't believe him for a nano second and shook my head. I had Sugar, if what Prin did to me was truly unbearable. She was still my salvation.

Prin released me with a grimace. He really didn't like to touch me. I dropped down on my cot, exhausted by the wild bout of laughter, and lack of air. Prin moved to the corner furthest from me. "Even clean, you reek of rot. Now, listen well and remember everything I say." He listed the answers I was to provide, when questioned. What he told me was so alarming, it penetrated the numbness that had become so much a part of me, it could have been a cloak I wore.

For the first time, I heard that my planet's surface was cracking apart. The answers Prin wanted me to give would help the Ice Planet—if he was speaking the truth. Yet that made no sense. He claimed to have started the cracks in the planet's perma-ice to prove it was the original Green World, so why would he suddenly want to stop that destruction and abandon his dream? His words confused me. I had no reason to trust my cousin, and every reason to disbelieve what he said.

After he left, I tried to analyze the situation. Owing to the sedatives in the food, I couldn't even stay awake. I curled up in a fetal position and succumbed to sleep.

The next time I awoke, it was because I was being hauled roughly out of my cell. My crushed hands were cuffed behind my back. A small audience was waiting in a larger outer chamber, sitting in a half circle on fur-padded chairs, as if I was to entertain them, perhaps start tap dancing. I giggled at the wayward image.

I was slammed into the only chair that had no fur padding, bruising my bones. It was a lonely chair, facing those I called family and friends—Kyar, Noel, Oran'Jay, Hanis, Mo. There were others that I didn't recognize, stern-faced and glaring. Prin and Greely were also in attendance, I wanted to end them both so badly, I could taste the bitterness welling up in my throat, threatening to choke me. I shifted my gaze, preferring to see my brother. Why was Sephine not seated by his side?

Noel looked tired, with faint circles beneath her eyes, and troubled. The little frown line between her eyebrows was quite evident. She looked lovely to me nonetheless. Mo was battered. Hanis appeared huge after my time with wasted prisoners. I gazed hungrily at them, simply enjoying the sight, until Prin approached. He was playing the part of me—the Nomad Megal. He circled me as if I was his prey, making a show of the questioning. "Prin, you've been treated well, better than you deserve after all the crimes you've committed," he began.

I really hoped that I had never sounded that pompous. I shrugged with false modesty. Perhaps it was the edge of insanity that still clung, but my lips twitched, trying to suppress more laughter. First Prin had masqueraded as me, and now I was supposed to return the favour and pretend to be him. It truly was a ridiculous farce.

Prin kicked the chair. "You have done great damage to the Ice Planet. Two of the cracks are continuing to destroy the southern glacier. We need to know where you have hidden the remaining nanos that will save the planet."

I wasn't even sure why he wanted me to cooperate and act the part of him, unless it was to convince everyone that he really was Megal, since I was Prin. Maybe he suspected that someone was suspicious of him. Kyar had recognized the imposter in my skin in the past. Did he see Prin squatting in my clone now?

Another piece of the puzzle clicked into place in my lumbering thoughts. Prin was the Nomad again. Maybe he really did want to stop his own destruction, and appear a hero, then no-one would doubt that he was me and I was Prin. Plus, he did crave a planet to lord over.

"Will you cooperate? Will you tell us where to find the nanos?"

I nodded, as he had instructed me to do.

Like a magician, Prin produced a tablet with letters and numbers. He held it in front of me, before the witnesses he had assembled. "Point to the letters—name the location."

He had instructed me to communicate that the nanos were hidden on the FarGone 5, although I wasn't sure how I was supposed to do that. My broken fingers were tied behind my back and my nose was so badly smashed in, I didn't even know where it pointed anymore, so how was I supposed to point? I looked at him like he was nuts, and raised an eyebrow questioningly, hoping that one eyebrow could convey a wealth of sarcasm and disdain.

Prin simply removed a mini-beamer from his pocket and stuck the thing in my mouth, between the broken teeth that were all I had left. He had come prepared, and I was supposed to reveal the location of the nanos—the location of his choice.

Alas, I simply hated Prin too much to cooperate, and when Sugar whispered instructions to me, I knew what I had to do. I stopped cooperating. I was going to make sure this scene did not unfold as my evil cousin had plotted, but as Sugar wanted it to.

I spat out the beamer and kicked Prin. He swore and shoved my chair over backwards, with me still in it. The metal deck was as hard as ice when my head bounced off it.

Kyar intervened, as Sugar and I had hoped someone would. He picked up my chair and shoved me back into it, holding me in place. "Point to the letters, where are the nanos," he ordered, replacing the beamer in my mouth. I obligingly pointed at the letters Sugar had proposed, now that Kyar had my back, sort of. And they were not the letters Prin wanted.

"Earth? He stashed the nanos on Earth," Kyar announced to everyone.

"Makes sense," Mo agreed. Oran'Jay nodded. I was glad they agreed with my planet of choice, because I had a very good reason for wanting to travel back there. In spite of all that I had endured, a small corner of my heart must have still believed in miracles.

Prin looked furious enough to strangle me, but he couldn't, not in front of everyone, and not when I appeared to be helping.

"Where on Earth?" Kyar demanded, motioning for Prin to hold the tablet in front of me again.

I wasn't going to reveal that, not until we were a lot closer to the restricted planet. If I withheld the vital information, the rest of the crew would want me kept alive. Prin couldn't kill me yet, not if he planned to produce these nanos that only I supposedly knew the location of.

I needed to be uncooperative again. I just hoped it wasn't going to hurt too much.

Dreading what was to come, I spat out the pointer and kicked Prin again, this time where it would cause the most pain. Prin never had been able to control his temper, and he lost it now, in a big way.

Kyar was still holding me in the chair. Prin used that position to his advantage. He smashed me in the face, once, twice, thrice. He had a brutal punch and hard boney knuckles. Kyar released me when I sagged against him.

'Kyar! Can you see Prin now?' *He can't hear you, Baby.*

Prin hauled me up and out of the chair, so he could pummel me some more. There was no doubt in my mind that he would have beaten me to death if Kyar hadn't intervened.

"Stop, Megal. We need him alive. He's the only one who knows where the nanos are. Stop!" Kyar said most commandingly.

Prin let me go. And Kyar hadn't recognized Prin. I dropped to my knees and started sobbing, sounding more animal than man. My heart was breaking. It hurt more that Prin's blows. Big green feet crossed my field of vision. Had Oran'Jay been about to jump into the fray? Prin had knocked out one of my remaining teeth. It gave me an inspired idea. 'Goodbye, Sugar.' I spat a mouthful of blood, a tooth, and a small silver capsule right in front of those big green feet, praying Oran'Jay had sharp eyes.

I was dragged away, before I had a chance to see if he had found my gift.

It was two long days before Oran'Jay came to see me, and by then, I had given up hope. When the door opened in the middle of the night, I was relatively alert. Much of my drugged food was now going directly down the toilet. I wasn't sleeping nearly as much, but I was hungry enough to eat my pillow.

Oran'Jay slipped silently into my cell, and eased the door almost closed.

I whispered, 'Frog'. It came out as a grunt.

"Who are you?" he whispered sourly.

I raised my hands questioningly. How did he expect me to answer that question? Returning his little pill should have proven who I was.

He reworded the question. "Megal, is that really you?"

186

I rolled my eyes and nodded impatiently.

"Slush, I wish you could talk."

'Me too, Frog.' Grunt.

"Do you know what Prin is up too?"

I nodded and shrugged at the same time. I had some idea.

"Greely must be in on this, faking the surgery?"

I nodded again, emphatically.

Oran'Jay paced twice across the tiny space. "Okay. Your cell is guarded around the clock. Guess Prin doesn't want anyone talking to you, not that you can talk." Oran'Jay peeked outside the door. "I only put the guards to sleep for a couple of minutes. I didn't want them to figure out they'd been drugged. I'm going to have a couple of drinks with Greely. Slip a few extra red drops into his brandy and buddy up to him. He'll spill his secrets. The man can't hold his liquor worth shit."

I raised my hands at him, in a questioning manner.

"I need proof that you are Megal, before I'll help you," he declared.

I pantomimed removing the pill from my mouth. I had given him proof.

"More proof. If Greely confirms your tale, I'll be back to talk. I'll bring one of those lettered tablets next time. Or can you hold a pencil?"

I waved my gruesome, mangled hands in front of his face.

"Guess not. I'm starting to think you are Megal, the way you're acting all ornery."

With another guttural growl, I flung myself back on the bed.

Oran'Jay chuckled and left. Even though he might be my saviour, I still didn't like him. I liked him even less when he didn't show up for two more days.

He arrived in the middle of the night again, with all the stealth of his previous visit. This time I was asleep and dreaming of rats. I awoke with a holler. His hand clamped over my mouth almost smothering me.

"Shush and listen. It took two days to get Greely alone, and half a bottle of red brandy, and then some, but he's blurted out the truth. He was paid a bloody fortune to leave Prin's brain exactly where it was." Oran'Jay sounded terrified. "Now that I know what's going on, I'll help you. We can't have Prin ruling, or misruling, again." He paced, his big feet slapping the deck. "The main problem now is that Prin is in charge of the Ice Guard and all the ships, and every bloody thing on your nine planets. They'll listen to him. They have to, so I'll have to act in secret.

As soon as I leave here, I'll wake Kyar up and tell him what the hell is going on."

I gripped Oran'Jay's arms between my palms, as firmly as I could. I looked into his face, raising my eyebrows in a question, desperately wishing I could speak again. He took a guess at what I was asking. "I haven't told Kyar yet, haven't told anyone. Is that what you want to know?"

The cell door rattled. We both jerked in that direction. It opened quietly, and I had a second visitor—a most unwelcome one. I prayed I was still having a nightmare, but I knew I wasn't.

Prin looked delighted by what he found. "Bit late for a visit, Oran'Jay. I was wondering why the guards were asleep on their feet. Now I know. What are you doing here?" he asked, as if he didn't know.

"I felt an urge to get the truth out of Prin. I was going to torture him until he spilled his guts, one way or another. We need to know the location of the nanos," Oran'Jay lied, and quite well.

Prin slid the door shut behind him. "Greely mentioned that you'd had drinks with him this evening, a lot of drinks. He was rather surprised to fall asleep in the middle of your visit. When he awoke, you were gone. He thought he might have opened his big mouth. Up to your old tricks, Oran'Jay?" Prin stepped closer. A small dartgun appeared in his hand. It looked like a toy, but we all knew it wasn't.

Oran'Jay backed up a step, there was no room to go further. "Fuzion nanos?" he gulped.

"Yes, but I won't shoot you unless I have to," Prin said calmly—too calmly. Oran'Jay nodded, eyes fixed on the gun. I simply shook my head at Prin, all I could do. "Have you told anyone else that Megal is the one locked in this cell?" Prin asked.

"No, no. I haven't had a chance. And I won't, I promise I won't. I have a family waiting for me." Oran'Jay shot me an apologetic glance. "I won't tell anyone, not if you let me go."

Prin appeared to be thinking it over. "You need to get home to all your little Amphaxions?"

Neither of us knew what Prin was talking about. "Little Amphaxions?" Oran'Jay said.

"Nothing you need to worry about. You can leave, I'll stay and have a chat with Megal. But don't tell anyone what you know. I control this ship and everyone aboard, so keep your mouth shut or you'll join Megal in the brig. Clear?" Prin opened the door and Oran'Jay rushed for it.

I didn't believe that Prin was letting Oran'Jay go, but I couldn't stop his hasty retreat. When Oran'Jay passed Prin, Prin clapped him on the shoulder as if they were pals. The dartgun didn't fire, yet Oran'Jay collapsed to the ground, writhing in agony. The writhing became twitching, then nothing—not even the sound of laboured breathing. Oran'Jay was quite dead.

Prin raised his left hand in a flashy gesture, displaying a tiny object. "Goran spine. I heard you almost killed Sephine with one. I guess you had acquired another one on Gehenna, and kept it hidden on your person, and Prin found it. Now Prin has killed Oran'Jay the same way. The crew won't like that, will they?"

My temper exploded and I lunged for him. Prin was quicker. He dropped the spine and jerked the door shut, sealing me in with Oran'Jay's corpse, and the evidence of how he had died.

Out of control, I attacked the door, banging and kicking and howling like a lunatic. I didn't even have Sugar to comfort me. She was gone. I made enough noise to wake the guards—not the smartest thing I could have done. They opened the door to investigate and found a green body on my floor. And Prin was right, I was believed to be the murderer. Since I was the only person locked in the cell with the body, there really was no question as to my guilt.

Prin and Kyar were summoned immediately, with no regard for the fact that it was the middle of the ship's night. Enough of a hew and cry went up that others were roused from sleep. Some of them were curious enough to trot along to the brig. Noel arrived as Prin and Kyar were leaving my cell. Prin was doing a stellar job of acting tragic and comforting Kyar. Prin—the murderer! I hated him so completely that it filled my chest and I could barely breathe.

The guards dragged me out of my cell and Prin made a show of this moment, too. "You have murdered one of the loyal members of my crew. That crime will not go unpunished," he orated. "You will reveal where the nanos are hidden, and tomorrow you will pay for murdering Oran'Jay. You will pay with your life."

I shook my head, denying my crime.

"You deserve no mercy. Your fate is mine to decide. Tomorrow, you will carry the murdered man's soul to the stars." His words were vague, almost poetic, yet I knew exactly what he meant to do with me, as did everyone. Some gasped. It was a cruel and outdated punishment, one that I had heard only pirates still embraced. The murderer, in this case me, was space-suited up with a supply of air, lashed to the body of his victim, and set adrift. It took days to die, slowly and agonizingly, drifting in space with only a corpse for company. I shook my head wildly.

Prin didn't lay a hand on me in front of the others. Perhaps he doubted his ability to control his violent streak. He turned to Kyar and said, "I'm going to get the truth out of Prin, now. And alone. This won't be pretty, but I won't kill him. I want Prin alive to suffer his punishment."

Kyar made no protest on my behalf, proving he still didn't have a clue that Prin continued to wear my skin. Prin ordered everyone back to their rooms. My hands were lashed behind my back, before he followed me into my cell and sealed the door.

A forceful shove from behind sent me sprawling face-down on the floor. Prin claimed the only comfortable surface—my cot. I tried to rise and his boot heels dug into my back, as if I was his own personal footstool. "Stay there. We've got a few hours to kill before your punishment will be carried out. I can lament poor Oran'Jay's passing at the same time. I'm so glad I had a chance to kill the Amphaxion," he drawled.

My face was pressed against the floor, but I could hear the satisfaction in his voice. Everything was unfolding as he had plotted. Prin began to ramble on about what he had discovered on the Ice Planet. I was shocked to learn that my home truly was the original Green World, but not in the way Prin had dreamed. And I finally understood why he was willing to cough up the nanos to stop the ice from disappearing. He didn't want any evidence coming to light—evidence that proved our race began as nothing but lowly prey, and had been seeded across the Universe as a convenient food source.

I began to laugh again and couldn't stop. Prin's dream had transformed to become his worst nightmare. Now he was trying to hide the evidence of the truth he had dedicated his life to revealing. He had ruined my life for *this*! I laughed harder, the madness creeping closer and closer.

Prin didn't like my noise. He stood up, on my back. He wasn't the biggest man, but I wasn't strong after Gehenna. I couldn't draw any air into my lungs. I writhed wildly, fighting to dislodge his weight. I must have passed out before I could. A fist banging on the cell door roused me. I groaned and rolled onto my side, so I could watch Prin open the door.

Kyar stood outside with Noel. "We wanted to make sure you were unharmed," he said, entering uninvited. The tiny room was getting crowded, and I was taking up most of the floor space.

Noel added to the crush, carrying the lettered tablet. She said, "We thought you might need this, to learn where the nanos are hidden."

"The tablet will come in handy. Thanks for bringing it."

Noel laid it on the cot and Prin pointedly motioned them toward the door. I had regained enough strength in my legs to kick out at Prin, tripping him. He hit the wall with a hard thud. I laughed.

As I had hoped, his true character was revealed. He kicked me where I lay, more than once, his face all twisted up in rage, his cheeks flushed an ugly purple.

Noel laid a hand on his arm. "Megal, get the truth out of him before you kill him."

Prin had not vented all of his temper yet. He flung her hand off. "If you don't like it, you don't have to bloody watch," he snarled, right in her face, spraying spittle on it.

She backed up a step and wiped her cheek. "I know you hate him, I know your cousin has made your life a living hell, but the Ice Planet still needs to be saved."

Prin's mouth pinched. "You're right," he said magnanimously, making an obvious effort to calm himself. "Don't worry, I'll get the truth out of him, and in a few hours, he will suffer the fate he deserves."

Noel nodded, and my brother and my wife left me alone with Prin again. At least he was calmer. He reclaimed the bed. I was still assigned the role of footstool. I pointed at the tablet, trying to ignore the waves of pain surging through my frame. Both the toes and heels on Prin's boots felt as hard as hammers.

"You want to talk? Some final words, Megal?"

I nodded.

He leaned forward, elbows on knees, holding the tablet so I could see it. Noel had thoughtfully included the small pointer. I rationed my words to one—nanos.

"Wondering what's going on, are you?"

I nodded.

"Then I'll tell you. Once I've apparently broken you and you've revealed the exact and true location of the nanos, I'll save the Ice Planet and hide the evidence of our pathetic history. I'll be a hero after I save the planet. I can't wait to rule again. It's great being you, Megal."

No, it wasn't great being me. It was a hell that seemed to have no end, but he didn't notice the irony in his own words. I signaled 'nanos' for a second time, adding the word 'where'.

Prin deigned to tell me, so I could admire his cleverness, I suppose. "I had the only remaining vial of the nanos on me, when I was captured by your brother. I was quick to stash it, before I was searched and locked in the brig on the FarGone 5."

I repeated the word 'where'. I suspected Prin was dragging this out, because he liked to watch my pathetic struggles to transmit the most basic information.

"The big fellow—Hanis, he carried me out over his shoulder."

I nodded, I had experienced the same ride myself in what seemed like another lifetime.

"I managed to slip the little vial into the lining of the ratty fur coat he was wearing. There was a little tear in the seam, just big enough to slide the vial through. Once I was free—once I was *you*, I searched his room on this vessel, but he must have left the coat in his quarters on the FarGone 5, and that is where you'll tell me the vial is located. I'll retrieve it from that ship and stop the ice from deteriorating and continue to rule as Nomad again." Prin gloated as well he might. It was a good plan, with little risk once I was forever silenced.

Alas, Prin would be the one left to care for my nine worlds, and knowing Prin, it wouldn't be long before he latched onto another idiotic scheme that would put the population at risk.

With a moan, I sagged into the floor, beaten. Prin would continue to abuse my clone, abuse my planets, abuse my life! Everyone would think it was me, and I was truly impotent to stop him. Since I didn't see a way out of my death sentence, I signed three short words, 'Sorry about Karina'. I had finally remembered the name of the pretty girl I had lured away from him, and I did regret my callous actions.

Prin snorted. "Karina. She died you know, not long after you bedded her."

I raised an eyebrow inquiringly.

"Murdered. They never caught her killer. She deserved to die after whoring around with you." He winked, and gave me another little kick.

I closed my eyes, so I wouldn't have to see my cousin's exultant face. It was a shock to learn he had been a murderous madman, even back then. Or had my actions helped to push him over the edge?

Prin didn't risk leaving me alone in my cell again. He napped with his feet on my back, holding his dartgun across his lap. Every time I moved to edge closer and murder him, he woke up. When morning came, he was still with me. Prin summoned half a dozen of the armed Ice Guard. I was grandly escorted to Prin's private quarters. He was taking no chances.

I had the displeasure of standing and watching him eat breakfast and sip hot cocoa. He took his time, ignoring me as if I truly was a piece of furniture. Apparently, there was to be no last meal for the condemned man.

From there, the six guards escorted me to a room lined with spacesuits. One was found in my diminished size. My bonds were cut free, so I could be stuffed into the padded metallic body. A full and heavy air cell was inserted into the back of the suit—Prin wanted me to die as slowly as possible. I'm sure his only regret was that he couldn't watch as my extremities froze solid, while I was still drawing breath. The helmet and gloves were shoved into my arms for me to carry.

Prin led me and my impressive escort to the ship's ejection hatch. Oran'Jay was there, laid out in his finest. He didn't need a spacesuit. Kyar and Noel were keeping his body company. Both looked tense and rather miserable.

"Almost time," Prin announced cheerfully.

I was shoved aside, and leaned against the wall beside Oran'Jay. My legs were shaking with weakness, or terror, maybe both. When they gave out, I slid down the wall and came to rest beside his body. Oran'Jay had died because he tried to help me. A wave of regret and affection flooded me. Tears welled up and I felt no shame when they washed down my cheeks. I touched Oran'Jay's still face with my palm, thanking him. Soon, we would be joined together for all eternity.

"Uh … Megal?" I looked up, but Kyar wasn't talking to me. He was addressing Prin. "Has Prin told you the location of the nanos?"

"He has."

Kyar did not look reassured. "Don't you think we should retrieve the sample, before you send him into space? What if he's lying? He does that a lot. I think we need Prin alive, until we actually have our hands on the nanos."

"He wasn't lying. Given the level of pain I inflicted, truth was the only thing he could speak, or grunt, as it were." Prin chuckled coldly.

Noel wasn't watching their exchange. Her eyes were on me. I didn't want her last sight of me to be a crying man. I shook my head to deny

Prin's words. Even though my face ached everywhere, I tried to smile at her one last time.

"But you know how diabolical Prin can be. I don't think you can trust anything he says. We should retrieve the nanos from Earth, before you jettison him into space. We're only a couple of days away from the planet. You wouldn't have to wait long."

"The nanos aren't on Earth," Prin said.

"They're not?"

"Prin was lying about that. The nanos are somewhere much closer to the Ice Planet." But Prin did not say where.

Kyar asked pointblank. "Where?"

"We will discuss that later. After Prin is gone." It sounded markedly like a threat, wrapped in a layer of blackmail.

It was clear to me that Kyar's unease was growing. Alas, he was no longer Nomad, and had no power to stop what was happening. Noel excused herself quietly. Did she not want to witness my end, wave goodbye to the man she had called husband, as he floated off into the blackness of space? I was deeply sad that I would never see her again. But I was wrong.

Noel wasn't gone long at all. She returned with the lettered tablet, and Mo and Hanis. "Every condemned man has a right to his last words," she said, explaining the tablet.

"Not this one." Prin jerked the tablet from her hands and smashed it over his knee. The fragments were tossed aside. One of the six Ice Guards kicked them away. They were still hanging around, making sure I didn't escape. "Enough delay, let us proceed." Prin picked up some straps, yanking on the lines to untangle them.

It looked like there really was no way out this time. 'Goodbye, Kyar.' It came out as a choked grunt. Our eyes met. I drank in the last sight of my brother, knowing that someday, he would know it was me who had been sent to the stars, while he watched.

Then Kyar winked at me. I blinked at him. Had he figured out the truth? Regardless, he was in no position to stop Prin. He had tried and failed.

Several of the Ice Guards moved forward, blocking Kyar's gaze. The gloves were sealed onto the suit, over my ruined hands. The helmet came next, locked in place. Lastly, Oran'Jay was held upright. My arms were wrapped around him, in what must have looked like a warm embrace.

194

My wrists were strapped tight together, holding him, and ensuring I could not remove my helmet to hasten my slow, torturous end.

Oran'Jay's greater weight tipped me over, onto the decking. I couldn't move or stand. His green face filled the helmet's visor. I could see nothing but his death. I cried out, losing control. The madness was slipping back into my head. Aware of how I would suffer in the days to come, I welcomed it like an old friend.

Strong, careful arms lifted me from behind. I knew Hanis' touch and fell against him. He tucked a hand under my armpit, holding me upright. A hard lump remained behind when his hand was removed.

Prin was the one who shoved me into the ejection hatch. I fell to the ground with Oran'Jay. There was a violent whoosh and we were sucked into space together, weightless. We spun in a slow spiral. The ship's lights circled us several times, before they flashed away. They were gone and I was alone with my dead companion.

'Sugar?' She wasn't there and I started to shake.

Already, the cold was seeping into the suit. I closed my eyes and tightened my shoulders, trying to feel the hard lump Hanis had hidden there. It was vibrating slightly. Maybe he had planted a small explosive device to kill me quickly. I prayed that he had.

There is no way to judge time in open space. I floated for hours or days, growing colder and colder, until I couldn't feel even that. Hanis's bomb did not go off. I eventually came to the conclusion that the mysterious lump must be something else, something that was not a bomb.

At some point, I started talking to Oran'Jay in my head. He was a great listener, but even in my wandering thoughts, he never once answered back. He was simply too dead.

I was humming him a sad lullaby when something banged into us. I tried to guess what it could be, since I couldn't see a thing. The stars were disappearing, and suddenly I wasn't weightless. I crashed onto something hard. The world lit up like a sun. I didn't know what was happening, not until my arms were cut free from Oran'Jay and my helmet was removed.

I blinked up at Lillyth. She was struggling to remove the rest of my suit, as Borelle lifted me up. Even Captain Glass was there to welcome me aboard. Perhaps she believed me dead, or I was dead, and the FarGone 5 was my nirvana.

Lillyth finished stripping my outer garments and said, "He's frozen, Borelle. Take him to his room."

Borelle carted me off. He wasn't as gentle as Hanis, when he dropped me on my fur-covered bed. Lillyth tended me, rubbing my feet and hands, and lamenting over my crushed fingers. Heated blankets were dropped over me. I began to shiver hard. My thawing limbs screamed with pain, and I came to the realization that, against all odds, I was still alive. And I truly was on the FarGone 5.

While I defrosted completely, Lillyth kept me company. She held warm drinks to my lips, and answered all the questions trapped in my head. She solved the mystery of what Hanis had hidden on my suit. It was a beacon, which had allowed the FarGone 5 to track me in space. Noel and Kyar had begun to suspect that Prin was still in my clone, but they couldn't stop Prin from jettisoning me into space, so they had Hanis place the beacon. They had sent the FarGone 5 an encoded message to pick me up. I decided then and there that I loved them both dearly. I had always loved Kyar, but now I loved Noel, too. And Hanis, and Lillyth, and everyone on the FarGone 5.

I fell asleep smiling. When I awoke, I was alone. I wasn't cold anymore, nor was I dead. My life was about as good as it got these days.

Lillyth walked in when I was struggling to dress. She suggested a steam-shower and turned the water on for me. I managed to rinse and dry myself, and found Lillyth waiting when I reentered my quarters, seeking fresh clothes.

With nimble fingers that I envied, Lillyth helped to dress me as if I was a tot. I definitely wasn't a child. I quirked an eyebrow at the bed. She frowned and shook her head. "Stop that, Megal. You have much more important things to attend to."

I shook my head emphatically, to disagree with her. She didn't take me seriously and tucked an arm through mine. She escorted me to the galley, where I was served hot cocoa, oatmeal, eggs and fried walrus. My life just kept getting better and better. I was too starved to feel shame when Lillyth fed me.

There was some strength in my legs when I limped for the bridge. Only six crew members were present, including Captain Glass, Venus and Borelle. Captain Glass welcomed me with surprising warmth. I had been cozying up to death again, so maybe she wanted to cozy up to me. I absently wondered what had become of Oran'Jay's corpse, then avoided thinking about it at all.

I sat in the Captain's chair while I was brought up-to-date. The ship was flying with less than half the crew, because the rest were on the Glacius.

Once they had gotten the message to retrieve me from space, the FarGone 5 had flown with all haste, to save me from freezing to death. It had taken them a day and a half to reach me, and another day to thaw me out.

In that time, the imposter Nomad Megal had been sending repeated messages. He had ordered the FarGone 5 back to the Ice Planet, to rendezvous with the Glacius. With a worried expression, Captain Glass said, "I don't know why he wants us to meet with him so urgently, unless it's because he has somehow learned that we've rescued the real Megal."

I grunted and shook my head.

"You know why he wants us to return to the Ice Planet?" Captain Glass asked.

With a frustrated sigh, I nodded. I needed a lettered tablet. I scanned the bridge, until I spotted the next best thing. I stepped in front of the main console and banged a couple of buttons with my elbow. A standard message appeared on the large clear screen—a message with lots of letters. Perfect. Before anyone started asking questions, I approached the screen and pointed to letters, spelling 'Hanis room'.

"I'll go with you," Lillyth said.

When we reached Hanis's room, she slid opened the door of the tiny cabin that had two bunks. After an awkward search, I found the ratty coat draped in the closet. I tried to lift the coat out, but couldn't, and knocked it onto the floor. Everything was so damned difficult without working fingers and a voice. I motioned Lillyth over with a grunt and a tilt of my head. She lifted the coat. I pawed around until I found a small tear in the side seam. I patted it and grunted.

Lillyth bit her lip. "What do you want me to do, Megal?"

In answer, I wormed my least damaged finger into the hole in the seam. Lillyth clued in and tore the seam opened. Nestled inside was the small vial of nanos.

Lillyth picked it up. "This is what you're looking for?"

I grinned and kissed her cheek. She blushed and we hurried back to the bridge. With great reverence, I held the vial between my palms and presented it to Captain Glass. I returned to the console to sign, 'nanos to save Ice Planet'.

Everyone on the bridge was momentarily stunned by what had been hidden aboard the ship. I spelled 'Prin hid nanos, last ones'.

"That's why he wants to rendezvous with us?" Captain Glass said.

I nodded.

"And … do we want Prin to have them?" Captain Glass asked.

It seemed I was calling the shots in spite of my infirmity. I shook my head.

"What should we do?"

I answered with, 'How far to Earth'.

Captain Glass checked her coordinates. "We're close. When we picked you up, you were only two days away from the planet. We've kept going in that direction, to avoid Prin. We're about a day away now. Why?"

I pointed at Venus and spelled, 'Fastest speed to Earth'.

"I could have us there in eight hours. Is that what you want?" she asked.

An idea was growing in my head. Eight hours to reach Earth was not so long. I decided we should risk it, avoid Prin a little longer, and hopefully persuade someone on that planet to come along with us—someone who would be very helpful indeed. A miracle worker in a sense. It was a gamble, but one worth taking. I signed, 'Earth fast Liena'.

"Yes, Nomad." Venus flashed a smile, and for just a second, she looked as solid as the ship's captain. She headed for her engine room.

I stayed parked in the comfy captain's chair, deeply content to be on a mission to save the Ice Planet—a mission that might actually have a chance of succeeding. I mulled over my half-formed plan, tweaking it, developing it, trying to prepare for all possibilities.

By the time Venus had us over the planet, I was satisfied with my plot to defeat Prin. With no time to waste orbiting, we landed in daylight. I couldn't show my ruined self on Earth, or walk any great distance, so Lillyth and Borelle went to fetch Liena. They returned with her as darkness was falling.

She stepped onto the bridge, looking surprised to find herself on the FarGone 5 again. It was great to see her and I smiled. When she saw me, her face went very still and tears dampened her eyes, but she did not hesitate to approach.

"Oh, Megal! I'm so glad they got you off Gehenna." She hugged me with such care, she must have believed me fragile enough to shatter to pieces. Her defenses were up, so she did not change into me, or relive my latest hell. Alas, she would have to endure those nightmare memories, if she agreed to help.

Lillyth and Borelle would have informed her of all that had happened, and was still happening, but I needed her to know my thoughts. As soon as she released me, I motioned that I wanted her to touch me. I tapped a knuckle against my temple, hoping she would understand that I wanted to communicate with her.

"You want to tell me something?" she said.

I nodded.

She took my hands in hers, and said, "Poor hands. Poor Megal." She drew in a shuddering breath and held them only briefly, then released them. It was enough for her to have read my most pressing thoughts, hopefully without any change occurring.

She said, "Of course I'll go with you, Megal. I only hope I can help save your planet. Captain Glass, we have to go to the Ice Planet as fast as the ship can fly, okay?" Liena wasn't used to giving orders and she made it a question.

"Of course," Captain Glass said with a nod at me.

The ship took off like a rocket, heading for home. I motioned the crew to gather around and Liena outlined my plan. She knew it as well as I did now. And she suggested some clever improvements of her own. She had a creative mind and one heck of a survival instinct.

I began to feel hopeful that we could actually carry it out, and save both the Ice Planet and my clone. All we would need was a little luck, or a lot of luck. We would be facing the seemingly indestructible Prin, one more time.

14. The Ice Planet

All the way back to the Ice Planet, we agonized over the details of how to beat Prin at his own game. It would not be easy, now that he again wore the Nomad's cloak, and possessed the absolute power that it granted him.

With Liena by my side, I had a voice again. We barely had to touch skin and she would speak my words and ask my questions. If our minor contact was creating any ongoing change, we couldn't identify it. Liena herself wasn't sure if the brief touches were enough to generate any side-effects.

I learned all about what had happened on the Ice Planet, and about how Prin had been captured. I was less than pleased to discover that by saving Sephine from Gehenna, I had caused Kyar nothing but grief.

Speaking for me, Liena asked if Kyar and Noel knew that I had been recovered safely.

"No, Megal," Lillyth answered. In the absence of key crew members, she was in charge of communications, and she was doing a great job. "Noel got her message out to us in secret, but we couldn't return one to her. There was too great a risk that Prin would intercept it, so we didn't send one at all. They won't have a clue what's happening, but they must be wondering why we haven't responded to all the urgent communiqués. Maybe that will tell Kyar and Noel that we found you in space, before it was too late."

I certainly hoped so. "But Prin will not know Megal survived space?" Liena said.

"There's no way he can know that. He must believe Megal long dead by now."

"So seeing Megal will be like seeing a ghost to Prin. That will be a bit of a shock, won't it?" she said.

And I was counting on that to keep my cousin unbalanced, and off his evil game.

It took four days to get home. The ship was traveling faster than ever before, and the wormholes the FarGone 5 generated were carrying us impossible distances. It was as if the ship shared the urgency of our mission. It was galloping through space like some sort of cosmic metal racehorse.

More messages arrived from the flagship. We didn't respond. The crew had agreed that this was the best tactic to keep Prin frustrated. He was probably throwing temper tantrums all over the grand flagship by now. If I was lucky, at least some of the crew on the Glacius would begin to doubt his inner identity.

When the FarGone 5 passed over Coldstar, Captain Glass ordered the ship halted on the far side, veiled from the Ice Planet. An encoded message was sent to Jann. We stayed hidden, awaiting his response. It was quick to arrive. Jann informed us that the flagship was already orbiting the Ice Planet. Prin had taken a shuttle down to enjoy the luxury of my tower. Kyar and Noel were also in the Ice Palace.

Jann confirmed that the two fissures were still growing, destroying the southern glacier, and edging dangerously close to a large inhabited crater. If the cracks got that far, a major city would be destroyed. Ships should have been rescuing the population, moving people out of harm's way, but no ships were available. Jann reported that Prin had every last vessel in the Nomad's fleet, except for the Glacius, scouring the galaxy for the FarGone 5.

It was a miracle that we had gotten as close as Coldstar, without being detected. I attributed that to our extreme speeding. But we could go no closer without being spotted. And Liena and I needed to reach the Ice Palace, without being waylaid, to pass the precious nanos to Jann.

As per our instructions, he had icers and a shuttle standing by, ready to transport the nanos south. In preparation for the nanos, molers had been hard at work, tunneling down under the encroaching ends of the fissures. Jann wanted to come to us, to pick up the nanos. Alas, the planetary shuttles weren't built for space travel, and there were no other ships available. Plus, I was convinced that Prin would be tracking Jann's movements. He knew we were friendly, and could surmise we were allies.

With the FarGone 5 hidden and safe for the moment, the entire crew met around the familiar scarred table in the galley, to discuss our next step.

I brushed Liena's hand and she said, "Venus, Megal would like to know if there are any small vessels on Coldstar's surface that could be raised to travel as far as the Ice Planet, without wasting time on repairs."

"There probably are, but to find one ... that would take time we don't have. The FarGone 5 could have us there in an hour," she estimated. "Far faster than any other ship can fly." Her body flashed briefly solid and her eyes glowed with light, as they did when she talked about racing her engines.

"Yes, but it's the Glacius that we have to worry about. We'll be flying right at her, and she has more guns than ten ships," Captain Glass said.

I touched Liena. "But they won't blast us, not with the nanos aboard. And they don't know Megal or I are on the ship," Liena said for me. "The FarGone 5 is small enough to land on the planet's ice. The Glacius can't."

"True." Captain Glass stroked her braid absently. "True. Okay, say we do make a mad dash for the planet and land beside the Crystal Crater. We'll be intercepted before we can descend into the crater."

My thoughts were stretching wildly. I grinned and touched Liena. She laughed and said, "Captain Glass, the Nomad Megal has such faith in your skill as a pilot, that he challenges you to land on the very lip of the Crystal Crater and coast gently down the side, without destroying his beautiful Ice Palace, the one he hasn't seen in four years."

"Oh slush!" Captain Glass cried.

I cocked an eyebrow in her direction—a challenging eyebrow.

"I can land the ship anywhere. I can land the ship on a snowflake, so if you want me to park beside the Ice Palace without smashing it into icicles, I will do just that, Nomad Megal," she declared, rising to my challenge.

I bowed my head in respect and gratitude. A spectacular homecoming was just what I was in the mood for. I stroked Liena's hand with my palm. She said, "Warn Jann what's about to happen. He should be ready to receive the nanos and take them south. And tell him to let Kyar and Noel know to expect us."

Lillyth nodded and went to send the encoded communiqué. Captain Glass and Venus also left to carry out my instructions. I knew my small crew would see me and the nanos safely to the Ice Palace. After that, it would be up to Liena and me to carry out the rest of our crazy plan. Perhaps I had been keeping close company with madness for too long, for I relished the drama that was about to unfold.

Venus was never slow. It took only fifty minutes to reach the Ice Planet. The Glacius was chasing our tail at that point, but she couldn't catch us, and she didn't fire on us.

The FarGone 5 dropped toward the planet as if we intended to crash into it. We landed much too hard and fast, with a bone-jarring thump, and bounced twice. In what seemed like an out-of-control slide, we skated toward my Crystal Crater.

For a fraction of a second, we balanced on the lid of the depression, then we picked up speed again. Brakes screaming, the ship slewed as it skidded down the steep slope into the crater. A wall of ice came rushing at us. I closed my eyes when we hit a corner pillar. It was not hard enough to bring down the palace. The ship came to rest with a shuddering groan that both felt and sounded disturbingly alive. Everyone released a pent-up breath.

"Now get the hell off my ship," Captain Glass ordered everyone. She would be doing the same, before Prin captured her for information.

I saluted her. I like to think that I ran off the bridge. In truth, I limped. Liena stayed by my side, her small face a picture of worry. Before I set foot on my home planet, I pulled the hood of my cloak over my head. I had to keep my identity hidden, not that anyone would recognize me as the Nomad Megal now. They would, however, remember such a monstrous sight, and I wanted no word of my arrival getting back to Prin.

"My first time setting foot on another planet, and I'm walking into the lion's den," Liena whispered, as we exited the hatch. It wasn't an expression I knew; her meaning was clear nonetheless.

Jann was waiting, flapping his arm for us to move faster. I tried my best and tripped, flat on my face. Jann hauled me up, almost dislocating my shoulder. He didn't let go, and rushed me along. We skirted the hot pools and stepped into an elevator, barely ahead of the rush of Ice Guards that were rampaging toward the ship. They would find no-one, only a deserted hull.

Jann had a frank look at me as the elevator rose. He wasn't able to mask his shock. "Megal, it's really you?" he gasped. At least he didn't blurt out how ugly he found me.

I nodded and pressed the precious vial into his hand.

"Thank you, Megal. Gods, lad, I'm glad your father isn't around to see how you've suffered, but he'd be proud of how you turned out." He hugged me so hard, I think he cracked a rib.

203

The elevator lurched to a stop. I motioned him off. Liena was my voice and said, "Megal says to get as far away from us as you can. Get the nanos to the southern glacier, and fast. We'll take care of Prin." She was getting better at giving orders.

"As you say. Luck be with you. Luck be with us all, except Prin. We'll have a proper reunion later." Jann pulled me into another bone-crushing hug and disembarked.

We rode higher. The elevator stopped and we stepped off. Liena knew the layout of the palace from my thoughts, and led the way to Kyar's rooms. We walked straight in and my brother was waiting with Noel.

"Anyone see you?" Kyar gasped, slamming the door quickly and locking it.

I shook my head.

"Heavens, Megal, I swear, you are both cursed and blessed." He brushed my hood back, gripped my face between his hands and kissed me exuberantly on both cheeks. Even then he didn't let me go. "I can't believe you survived open space. I didn't even suspect at first... after the surgery. Prin kept you locked away. He kept to himself, said he was recovering. I didn't see him enough to know it wasn't you. And when you didn't seem like yourself, when you were so filled with anger, I attributed your behaviour to ... to Gehenna and what happened to you there. But then, when Prin interacted with you, it became quite obvious that he wasn't you, which meant that you were not Prin. Please forgive me for not seeing it sooner," he said, as if there was anything to forgive.

I touched Liena. "Kyar, Megal says there is nothing to forgive, and to shut up about it."

"Shut up about it?"

"Well, those aren't his words, but the thought is the same. I'm his voice, for the moment." We had a lot to tell Kyar. I was so very glad I didn't have to point laboriously to one letter after another.

Noel welcomed me with a warm embrace and even some tears. I returned the embrace, and it felt so right, like she was my home as much as the Ice Palace. She released me and ushered us all to the comfortable furniture. I sank down, utterly exhausted. I had been running on adrenaline, and that had been completely tapped. Liena sat beside me, so that we could communicate.

The first thing we told Kyar was that the nanos were secretly winging their way south, in the trusted hands of Jann. Kyar was so relieved to hear it, I thought he was going to kiss me again.

204

In turn, he informed me of all I needed to know. Prin still believed that no-one knew who he truly was. He was acting the part of the hero, desperately fighting to save his world. He hadn't postponed even one banquet dinner, saying his people needed to keep their spirits up.

"And he gets to be the center of attention. He tries to look all brave and noble, as if he ever could," Noel snapped.

I growled at that and Liena said for me, "While he risks the lives of the population, by having no ships available to transport them out of harm's path. What a jerk!" The last part was hers.

"That's Prin," Kyar stated. "Now, we have to prove that he is the imposter, while he holds absolute power and keeps himself surrounded by a dozen Ice Guards at all times. It is not going to be easy."

It wasn't. But I had come armed with my plan, honed to sharpness by those on the FarGone 5, with Liena playing the key role. Liena outlined our scheme to Kyar and Noel. I was just glad that Prin hadn't cancelled the evening's banquet. The safest setting for us to confront him, was before a vast audience of my people as witnesses.

One of our main advantages was that, by now, Prin would have searched the FarGone 5. He would know the vial of nanos was gone. He would be panicking. When I appeared before him, as if back from the dead, he would be stunned. He couldn't kill me outright, not only because of the many witnesses, but because he needed me to tell him the new location of the nanos. Prin would know I had them. He had told me their exact location himself, and it didn't take a genius to deduce that I had arrived on the planet aboard the FarGone 5.

Believing Liena would be safe was the only reason I was allowing her to take my form, to face Prin as my ruined self. And if our plan unfolded as it should, Liena would lure Prin into a private meeting, so they could speak alone, and she would do what only she could.

When Kyar and Noel knew the whole convoluted plan, Kyar glanced at the clock and said, "It's another hour and a half before the evening banquet begins, if it begins on schedule. Might not, since a spaceship crashed into the palace." A hint of his saucy grin flashed across his features, almost lightening the tension we were all feeling.

Noel said, "We'll have to time this carefully, otherwise Prin will wonder why both Kyar and I are late to arrive. We have been trying our utmost not to arouse his suspicions. If we leave here in an hour, the hall will be almost full, and we won't be conspicuously late."

"You should go to the banquet ahead of me, so we both won't be late," Kyar said.

Noel worried her lip, then nodded. "Yes, that would be better. I'll dress now, and check back in before I head to the hall."

She hurried away, and I didn't waste that hour. I made myself at home in my brother's kitchen, and then in his bed. Sleep had been rare of late, and my body was still fighting too many infections, draining my meager strength.

After my second stint on Gehenna, Kyar woke me gently, laying his hand on my shoulder and turning me toward him. "It's time, Megal."

I nodded and sat up. Kyar was dressed formally for the banquet, in a fur-trimmed cloak. He adjusted my tunic, retying the top tie, not that it mattered how I looked. His help didn't embarrass me. I was simply grateful to have Kyar as my brother. I had hurt him in the past, and he had forgiven me. I would never hurt him again, and I would die before I let anyone else harm him.

I stood up and hugged him for a long moment, then we rejoined the others. Noel was gowned in silver-blue, and looked quite beautiful to my eyes, and heart. I wished I could have told her so. Liena was dressed in some of my casual clothes, including a worn hooded cloak.

At our appearance, Noel said, "All set then? Well, time for me to make myself scarce, and sit by my dear husband's side. May we all survive this night."

I approached her, and for want of a better way to communicate my feelings, I touched my heart. I wanted to express so much—my gratitude for what she did now, my regret over my disregard for her in the past, an apology for both the ass I had been and the wreck of a man I was now, a man no woman could ever love. And what my heart felt for her did seem to be a burgeoning love. It would no doubt be an unrequited one, unless we successfully captured Prin, and I was restored to my last clone.

Noel stroked my cheek gently. "May we all survive this night," she repeated. I nodded, drinking in that little touch of her hand. She departed, her head high and her gown swirling around her.

I returned to Liena's side and touched her hand. She spoke my thoughts. "Time to summon the guards, Kyar. You have an intruder."

He groaned for what was to come. He moved to the wall panel, then awaited our signal. Before Liena turned into me and absorbed all the latest tortures I had endured, I brushed my hand against hers, warning her that my new memories of Gehenna were even worse than the ones that came before. She needed to be prepared.

"Oh Megal, I'll try to block the worst of them," she said. She took my broken hands gently, and didn't let go. I felt like I was spinning through a blackhole and then I faced my twin.

I was so much more gruesome than the last time I had laid eyes on myself. I wouldn't have believed it possible, if I hadn't seen it with my own eyes. The eyes that gazed back at me were devastated. Liena was lost in my torments, drowning in my madness. She hadn't been able to block all the torments I had endured. I shook her gently, trying to bring her back from my memories, as the walls began to melt around us.

Liena blinked and refocused on my face. I pressed my forehead against hers, trying to communicate reassuring thoughts, as the floor turned into a puddle of icy cold water.

"What's happening?" Kyar said.

Liena took a shuddering breath and her eyes cleared. She tried to answer Kyar, but could only grunt now that she had no tongue. She settled for pointing at herself.

Kyar said, "The ice is changing around us, interesting. We better not linger." Already, we were up to our ankles in frigid water. "Time to hide, Megal," he prompted.

Liena seemed to be recovered enough, so I limped into my brother's bedroom. I stayed near the door to hear what transpired, standing atop a chair. My soaked feet were aching from the cold.

The guards were quick to arrive. There was the sound of a splashing tussle. Kyar shouted, "Take it easy. He's not putting up a fight, is he?"

Things settled down after that. There was some garbled explanation about the heat-vents accidentally being left fully opened, to explain the melting, then Liena, as me, as Prin, was escorted from Kyar's rooms. Kyar went with her.

Once my pounding heart calmed, I donned one of Kyar's outdoor cloaks. It swamped me, but that was good as a disguise. I pulled the hood over my head and sloshed from the room, to see if events played out as we had planned. If it all went wrong, I could try and save Liena at least. Somehow.

As we had hoped, the guards obeyed Kyar and brought Liena directly to the banquet hall—to Prin. I trailed at a discreet distance, and boldly entered the grand hall itself. The rows of tables were already filled with bodies, talking in the subdued tones of those who were facing a disaster.

It had been four impossibly long and appalling years since I had stood in this room. I pictured myself as I had been in the past—beautiful, arrogant, probably drunk and strutting about in the latest fashions. I smiled ruefully at the picture I made now, skulking at the back of the hall, a monster of a man with no voice and no power, and barely useable hands. Oh how times had changed. I must have been truly mad because, in spite of it all, I did not want to go back in time and be that shallow, swollen-headed young fool again.

At the raised head table, Prin squatted in my place as the Nomad Megal. He was flanked by Noel, her face expressionless, and Sephine, my brother's wife. Beside Sephine was an empty chair, meant for Kyar. I knew he did not want to be within a hundred galaxies of Sephine, so the seating arrangement must have been Prin's doing.

Sephine looked as beautiful as a goddess. Perhaps her bite's potency had worn off, after so long, for in spite of her splendor, she held no appeal to me now.

Prin was playing the hero, showing a brave face to his people. My people. I contained my rage and limped along the back of the room, staying in the shadows as an observer. My mother sat further along. She might have been frozen in time for four years, for she had not changed one iota. She was still haughty and cool, with not a hair out of place.

Liena was hauled down the central aisle, her hood pulled low over her bowed head. Her limping pace was too slow to satisfy the guards, so she was being half-dragged, straight to Prin. A more pitiful figure was hard to imagine.

When she was presented to Prin, Liena reached up and pushed back the hood. As soon as my cousin's eyes rested on who had been brought before him, he thrust to his feet, his mouth dropped opened like a beached fish's. Even his scheming mind could not have foreseen this.

"How do you still live?" he asked in a shaken voice. Did he think my tongue had grown back? No, the shock had made him stupid.

Liena raised both hands in an exaggerated shrug that managed to mock Prin. She had a nice flair for the dramatic, did Liena.

"Do you know how Prin survived space?" Prin asked Kyar, his eyes narrowed suspiciously on my brother.

"How could I? I was with you on the Glacius. Prin just turned up in my room, probably trying to kill me for revenge. Luckily, I caught him before he could, and summoned the guards immediately."

Prin mulled that over for a moment. "Yes. It is indeed fortunate you caught Prin before he could do more harm," Prin orated as if performing in a play, and not a very well-written one.

He strutted around the table and down the two steps to level ground, to stand before Liena. Noel followed, staying by his side. "You have the audacity to return to the planet you've tried to destroy, Prin? I suppose I shouldn't be surprised, knowing you as I do." Prin turned to the guards. "Does he have the vial of nanos on him?"

"Not unless it's up his arse. Searched him, but didn't check there," one of the guards reported.

"Where are the nanos, Prin?" Prin asked, mildly for him.

Liena didn't answer with a nod or shake or shrug. She stood unmoving.

Prin's eyes narrowed to slits, and I knew he had decided on his next move. He beckoned to Sephine. "I think we need your special assistance, my dearest sister-in-law."

My breath caught in my throat. We had not anticipated this.

Sephine strolled gracefully down the two steps in a swirl of shiny blue cloth, vermink fur and bouncing curls. "Of course, Megal. I'm so pleased to have an opportunity to help save the Ice Planet. Prin will be spilling his secrets to me in no time, once I give him a little encouragement." Sephine stepped closer to Liena as me and shuddered.

"Can you bear to bite someone so hideous?" Prin drawled.

"I'll close my eyes." Sephine did just that. There was no way to stop the bite, not without giving ourselves away. Kyar and Noel stood tensely while Sephine sank her fangs into Liena's neck. The bite was short. Sephine fell back from her victim, her eyes wide with shock. She gripped her throat and began to choke. When she fell to her knees, no-one knew what was happening.

"Sephine, Sephine?" Prin dropped to kneel by her side. "What's wrong?"

Sephine couldn't answer. Her eyes began to bulge. Her lips swelled and turned yellow, as she fought to breathe and couldn't. Prin shook her, as if that would help. It didn't. There was a last long and awful wet gurgle, before Sephine slumped limply to the ground.

Kyar was the one to bend over the body and verify that there was no life left in Sephine. "She's dead," he stated without emotion, and backed away. I felt nothing, except relief. Prin was in a terrible state, sobbing over her prostate form. His heartbreak would feel real to him, since he'd been bitten recently.

After a few more ragged sobs, Prin fell silent. He surged to his feet to face my ruined skin. Liena stood firm, yet she must have been terrified. Prin was showing every sign of losing control in a big, violent way.

"What did you do?" he snarled.

Liena simply shook her head and shrugged emphatically. Her answer of 'I don't know' was crystal clear.

"Did you take poison that would kill her? Anticipating this?" Prin raged. Liena shook her head. "You're lying!" he screeched.

Liena kept shaking her head. Our plan was disintegrating before our eyes. Kyar leapt between them once more. "Megal—nanos first! Then you can do whatever you want to Prin, but nanos first!" He gripped the imposter's shoulders, trying to calm him down. "The planet must be saved," he stressed.

Prin dislodged Kyar's hands and panted as if he had run a hard mile. "Nanos first," he gasped, wiping sweat and traces of tears off his face with the fur cuff of his robe.

Kyar turned to Liena. "Prin, you will tell us where you hid the nanos," he stated.

My repulsive head nodded, eyes on the corpse of Sephine. Even from a distance, I could see that Liena was deeply shocked, yet she was still managing to play her part.

"In private," my traitorous cousin said. Of course he could not trust what might be revealed before the large gathering.

In a thoughtful gesture, Prin covered Sephine's face, before motioning for the guards to escort his prisoner from the great hall. As Nomad, Prin took the lead. Kyar followed with Noel, as if 'private' naturally included them. The guards trailed after, with Liena limping between them. Prin had had no time to plan for these unexpected events. His mind had to be churning with machinations.

A frantic buzz of voices filled the hall as soon as they left, discussing all that had just happened. Discreetly, I edged away from the cacophony, trying my damnedest not to limp, in case it gave me away.

I assumed that Prin would choose to interrogate me in my own tower, to flaunt my cursed life in my battered face. I headed that way, via the narrow servants' corridors that I had so often played in as a child. The passages were deserted during the banquet hour. I moved unseen through the palace, all the way to the base of my tower. I had not walked the route in four years, yet it was as familiar to me as if I had walked it yesterday.

I peeked around the corner. Six Ice Guards were standing sentinel outside the main door of my tower, proving that Prin had indeed taken Liena there. Kyar and Noel had not been permitted past that point. They perched on a bench outside, waiting anxiously. I did not dare approach them, under the watchful gaze of so many attentive guards. I stayed put, leaning against the wall for a much needed breather, and biding my time.

I was still recouping my strength when the floor beneath me shook and a sharp cracking noise came from the direction of my tower. Ice cracking? Had something impacted with my castle, in addition to the FarGone 5? Or could this be blamed on Liena creating change? That seemed much more likely.

I peeked again. The guards were facing the tower, heads cocked. I waved an arm and Kyar spotted me out of the corner of his eye. With a backward glance at the guards, he and Noel trotted my way. They joined me, around the corner and out of sight.

"Do you think Liena has transformed?" Kyar whispered.

I nodded.

We didn't have to wait long for proof. We heard my tower door open and voices. The guards were inquiring about the odd noise, asking if everything was alright. A voice that sounded like mine assured them it was. Kyar hurried back toward the guards.

"There you are. Get in here. Bring Noel," my voice called petulantly.

"There is another here who wishes to speak with you, and might have information about the nanos," Kyar said.

"Bring them, if you think their information is credible."

Noel jerked my hood lower and walked ahead of me to the tower door. We paraded right past the guards and Noel shut the door on them. We climbed the stairs to the top.

I kept my face covered until I heard my voice ask, "Megal, is that you under there?" The tone of the voice had softened.

"Liena?" Kyar asked.

"Who else?" She still looked like me, but the pretty version now. She had donned one of my finest robes. Her face smiled sweetly, girlishly. It definitely wasn't Prin. I pushed back my hood and grunted a greeting.

"You did it!" Noel cried. "Where is Prin?"

"Come see." Liena led the way into my lavish sitting room. Prin was all tied up and barely conscious. A bump was sprouting on his forehead.

The room was also cooling rapidly. A wide crack had split the ice overhead. Great chunks had fallen inward, onto my floor. Liena was lucky not to have been crushed. I could even see stars, through the wide crack.

"I knocked him out with a candle stick, while he was still confused by the physical change," Liena said. "Did I tie him tight enough?"

Kyar checked and tightened the bonds. He also added a gag, then stood back and surveyed the three of us—the prostate Prin in my clone, Liena masquerading as him, and the real me in my damaged skin.

"Three Megals," Noel said, with a shake of her head. "It's very peculiar."

"My worst nightmare," Kyar said, with a grin that belied his words.

I had another question and motioned to Liena. She brushed my arm. "Yes, I do know what killed Sephine. I found out when she touched me— bit me, and I knew her thoughts. It's quite fascinating, really. Only the females of her species have the venomous bite, and only after they reach sexual maturity. They can't bite other females. Otherwise they would all try to kill each other off, to be top dog, or alpha female, I suppose. Anyway, biting another female is like poison to them, deadly poison. Oh, and I'm not in love with her, in case you were wondering."

Prin moaned. He squirmed against his bonds as he came awake. I nudged him with the toe of my boot. He opened his eyes and blinked up at the two Megals who looked down at him. He must have thought he was having a hallucination. His eyes rolled back in his head and he fainted.

I wanted only one thing, to be put back in my clone. I wanted to have a voice again. Jann was taking care of the nanos and there was nothing I could do to help him. It was time to take care of me. I brushed Liena's arm. She said, "Kyar, we need to get Megal and Prin aboard the FarGone 5."

"Yes we do, and quickly." He heaved Prin on top of a fur carpet, and rolled him up inside it. Noel helped. Once Prin was a tightly wrapped bundle, Kyar tossed him over his shoulder. He staggered under the weight. "Let's go," he said.

I replaced my hood and we filed down the stairs and out of the tower.

The guards snapped straight when Liena/Nomad Megal appeared, leading her odd little parade. "Accompany us to the FarGone 5. Make sure we are not delayed. It is time to retrieve the nanos that will save the Ice Planet," she ordered curtly, sounding every bit the commander.

The guards moved to surround us. With a curious glance, one offered to carry Kyar's burden. Kyar was sweating and panting from exertion, nonetheless, he refused.

At a reduced pace, we reached the elevator. I know my limp raised some eyebrows, but the guards did not question who I was. When we reached the base of the palace, the FarGone 5 sat where she had impacted with the corner of ice. A new dent decorated her hull, barely noticeable amongst all the rest.

"Will she fly out of here?" Kyar asked, surveying the ship's position at the bottom of the crater. Only one person could answer that question.

We bypassed the dozen or so guards who were keeping an eye on the FarGone 5. We boarded the ship and settled on the bridge, to wait. Captain Glass had also been keeping a covert eye on her ship. She turned up within five minutes, and was escorted inside by a pair of Ice Guards.

Liena as Nomad Megal frowned deeply, doing a good job of looking displeased. "Leave the ship's captain with me and get out," she ordered the pair, with a dismissive wave of her hand.

"Yes, Nomad." They bowed before they departed. As soon as we were alone, I tossed my hood off.

"Any more guards aboard the ship?" Liena asked, eyes darting around.

Captain Glass checked the sensors. "No. Liena? Is it you?"

"Yes, me—Liena." Liena patted her chest, then pointed at me and said, "The true and honourable Nomad Megal." She kicked the squirming, fur-wrapped bundle on the deck. "And the evil imposter Prin in Megal's clone. We're all here. Time to rock and roll."

"Rock and roll?" Captain Glass said, puzzled.

"Time to get the party started." Liena grinned. "You know, put everything back the way it should be."

Captain Glass grimaced. "I'm not sure I would call it a party. The rest of the crew should be turning up directly. You better let the guards know that you want to interrogate them aboard the FarGone 5," she reminded Liena.

Liena glanced at Kyar. "Can you tell them?"

Kyar nodded. "Sure. I just hope Mo and Hanis succeeded in rounding up Greely. We can't proceed without him."

Greely was integral to our plan and I was terrified that he might manage to elude Mo and Hanis. I sank into the captain's chair and rested my boot heels on Prin, who was conveniently laid out in front of me. I dug my heels in when he tried to wriggle away like the worm he was.

The crew of the FarGone 5 was quick to turn up. The only ones we had to wait for were Mo and Hanis, and Greely. The longer we waited, the more convinced I became that he had escaped. Optimism was not something I felt easily, or at all, after two lifetimes in hell. If I could have drummed my fingers, I would have.

I was counting stars on the viewing screen when the sound of approaching footsteps had everyone watching the arched entrance to the bridge.

"Sounds like them," Kyar said quietly.

I yanked my hood over my head and tucked my hands out of sight. Greely appeared, flanked by Mo and Hanis, and backed by a pair of Ice Guards. Mo had a limp that rivaled mine.

"Excellent," Liena/Nomad Megal said. "You two, back to your post outside the ship."

The Ice Guards bowed and left. Hanis took up a silent position at the door, arms crossed. Everyone looked at Greely, who didn't seem to have a clue that we were on to him. "Nomad Megal, you summoned me? No troubles with your nice new clone, I hope?" he said to Liena, darting curious glances at my hooded figure, and the squirming roll of carpet my heels rested upon.

I wanted to toss my hood off dramatically and unmask myself to the traitorous doctor. Instead, I fumbled the hood off, and by then Greely had seen my hands. He knew my hands. His skin lost its healthy flush of colour and turned as pale gray as dirty snow. I rose and looked him in the eye, wishing I had hands to strangle the life out of him, yet I knew I could do no such thing. He was the only one who could liberate me from my ruined skin.

He glanced at who he believed to be Prin and maintained the charade. "Nomad Megal, what's going on? What is Prin doing here? How in the heavens is he still alive?"

"Drop the pretense," Liena snapped. "Your handiwork has been exposed."

I kicked the carpet roll that was Prin and my cousin groaned on cue. "Prin is in no position to help you," Liena stressed, in case Greely still wasn't getting it.

"That … that's Prin in the carpet? Then who are you? Another clone?" Greely stammered.

"No," Liena said. "I'm actually one of your former patients, Greely. I'm from Earth."

214

It only took him a heartbeat. "The Catalyst?" She saluted snappily. I didn't think Greely could turn any paler, but he did, in a waxy sort of way.

I stepped over Prin and limped a few steps closer to Liena, needing her voice. I brushed her arm and in my most scathing tone, she said, "You are going to undo your vile deed and put the rightful Nomad Megal in his clone. And Prin ..." She paused, because in my mind, I truly couldn't decide what to do with him. I wanted him to suffer as I had suffered. I had a grand thirst for vengeance that demanded satisfaction. At the same time, I was truly afraid to leave Prin alive. He was devious and destructive, and as evil as a man can be. He had almost destroyed the Ice Planet, and even in my ruined skin, he might wreak more havoc.

"What would you like done with Prin?" Kyar prompted me, moving to stand by my shoulder.

I brushed Liena's arm and she said, "For Oran'Jay, he will die." My words coming out of her mouth had a fatal ring. The squirming Prin stilled.

Kyar nodded. "Fair judgment." Everyone on the bridge nodded. Prin was responsible for countless deaths on the Ice Planet, but Oran'Jay's murder was personal to the crew of the FarGone 5.

Greely had been thinking. "I won't do it," he said.

I hadn't realized quite how stupid he was until that moment. In hindsight, the fact that he had worked for pirates and smugglers should have clued us in to his corrupt nature.

"What?" Liena said incredulously, for me.

"I won't do it without a written pardon in hand, beforehand, from the Nomad Megal. And a ship. I want a ship to leave here. A speedy little Scarnivian disc, fully fueled."

Before he foolishly demanded a fortune in bizoux, I touched Liena. She turned to gape at me, turning rather pale herself. She rested her fingers on my arm for a second, perhaps to verify my thoughts. She swallowed sickly and murmured, "Oh no, Megal. I couldn't. Please, don't ask that of me."

While we were eye-to-eye, I rested my forehead briefly against hers, trying to impart a wealth of intertwined emotions and thoughts. She pulled back in alarm, and nodded so reluctantly, I wasn't sure she meant it.

"I might make a mess of it, Megal," she whispered to me and only me. I brushed her arm, sharing the faith I had in her, and warning her not to reveal our strategy to Greely or Prin.

Everyone on the bridge must have been darned curious about what we were communicating, yet no-one asked questions. Liena said, "Time to fly. Captain Glass, can you take off from this crater, without causing more damage to the beautiful Ice Palace?"

She considered that. "It would be better to be towed up the side to the crater's edge, but I think I can manage the maneuver, with a little luck."

That was good enough for me. I nodded and pointed to Greely.

"I'll put him in the brig for the time being," Mo said.

I limped over to Mo, and since we hadn't had a chance to reunite, I hugged him. I had missed my friends. Mo harrumphed a bit, embarrassed, and clapped me on the back. "Good to see you again, Megal. Well, maybe not *see* you, but good to have you back."

I touched his leg and raised an eyebrow.

"The leg is going to be fine, it just needs a few more weeks to recover," he said.

I was deeply relieved to hear it and hugged Hanis next. He hugged me back. I wanted to thank him for saving my life with the little tracking beacon he had hidden on my spacesuit. I patted the spot under my arm, where the tracker had been. If he had been caught stashing it on me, Prin probably would have jettisoned Hanis into space with me, so I knew he had risked his skin to save mine.

"Just glad it worked," he mumbled, flushing.

I nodded deeply, happy he had understood my message.

Together, Mo and Hanis escorted Greely away, with the doctor whining about his pardon. It was a relief when I couldn't hear his grating voice any longer. Venus headed for the engine room.

Kyar said, "I'll go tell those guards outside that we're going to take off, and that they better put some distance between themselves and this ship."

"I suggest everyone belt in securely, very securely," Captain Glass said. Everyone did.

As soon as Kyar, Hanis and Mo returned, and had belted in, she revved up the engines. The ship hummed and shook. She fired one of the thrusters so the hot end of the tail turned to angle away from the Ice Palace. "Hang on tight," she warned and reversed hard, partway up the

216

crater's bowl. With a flashy move, she slammed the ship into forward thrust and gave it full power.

The FarGone 5 slid partway down the crater before momentum took over and the ship raced around the bowl like water going up a drain, rather than down it. There was a bone-rattling lurch when the ship impacted with the crater's edge, smashing a huge chunk out of the ice, then we were airborne.

Everyone cheered to be off the planet and in one piece. And my Ice Palace was still standing. In a few short days, I would have a home to go home to.

Liena/Nomad Megal contacted the planet. She informed them that the nanos had been found, and were on their way to the southern glacier. She also contacted the Glacius and told them that all was well, and that we were taking a little jaunt across space. They offered a protective escort. She didn't even consult me. "Yes, an escort would be most welcome, and fitting, I think." She flashed me a sweet smile and ended the transmission. Before all our eyes, she transformed to look like herself again.

Captain Glass adjusted our course, murmuring dryly, "That threw us off by a few degrees, or all the stars in the galaxy shifted position. I think it was the stars." She sounded rather terrified.

I unbelted and rose on unsteady legs. It was time to lie helpless under a laser-scalpel again, but this time I wouldn't be alone. I nodded around to the crew and touched my heart. My eyes stopped on Noel's face for a long moment. Soon, I would have a voice to tell everyone how much they all meant to me. Including Noel, if she wanted to hear it.

I limped off the bridge. Kyar followed, with Prin draped over his shoulder. The villain was struggling with renewed energy. Liena came, too.

I motioned for Kyar to keep going and slowed for a last word with Liena. I touched her arm. She said, "Oh Megal, I hope you know what you're doing." I nodded. She swallowed hard, whimpered once, and detoured to do what I had asked of her.

The medical facilities on the FarGone 5 were rudimentary, but they would have to do. Hanis had readied the treatment room with two stretchers, purified air, and a reduced temperature. He helped Kyar unroll Prin. Between them, they strapped him tight to one of the stretchers, by his arms and legs, and neck. The ship wobbled, throwing us all off balance.

217

"I wonder if we damaged the hull when we hit the edge of the crater," Mo mused, giving Prin's bonds a few extra tugs to tighten them. I didn't think the ship was damaged at all. The wobble was something else entirely.

When Prin could barely move, I gazed down at him, wearing my clone, and marveled that one being could be so evil, and cause so much destruction. And it was one who was directly related to me. We shared the same blood, so why was Prin's so tainted?

Prin glared up at me. "You think you've won?" he said with a smile that was as twisted as his nature. It made the hair on the back of my neck stand up.

I shook my head. We might have beaten Prin in the end, but as far as victories went, it was far more bitter than sweet. My home and people had paid a terrible price, as had I. When I ruled again, I would do it properly. As the man I was now, I could see that my birthright was both a great honour and an even greater responsibility.

"You haven't won," Prin snarled when Mo and Hanis escorted Greely in. It made the small room overly crowded. I preferred it that way. I perched on the edge of my stretcher, not quite prepared to prostate myself. I shared a long look with Greely.

"Shall we proceed?" he said, with a wink just for me.

Reassured, I reclined. The temperature in the room was lowered even more and all superfluous personnel exited. Kyar stayed beside my stretcher. I pressed his hand between my two palms, afraid to let go. 'Stay with me,' I tried to tell him with my grip and my eyes.

He must have understood, or he could see how frightened I was. "I won't leave you, Megal, not for a second," he promised. "I'll make sure it's done right this time."

I nodded and smiled, and kept clutching his hand.

As the surgeon prepared several nano darts of tranquilizers, Prin was surprisingly calm. In my experience, that meant he still had one more nasty trick up his sleeve. I only hoped my safeguards had eliminated any and all possible threats.

Prin was sedated first. "I'll see you in hell, cousin," he said, his words slurring.

I turned my head to look at the flawless skin I would soon wear. Prin's icy silver-blue eyes fell closed and I felt the prick of a nano dart in my arm.

Liena as Greely had all the doctor's medical knowledge, and far gentler hands than the slapdash surgeon himself. Trusting her hands, and the brother who stood by my side, I succumbed to the frigid darkness, whispering farewell to my ruined skin. We had been through a lot together, including two eternities in hell. Soon, my body would lie cold and unmoving, abandoned by me. An empty husk.

I wished it farewell, as I was sucked into the black hole in my head, to the sound of Kyar's panicked shouting, Greely's voice hollering for a laser-scalpel, and Mo cursing up a storm from the doorway. It did not sound like the operation was going as planned. Perhaps I would see Prin in hell after all.

15. Live Long & Prosper

I t felt like it took weeks rather than days for me to make the long journey back to the light. When I finally managed to lift my eyelids, I was in my own bed. Someone was slumped in the corner chair, snoring softly. I would have known that snore anywhere.

I tried to speak my brother's name, but my mouth stung like hell. I wasn't sure why that would be, since there shouldn't have been any pain, at least not in my mouth. I tried to reach for the glass of water that was so temptingly close. I couldn't lift either of my arms. That wasn't right either.

Suddenly terrified that I was still trapped in my ruined skin, I bellowed like a madman. Kyar leapt to his feet as if he had been stabbed. "Megal, you're awake! Thank heavens."

"Kyar, what's wrong," I said, and stopped there. I was infinitely relieved that I could speak, yet the pain of uttering those three words made my head swim.

He laid a hand on my shoulder and said, "Try not to talk, Megal. I'll explain everything. There's good news … and bad, I'm afraid."

I opened my mouth to blurt out questions, thought better of it, and sagged back into thick fur, becoming aware of new pains in unexpected places. Far too many pains in far too many places. I waited for my brother to tell me what was going on. He didn't seem to be in any rush to do so.

"Kyar," I prompted, when the suspense almost killed me.

He settled carefully on the edge of the bed and sighed. "Good news first." He gently lifted one of my arms. From elbow to wrist, it was encased in hardened micro-resin.

I blinked at it, as if I had never seen an arm before. At least there were four complete fingers and a thumb on the end of that arm, although I couldn't move them at the moment. "You have functioning hands again, and a tongue," Kyar said. "They just need to heal for a few more days, then you'll be able to use them perfectly well. And I'm sure you'll never shut up, after having no voice for months."

I scowled at Kyar, since he was doing a very poor job of explaining things. Gritting my teeth against the pain, I muttered, "Bad news?"

"Prin had booby-trapped his body—your clone," Kyar said baldly. In truth, I wasn't surprised to hear it. "As soon as Liena made the first incision to remove the brain, it ruptured an implanted capsule of vulture nanos. According to Liena, even Greely didn't know about it."

"Liena was Prin," I managed. She should have known all his thoughts.

"I asked her about that. She said Prin's thoughts were so vile and disturbing, all the terrible things he had done ... well, she had blocked some of them out, when she became him for a second time, including the knowledge of the implanted vulture nanos, I guess. He probably had the capsule implanted very recently, when his plan wasn't going as planned."

I nodded. I had known Prin was insane, but to implant vulture nanos into the skin he wore, that was beyond madness. Clearly, he would rather be eaten alive, than allow me to be whole and happy again.

"To make a long story short," Kyar continued, "Liena figured it out at once. She knew your clone would soon be devoured completely. She grabbed a laser-scalpel and sliced off Prin's tongue, and lower arms and the one leg, before the vulture nanos could spread into them."

"Leg?" I tried to touch my lame limb and still couldn't move my arms.

Kyar shifted the blanket aside and bared my legs. I almost laughed. The two limbs were similar, but not the same. Even through the translucent micro-resin, my new leg was pale, unscarred, and more muscular than its partner, which was deeply tanned, stick-like and scarred just about everywhere. In time, they would look more alike, but they didn't yet. At least neither was crooked.

"Walk," I said. I wanted to try out my new leg.

Kyar shook his head. "It's too soon, Megal. Give it a few more days. Liena made some other repairs while you were sedated, fixed your nose and teeth, and a few other things. You're going to be sore all over for a while, so just rest."

I wilted back into the bed. "Water please."

Kyar held the glass and I drained it. The coolness eased the pain in my mouth. "More?" he asked.

I shook my head, exhaustion claiming me. "Ice Planet?" I asked.

"All is well. Jann and the icers got the nanos into both cracks and the ice stopped disintegrating. No new cracks have developed. The crisis is over." The sound of Kyar's voice soothed me, as did his news. The knot of anxiety inside me began to loosen.

"Sephine?" I said next, not sure what I was asking.

Kyar sighed. "That's a long story, Megal. I'll tell you when you're more alert, because I don't want to tell it twice, although I'm sure you heard some of it." He paused and I waited for more. "Okay, short version, she tricked me. I was unknowingly addicted to her, twice, it made me think I loved her. When I was transplanted into my clone, I didn't love her anymore, which made me realize that something wasn't right." He sighed again. "And still, I was fool enough to let her do it again."

"Not your fault." I wished I could say more, but it hurt too much to speak.

"I'm so sorry that things turned out this way, Megal, for you. After all we went through to capture your clone undamaged." He sighed heavily. "At least Prin is gone. Dead. At least you have functioning parts again. Liena called it Frankenstein surgery, whatever that means." He tapped his own nose. "She did a great job on your nose. It looks as if it was never broken at all. She's better than Greely ever was, as a surgeon."

"See it," I said.

Kyar held a hand-mirror in front of my face. I wasn't sure I wanted to look, but I did. The face that gazed back at me was familiar, and told the story of my life. It was scarred and sun-damaged and skeletal tight over cheekbones and my skull. Soft white stubble was already sprouting on my head. My nose was perfectly straight and quite nice looking, at least. I smiled, to see my mouthful of teeth. Always nice to have teeth.

This was my face, and I suddenly realized that it was the right face. The clone's face would have been a stranger's mask, and a lie.

I shared a true smile with the skin that I would be keeping for the rest of my days. "Handsome," I said, trying to tell Kyar that it was okay, in as few words as possible. It was the truth. To have a voice and hands again, and to be able to walk properly, that was more than enough. I would stride freely across the ice on my home planet as the Nomad Megal, as the man I was now. A beautiful skin and flawless face would have been an ill-fitting suit for that man.

In time, my hair would grow and I would put some weight on my bones. Regular skin regeneration treatments would reduce the scarring on my face. I wouldn't always look as damaged as I did now, but I would never be beautiful again. Would Noel be able to care for me as I was now? She wasn't shallow, so maybe she could, if I earned her love.

Too exhausted to resist the pull of sleep, I closed my eyes. When I awoke clear-headed, several days had passed, yet Kyar still wore an anxious face. I again reassured him that I was not disappointed with how things had turned out. I think this time he believed me.

Liena, as my vigilant physician, removed the micro-resin casts and said I could get up. The first walk I took was to escort her to the main hatch. We had reached Earth. We were trespassing on her planet one last time, and she was going home. The Glacius had been sent back to the Ice Planet, with the promise that we would rendezvous with my flagship there.

Liena had already said her farewells to everyone else on the ship, except me. She opened the hatch and we both stood unmoving, inhaling the fresh air. It was a lot colder than the last time I had visited Earth. Everything was coated in snow. It was like my Ice Planet, but with a lot more hills and trees.

"I thank you, Liena, for all that you have done. You saved my life, and my world," I said, still thrilling to the sound of my own voice. It was deeper and more musical than I remembered. I simply liked to hear the sound of it. I had even started singing, something I had never done in the past, and I could sing beautifully, like an angel. Perhaps it was a change caused by Liena.

"You are most welcome, Megal. It was a real adventure, wasn't it?"

"It was that," I agreed.

We smiled at each other. "Live long and prosper, Megal."

"Is that an expression on Earth?" I liked the turn of phrase.

"Sort of," she said with a quirky grin.

"Live long and prosper, Liena. And be vigilant on this planet, where you are an alien." We had offered to transport her anywhere in the Universe, and she had chosen Earth. She had insisted on Earth. She wasn't ready to meet, or forgive, the father who had abandoned her to be experimented on and imprisoned as an extraterrestrial.

"I'll be fine, Megal. I am going home with a head full of advanced, outer space medical knowledge, as well as some nifty surgical tools. I think I'm going to become a doctor." She patted a bulging medical bag. "What will happen to Greely?"

"He will be tried on my planet. His fate will be decided there." He would be iced there, but I didn't say that. She probably knew.

Liena leaned forward to brush my cheek with her lips. "Don't forget your daily skin regenerations, Megal. I've left the machine set for you in the treatment room. Fifteen minutes a day, every day. In no time, your face will be as smooth as a baby's bottom."

"I certainly hope not, but I won't forget. Farewell, Liena. I will miss you." I stroked her soft cheek with an unblemished hand.

"Me too, Megal. Me too." She turned and walked away, disappearing into the snowy trees. I closed and sealed the hatch, wondering if we might meet again someday.

When I walked onto the bridge, the crew stopped what they were doing. They embarrassed me by standing up and applauding to see me on my feet. Noel was hanging around, even though she had no bridge duties. She applauded, too. Our eyes met and held. She looked proud of me, and happy to be on the FarGone 5 with our ragtag crew, with me. Yes, perhaps I could earn her love. I could certainly try.

Kyar said, "Megal, stop limping!" I kept limping for no reason whatsoever, since I had two perfectly good, if mismatched legs. I think it was just a bad habit.

I sat down in the captain's chair and grinned around at everyone, showing off my teeth. I focused on the viewing screen. The stars seemed brighter than usual, and twinklier, perhaps because my eyes were damp. I cleared my throat, and relishing the words, I said, "Set course for the Ice Planet, set course for home."

"Yes, Nomad Megal," Captain Glass said with a jaunty salute. The crew turned back to their consoles and the FarGone 5 hurtled off the planet and into space, as if the little ship was every bit as eager to go home as her passengers.

 The End

Visit SrigleyArts.com and join the author's mailing list, to receive updates and win give-aways.

www.ingramcontent.com/pod-product-compliance
Lightning Source LLC
Chambersburg PA
CBHW031325170626
46807CB00002B/572